FORGER OF LIGHT

A CELINE SKYE PSYCHIC MYSTERY

NUPUR TUSTIN

Foiled Plots Press

Forger of Light
A Celine Skye Psychic Mystery
Foiled Plots Press

Copyright © 2021~Nupur Tustin
Cover Design by Crowe Covers / crowecovers.com

Published by Foiled Plots Press

ISBN 978-0-9982430-9-2

Typesetting services by BOOKOW.COM

Acknowledgments

As always, I've relied on a number of experts to get it right. Many thanks to: Lisa Caprino and Melinda McCurdy, Huntington Library; Jeffrey Holman, MFA; Manon van der Mullen and Erik Hinterding, Rijksmuseum; Gloria Williams, Norton Simon Museum; and art historian Gary Schwartz.

For police procedure, I'd like to thank Adam Richardson and his Writer's Detective Bureau as well as the ever helpful members of his Facebook group.

Many thanks also to my author friends, Grace Topping, Jane Gorman, and CJ Peterson.

Finally, thanks also to my three adorable musketeers for being good while Mom wrote! And to my husband, Matt, for keeping them out of my hair when they weren't!

ALSO BY NUPUR TUSTIN

JOSEPH HAYDN MYSTERIES
A Minor Deception
Aria to Death
Prussian Counterpoint

CELINE SKYE PSYCHIC MYSTERIES
Visions of Murder: Prequel
Master of Illusion
Forger of Death

ANTHOLOGIES
Murder in Vienna: A **FREE** Joseph Haydn Mystery
Murder in the Sun: A **FREE** Women Sleuths Mystery
The Baker's Boy: A Young Haydn Mystery
In **Day of the Dark**, Edited by Kaye George
The Christmas Stalker
In **Shhh. . .Murder!**, Edited by Andrew MacRae

FREE Mysteries Available from NTUSTIN.COM

Cambridge, Massachusetts

The image looked instantly familiar.

"Where did you get this?" Anthony Reynolds struggled to keep his voice calm.

He carefully set the work on his coffee table and regarded the expensively outfitted man seated across from him.

He was a client of long standing; a man Reynolds quite liked. An accountant with a taste for art. A bit of a fusspot.

"Got it from a client." Fussy Phil shrugged off the question, his insouciant response suggesting a disturbing lack of awareness of the image's dark history.

"Did he tell you where he got it from?"

"From some dealer or other. Look, what does it matter? Will you do what I want or not?"

His client sat at the very edge of his armchair now, an uncharacteristic edginess replacing his usual placid manner. The divorce—and its inevitability—were beginning to get to him.

Reynolds felt sorry for the guy. He himself had no illusions about women. But Fussy Phil had been happily married—or so the poor sap had believed, erroneously as it turned out—for years.

"Yes, but . . ." Reynolds stared at the work on his coffee table. "You've checked out the provenance, I assume?"

"Why? You think it's fake?" His client stared suspiciously at him.

"No." Reynolds felt a dull thud in the pit of his stomach. "No, I'm pretty sure it's not."

Unless he was mistaken, it was much worse than that.

"All right, then." His client rubbed his hands together. "Good."

Reynolds wasn't so sure it was. But he hesitated to share his suspicions. The man was just beginning to come to grips with the news that his ex would be taking him to the cleaners. Now to find out that the money spent on this work—God alone knew how much he'd shelled out for it—had in essence been flushed down the drain. It was a cruel blow.

"Listen." Fussy rose, indicating the meeting had come to an end. "This thing's valuable. I don't want my wife getting her gold-digging claws on it." —Reynolds noted Fussy still couldn't bring himself to refer to her as his ex —"Bad enough I'll have to sell most of my collection to satisfy the bitch's demands. I don't need her accountants finding out about this little gem. I can't let it go."

"Understood." Reynolds stood up too. "I'll figure something out." He waited a fraction of a beat, then said: "But it might take me a while. I have several new commissions, new clients, an exhibition."

And he wanted to assure himself that the work wasn't what he suspected it was.

"No problem." Fussy pulled out a thick envelope from his jacket pocket —the initial deposit for the commission—and handed it to Reynolds. "Take your time. It's safe here with you. And listen"—he tipped his chin at the money—"keep this off the books, will you?"

"Yup." Reynolds took the money, saw his client out, and returned to his living room.

The piece stared up at him, drawing out the misgivings he'd squelched for his client's sake.

If he was right, it was an old master. One that had been made famous —or infamous—by the most outrageous art heist in the history of such thefts. Stolen, along with twelve other works, right here in Boston from the Gardner Museum.

The sculptor sat at his desk and pulled his laptop toward himself. He double-clicked on the Chrome icon. It didn't take him long to access the page he wanted. The URL came up seconds after he typed the first few letters into the address bar.

When the Gardner Museum page devoted to the theft downloaded, he scrolled through its gallery of stolen works until he came to what he was looking for.

He enlarged the digital image and zoomed in. He could detect no discernible difference between it and the piece on his coffee table. There were the same velvety strokes, the same subtle gradations in tonality that he'd admired in the work his client had left behind.

He reached for the thick leather-bound book on the shelf above his desk and thumbed through its pages.

Thomas Wilson's *Descriptive Catalogue* was quite clear on the subject. There were only two known copies of this work. The Museum of Fine Arts had one—he opened up a second tab to confirm this. The Gardner had the other.

And, as if to drive the last nail into the coffin of truth, the Gardner website described the work as being extremely rare.

He'd gotten it from a client, Fussy had said.

If the image was stolen, there was just one person he could've gotten it from. And if that were the case, the work was neither a gift nor a legitimate purchase. Fussy was merely its custodian, tasked with keeping it safe from the prying eyes of law enforcement.

That meant, too, that this commission—Reynolds felt the thick wad of cash his client had handed him instead of the usual check—was actually a commission from . . .

A sickening sensation of dread arose within him. He thought he'd put all that behind him—the associations with criminals; his dealings with the men who'd masterminded the Gardner Museum heist.

But every time he managed to get away, he was dragged back again. Back into the murky depths of crime. He had no intentions of drowning there, though.

A yellow popup glided up on his laptop screen. Bolded text urged him to call the number listed for more details.

He hesitated, but only for a moment. Then he reached for the holster clipped to his belt and yanked his phone out of it.

Chapter One

Paso Robles, CA. July 2019.

"Where are you, Celine?"

Julia Hood's voice filtered through the swirling yellow-gray mist. The former fed's husky cadence was so soft, Celine Skye could barely hear it.

She strained her ears. But the words eluded her, fading into tenuous vibrations of sound.

Too far . . . so soft . . .

Celine's mind sank back—unresisting—into the pillowy clouds of sleep surrounding her.

"Celine?" Julia's voice, louder and sharper, pierced the heavy stupor that had fallen over her.

"I hear you," Celine responded. Her mind was alert now, eyes trained on the mist, waiting for the wisps of yellow-beige and gray to completely dissipate.

A building emerged. Large, square. Celine counted the windows—long rectangles of glass. Four stories. Then a tiled roof.

"I'm in front of the Gardner." Standing before it, shivering, even though her body was ensconced in an armchair in the Delft Coffee & Wine Bar.

"Where exactly?" Julia's voice came through crisp and clear.

They were sitting—the four of them—in the space concealed behind the wall panel that had once been her departed employer Dirck Thin's sanctum.

Through the depths of her trance, Celine could hear the sounds they made. The rhythmic tapping of Julia's pencil against the small notepad on her lap; Annabelle Curtis's soft breathing; and the rustle of denim against upholstery as Jonah Hibbert restlessly shifted position yet again.

Celine smiled, amused and exasperated at the same time. Jonah, a rookie journalist and wannabe author, just could not sit still. She wished she hadn't agreed to his presence at this session.

Jonah had insisted upon it, however. "It's good research for my book, Celine. People will want to know more about your psychic visions; how you do it. I need firsthand information. Look, I'll be so quiet, you won't even know I'm there."

But she did know. And he was distracting her.

Annabelle, Dirck's sister, shushed Jonah and gently chided Celine.

"Concentrate, Celine. Focus on Julia's voice; turn your mind inward. Where are you?"

Celine felt the cotton fabric of her armchair chafing the skin behind her knees. Deliberately, she turned her mind away from the sensation toward the scene unfolding before her mind's eye.

The cold early hours of dawn. The building before her. March 18, 1990. St. Patrick's Day. Where exactly was she?

She turned her head, shivering as the wind whipped around her neck, whistling and crackling through the branches of the trees above her. The building was shrouded in darkness, but a lighter gray, box-like structure—the portico to the entrance—projected out from it, centered between the rows of windows on the first floor.

"Fenway. I'm at the front entrance of the Gardner."

"The front entrance of the Gardner Museum?" Jonah's voice rose, heavy with skepticism. "On Fenway?"

"She's right. It used to be on Fenway, Jonah," Julia responded sharply. "Could you please stop interrupting? You'll bring her out of the trance if you keep this up."

"I'm walking around to Palace Road," Celine said. It was the routine they usually followed. She'd emerge from the mist at the front entrance of the Gardner Museum in Boston, Julia oriented her and then guided her toward the side entrance—the one the thieves had used to enter the museum.

This time, however, Celine didn't wait for Julia's voice instructing her to move to Palace Road.

"The hatchback's still there, parked in front of the employee's entrance." The car that thieves George Reissfelder and Lenny DiMuzio had driven to the Gardner Museum that awful March day in 1990.

A drunken couple—huddling close to each other, smooching—zigzagged past Celine. She winced, turning her face away from the stench of beer and their energy clashing into her aura as they brushed by her.

A sudden gust of wind made her shiver again.

"Get the blanket, Jonah," Annabelle softly ordered. "She's cold."

"No, it's all right," Celine said. "I need to feel this."

Maybe—just maybe—a few more details would emerge this time. She doubted it.

Relax, Celine. You know more than you think. But her guardian angel's whispered words, meant to reassure her, only served to increase her frustration.

It had been months since Celine had helped Julia Hood, a retired FBI agent, recover the Gardner's Vermeer and its eagle finial. Months since Celine had pored over Julia's files with no further leads in sight.

No, Sister Mary Catherine was wrong. Celine didn't know more than she thought.

And the pressure just kept mounting. Penny Hoskins' anxious calls: "Any new insights, Celine? The Gardner would just love to recover the rest of its stolen treasure. And you, my dear, are our only hope."

But worse than the museum director's breathlessly expressed hopes were the insidious comments of the journalists.

"How can you be so sure, Ms. Skye, that Dirck Thins and John Mechelen didn't spirit away all the stolen art to California? After all, two of the stolen works were found in your winery."

Anger surged through her and her eyes flew open.

"I can't do this anymore. I need a break."

Julia, a short, heavyset woman with her gray hair pulled back into a ponytail, and Annabelle, taller and slender with curly hair framing her face, exchanged a worried glance.

"I don't know much about these things," Annabelle said. "But I don't think you can force it."

"Fine, we'll take a break." Julia glanced over at Jonah Hibbert's tall, ungainly form sprawled upon the couch next to her.

"But when we get back, let's get him out of here. He's a distraction."

Jonah sat up; his wire-rimmed glasses slid down his nose. "I'm not going anywhere." With a firm forefinger, he pushed his glasses back up and jerked his chin at Celine. "We have an agreement. I get a seat on this train —in return for—"

"Not giving into rampant speculation." Julia snorted. "Some agreement."

But after the FBI had made an *utter fool* of itself—Julia's words, not Celine's—some kind of damage control had been called for. The bureau had felt this *Faustian deal*—Julia's words again—was the only way to contain the media. In particular, the prestigious arts section of Jonah's newspaper, *The Boston Gazette.*

And Blake Markham, the member of the FBI's Art Crime Team who was most directly involved with investigating the theft, had agreed.

Chapter Two

FBI. Boston Field Office, 10 a.m.

Special Agent Blake Markham took a sip of his coffee and glanced at the newspapers his personal assistant had left for him to peruse.

Jonah Hibbert is a jackass, he thought, grimacing at the size of the stack.

Blake was an FBI agent, a member of its Art Crime Unit.

And this was how his mornings began—with a review, not of case files, but of Boston's major newspapers. The arts section of each outlet, to be precise.

It should've been a job for Ella Rawlins, his assistant, or some lowly intern. But Special Agent-in-Charge James Patrick Walsh had insisted that Blake personally scour the newspapers to staunch any further embarrassing leaks of information.

All thanks to the ill-advised article Hibbert had published—with the single push of a button on his laptop—four months ago in the arts section of the online *Boston Gazette.*

Clueless FBI Calls in Psychic to Recover Gardner Art.

An unconfirmed piece of news based on an anonymous press release faxed to Hibbert's credulous desk. The idiot hadn't bothered to call either the Gardner Museum or the FBI for verification of the news or any comment on it.

Apparently the FBI, with exactly zero leads to go upon, had gone running to a psychic for clues!

What exactly did they teach in Journalism school these days—anything?

"But the news release," Hibbert had whined when tasked on his dereliction of journalistic ethics. "Why would I call the Gardner when they faxed the news over?"

He'd jabbed at the sheet of paper. In his defense, it *had* looked like it had come from the Gardner Museum.

But that was no excuse. Hibbert should've known better. Should've called the FBI for comment. But, of course, he hadn't.

And as it happened, the Gardner had sent no such fax. "Don't be ridiculous, Blake!" Penny Hoskins, the Director of the museum, had retorted when he'd asked her about it.

Nevertheless, Hibbert had run with that bit faux news, even questioning the FBI's existence based on it. If psychics could successfully investigate and solve crime, were law enforcement agencies absolutely necessary?

No, Hibbert had answered his question. Law enforcement was simply "*a colossal waste of taxpayer dollars!*"

A sound bite that every television station had gleefully run with.

But being anti-law enforcement didn't mean the journalists were pro-psychic. Celine and her powers had also come under fire. Was it really her visions—or more likely, access to the stolen stash—that had resulted in her recovery of two of the Gardner's stolen works?

The insinuations were so pervasive, they'd forced the FBI—SAC James Patrick Walsh, to be precise—to launch a raid that was a spectacular bust.

Not only had it yielded zilch, it had also, at the end of the day, proven Hibbert's point.

The FBI was clueless!

Blake shook his head and scowled at the newspapers. Jonah F-in' Hibbert! What an unrepentant dipshit that guy was.

SAC Walsh had for once done something useful—ensured the failed raid didn't receive too much media attention. In exchange, he'd struck a bargain with Hibbert's paper.

A deal that would've meant allowing Hibbert to tag along with Blake as he worked the Gardner case.

Blake had reluctantly agreed, mentally preparing to endure the insufferable Hibbert, when he'd caught a profoundly lucky break. It wasn't Blake the bozo wanted to follow. It was Celine. Apparently the smug, self-satisfied prick had become an overnight believer in psychic phenomena and was now more interested in covering Celine's psychic methods.

Thank heavens for small mercies!

With a barely suppressed shudder at what might have been, Blake pulled the newspapers toward himself. What piece of garbage was he going to unearth today? What idiotic notion that could hobble an investigation?

He'd just started scanning *The Massachusetts Post* when his phone rang. *Penny Hoskins.*

Somehow Blake didn't think this was going to be good.

❧

"Blake, what is the meaning of this?" The Director of the Gardner Museum began without preamble.

Blake pulled the phone away from his ear. Penny's voice—breathy and high-pitched—tended to get unpleasantly shrill when she was agitated.

"I'm looking into it, Penny," he replied calmly. He had no idea what she was talking about, but to admit it would have enraged her even further.

Now, how in the hell was he going to elicit further details from her?

"I've been fielding calls from reporters all morning, Blake. This has simply got to stop!"

Fielding calls? From reporters?

Jesus Christ, that meant another f-in' leak!

"I know. It's simply outrageous." He turned to his laptop, called up Google and began typing rapidly into its search bar. "I'm as appalled as you are."

"The reputation of the Gardner Museum is being called into question, Blake. It's worse than outrageous." Penny seemed almost in tears now.

God! What had that idiot Jonah published now?

His search results had by now populated the screen; Blake clicked on the topmost link. *The Arts Gazette*, the pompously named arts section of the *Boston Gazette*. It was an online-only newspaper; there was no print copy to peruse on his desk.

Even so, it carried considerable weight in the art world—at least in New England. If you saw it in the *Arts Gazette*, it had to be true. That's why Hibbert's article had been so reprehensible.

But a quick scan of the homepage and sidebar yielded . . . nothing.

Nothing?

"There's . . . nothing in the *Arts Gazette*, Penny," he stammered.

"I don't care, Blake. It's in every other paper. And if people think there's even a grain of truth in that foul accusation, we could—" Penny broke off.

She didn't have to spell it out for Blake. Any suspicion of scandal, and the Gardner could lose its collection. As stipulated by the eccentric Isabella Stewart Gardner in her will. Any replacements of the art she'd assiduously collected, the slightest change to the way she'd arranged it, or the merest hint of disrepute, would result in her art being entrusted into the care of Harvard University.

It was a blow from which the Gardner would never recover.

The reason for the clause eluded even Gardner insiders. A way for Mrs. Jack to assert control over her beloved museum in death as much as in life, maybe?

To Blake it made about as much sense as cutting your nose off to spite your own face. But that didn't change the issue. He could see why Penny was near hysterical over the situation—whatever it was.

"The FBI needs to put a stop to this, Blake," she continued a minute later, her voice hard. "It really does."

Chapter Three

"Some deal this is turning out to be," Jonah muttered under his breath as he tucked his notebook into his shirt pocket. "She's given us nothing we don't already know."

Celine flinched. She realized Jonah probably hadn't meant for her to hear his complaint. But, nevertheless, she'd heard. And the words were like a hard, stinging slap across her face.

"I'm sorry, Jonah," she said quietly. "I'm as frus—"

"Oh, don't apologize to him." Julia's eyes blazed. She shot up, a sturdy forefinger pointing to the door. "Why don't you just get the hell outta here, Jonah Hibbert?" She thrust her finger at his chest. "You should've lost your job for that hit piece you published."

Jonah stumbled back against the onslaught of her fury; Annabelle looked on aghast. But Julia wasn't done.

"Frankly, you should've been prosecuted. You compromised an ongoing investigation with your idiotic insinuations. Instead, you get a front seat at the table because—"

Celine could stand it no longer. "That's enough, Julia. Leave him alone."

Wave upon wave of Jonah's confused emotions—frustration mingling with desperation—crashed upon her psyche.

"You're worried about your mother, aren't you?" She turned to him.

"What do you think?" he snapped. "It's always at the back of my mind —the treatments she needs, the constant care."

And the money he could ill-afford to spend on a reporter's salary. Celine understood his fears all too well.

The reporter was an irritant—she would've been the last to deny that. But his devotion to his mother—confined to a nursing home, a victim to Alzheimer's—had elicited Celine's sympathy from the start—and Annabelle's maternal instincts.

Jonah's glasses misted over. "And there's no one to shoulder the burden."

"Oh, Jonah!" Annabelle put her arm around the young man's shoulders. Although she'd never mentioned it, Celine was aware that Annabelle worried about becoming a burden on her only son as she aged.

In Jonah, Annabelle saw her son, Bryan, and despite his flaws, he'd earned a place in Annabelle's heart.

Julia snorted. "Oh, good grief! You've gotta be kidding me!"

Celine ignored the former fed. Julia was single, childless, and she hadn't had a particularly loving relationship with her mother. That coupled with a lifetime in law enforcement had given her a cynical attitude that very little could shake off.

Celine concentrated on Jonah instead.

"You may think there's no one to shoulder the burden, Jonah. But there is. Your mother will be taken care of. You have to believe."

"In what? Whom?" He rolled his eyes upward. "A God that doesn't exist?"

"That's not what I meant." Although what she had meant, Celine didn't know. She'd simply conveyed the message Sister Mary Catherine had passed on to her.

He's on the wrong path, the nun said. *This impatience will get him nowhere.*

"You have to be patient, Jonah," Celine said, but the reporter was in no mood to listen.

He surveyed his opulent surroundings. "Yeah, says the woman who, lucky for her, inherited a lucrative business. Wish I had it like that."

It was another wound that dug deep. Celine's nails dug into her palms, willing him to stop. But steeped in his own pain, Jonah was oblivious to hers and blind to the misery in Annabelle's eyes. Dirck had been her beloved younger brother.

"You know, even if O'Rourke"—that was Jonah's editor at the *Boston Gazette*—"died on me, I'll bet he doesn't have much to leave. And if he did, he certainly wouldn't leave it to me."

He had no idea what he was talking about. *Dear God*, he had no idea. If he'd lost someone he loved, he'd realize that money wasn't everything.

"I'd give it all away in a heartbeat, if I could bring Dirck back." The words forced themselves out of Celine's constricted throat.

The shock of finding Dirck's murdered body four months ago still hadn't subsided. It had been second only to the raw pain she'd endured as a twelve-year-old when she'd learned she'd never see her parents again. She'd failed to secure justice for their death. But at least the men who'd tortured Dirck were behind bars.

Julia turned to Annabelle.

"For God's sake, get him out of here."

Flustered and somewhat taken aback, Annabelle could only nod. She brushed the tears from her eyes, struggling to regain her composure. "Let's get you some breakfast, Jonah," she said briskly.

Promising to return with a cup of tea for Celine, she pulled Jonah out of the room.

❧

"I swear, that woman has the patience of a saint." Julia sat back down. "Sure you're okay?" she turned to Celine.

Celine smiled wanly. "I'll be fine. I don't think he means any harm, but he sure has a knack for grating on one's nerves." She sighed. "I guess I need to learn how to deal with it."

"Nonsense!" Julia's hand swept the air in a gesture of impatient dismissal. "If he's interfering with your process—and I can see that he is—he shouldn't be here."

Celine didn't respond. The door was ajar, and she watched as Annabelle led Jonah to the Delft's kitchen. She'd put the reporter off for as long as she could. But they'd promised to work with him, and a deal was a deal.

Julia, however, wasn't so easily fobbed off.

Leaning forward, she placed a gentle hand on Celine's knee.

"I'm serious, Celine. I don't like the idea of Jonah being here."

"And I don't like him being in my kitchen at this hour," Celine responded, seeing Jonah push open the bar's kitchen door. "He gets on Wanda's nerves."

She wasn't being entirely flippant.

She was grateful to Annabelle for offering their visitor some breakfast and heading off a potential argument with Julia. But the Delft's new assistant manager, Wanda Roberts, and Jonah had never quite hit it off either.

Having the reporter in the kitchen while Wanda supervised their staff, just hours before the bar opened, was a recipe for disaster.

"He's a distraction at best," Julia went on, undeterred. "And I strongly suspect he's blocking your vision."

Julia had the typical law enforcement agent's aversion to journalists—in particular those as abrasive as the *Boston Gazette's* Jonah Hibbert. That antipathy hadn't abated one whit since she'd retired. With good reason, Celine had to concede.

She herself hadn't been particularly happy about Jonah's bombshell revelation a few months back—in Boston's most influential online newspaper at that.

Celine had asked that her role in the recovery of some of the Gardner Museum's stolen art be kept quiet. The FBI had agreed. Giving out any more details than necessary could jeopardize an ongoing investigation.

There was also—they'd all agreed—absolutely no need to drag the names of Celine's former employers, Dirck Thins and John Mechelen, through the mud.

But Jonah—Jonah had done just that.

Celine gripped the edge of the couch, her anger surging again. She could forgive Jonah everything but that. The media scrutiny she'd been forced to endure, the name-calling—"science-denying kook" had been the worst of it—had been bad enough.

But suggesting that Dirck—who'd been murdered trying to return two of the Gardner's stolen items—was behind the 1990 heist was simply beyond the pale.

Besides Dirck Thins, owner of the Delft Coffee & Wine Bar, and John Mechelen, founder of the Mechelen Winery, had given Celine a chance when she most needed it.

She could feel the heat rising in her cheeks, her breathing becoming shallow.

Julia's hand squeezed hers. "Anger is your enemy, Celine. It blocks your vision."

Celine took a deep breath, an effort to calm herself down. "I know." She inhaled again.

"You can cut him loose, you know," Julia suggested yet again. "There's nothing Jonah Hibbert can publish without it going through his editor. And O'Rourke's agreed to get the FBI's blessing before printing any news on the Gardner case."

Celine sighed. "I know," she said again. "But I promised I'd let him see what I do."

Jonah was every bit as obnoxious as Julia considered him. But his hustling was due in large part to his anxiety for his mother—slowly but surely succumbing to dementia. His dogged persistence fueled by his determination to get the woman who'd singlehandedly raised him the very best care he could afford.

It was the only reason Celine had agreed to help him.

She got to her feet now and gave Julia a weak smile. "I think I'd better go see about that tea Annabelle promised me."

She walked away before Julia could stop her.

✖

So much had changed at the Delft since Dirck had died and she'd taken over. Wanda, her new manager, had taken over much of Celine's former duties. And Annabelle, Dirck's sister, had become an unofficial partner—creating unique blends of tea that were now on the Delft's menu.

If only Bryan would come around, she thought. Annabelle's son resented her—whether for inheriting Dirck and John's wine bar and winery or for offering the Curtis family a share in her newly acquired business interests, she didn't know.

He's hurting, Celine, Sister Mary Catherine whispered into her ear. *He feels betrayed. Just like you did.*

And he's taking his pain out on me. Celine communicated back. *I tried not to do that. I tried very hard.*

She pushed open the kitchen door. God, she really needed that tea!

Chapter Four

Blake found it at last—the news story that had gotten Penny Hoskins' hackles up. It was in the *Massachusetts Post*. Not on the front page, but on page three with a prominent headline that sprawled across the page:

Gardner Heist—Orchestrated From the Inside?

It was a headline calculated to get hits. Deliberately couched as a provocative question to make the situation appear far worse than it actually was, Blake bitterly reflected. The first line was absurdly inane:

The FBI has long suspected an insider angle to the Gardner Museum heist.

Blake rolled his eyes. *The FBI had suspected an insider angle.*

Of course it had! Any self-respecting investigator would. That someone on the inside was in cahoots with the thieves was obvious right from the start.

He skimmed the article, the facts of the case—so well-rehearsed they were easily recalled—coming to the forefront of his mind.

The FBI had zeroed in on Richard Abath—the night guard who on two consecutive nights had acted against security protocol to let outsiders into the museum after hours.

But—

Blake's gaze caught on a paragraph. His eyes scrolled up, and he re-read it.

Jesus Christ! The *Post* had concocted quite the theory from a single mundane fact.

*

Celine stood by the front window of the Delft, nursing the mug of tea Annabelle had brewed for her. It was too hot to drink, but Celine welcomed the warmth that seeped into her icy hands—cold from the trance she'd snapped out of fifteen minutes ago.

Going into a psychic trance state usually drained all the energy—and heat—out of her body.

She bent her head to the rim of her mug and sniffed deeply. The fragrance of chamomile, mint, and hibiscus in Annabelle's tea was beginning to restore her, calming her ragged nerves.

Outside, washed-out gray clouds hung low over the city and a light drizzle fell on 13th Street, nearly deserted at this hour. Few businesses in downtown Paso Robles opened before 10 am; it was just about a quarter past seven now.

She closed her eyes, took a cautious sip of her tea, and sighed. The Delft would open at eleven. There was no prep work to be done; the kitchen staff, under Wanda Roberts, was taking care of that.

It had been her Italian winemaker who'd suggested Celine hire Wanda to help with the running of the wine bar.

"You cannot chase around after lost art, *cara*, and make and sell wine at the same time," Andrea Giordano had said. "Get some help. You can afford it."

Thank God she'd acted on his advice. She had less than four hours to go into another trance before the Delft opened. She fervently hoped nothing would make her snap out of it before she succeeded in getting something.

Anything.

Please, Sister Mary Catherine, she prayed to her guardian angel, *help me see.*

All you have to do is open your eyes, Celine. Open your eyes.

Celine opened her eyes. A red Mustang parked diagonally across the street—between the Italian Cheese Market and the tasting room of a rival winery—caught her eye. It hadn't been there before, had it?

The driver, a tall man in a beige jacket and dark slacks, slid gracefully out of the sports car, adjusted his shades, and looked straight at her.

As he strode purposefully across the street, Celine had the oddest sensation he was gunning for her. She took a step back; a flash of black caught her eye as her body crashed against a soft obstacle.

"A-a-ah!" Her low scream pierced the stillness within the Delft.

✍

Why Richard Abath openly flouted security protocol has long been a mystery. But not anymore. New evidence suggests the night guard may have been following orders.

Orders issued by a high-level museum official—or the museum itself.

This was some accusation. Blake put the newspaper down, stunned. He understood now why Penny Hoskins had been so incensed.

Worse still, the writer claimed to be citing an "anonymous source close to the investigation."

That was an outright lie. There had never been any evidence that someone high up in the museum's hierarchy was involved.

What the FBI had strongly suspected was that several low-level museum employees had been conned into helping the thieves.

The theft of the Manet was a clear indication of that. Its gold frame had been left on the chair of the Gardner's Security Director—clearly a brazen gesture of defiance.

But the *Post* had managed to twist even that fact.

Abath and his colleague Grayson Pike, investigators now surmise, took Manet's Chez Tortoni off the museum walls during their security rounds— hours before they let Reissfelder and DiMuzio in.

Clearly, the thieves didn't order the removal of the painting. The question is: who did? The same official who encouraged the guards to violate security protocols?

Blake's stomach churned. It was a supremely clever twisting of the facts. The theft of the Manet had never fit. But had someone else—some individual not connected to the thieves; some person associated with the museum —commissioned its removal?

That was a question the FBI had never considered. One that no journalist—in the thirty years since the theft—had ever speculated on.

There'd been no reason to.

So why now, Blake wondered.

What had changed?

Chapter Five

"Celine! I'm sorry." Annabelle's fingers grasped her arm. "I didn't mean to startle you. Are you all right?"

"Yes, I—er—thought we had a customer." Her head swiveled around to the window. She'd need to head the stranger off—tell him they weren't open yet.

But the man had disappeared. Her eyes shifted toward the curb across the street. The red Mustang was gone as well.

"What customer, dear?" Annabelle peered out the window, mystified.

"I—" Celine shook her head. "He was right there." She pointed across the street. "I even saw a red car, but . . ."

"A vision, perhaps?" Annabelle looked anxiously up at her.

"I guess."

"Do you recall seeing anything else?"

Celine was beginning to shake her head when she remembered the flash of black she'd glimpsed. It had been just a flicker, but accompanied with a brief, familiar twisting of her heart muscles that could mean only one thing.

Death was near.

"I think I caught a glimpse—just a glimpse of—"

"Belle Gardner?" Annabelle interrupted, her eyes wide. She understood the implication of the vision.

Celine nodded. "The Lady," she confirmed. Referring to her as Belle seemed just too familiar—even though Sister Mary Catherine insisted the Lady preferred it that way.

You can call her Belle, Celine. She would like it if you did.

Annabelle's face had turned pale. "Is someone going to die?"

Celine silently put the question to her guardian angel.

Yes, Celine, Sister Mary Catherine whispered. *Death is near—closer than you think.*

"And the man? Annabelle wanted to know.

"I don't know." But he had seemed to know her—had been heading straight for her.

Gunning for her.

The words repeated themselves in her head.

❧

Feeling like he'd been punched in the gut, Blake forced his eye to run down the *Post* column. How much worse could it get?

Investigators have yet another fact to hang their theory on.

During the eighty-one-minute theft, the Gardner's motion sensors detected no movement in the Blue Room, where Chez Tortoni was displayed.

But police reports confirm the Blue Room's sensors were fully functioning at the time of the theft and would have picked up Reissfelder and DiMuzio's presence had they entered the gallery.

The sinking feeling in the pit of Blake's stomach intensified. The facts were undeniable. Would anyone understand they'd been bent out of shape to fit a cockamamie theory?

He doubted it. If you couldn't refute the facts, could you really discount the theory?

The lack of motion sensor activity in the Blue Room had led the FBI to the only reasonable conclusion an investigator could draw.

That one or both of the guards on duty that night must have been responsible for the theft, plucking the painting off the walls of the Blue Room during their regular walk-through of the galleries.

But the *Post* was taking the FBI's logical conjecture as proof positive that Abath and Pike had been taking orders from someone in the upper echelons of the museum's staff.

The evidence points strongly to an internal motive for the crime.

Where had they gotten this garbage from?

A loud trill interrupted his thoughts. He glanced at his phone.

Lawrence O'Rourke, the editor of the *Boston Gazette. Great! Another newspaper shark alerted to the scent of blood.*

Chapter Six

The hum of the air conditioner filled Celine's ear as Julia guided her back into a trance. They were back in the sanctum—what had once been a sanctum before Dirck had been murdered. A secret space concealed behind a wall panel in the Delft.

Let that thought go, Celine.

His killers were behind bars, but faint traces of their energy still contaminated the space.

Let it go.

A rush of cold air made her shiver. The air from the vents in the ceiling? Or was it the cold wind blowing on the morning of March 18, 1990, in Boston?

She was back on Palace Road, standing directly across from the Gardner Museum. The door to the employees' entrance opened. A man glanced furtively out, peered left and right, and then emerged onto the sidewalk.

He whistled—a low sound that brought his companion out. And a third man.

A burly Liam Neeson-like figure. Grayson Pike. Younger. Not quite as burly as when she'd last seen him, but with the beginnings of a beer gut.

"Wait!" Jonah's voice seemed to come from a great distance. "Pike was one of the guards on duty that night? I thought the thieves restrained those guys before going into the galleries."

"He's helping them," Celine explained. "They've all agreed to help." But that had been before they'd known the works would never be returned. "There's no turning back now."

"Helping with what, Celine?" Julia asked. "What is Grayson helping the men do?"

Celine peered through the darkness. "He's helping them bring out the stolen items. There's too much for two men to carry."

The taller of the two thieves adjusted his glasses and turned to Grayson. "The fella in the hat goes with you. You know where to take him?"

Grayson nodded.

"Where are you parked?"

Grayson pointed to a beat-up old gray sedan a few feet behind the hatchback.

The taller man—DiMuzio—jerked his chin at the small, flat rectangular object Grayson clutched to his chest. "Put that in your car first and get back here."

"What are they talking about?" Julia's voice was low, soothing. "Can you tell?"

"One of the works they stole. It's small. About ten inches by thirteen. I can't see it."

The rustling sound of paper being shuffled reached her ears. Celine knew it wasn't coming from the scene before her. The file Julia had compiled on the Gardner heist was on Annabelle's lap; she was paging through it.

"The Manet," Annabelle said. "I think she means the Manet."

"Grayson Pike had the Manet?" It was Jonah. "This whole time?" His voice rose. "That can't—"

Celine frowned, the image before her threatening to fade. "No, no."

"Shhh!" Annabelle hissed.

❧

"O'Rourke," Blake greeted the other man curtly, not bothering to identify himself.

"Listen, I just wanted to tell you they didn't get it from us," O'Rourke informed him.

"I beg your pardon?" Blake was still reeling from the brazen lies the *Post* had spun.

"I take it you've seen this morning's newspapers."

Blake confirmed that he had.

"That didn't come from us."

"Yes, I know." Was that the only reason O'Rourke was calling?

"Both the *Globe* and the *Herald* have a watered-down version of the story." O'Rourke paused. "I have to ask: Is any of it true?"

So that was it! O'Rourke wanted permission to dish out the dirt as well.

There was a moment's silence, then O'Rourke continued: "*The Gazette* can't be the only paper without a story as juicy as that."

Left unspoken was the deal the *Gazette* had struck with the FBI: an exclusive scoop on major developments in the Gardner case in return for keeping a lid on any inconvenient details that found their way to Jonah Hibbert's desk.

"The insider angle?" Blake leaned back in his chair, considering his words. "We always suspected something like that. After all, Abath knowingly flouted museum security when he let Reissfelder and DiMuzio in after hours."

"They were dressed as cops."

"On the night of the theft, sure. On the night before, they were just regular guys. He had no reason to let them in."

"And the *Chez Tortoni*?" O'Rourke probed. "Any truth to that?"

"The motion sensors were on—the whole time. We know Reissfelder and DiMuzio went into the Dutch Room. We know they entered the Short Gallery. They were nowhere near the Blue Room."

"So it's true, Abath or Grayson Pike took the Manet?"

"It sure looks like it. It was the only thing stolen from the Blue Room. And whoever took it left the empty frame standing on the security director's chair."

"Someone was deliberately thumbing their nose at the guy."

"Possibly. But it doesn't follow they were doing it on orders from above."

"No, I guess not. And Ms. Skye's statements—what do you make of them?"

Blake had yet to read them. His blood boiled as he took in the offensive paragraphs in the *Post*.

Chapter Seven

"Grayson never had the Manet." It was Julia's voice—calm, low. "He was in charge of delivering it." They'd discovered that in a previous trance session. It had confirmed the FBI's suspicion that museum employees were involved.

Celine heard Julia's voice and allowed her mind to turn inward. She looked across the street.

DiMuzio stood still, watching as Grayson hurried to his car. Then he pulled out a key from his jeans pocket, unlocked the hatchback, and tossed in a clear plastic folder.

Celine stepped into the street, eager to take a closer look. But Sister Mary Catherine's voice stopped her.

You don't have to walk across, Celine. Will yourself over.

As Celine focused, the scene did a three-sixty-degree rotation around her. The shift in perspective was sudden and disconcerting. Instead of facing DiMuzio, she was staring at his back. Reissfelder was on his right.

She moved forward to DiMuzio's left.

"The sketches," she said. "He's taking the sketches with him."

She turned to face the man. She was standing so close to him, it would've been impossible for him not to be aware of her. He stirred uneasily, his head swiveling from left to right.

"It's like I'm being watched by a ghost," he muttered.

"It's just your mind playing tricks on you, Lenny." Reissfelder, the shorter of the two men, chuckled. A goofy grin spread over his square face. "There's nothin' here. We got this."

DiMuzio nodded curtly. "You got the vase?"

"Right here." Reissfelder waved the black velvet drawstring bag dangling from his left hand.

"Quit waving that thing around like an idiot. Put it in the car."

"Don't get all cranky on me now, Lenny." But Reissfelder obeyed the command, dropping the bag in the rear passenger seat just as Grayson hurried back.

"What now?" Grayson looked from Reissfelder to DiMuzio. The taller man was clearly in charge.

"You two take the rest of the stuff to the truck. And tell those kids"—DiMuzio meant Simon Duarte and Earl Bramer—"to drive straight to the warehouse. No funny business now. You understand. They drive the truck in, lock the warehouse, and scoot—just like we discussed."

"And then what?"

DiMuzio's lips widened. He seemed to be enjoying this. "And then we tie you down like a hog in the basement, and you wait for someone to find you."

Grayson's eyes widened. "Hey, that wasn't part of the deal. I'm supposed to be—"

"They were in on it!" Jonah's voice exploded, shocked. "The guards were really in on it. It was an inside job?"

❧

"Well?" O'Rourke asked.

"I'm still reading this," Blake replied tersely. He was actually re-reading the passage, trying to process the stuff the *Post* writer had casually bandied around. Attempting to fashion an appropriate response as well.

Although the FBI and its psychic consultant, Celine Skye, have yet to verify the identity of the individual who masterminded the Gardner heist, our source confirms Skye's visions have unearthed a valuable clue.

Our source? Blake was troubled by those words. Who was the *Post's* source?

The question niggled at his consciousness as he read on. And why were these details being so publicly revealed?

The person behind the theft, according to Skye, is associated with the museum at its highest levels, is well connected, and has a deep appreciation of Impressionist art.

In fact, Skye suggests, the target of the theft may well have been the Degas sketches, and not, as is widely believed, the more valuable Dutch works by Rembrandt, Vermeer, and Flinck.

The problem was there was a small nugget—a tiny kernel, really—of truth in the story. Celine had tentatively suggested that the General was working on behalf of someone else—and had been paid in kind with some of the works stolen from the Dutch Room.

But there were only a few people who were aware of that. And none of them would have taken it to the press.

"You still there, Markham?"

"My guess would be that Celine didn't make these remarks," he hotly informed O'Rourke. At least, not to the *Post*. To Jonah, perhaps?

"Did Hibbert send you any details of this?"

If not, Blake had an even bigger problem on his hands than he'd suspected.

"No. That's why I called."

Damn! This wasn't good.

"Wouldn't want to see another paper get an exclusive when we have a deal." O'Rourke paused. "Want me to set the record straight on this one?"

"Nope." Blake was decisive. "Ignore it. No need to fan the flames."

He was beginning to understand what was going on here. And it was a very dangerous game.

❧

Inside job. The words were swirling in Celine's brain, sounding faintly in her ears. She repeated them. An image was coming through.

"He's connected to the Gardner."

"Who is, Celine?" Julia's voice was gentle, careful not to disturb the fragments emerging. They'd done this before. Julia had learned how to guide Celine toward her insights.

"Associated with the museum. Affiliated with it." Her mind was wandering. She felt her right hand lift up, moving energetically. "Quick strokes that capture an impression. He's fascinated by that. That's why he took them." Her hand moved. Black-and-white images flashed through her mind. "Just a few quick strokes."

"Celine. . .?" Julia sounded puzzled, worried.

A phone was ringing, its tone getting louder and closer.

"You need to answer that, Celine."

Julia? Could she hear the phone ringing in Celine's trance?

"It's for you, Celine."

Celine lifted the receiver, glancing down at it in surprise. It was black, the receiver of an old-fashioned rotary phone.

"Hello?"

"Ms. Skye," the icy voice of the General's assistant sounded in her ear. "I have a message from the General. He doesn't want to kill you. But you leave him no choice."

The ringing continued.

You must die.

Celine's eyes snapped open. She stared at the three people in the room with her.

"He wants me dead," she announced. "The General wants me dead."

Chapter Eight

"No, it's not true!" Celine resisted the urge to slam down her phone. She'd been jolted out of her trance by a ringing phone. Had heard it ringing, even though the ringer was on mute.

Now she was regretting answering the damn thing.

"But the Boston newspapers say—"

"I don't care what they say," Celine interrupted the reporter from the *Paso Tribune*, her voice shrill. "I've never said anyone from within the Gardner Museum orchestrated the heist."

The July sun beat down upon her—hot and muggy after the morning drizzle—as she paced the parking lot behind the bar, phone clutched to her ear. It was making her feel feverish.

Finding herself at the edge of the lot, facing the alley that ran behind the row of businesses on 13th Street, she turned back.

Jonah was staring at her from the back door of the Delft. She glared back at him; he was responsible for this debacle, she guessed. Had to be. Who else could it be?

The urge to sock his pasty-white face and the round wire-rimmed glasses that gave him such an owl-like look was overwhelming.

Calm down, Celine, Sister Mary Catherine whispered. *Anger blocks your sight.*

I know. But her heart continued to palpitate rapidly, her breath came in shallow gasps.

The *Tribune* reporter's words filtered through the haze of red-hot fury that surrounded her.

"But you do think whoever was behind the heist wanted the Degas sketches and not the Dutch works, right?"

The guy was persistent, Celine had to give him that. Not wanting to lie, she deflected. "Do the Boston newspapers say that as well?"

She inflected an intentional note of sarcasm into her voice. It seemed to work.

"I'm afraid so, Ms. Skye." The *Tribune* reporter sounded sheepish. "Care to comment."

"I'd prefer not to dignify that kind of nonsense with any comment," she said firmly.

She hung up and strode over to Jonah.

"You're behind this, aren't you?" She stopped inches from him and glared. "I thought we had a deal. I let you sit in on my trance."

Jonah staggered back, palms raised in a gesture of surrender. "I have no idea what you're talking about, Celine?"

"Apparently every newspaper in Boston thinks the Gardner heist was an inside job—organized by someone high-up within the museum. You told them that, didn't you?"

Jonah withdrew a couple more steps, shaking his head. "No, I didn't. How could I? I only just heard you mention it in your trance."

Celine stopped, fists clenched. "I said no such thing." She frowned. "Did I?"

She didn't always remember every single word she pronounced in a trance. But surely she'd have recalled a bombshell like that.

Jonah plucked a notebook from the back pocket of his skin-tight jeans. He quickly flipped through the pages until he found what he was looking for.

"You said, quote: *Associated with the museum. Affiliated with it.*"

"That could be anyone." She'd had a vague impression of a man. It was gone now—fading away like a wisp of smoke. "And it could mean any-thing," she muttered to herself.

Her words had been vague enough to refer to a gardener, a guard, a receptionist. But there'd been an aura of power and authority about the man she'd caught a glimpse of.

She felt Jonah's eyes on her—dark brown, avid, a hungry hyena waiting for tidbits to fall from her mouth.

"So you had nothing to do with the reports in the Boston papers this morning?"

She studied his face. Was it her imagination—or was he looking paler than usual?

"Look, Celine, I swear"—Jonah held up his palms in a gesture of sur-render—"on my mother's honor."

She kept her eyes on his face.

"I've said nothing, published nothing. You have to admit, you've given me very little to work with."

That was true enough.

"Fine," she said, brushing past him back into the bar. She had to find Julia.

Chapter Nine

Julia was still in Dirck's sanctum, poring over transcripts from the morning's session. Celine stormed in, hitting a button on the wall. A panel slid out, closing them off from the main area of the bar. She didn't want Annabelle hearing about this.

"We have trouble," she said tersely.

"I can see it on your face. What's going on?" Julia's blue eyes were narrowed, but her face remained restful, impassive like the Dalai Llama.

Nothing ever seemed to take Julia by surprise, Celine reflected. The former fed was like a rock, ready for anything. Her manner brought a measure of calm to Celine.

"That was a reporter from the *Paso Tribune*. You won't believe what the Boston papers are saying." She filled her friend in.

"They've twisted my words. It's . . ." Words failed her. It felt like a betrayal. As though someone had breached her mind, filtered its impressions, and put the worst possible interpretation on them.

"It's what reporters do, Celine." Julia's head was bent over her phone's browser. "*Unconfirmed reports*," she read aloud. "At least they say that. But they couldn't resist publishing it all the same."

She gave a wry shrug. "Sounds like the kind of thing Jonah would write."

"It wasn't him," Celine told her. "I confronted him, and he categorically denied having anything to do with that tripe."

"There's nothing in the *Gazette*. So that does bear out his story, I guess."

"I just don't understand why," Celine repeated. She ground the heels of her palms together. The whole situation was so frustrating. "Why now? And Penny must be—"

"Furious. I know." Julia looked up at her. They'd promised to keep the director of the Gardner Museum in the loop. "But she'll understand you had nothing to do with this."

"Yes, but I still feel like I've betrayed her trust." Celine raked her fingers through her long red hair.

"Some of it's true, that's the worst of it," she continued. The silken strands of her hair felt pleasantly cool against her feverish fingers.

Julia gave her a piercing look. "Some of it sounds like what you said this morning. A connection to the Gardner. You've never mentioned that before—not in the context of—" She broke off. "What exactly did you see this morning when you mentioned that?"

Celine closed her eyes, trying to recall the images that were already receding from her mind. Hazy wisps of them returned. She drew them toward her like strands of cotton candy.

"I smell cologne," she whispered. "A man in a suit. His back is turned to me. Broad shoulders. Powerful."

"Can you get him to turn around?"

"No." She knew why instantly. "I've never seen his face."

Although the explanation didn't make sense. She couldn't recall seeing the General's face either.

"And the impressions? What he likes?"

"Black ink. Black chalk." Celine's right hand jerked up, executing swift movements. "Movement. He captures it so well. A moment in time. Sepia tones."

"The sketches," Julia said. "The stolen Degas sketches. Is that what you're seeing?"

The images receded from Celine's mind; she opened her eyes. Julia was still talking to herself.

"A man with an appreciation for Degas and with a connection to the Gardner Museum. A trustee?"

"I'm not sure." The image on Celine's mental screen had been from a zoomed-in perspective, too fuzzy to be interpreted in any meaningful fashion. "I don't understand what I saw or even why I saw it. My mind just seems to wander at random from one impression to another."

Julia shuffled through her notes. "It may not be quite as random as all that."

"What do you mean?"

Julia looked up. "There was something Jonah said that triggered those impressions. And you went from there to sensing the General wants you dead."

"He does want me dead." It was the one thing Celine saw quite clearly. "He may be reluctant to do it. But his mind's made up. He feels compelled."

"I believe you." Julia picked up her phone stared at it. The screen was still on the *Massachusetts Post* article. "Maybe now we know why."

✦

"Celine? You in there?" Wanda Roberts' voice followed the hard rapping on the wooden panel that concealed Dirck's sanctum from the bar.

Celine glanced over her shoulder, reluctant to end her conversation with Julia.

"You better get out here, girl!" Wanda called again. Her voice was raspy, gruff. "Your wine tasting group is gonna be here in a few."

Damn! Celine had forgotten about that. She was half-tempted to ask Wanda to cover for her, but what kind of example would that set? Not for Wanda, who had a no-nonsense, take-charge manner when it came to work. But for the rest of their employees.

"I'll be there in a minute."

Celine turned back to Julia.

"I'm not scared," she assured her friend, but her voice trembled nonetheless. She swallowed. "It's just that I don't know where the danger is coming from. Or how? And it—" She swallowed hard again.

"It unsettles you," Julia finished for her. "I know. Just go out and do your thing. I'm here. I'm always here. The General can't get to you."

Yes, he can. The words floated across her mind. *If he wants you dead, you will be.* She decided not to repeat the message to Julia.

She got to her feet. "Don't underestimate him. He's very good at killing people. It's what he does."

A customer was walking out of the Delft, arms laden with black fabric wine carriers, as Celine emerged from the sanctum, Julia behind her.

"Came in for coffee," Wanda informed her proudly, seeing Celine's gaze following the departing customer. "Walked out with Pinot Noir, Chardonnay, and a couple of bottles of Viognier."

Celine grinned. "You talked him into a tasting and sold him on our wine? Great job!"

Wanda's smile widened, brightening the expression on her smooth brown face. Her tight dark curls bobbed. "Yes, ma'am, I sure did. But I just brought the guy to the proverbial well. It was Andrea's fine winemaking skills that sold him on our product."

"You're pretty amazing, Wanda, you know that!"

Her gaze swept across the bar to the horseshoe-shaped counter—set for a wine tasting. Barely four months ago, Dirck had stood behind it.

A ball of pain swelled within her throat. It was hard to believe he was gone.

"I set the wine glasses out for you." Wanda's voice cut through the haze of pain. "And the menus." She pointed. "Plates of cheese sticks and bowls of pistachios."

The nuts were grown on the estate. No one had thought to package them up and serve them to the customers until Wanda came along.

Celine bit back the tears threatening to well up in her eyes. "Thanks, Wanda. I don't know what I'd do without you."

Chapter Ten

The wine tasting was going well. At least something was, Celine thought.

She brought out another bottle as her guests downed the last drop and held their glasses out, ready to sample the next item on the tasting menu.

"Next up, is our Chardonnay." She tipped the wine bottle; the straw-colored wine sloshed into the wine glass. "You'll notice hints of apricot and pear."

She pushed the glass toward the young woman leaning eagerly forward.

The Sauvignon Blanc she'd served earlier had been favorably received. It was light with a bright, crisp, citrusy note that most patrons—even those new to wine—found extremely pleasing.

Celine hoped the party of six—a young bride-to-be, her fiancé, the bride's parents, and the groom's father and stepmother—enjoyed the Chardonnay as well.

"This is really good!" The bride-to-be, an attractive, dark-haired woman, nodded in appreciation. "Isn't it, Jordan?" She turned to her fiancé.

"Yup," Jordan agreed, his lips squished against the rim of his wine glass.

He doesn't like it, Celine thought. *But he thinks he'll be sleeping on the couch if he gives her an honest opinion.*

It was no way to start a relationship, but he wasn't entirely wrong about the wine.

The Chardonnay was harder to like—aged a little longer than the Sauvignon Blanc, it had an oaky aftertaste that took some getting used to.

The relief on her guests' faces when Celine mentioned this was unmistakable. People new to wine tended to think they had to appreciate every bottle they tasted.

"Yes, it is a bit. . ." The bride-to-be wrinkled her nose daintily.

"Definitely," Jordan said, feeling himself on firmer ground now.

"It gets a creamy, buttery flavor as it ages," Celine informed the couple.

They'd have a good marriage—if only Jordan didn't feel pressured into telling white lies so as not to rock the boat.

"And that woodsy taste mellows out." She gave them a dazzling smile. This was the best part of the job—guiding new people into an appreciation of fine wine. It was helping to take her mind off the other, darker events relentlessly pressing into her consciousness.

"This'll be a good bottle to keep for your second or third anniversary."

"Ooh! That's a fantastic idea." The bride tipped her glass up, swallowing the rest of her Chardonnay. "I think we'll take a couple of bottles. What do you think, honey?"

"Absolutely!" Jordan was appropriately enthusiastic. But then he'd have been just as eager to please if his fiancée had suggested he jump off a cliff.

Celine suppressed a grin, but as she glanced up, her amusement faded.

There was the red Mustang she'd seen earlier that morning. A tall figure swept out of the sports car. Then the image faded, the sun glinting against the window making her squint.

This was the second time she'd had a vision of the man. What could it mean?

Her heart muscles clenched.

Was she seeing the General's agent? The agent of her death?

"You look really pale, miss." The gruff male voice—the bride's father—brought her out of her reverie. "Everything okay?"

"You look like you've seen a ghost." This from the groom's stepmother, a slender woman in her forties with wavy hair dyed platinum blond.

"Wait!" Her jaw dropped. "You're the psychic who helped recover those paintings stolen from the Gardner Museum, aren't you?"

"I do believe you're right, babycakes!" The groom's father slapped his thigh. "That's her all right." He leaned forward, chest hairs poking out of his baggy floral-patterned shirt. "So, you really think that heist was an inside job?"

"It's in all the papers," the bride's mother explained apologetically. "The Boston papers."

"You're from Boston?" Celine surveyed the party. She'd grown so accustomed to hearing the Boston tones in Annabelle's voice, her guests' distinctive accents had escaped her.

The bride nodded. "You really are psychic, aren't you?"

"Were you having a vision just now?" The bride's mother stared at her, eyes wide. She was dying of cancer—Celine could see it in the fading colors of her aura and the yellowish hue of her skin. But the woman's curiosity remained undiminished. "Something to do with the Gardner heist?"

Everyone leaned forward expectantly.

Celine felt her cheeks flaming. Some wine tasting this was turning out to be. *Don't comment*, Julia had warned her. But if she refused to say a word, wouldn't that just lend credence to the *Post*'s wild speculations?

Speculations that Julia was beginning to think might have some basis in fact. Although Celine still wasn't sure.

The faint whisper of cologne assailed her nostrils again. An expensive suit. Broad shoulders. A powerful male presence.

Was Julia right? Was this someone high up in the museum's hierarchy?

"*Connected to the Gardner*, your words. What else could that mean?" Julia asked when Celine questioned her leap in logic. They'd managed to sneak in a whispered discussion when Celine had hurried into the kitchen for refills on the cheese sticks and pistachios. The men in the group had made short work of those.

"Besides I can't think of anything else that would've put a target on your back, can you?"

Celine had been forced to concede she couldn't. Dismaying as the prospect was, they'd have to at least consider the possibility Julia was right. What Penny would have to say about that when she heard, Celine didn't know. The thought brought back the queasy sensation she'd felt earlier, as though her stomach were in free fall.

The loud buzzing of her guests' voices invaded her thoughts.

"Oh, do tell us what you think!" the bride was urging her.

"It's an ongoing investigation." Julia had appeared from nowhere. "Ms. Skye can't comment on it."

"But she told the papers it was an inside job," the groom's father argued.

"Actually, no, I didn't," Celine said, taking matters into her own hands. "I'm sorry to say the *Post* never reached out to me for comment. If they had, I would've corrected their impressions."

"So, what do you think?" The groom's father wasn't about to let go. Julia looked as though she wanted to sock him. She opened her mouth, her expression stormy.

Celine could hear the former fed's thoughts as clearly as though she'd uttered them. *Put a sock in it, buddy!*

She reached out for her friend's hand; her gaze bore into Julia's. She couldn't allow the former fed to drive away potential customers.

You could easily put a stop to this, my dear, Sister Mary Catherine murmured. *Sometimes tact and circumspection are vastly overrated.*

Her hand still covering Julia's, Celine turned to the groom's father and smiled. "I think fidelity is very important in a relationship." She gazed meaningfully at the florid-faced man. "The older one grows, especially."

The man reddened as did the bride's mother. The groom's father sputtered into his wine, his question forgotten.

It had been a momentary indiscretion, Celine knew—embarrassing to both parties in the clear light of day. She wouldn't have exploited it, but she'd been left with no choice.

She turned to the young couple. "Why don't we drink to that with our next wine—a lovely Viognier with notes of ripe melon and fragrant pear?"

Celine was about to introduce the bridal party to Mechelen's red wines when her winemaker called.

"The man you wished to meet is here, *cara*."

"What man?" She didn't recall having made any appointments.

"A sculptor." Andrea's voice rose, making it seem like a question. She saw him in her mind's eye shrugging and spreading out his palms. "Referred, he says, by the lady from the Gardner Museum."

"Penny. Oh, yes!" The details rushed back into her mind. She'd agreed a few weeks ago to meet a sculptor Penny had recommended. A rising New England artist the Director of the Gardner had insisted she meet.

"A bronze or marble here and there would liven up the place, my dear. And I know just the right person."

"He's here now?" Celine glanced at the wine-tasting party in dismay. She couldn't abandon them halfway through the tasting.

"For a few hours, yes." Andrea sounded regretful. But she knew he'd draw the line at taking her place to discuss artworks with their visitor.

"Damn," she softly cursed. She'd known the man would be flying in that week, but she hadn't realized it would be that morning. She scanned the bar.

Wanda was busy attending to another group. Annabelle knew nothing about wine. No, Celine couldn't leave. The meeting would have to be delegated.

"It's Andrea," she said, catching Julia's eye. "Penny's sculptor is here."

"No problem. You go on." Julia fished out a black apron from under the bar counter, looping it around her neck before Celine could voice her request. "I can manage this lot."

"No, Julia, I—"

But Julia had already swooped up a bottle of Grenache and was approaching her guests.

"Alrighty folks, we're moving on to the funky reds now."

"*Funky*?" The bride asked doubtfully. Her eyes skittered toward Celine who lingered midway between the horseshoe-shaped bar counter and the door, watching nervously.

"It's not funky at all," Celine assured her. They'd lose customers if this continued. But Julia seemed blissfully unaware of the effect she was having on the tasters.

"A little more earthy, harder to like." The former fed sloshed a small quantity of the dark red wine into the bride's glass. "Higher alcohol content, on the plus side. So you get more of a buzz."

The bride took a tentative sip. "Mmmm." She licked her lips and glanced at the tasting menu. "It says here it has cherry notes."

Julia nodded sagely. "Black cherry. Word to the wise?" She leaned closer and dropped her voice. "Those cherry notes come out a lot stronger with a packet of Equal."

Oh God! Celine groaned. Julia hadn't really suggested adding artificial sweetener to their wine, had she?

"*Equal?*" The bride's mother sounded just as scandalized as Celine felt.

"Sure. Brings out the sweet tones. Makes it more palatable. I do it all the time."

"Julia!"

The former fed looked up. "Shouldn't you get going?" She wiggled her fingers, gesturing toward the door. "You'll be late for your appointment. Trust me, I got this."

She pushed a glass caddy filled with tiny packets of sweetener toward her guests. "Wanna give it a try?"

"Uhmm." Jordan eyed the caddy; his gaze slid guiltily to his bride-to-be. "Sure, why not?"

All right, there was officially no way to salvage the situation. Celine pushed open the heavy glass door and fled.

Chapter Eleven

The phone rang as Celine sped away from downtown Paso Robles. Reluctantly, she brought it up, resting it against the wheel before lowering her eyes to the screen.

Penny Hoskins. Celine's stomach clenched. She wasn't in the mood to talk. Not to Penny. Not to anyone else, for that matter.

She'd been looking forward to a quiet drive.

Away from the narrow streets of downtown Paso Robles, the road opened up, areas of undulating green stretching out on either side of her. It had promised to be a restful drive.

Her ringtone—the opening section of Vivaldi's *Summer*—completed its allotted segment and looped back to the beginning. Shriller and louder on its second rendition.

Celine was tempted to ignore it. But she owed Penny an explanation.

"Penny!" She answered the call, putting herself on speaker. "I'm driving," she said by way of apology. "I'm really sorry about—"

"Oh, don't worry about that." Penny's breathy voice interrupted her. "Don't get me wrong, I'm furious. But I know you had nothing to do with it."

True. But she couldn't help feeling guilty all the same. A whiff of cologne filled the Pilot—a psychic sensation from earlier. She was certain the mysterious male presence she'd felt was connected to the heist—behind it, possibly.

But she couldn't be certain—as Julia now was—that he was connected to the Gardner—a powerful figure on the inside.

Inside job, her consciousness whispered, contradicting her certainty.

Julia had shown her the transcript. There was no denying that the images she'd seen had been triggered by Jonah's use of those words.

After she'd heard them, her mind had gone straight from the scene outside the museum to a different place, a different time.

But . . . she hadn't mentioned that before. Hadn't told the *Massachusetts Post* about it either. Where had they gotten that from?

"Celine?"

She started guiltily at the sound of her name. Penny had been droning on, and Celine had tuned her out. She tuned back into the conversation.

"Sorry, I, eh . . . I was concentrating. There's a bend in the road."

There was. But she'd driven this route thousands of times and could take the turns blindfolded.

"I was just saying that I think you'll like Tony Reynolds."

"Reynolds?" She was about to ask who he was when Penny filled her in.

"The sculptor I was telling you about. He should have arrived by now . . . Hasn't he?"

So that was the guy's name. Reynolds.

"He has," she informed Penny. "I'm on my way to meet him now."

"Brilliant. Hope it goes well. I think you'll love him!"

Celine smiled as they exchanged goodbyes and she hung up. Penny's ebullience was as potent as a psychic defense charm. It buoyed Celine's sagging spirits.

She pushed the pedal to the floor, enjoying the ride. She was on Linne Road now, passing through neighboring wineries. The first signs of *Veraison*—that exciting moment when the grapes begin to show their colors—were visible. Clusters of grapes tinged with red dangled from leafy vines.

The leaves would have to be pruned back, poorer clusters taken off the vine. The added sunlight would enable the best specimens to ripen to an optimal level of sweetness.

But as she approached the Mechelen—the vineyard and winery she owned now—the sight of workers in gloves and boots moving through the rows of vines failed to cheer her.

A black cloud seemed to brood over the vineyard. The dark memory of being held captive in a Boston shed returned. She felt like a fly walking into the General's web. Only this time there would be no escape.

Be careful whom you trust, Celine, Sister Mary Catherine warned her. *Be careful.*

Her Pilot entered the gates of the Mechelen, scrunching slowly over the gravel-strewn driveway.

She clutched the wheel, her palms clammy. This wasn't a fight she was prepared for.

❧

A car parked outside the Mechelen Estate Tasting Room caught her eye. A red Mustang.

The same red Mustang she'd seen twice before outside the Delft. She rubbed her eyes. Another vision?

Celine climbed out of the Pilot. Her palms were sweaty. She rubbed them down the sides of her black jeans and stepped gingerly toward the sports car.

It remained where it was. She was inches away from it now. Slowly she stretched her hand toward the door, half-expecting her fingers to go through.

But the vehicle's smooth red metal stopped her probing fingertips, the heat from its sun-warmed surface penetrating her skin. Definitely not a psychic experience.

"That is our visitor's car, *cara*. Mr. Anthony Reynolds."

Celine pulled her hand back with a start.

Andrea was standing on the stone porch of the Tasting Room.

"He is waiting inside for you." He gestured toward the double wood-and-glass doors behind him.

"Thanks, Andrea." She walked briskly toward him, trying to shake off the feeling of unease that enshrouded her like a fog. Forcing a smile on her face, she stepped up alongside him on the porch. "I'll take it from here."

"*Cara*?" Her winemaker stopped her. "Have you given any thought to the vineyard on sale?"

"Yes, I—" Celine paused, unsure how to continue. Her gaze shifted away from her winemaker's eager face.

The small vineyard nestled in the foothills of the Santa Lucia mountains was ideal for the kind of wines Andrea wanted to develop. It was some minutes north and west of the Mechelen, but it wasn't the distance between the properties that bothered Celine.

The Mechelen was doing remarkably well at the moment—business was booming. It was tempting to expand, to buy new properties. But Celine sensed a cloud of impending doom. The estate would weather the storm, but only if they conserved their financial resources.

Her eyes returned to Andrea's face. "I don't think this is the right time, Andrea."

His face fell.

She reached out and gently squeezed his hand.

"Trust me, it's not. If we buy the property now, we'll find ourselves in deep trouble."

"It's a steal at the price," he protested. "Someone else will take it"—his arm swiped forward and upward—"out from under us, *cara*, and—"

"And they'll be eager to sell it next year."

He straightened up. "You are mistaken, *cara*. It's not bad land. The soil is rich, the grapes will get plenty of sun."

"It's not the land," Celine cut him short. "It's the economy. It won't last."

In her mind's eye, she saw the silken red folds of a five-starred flag fluttering in the wind. A dark cloud hung over it, spreading outward.

It will come from China, she murmured.

"What will, *cara?*"

Andrea's voice snapped her out of her reverie. She wasn't aware of having spoken aloud.

"The illness that will imprison us in our homes," she said. The image had vanished. But it was replaced by a sense of nausea so strong, she nearly doubled over.

"*Cara?*" Andrea gripped her arm.

"I'm okay." She swallowed hard. "Let's not keep Mr. Reynolds waiting."

Chapter Twelve

The man who greeted Celine—"Hello, I'm Tony!"—as she emerged from the Tasting Room into the garden behind it was in his forties. Tall, muscular, a carbon copy of the phantom man who'd stepped out of his phantom vehicle outside the Delft and headed straight for her.

Tony's arm was extended out to her, not quite bridging the distance between them. She ignored it, wondering why she'd been shown a vision of him—not once, but twice—before they'd even met.

To a psychic, a prevision like that was usually indicative of a warning. But what kind of warning did Tony represent? Death?

The sculptor had been nowhere to be seen when Celine had followed Andrea into the Tasting Room. She'd glimpsed him in the garden, instead —restlessly pacing the narrow flagstone path that meandered through it.

He'd leaped forward the moment he caught sight of her, hand outstretched—like a leopard that had sighted its prey.

"Afraid of germs or do you just not believe in shaking people's hands?"

Tony Reynolds smiled down at her. A friendly smile that held no menace.

Aware she'd been gaping at the sculptor, Celine closed her mouth.

"Umm, sorry." He didn't seem particularly threatening now.

Although she'd flinched when he initially homed in on her.

Her gaze dropped to his outstretched hand. Beyond it, she saw the corner of his bulging leather briefcase sitting on the grass.

If he represented some sort of danger to her, she couldn't identify it. Yet, she'd seen him twice before encountering him in person. Why?

"Ms. Skye? Everything all right?" Reynolds kept his hand out, still waiting for her to clasp it.

Her own arm moved stiffly forward. Her fingers encountered his warm palm, feeling the fine brown hairs that covered the back of his hand and muscular wrist.

Images jolted through her almost immediately—like an electric shock through a circuit she was powerless to disconnect.

A large, furry, gray spider crawled along a slender bronze vessel. *The real thing*, Tony had thought when he'd grasped it, oblivious to the spider's presence.

Green-patterned wallpaper—where had she seen it before? A gold-framed portrait of a young man in a plumed cap. Tony was drawn to the work, she could tell.

A jagged fracture slashed the painting. The spider hoisted itself out, lifting one furry leg, then another out from behind the ragged edges. It crawled onto the wallpaper.

Snatches of words from a cold, familiar voice.

A liability . . . you must eliminate . . .

"The General?" As her mind felt its way to the interpretation, her gaze collided with Reynolds'. "You know him?"

The voice she'd heard belonged to the General's assistant. Although if Reynolds had been hired by the man, surely he knew the General as well?

Was that why she'd sensed his presence, seen him gunning for her? Had he been sent to eliminate a liability? *Her?*

"You do know the General." She held Reynold's gaze. "You work for him. That's why you're here, right?"

"I have no idea what you're talking about." The sculptor's eyes were cold. He abruptly pulled his hand away mid-shake.

Out of the corner of her eye, Celine saw the Lady—Belle Gardner—shimmer in and out of the noonday sun.

A warning for her? Or for Tony Reynolds?

On the sunny patch of grass between them, their shadows intertwined. That meant their paths were connected—flowing together for however short a time.

Celine squinted suspiciously up at him. "Why are you here?"

"Penny Hoskins thought you'd be interested in my work. But if you're not"—the smile was gone, his tone brusque—"I won't bother wasting any more of your time."

Reynolds swept up his leather case and brushed past her, ready to leave.

"No, wait." Celine caught his arm. If he was on the General's payroll, she didn't want him leaving. Not before she had a chance to find out more.

"I know Penny sent you," she said. "But that's not the only reason you're here, is it? There's something else . . . ?"

She let her voice trail off, certain the sculptor had sought her out for a purpose other than the works she was going to commission.

Reynolds faced her. A flicker of uncertainty shot through his eyes—green like her own.

You're psychic.

She received the thought foremost in his mind. The rest of it was blocked to her.

"Whatever it is, you should get it off your chest," she urged him.

Before it's too late. The words crossed her mental screen, but she didn't utter them.

Could she persuade him to break his silence?

Reynolds turned away. "Trust me, there's nothing."

He's nervous, Celine, Sister Mary Catherine said softly. *You'll need to put him at his ease first.*

"Fine. Let's talk about the work." Celine forced herself to smile at him. "You've had a chance to see the grounds. Most people gather here behind the Tasting Room or in that area there." She pointed to the gently sloping area to the left of the garden.

Trees dotted it and a scattering of round stone tables encircled by benches and shaded by green umbrellas spread far into the distance.

"We'd like our sculptures to be displayed here, out in the open. I want the pieces to be a testament to Dirck and John, the men who started the business. I have some ideas, but I'd like to hear your thoughts first."

"I'd be happy to show you what I've got." His tone was polite but something in him had shut down.

You'll need to win his trust back, Celine, Sister Mary Catherine reminded her.

I know, Celine thought. "I'm ready whenever you are," she said out loud, lips curving into what she hoped was an inviting, hospitable smile.

"Can we sit there?" Reynolds gestured toward the umbrella-shaded stone benches beyond. "I like to spread out my drawings and scale models."

❧

"These are really good!" Celine marveled at the large-scale, three-dimensional drawings spread out on the table before her.

She raised her eyes toward Reynolds and repeated her praise: "Really good!"

Her smile this time was genuine, not forced upon her face to put the sculptor at his ease. His draftsmanship was truly excellent, although when she'd complimented him on it, he'd confided he'd never been good enough to make it as a painter.

Now Reynolds smiled back at her. "I thought you'd like these ideas. I like to research my clients and their backgrounds before coming up with anything."

The tension had eased out of him as he'd shared his drawings with her, but he still seemed cagey. His mind remained closed to her. Celine knew because she'd attempted to probe it—feeling like a peeping Tom for doing so.

But Reynolds was concealing something—and she needed to know what it was. Behind his mental shield—in her mind's eye, Celine saw it as a copper plate—was information she had to get to.

What else am I to do? she'd responded when Sister Mary Catherine had admonished her. *It's not like he'll tell me if I ask.*

You wait for him to confide in you. Sister Mary Catherine was annoyed. *You don't wander into other people's minds any more than you'd wander in through their doors, Celine. It's an invasion of privacy.*

I know. And she did. But if Reynolds was connected to the General, she needed to know how.

She'd had a premonition of death and two previsions of Reynolds before meeting the sculptor. She was entitled to a little mental trespassing.

Reynolds seemed on the verge of a revelation, though. She sensed the hesitation in him—the desire to open up to her. Would flattery help?

"I love the allusions to Vermeer." She pointed to an apron-clad figure of John Mechelen standing by a table, pouring wine from a pitcher into a wine glass.

It was a reference to Vermeer's *The Milkmaid.* A very apt one, she thought. The names of the vineyard and bar she'd inherited alluded to the Dutch master.

"I'd heard from Penny Hoskins that Thins and Mechelen were instrumental in revealing Vermeer's technique," he said. "I figured this would be a good way to suggest a love of both wine and art."

So Penny had helped with his research. The Director of the Gardner tended to be voluble, giving out more information than she needed to. What else, Celine wondered, had she told Reynolds?

"She mentioned Simon Underwood using Vermeer's technique and becoming an artist of note," he said when she asked.

"That's a reference to *The Art of Painting,*" Celine guessed, pointing to a three-dimensional drawing of Underwood sitting before an easel.

Underwood—a friend of both Dirck and John from their Boston University days—had lost his life four months ago at the same time Dirck had been murdered.

The men who'd tightened the wire around their necks may have been apprehended. But the General—the man who'd ordered the kills—was still at large.

"Yes, but he's painting *The Concert.*" Reynolds indicated the unfinished painting on the easel.

Celine examined the drawing. Had Reynolds made the reference to *The Concert* because Simon Underwood had forged the Gardner's stolen painting? Or because Dirck had been instrumental in returning it?

"I'm assuming Underwood knew Dirck and John had it," Reynolds' voice broke into her reverie.

"Most likely he did." Celine nodded curtly. What was Reynolds getting at? More importantly, what did he know?

She was beginning to lose patience. Time to goad him into speaking.

I wouldn't, if I were you, Sister Mary Catherine warned, but the words were already out of Celine's mouth.

"Did Penny happen to mention I'm psychic?" Her gaze penetrated the green depths of the sculptor's eyes.

He met her gaze, his eyes veiled. "She did."

Damn, she'd blown it. His mental guard was all the way up again. There'd be no penetrating that burnished copper wall of defense.

It was too late to back down. She forged ahead.

"I have a strong sense you came here for a reason. To say or do something." She saw the Lady out of the corner of her eye. "I wouldn't leave it too late, if I were you."

"I've done what I set out to do." Reynolds got to his feet. He picked up his leather case. "You can keep the drawings and the scale models. Let me know if you want any changes."

"Listen." Celine stumbled to her feet. "You can't go back to Boston. You're in danger." Was he really? Or was she just desperate to keep him in Paso Robles until she could pry the truth out of him?

He looked at her. "I have to go back. My exhibition opens tomorrow."

She'd forgotten about that. The Gardner had offered to host an exclusive showing of Reynolds' sculptures.

"I can't let Penny down." His lips stretched into a slow grin. "Even if it means dying in a plane crash. At least she'll know I died trying to make it to the show."

Chapter Thirteen

Minutes after the sculptor had left, Celine remained seated at the outdoor table. A woodpecker's rhythmic drumming on a nearby tree trunk the only sound punctuating the stillness around her.

She'd scared Reynolds away, Celine was convinced of that. But why? Because she'd sensed he had a purpose in visiting Paso Robles—a purpose that had little to do with her commission?

Of course, if he'd been sent to kill her, he hadn't accomplished his task. She'd come out of the encounter still alive.

On a whim, she reached into her purse and took out her phone. Blake answered the phone on the first ring.

"Good timing. I was just about to call you."

"Why?" she wondered, genuinely curious.

"The articles in the Boston papers."

"Oh that." She'd forgotten about it, her mind focusing on more pressing matters.

"You've had reporters plaguing you, I'm told."

"Then you also know I've told them nothing," she responded. "Did Julia call you?"

"Wasn't she supposed to?"

"No, it's just that she's supposed to be attending to my wine-tasting party."

"Julia? Helping with a wine tasting? Wow!" Blake chortled. "If you don't want to be in the wine business, Celine, sell the estate. There's no need to deliberately run it into the ground."

She laughed along with him. "I'm sure Julia's managing just fine." At least Celine hoped she was. "Listen—"

But Blake interrupted before she could explain her reason for calling.

"Look, I'm glad you're not as bothered by those goddamn articles as I feared you might be. The TV stations have been sniffing around, but we've been able to convince them it's nothing but errant gossip.

"Even so, we've got to be careful now, seriously watch our steps. Especially after those startling revelations you had this morning. We need to keep a lid on insights like that."

"I had them *after*"—Celine emphasized the word—"the article had already come out."

"You're sure about that?"

"Yes, why?" He was acting like she'd personally leaked the information to the press.

Blake blew out a pent-up sigh. "We've always suspected the General was behind Hibbert's hit piece, right?"

"Yes, it was a great way of finding out whether the other stolen items were in my backyard."

"Right." Blake released another breath. "But what would the General's motive be for divulging this information—that a high-level insider might be involved? Why release that fact—especially if it might be true?"

"Clearly, he didn't." Celine wasn't sure where Blake was going with this.

"Then we have to consider the idea of a mole in our ranks. Someone who's leaking information to the press—and it would be easy to do with Jonah Hibbert dogging your steps—as a way of communicating with the General."

"You mean someone's watching us." The skin on her nape prickled. "And passing the information along via what looks like sensationalist gossip in the media?"

"Yes, and with Hibbert—"

She shook her head. "It wasn't him." Jonah hadn't been privy to any of her prior sessions. "If you're worried about a leak, it's gotta be someone in the FBI. Although I can't imagine where they got the information they did leak."

"Fact is, none of it was that much of a stretch from what you've said before. Sounds like you spooked someone, and this is his—or her—way of warning the General that you're getting closer to the truth. Your theory —that there were two people behind the theft and two different motives for it—has never been made public. But it's all over the news now. That can't be a coincidence."

Blake paused. "There are a lot of people around you these days. You've got Annabelle, Bryan, that new marketing manager of yours, Jonah. Anything you inadvertently let slip could fall into the wrong hands.

But these were all people she could trust. She didn't belabor the point, though.

"I'll be careful," she promised instead. Then before he could say anything else, she plunged ahead with her request. "There's a favor I'd like to ask." After that humiliating raid on her property, she figured he owed her.

Besides the hunch she wanted to follow up on could only be done with FBI resources.

"Sure, anything," Blake said without hesitation.

～

She was still sitting in the garden when Blake called back twenty minutes later.

"You were right," he informed Celine.

Celine clutched the phone to her ear, listening carefully.

"Reynolds was booked on a later flight out of SLO County. He made a last-minute change, taking the first available flight back to Boston."

"I knew it!" Validation surged through her being—a familiar electrifying tingle that lit up her body when her psychic senses were proven right. "I just knew it."

The afternoon sun warmed her back, dappling the wood and bronze models Reynolds had left behind. She fingered them absent-mindedly.

"He seemed in such a hurry to leave. He comes all the way from Boston. It's a long flight. You'd think he'd stay a while. But no."

She couldn't for the life of her figure out what she'd said to send the sculptor hurtling back to Boston. But at least she'd confirmed her suspicion that it had something to do with their encounter.

"Wish I knew what I said to drive him away," she mused.

Blake coughed. "What exactly is this about, Celine?"

The question took her by surprise, although it shouldn't have. She hadn't told Blake anything other than that she needed a favor. There'd been a reason for that.

There was nothing concrete she could offer the agent about Tony Reynolds. Just a strong inkling that something seemed fishy. And she hadn't wanted Blake to balk at using FBI resources for what, on the face of it, seemed like a flimsy reason.

She'd allowed him to think she was merely checking out Reynolds as an individual she'd possibly be contracting with.

"Listen, you're a grown woman," Blake broke the silence. "You probably know what you're doing. But . . . ahmm . . . Tony Reynolds might not be the best person for you to pursue."

"I thought you said he didn't have a criminal record."

She'd asked about that in her initial phone call, and Blake had confirmed that the sculptor seemed to be operating on the right side of the law.

That had shed some light on the connection she'd perceived between him and the General. Either Reynolds had no idea who he was dealing with. Or, until that point, the association had been entirely on the up-and-up.

No different than the connection the General might have with a house-keeper—if he employed one—or a gardener or a delivery boy.

"He doesn't," Blake confirmed her assumption. "But he has a reputation for being something of a womanizer. Treats women like playthings. Yet they keep running to him like moths to a flame."

He paused.

"I just don't want to see you getting hurt."

It took her some time to process the federal agent's concerns.

"You think I'm . . . you can't possibly think I . . ."

"Look, he's a handsome man. I get it. And you're a grown woman. Just thought you should know, he may not be interested in anything more than a casual fling."

"I don't think he's interested in even that." Blake was beginning to say something, but Celine spoke over him. "And neither am I. But I sensed a connection to the General."

She elaborated on what she'd received psychically since the morning.

"Jesus Christ, Celine! You could've told me that when you called."

She ignored the remark. "Before Reynolds left, he said he'd done what he set out to do. But if he was sent to *eliminate a liability*—me—he didn't do it."

Either he'd changed his mind. Or—

"He must have been trying to get the lay of the land—scouting out the place, determining the vulnerabilities in your security. Does Julia know?"

"I haven't spoken with her yet."

She hadn't wanted to know how many potential patrons Julia had driven away with her flippant attitude toward the wine they were selling. Doctoring their reds with Equal, for goodness' sake!

"Goddammit, Celine, you need to tell her. Neither one of us can protect you if we have no idea where the danger is coming from. And if you've identified the source of the threat . . ." His voice tightened.

She heard the tense drumbeat of his fingers on the phone. He was recalling the kidnapping he'd failed to prevent four months ago. Her kidnapping.

But that had been as much her fault as his. She was the psychic on the team.

"I'll put a tail on him." Blake had managed to get a grip on his emotions. "We know when his flight arrives. We'll be ready for him whatever he tries to do."

Chapter Fourteen

Wanda called just as Celine was gathering up the drawings Reynolds had left.

"I'm headed back," Celine said immediately, attempting to forestall any complaints her new marketing manager might have about Julia's handling of customers.

"There's no rush," Wanda assured her. "I just thought you'd want to know that Julia—"

"I know. I shouldn't have left her with the wedding party. I guess she drove them away, huh?"

"No—"

"No?" Celine nervously fingered the beautiful woodpecker made of English cedar Reynolds had left along with his other scale models.

Dear God, it couldn't be much worse than that, could it?

"What do you mean, *no*? What exactly did Julia do?"

"She sold an entire case of red wine to the wedding party."

"What!" Celine slipped the woodpecker into her purse. She'd need to find a place to display it.

Reynolds had spied a woodpecker in the images showcasing the Mechelen's ornate gardens on their website and had decided a replica would be the perfect installation. "It captures the spirit of the place," he'd told her.

The memory ran through her mind on a parallel track as she continued to speak. "You've got to be kidding me," she told Wanda.

"I'm not, God's honor." Wanda giggled. "They all loved the idea of adding sweetener to their wine."

Of course they had. Wine was an acquired taste—the reds, in particular, requiring years of familiarity before they could be fully appreciated. New to the world of wine, her guests had obviously not had the time to develop a taste for the robust reds the Mechelen's Italian winemaker loved to create.

An awful thought ran through her mind. "Julia didn't sell our entire supply of Equal as well, did she?"

Wanda burst out laughing. "No, of course not. But I have a feeling those folks just might be headed to the nearest grocery store. They've got a lot of wine to sweeten."

Wanda's laughter was contagious. Celine was about to join in when she caught sight of her winemaker near the Tasting Room. She bit back her grin. "Do me a favor, Wanda—make sure Andrea doesn't hear about this, okay?"

Andrea wouldn't find the story all that amusing. Quite the contrary, in fact.

"I won't," Wanda promised. "But you've got to admit it's a great way to sell red wine. Especially to newbies."

There was a pause.

"You might want to let Julia help out a little more, you know," Wanda suggested. "Seeing as how you're busy with . . . other stuff."

The marketing manager's words reminded Celine of something she'd been meaning to do for a long time. The morning's events and the encounter with Reynolds had cemented her decision.

"About that, there's something I need to say." She hesitated, unsure how to explain what she wanted. "This work that I do—helping Julia, Penny, the FBI—it takes me away from the business. But that's not the worst of it —"

"You're thinking of selling, is that it?" Wanda's gruff voice sounded harsher than ever.

"No, Wanda—"

"It's okay, if you are. It's your business. Just let me—let everyone—know when, so we can, you know. . ."

"Wanda, I'm not going to sell our vineyards and bar." Celine set her tote bag down and transferred her phone to her other ear. "I wanted to ask if you'd be okay with being named as a beneficiary on the Trust?"

There was silence on the other end. Unsure of Wanda's reaction, Celine hurtled along. "I mean, if something were to happen to me—which, it could. I can't pretend the work I do doesn't put me in harm's way. If that happened, would you be willing to take over?"

She hadn't told Wanda about the premonition she'd had that morning— that she was next on the General's hit list. Acknowledging the potential of danger was as far as she was willing to go. The sound of Wanda's breathing filled the silence between them—amplified by the phone's speaker.

Celine held her breath. Was she asking too much of Wanda? The twenty-six-year-old had been hired barely months ago. And now Celine was asking her to consider devoting her entire life to a business built by two men she'd never even met.

"You won't be on your own. Andrea will be named on the Trust as well." She was going to ask him to partner with her. If the General succeeded in executing his threat, he'd be the best person to take charge and continue Dirck and John's legacy. "But Andrea will need help."

She waited for Wanda to say something—anything.

"Wanda?"

"I—I don't know what to say. I'm so honored, I—"

"Then, you'll do it?"

"If you need me to, sure. You took me in, Celine. I'll never forget that. I won't let you down, I promise."

❧

"Putting your affairs in order, Celine."

Charles Durand, the lawyer she'd inherited along with the business, leaned back in his leather armchair and regarded her. He was a husky man in his fifties with prematurely graying hair, pink cheeks, and sharp, sapphire-blue eyes.

"You could say that." Celine placed her tote bag on the floor. She'd stopped by the lawyer's office on her way back to the Delft. The sooner she handled this the better.

"I'm glad you are." Durand interlaced his fingers. "Not many people your age would think to do it. No one realizes just how much bother they can save their family and friends when they give their eventual demise some thought."

"That's exactly why I'm doing this," Celine informed him. "To save everyone needless trouble."

The afternoon sun poured in through the plate glass wall panels of Lance, Douglass & Durand, bathing her cushioned chair and Durand's dark wood desk in a warm, golden glow. She was on the right path.

Ignoring the Lady's presence by the window, Celine launched into an explanation of what she wanted. Reynolds' abrupt departure had put something into motion; she just didn't know what.

"Naming Wanda Roberts as a beneficiary is no problem." Durand glanced up from the notes he'd been scribbling on a narrow white pad. "But have you spoken to Andrea about naming him a partner? You'll need his consent in order to proceed."

"I have it," Celine said. After much grumbling, her winemaker had agreed to her proposition. "You should name a younger person, *cara*," he'd said. "One more likely than me to outlive you."

"I'll do that," she'd promised, "the moment I find someone who knows as much about wine as you do."

"Do you need him here?" she asked Durand now. "To sign papers?"

Durand dismissed the idea. "I'll draw up the papers and have them sent over. You and Giordano can handle them at your leisure." He put his pen down. "I'm glad you're taking this step, Celine. But let's face it, you have plenty of time. Most of my other clients wait until they're actually knocking on Death's door."

He took a sip from the tall glass of water on his desk. "Anything else I can do for you?"

"I'm not sure." Celine chose her words carefully. "I'd like to name Bryan Curtis as a beneficiary, but . . ."

But Annabelle's son resented her so much, he'd find a reason to take offense at the gesture. And Annabelle herself had balked at the idea of having any formal association with the business.

"I'm too old for this kind of thing, Celine," she'd said, her gray curls bouncing as she shook her head strenuously. "I'm happy to help you. But I really don't want to run a business. I've no head for it."

Durand played with his pen, flicking it upside down as he regarded her. "Dirck's nephew. It would be fitting."

"Yes, it would, but"—Celine looked down at her clenched hands—"he'll see it as a burden at best. Throwing him a few crumbs to placate him at worst." She raised her eyes. "There doesn't seem to be anything I can do right as far as Bryan is concerned."

Durand nodded. "He's hurting, Celine. Grieving, I guess."

"It's not my fault Dirck walked away." Hot tears pricked her eyes as her temper flared. "I wasn't even born when he made that decision. I didn't know he had a family. No one did."

"Of course." Durand nodded again.

How could he be so calm, so unfazed?

"But Bryan needs to work through his feelings of hurt and betrayal—on his own. Your overtures of friendship—however well-meaning—don't make up for what Dirck put him and Annabelle through."

What have I been telling you, Celine? Sister Mary Catherine's voice boomed into Celine's ear. *You can shop around for advice, but you won't hear anything different. You can't erase the past. You can't make up for what Dirck did.*

Celine sat back, suddenly exhausted. Was that what she was doing—making up for Dirck's behavior?

"So what do I do, Charles?"

Durand smiled. "The only thing you can do, Celine. Nothing."

Chapter Fifteen

Back at the Delft, Celine murmured a quick apology—"Sorry it took me so long"—and hurried behind the counter. The bar was milling with customers—small, impromptu wine-tasting groups, couples sharing a bottle of wine, coffee and tea drinkers.

Julia glanced up, the bottle of wine in her hands tipped over a guest's wine glass, ready to be poured. Her finely drawn dark eyebrows were raised. She took a step back, prepared to retreat if Celine wanted her to.

Motioning her to stay, Celine took her place behind the cash register. She needed the former fed by her side. Between ringing up sales and typing up receipts, she filled Julia in on her meeting with Reynolds.

"He doesn't have a criminal record, meaning his association with the General is either innocuous or fairly recent." But even as she spoke, Celine realized neither explanation seemed entirely right.

An image of the bronze vessel in Reynolds' hands flashed into her mind again.

"He knows more than he's letting on."

"About the General?"

"And the heist. I think—" Celine hesitated. Had she seen the Gardner's stolen Chinese gu in Reynolds' hands? It had supposedly been sighted seven years ago when she was an under-appreciated, low-level employee at the Montague Museum.

But Julia had checked out the tip herself—she and Celine hadn't known each other at the time— and confirmed it was as bogus as the vessel alleged to be the Gardner's Shang Dynasty wine vessel.

"I think I had a flash of the Gardner's Chinese gu in—Will that be all for you?" Celine said brightly, addressing the woman who'd approached the cash register, wine purchases and magnets in hand.

She completed the transaction, but it was a while before Julia—occupied with serving customers—could return to pursue the conversation with her.

"You were saying . . ." Julia prompted. "Something about the gu?"

Celine shook her head. "I'm actually not sure what I saw. Reynolds' hands on the gu—he recognized it."

"You think he knows where it is? Or was that just your mind's way of confirming his connection to the General?"

Celine considered this. From what she'd seen in her visions, Reissfelder and DiMuzio had taken the gu. Ostensibly for the General.

"That was so if they'd been caught that night and been recognized as the men who'd broken into the Gardner, the entire haul wouldn't be lost," she said to herself. She looked up at Julia. "You're probably right."

You got a lot more than that, Celine, Sister Mary Catherine said. An image of a calendar's pages being rapidly flicked back occupied Celine's mental screen. It was a reference to time.

Reynolds had known the General for a long time. Okay, but what did that tell her? Hearing Julia's voice, she turned her attention back to the former fed.

"So Blake was right. Reynolds was here casing the joint, so to speak." Julia regarded her, concern making the fine web of wrinkles on her face stand out. When Celine didn't confirm her impression, she continued: "It makes sense. He's not going to make his move the very day he gets here."

She moved away to serve a waiting patron before Celine could respond.

He doesn't intend to come back, Celine, Sister Mary Catherine informed her. *And he likely won't be able to.*

Yet Reynolds had said he'd accomplished what he'd set out to do.

When Julia returned, she shared her impressions with the former fed. "I just don't understand what I'm getting," she said.

"It seems simple enough to me." Julia flicked her ponytail back—strands of graying hair escaped the confines of her navy blue hairband. "If Reynolds hasn't been tasked with the hit, then he was here to just observe —and to report back to the General."

"Or his agent." Something else Blake had said to her snaked up into her mind.

The *Post* reporter who'd responded to the anonymous tip that was the basis of his unverified article had recognized the incoming call as coming from a Boston phone number.

"It was a burner phone," Blake had told her, "discarded shortly after it was used. But the call was made from San Luis Obispo."

"A Boston number making a call from Central California?" Julia said when Celine shared the details with her. "That could be anyone—Jonah, Wanda"—she lowered her voice and surveyed the room—"and I hate to say this, but Annabelle as well."

"Or Bryan," Celine said flatly. Her mind had gone straight to Annabelle's son when she'd heard what Blake had uncovered. "The reporter thought the caller was male, and the call was made over the weekend. Bryan was still in Paso Robles at the time."

Julia's eyes targeted Annabelle, who was explaining the choice of brews available to a couple sitting across the room. "Are you planning to say anything to her about this?"

"No." Celine didn't even have to stop to ponder her decision. They had no evidence, but Bryan fit the bill. He was the only person she could think of—other than the General—with a motive to harm her.

Had the General ensnared Bryan in his web? She hoped not. Bryan would only end up hurting himself—and his mother—if he tried to destroy her.

When the last customer had left and Wanda and the rest of the Delft's staff had finished for the day, Celine sank into the cream-colored, floral-patterned couch in Dirck's sanctum.

In preparation for harvest time, Andrea had given her a list of items to order: stainless steel tanks for their white wines—"I want to create a batch without any oak flavors, *cara*," he'd told her—Hungarian and French oaks to replace some of their older barrels; yeast and nutrients; bottles as well.

Her laptop perched on her knees, Celine began to send out emails to her various suppliers. They'd need to book a time with the cleaning crews to clean out the grape bins.

Aware of Annabelle's slender form standing by the doorway, she looked up.

"How'd it go with that sculptor Tony Reynolds?" Annabelle walked over to her, sitting down on one of the matching armchairs on the other side of the coffee table. "Did you like his ideas?"

Celine nodded. "I did." She'd forgotten how enthusiastic Annabelle had been when Penny had first suggested installing sculptures on the estate to keep alive the memories of Dirck, John, and their friend Simon Underwood.

"He gave me his drawings." She tipped her chin at her tote bag, slumped on the coffee table. "Take a look, if you like."

She hadn't put away his designs or the miniature models he'd created of them.

"If you root around in there, you'll find these absolutely stunning wood and bronze models he's created. Take a couple for yourself if you like."

Annabelle looked at her, blue eyes tearing up. "Are you sure?"

"Of course. Help yourself. And Annabelle, if there's anything you want Reynolds to change, just let me know."

Annabelle leaned over and gently squeezed her hand. "Thank you, Celine. You have no idea how much this means to me. I wish Dirck and

I could've spoken or met while . . ." She drew back, clamping her lips together and brushing away the tears that welled up in her eyes.

"I understand why he couldn't, of course. It doesn't make it any easier to bear, though, does it?"

No, it didn't. Believing in an afterlife—knowing the soul survived death, however painful—didn't make you miss your family members any less.

The other side was as distant and unreachable to the living as the New World must've been to the mothers, fathers, and children the first Pilgrims had left behind when they crossed the Atlantic.

It was Annabelle, a retired schoolteacher, who'd come up with the analogy. "It must have been hard back in those days when there was no way of sending a message to let your loved ones know you'd made it across safely. No way of letting folks back home know that someone had died either."

"How's Bryan doing?" Celine asked. It was an attempt to change the subject for Annabelle's sake as well as to satisfy her own curiosity. He'd left in a huff a few days ago, tired, he said, of hanging around where he wasn't wanted.

"I think my dear dead uncle made his wishes quite clear, don't you? He didn't want us around, didn't want us sharing in all of this." Bryan had waved his arm expansively around the vineyards that surrounded the estate.

Annabelle managed a smile. "He's inundated. There was a backlog of jobs waiting for him." Byran was a master plumber in Boston. "Probably a good thing he returned. People with plumbing issues aren't exactly the most patient of clients. Neither are general contractors, of course."

"No, I guess not." Celine returned to her work, while Annabelle pulled out Reynolds' plans and spread them out on the coffee table between them.

"These are stunning," Annabelle said a few minutes later. "Reynolds must have missed his calling. He's an excellent draftsman."

"So, he is." Julia had walked in just then and was peering over Annabelle's shoulders at the three-dimensional drawings Reynolds had created of each piece from a range of perspectives—front, rear, and three-quarter view from either side. "Wonder why he didn't become an artist."

Celine raised her eyes from her laptop. "He wasn't good enough, or so he believed. Lacked originality of vision. It's the usual reason art students give up on their dreams." She had given up on hers—although in her case, it had been her visions of murder that had compelled her to do it.

It had been ages since she'd painted anything. She regretted that sometimes.

"It's hard to make it as an artist," Annabelle agreed. "And if your work is seen as derivative . . ." She turned to the next sheet. "That's why Dirck and John never believed they'd make it." She'd taken to calling her brother and his friend by the names they'd assumed thirty years ago when they'd fled Boston. Not Simon and Earl, but Dirck and John.

They'd died and been buried with those names, she'd explained when Celine had asked her about it.

"I'm so bushed." Julia suppressed a yawn. "Are you two ready to leave?"

As always, the former fed and Annabelle had hitched a ride with Celine. Parking spaces were few and far between on 13th, and the parking lot in the back was too tiny to accommodate more than two employee cars. The rest were reserved for customers.

"Yup." Celine sent the last email on her list, shut down her computer, and rose. Her Pilot was parked in the small lot behind the Delft. "Let's go."

Jonah was waiting for them by the Mechelen's Tasting Room. He approached Celine's car when it pulled up.

"I was just about to go to your cottage," he said, poking his head in through the driver's side window. "Your mail was in the office back there." He handed her a stack of envelopes with a slim rectangular box on top. "Andrea wanted to close up, so I uhmm . . . "

"Offered to help?" Celine finished for him. "Thanks."

She placed the stack on the center console and prepared to drive Annabelle to her cottage—the cottage that had once belonged to Dirck. Julia had taken over John Mechelen's place.

"Chocolates." Annabelle peered down at the slim box sitting on top of Celine's stack of mail. "From Boston? You don't have a secret admirer do you?"

Celine smiled. Out of the corner of her eye, she saw Annabelle opening the lid and prying up a chocolate-covered cube.

A quick succession of images flashed through Celine's mind. The gu. Laurie, the intern from the Montague Museum. The red inhaler she'd kept seeing before Laurie was murdered.

It took but a moment for their significance to register.

"Annabelle, no!" Her voice was shrill with panic. She jammed her foot on the brake.

But Annabelle had already popped the poisoned chocolate into her mouth.

"Spit it out, Annabelle. Quick!"

Eyes bulging with fear, mouth foaming, Annabelle spat out chocolate remnants and chocolate-tinged spit.

"What's the matter, Celine?" Julia leaned forward from the rear passenger seat.

"Cyanide." The Pilot's wheels squealed as Celine swung the car around and peeled forward. "We've got to get her to the Emergency Room."

Chapter Sixteen

The nearest Emergency Facility was in Templeton, seven miles from the Mechelen. The drive, even on a relatively quiet, traffic-free day, took nearly fifteen minutes. Celine made it in nine, turning off Las Tablas Road into the narrow, rectangular parking lot.

"Hang in there, Annabelle!" Celine pleaded. "Please, just hang in there."

Annabelle sat hunched in the passenger seat, arms wrapped around herself, mouth hanging open, softly moaning. The poison had already begun to take effect. Her features were flushed.

"My head's killing me. Oh God, dear God."

She retched repeatedly.

"Ahh . . . uhhh . . .ahhh . . ."

Julia reached forward to massage her back—firm, deep strokes designed to calm Annabelle down. It was all they could do at this time. "You'll be fine, Annabelle. We're at the hospital. It's going to be okay."

The tires screeched as the Pilot rammed to a stop.

"We're here. We're here. We're here."

Thrusting the driver's side door open, Celine ejected herself out of the car.

Someone had left a wheelchair in the parking space next to theirs. Julia commandeered it as Celine helped Annabelle out of the car.

The next several minutes passed in a blur, caught up in a whirlwind of activity. Celine sprinted ahead into the facility.

"Cyanide poisoning," she yelled as she pushed past the glass doors. "We have a case of cyanide poisoning." She locked eyes with a nurse. "Please, we need help."

She kept the door open as Julia trundled in with Annabelle, groaning now, about to vomit.

Her appearance triggered a sudden burst of activity.

"We'll take it from here, ma'am."

Nurses and interns in jade-green scrubs, masks, and eye-protecting shields swarmed around the wheelchair.

Someone brought in a stretcher. Annabelle was helped into it, then they started moving down a hallway.

"How do you know it was cyanide? How was the poison administered?"

The questions fell on Celine's mind like bullets.

"Chocolates," she said, sprinting alongside. "Poisoned chocolates. I have the box with me. In the car."

"Bring it in, please."

Celine raced back to her car. "I'll be back in a sec," she called to Julia.

When she returned, Annabelle had already been wheeled into a room. Julia paced the tiled floor outside.

"They're administering a dose of hydroxocobalamin. If it is cyanide, it'll neutralize the cyanide molecules at a slow enough rate to allow her liver to detoxify it."

"Will that work?" Celine asked, anxious. Would Annabelle's liver be able to handle the task? Wouldn't it have been better to let the medicine take care of the detoxification?

Julia shrugged. "I dunno. Depends on how much cyanide there was in those chocolates. At least, she didn't have more than one."

"And she spat out most of that," Celine remembered.

"Thanks to your warning. How in the world did you know?"

Seeing one of the nurses who'd been attending Annabelle pass by, Celine thrust the box of chocolates at her. "She ate one of these. Annabelle Curtis" —she jerked her chin in the direction of Annabelle's room—"the patient we brought in."

"Thanks, we'll have these tested," the nurse promised, walking briskly away.

Celine turned back to Julia. How had she known?

"Flashes," she explained. She gathered her fingers together and immediately sprang them apart in an attempt to illustrate the experience. "I saw the Gardner's gu—"

"A reference to the General?"

"Maybe." Celine wasn't sure that was what the gu signified in this case. "And I saw Laurie Robbes, the Montague Museum intern who was murdered seven years ago. You remember the case, don't you?"

Julia nodded. "How could I forget? It was the first I heard of you." The former fed frowned. "That was a case of cyanide poisoning, too, wasn't it?"

"Yup. I kept seeing a red inhaler in the days before Laurie was killed. That's how Keith"—Celine was referring to a mutual friend of theirs, psychic cop Keith Elliot, from New Hampshire—"and I realized she'd been exposed to hydrogen cyanide."

"It was the red inhaler that tipped you off?"

"Eventually, yes. I saw it again when Annabelle put that piece of chocolate in her mouth."

Another thought surfaced, driving away the rush of adrenaline that had kept her going thus far. It surged out of her body, leaving her exhausted.

"Here, sit down." Julia pushed her toward a chair upholstered in blue-gray serge. Her face was covered in alarm. "Are you okay? God, I hope you weren't exposed to the poison as well."

She looked around, in frantic search of a nurse.

"I'm fine." Celine put her palm up, a weak attempt at reassuring the former fed. "I just realized—" She took a deep breath. "I just realized those chocolates were meant for me."

Julia's head swiveled slowly toward her; the former fed's blue eyes dilated for just a fraction of a second before resuming their normal size. "Damn!"

The thoughts exploding out of her mind were powerful enough to reach Celine's without any mental trespassing.

Her kidnapping four months ago had been a dramatic, larger-than-life affair. Julia had been expecting the attempt on Celine's life to be similar. But poisoning—cyanide poisoning, in particular—was subtle, insidious. A threat that couldn't be seen or prepared for.

Nothing that bullets could save her from. Unless they shot the chocolates full of holes. The image made her giggle hysterically.

"What is it?" Julia demanded sharply.

"Nothing." Celine sobered up instantly at her tone. "It's just that none of us anticipated this."

"No, we didn't, shame on us."

"The chocolates had a Boston label, if that helps."

Celine had seen it when she'd retrieved the box from the Pilot.

Julia considered the information, lips pursed.

"I doubt we'll get any usable fingerprints. Did you see a postmark? I'd better get Mailand down here."

Fishing her phone out of her purse, Julia turned away to make her call to the Sheriff's Department detective who'd been assigned to Dirck's murder.

The case was closed, but they'd managed to forge a tenuous relationship with the detective since then.

"He'll be here ASAP," she reported a few minutes later.

❧

It was a mere twenty minutes after Julia's call that Rick Mailand, a detective with the San Luis Obispo County Sheriff's Department, strode into the waiting room. The black suit that clothed his tall frame—he was an impressive six foot four—was covered in creases.

"It's been a long day," he said, apologizing for his disheveled appearance.

"You okay?" His usually suspicious mahogany eyes softened as they fell on Celine.

"I am, thank you." She had to crane her head up to meet his eyes.

At five-eight, Celine was reasonably tall for a woman. But Mailand, towering over, made her feel positively petite.

"And your friend?" His gaze swept past her to Julia. He must have sensed she herself wasn't up to answering his questions.

"She'll survive," the former fed replied. A physician had informed them minutes ago that Annabelle's condition was stable. She'd been transferred to the hospital wing of the facility.

"We'd like to keep her under observation for a day or two. Just as a precaution," he'd said, peeling off his latex gloves. "But she'll be fine. You brought her here just in time.

"Fortunately," he went on, "she hadn't ingested enough of the poison to be permanently damaged. Every chocolate in that box had potassium cyanide, but you'd have to eat two or three to get a fatal dose."

The physician had scanned their faces, deeply curious. "I expect the poisoner was counting on that."

"I expect so," Julia had replied, noncommittally.

Now the former fed shared this information with Mailand.

The Sheriff's detective frowned, the lines etched into his forehead deepening. "Sounds like a half-baked way to do the job."

"Unless he—or she, we probably shouldn't be making any assumptions at this point—was expecting to be sharing a piece or two as well," Julia said.

"Or thought someone he knew would be having some," Celine softly added.

The chocolates had come from Concord Chocolates, a popular Boston chocolatier in North Boston. It wasn't anywhere close to Annabelle's home in Revere, but Celine wondered if Bryan Curtis had sent the gift box.

Getting rid of her while ensuring Annabelle stayed safe would certainly have been a motive for him.

"Meaning what?" Mailand turned to her, mystified.

"Nothing," she mumbled. She didn't want to get Bryan in trouble. For Annabelle's sake, not for his. She'd known Bryan resented her. She just hadn't realized he hated her enough to fall in with the General's plans to eliminate her.

Hands on her hips, she pivoted around to face the wall. The ghostly figure she saw made her heart stop.

Why was Dirck here? To take Annabelle away?

Oh, God, where were the nurses? It wasn't Annabelle's time, was it? She simply could not let that happen.

There's nothing you can do to prevent it, if it is her time, Sister Mary Catherine reminded her.

I know, but . . . Celine felt her eyes brimming over. *I'm just not ready for her to go.*

It's not her time, Celine. Dirck's here to see her. Annabelle's more receptive to him in her current state. In her waking hours, her grief is so intense, try as he might, she blocks him out.

Behind her, she heard the dim hum of Mailand's voice interwoven with Julia's husky tone. But when she finally turned around the Sheriff's detective had left.

"He's taken the box of chocolates in for further analysis," Julia informed her. "I suggested he speak with Jonah—and Andrea. We need to know how those chocolates got to your office."

"I'm not sure that'll help," Celine said wearily, "but I guess it's a start."

She hadn't confided her suspicions about Bryan to Julia yet. She wasn't even sure she wanted to. If Bryan was involved, she'd need to deal with him herself. He was—well, as Dirck's nephew, he was practically family.

"Come." Julia gently grasped her elbow. "Let's get you home. You're in shock. It's been a long day."

Chapter Seventeen

It was close to midnight when Julia dropped Celine off at her cottage. Celine had allowed her to drive the Pilot. She was in no shape to handle the seven-mile trip herself.

Flopping onto her bed, Celine glanced at the slim mother-of-pearl clock on her nightstand. Boston was three hours ahead of Paso Robles. Should she risk waking Bryan up in the middle of the night? Or would it be better to wait until morning?

Now. Catch him off-guard, a voice in her head said. It wasn't Sister Mary Catherine. Just her own intuition realizing that a surprise call made when Bryan was least expecting it would be her best chance of getting at the truth.

Decision made, she stared at her phone for several seconds before finally scrolling through her contacts to find Bryan's number. It was late, she was exhausted, and she wasn't too enthused about the prospect of triggering a confrontation. But she knew she didn't have a choice.

She hit dial when she found the number.

The first three rings went unanswered. In her mind's eye, she saw Bryan's hand emerging from the flat sheet covering his person to swat at the phone.

At the fourth ring, he picked up. "Shrivel up and die," he growled into the phone.

"Did you send your mother chocolates, Bryan?" Celine asked before he could hang up on her.

"Who is this?" he demanded. Her words hadn't registered.

"It's Celine. Celine Skye." She repeated her question.

"Is this some kind of joke?" Celine could see him sitting up in his bed now, wide awake. "Have you any idea what time it is?" He was glancing at his clock. "Jesus Christ, it must be past midnight in California."

But he'd answered her question. She rephrased it to confirm her impressions: "So you didn't send her any chocolates?"

"Why would I? It's not her birthday or Mother's Day? God, Celine, are you completely nuts?"

The image of him receded from her mind as she wondered how to break the news to him.

"Bryan—"

"Lady, could you please just let me get back to sleep?"

"Bryan, you've got to listen to me, please. Annabelle's in the hospital."

"What? Celine, if this is some kind of—"

"We received a box of chocolates. They'd been tampered with. Annabelle put a piece in her mouth before we realized that was the case. She's going to be fine. Julia and I rushed her to the Emergency Room. I just wanted to let you know."

"She was poisoned?" He was trying to wrap his mind around the fact.

"It was an accident."

"Some accident! If someone deliberately poisoned the candy, that sounds like murder to me."

"Yes, it is murder. But she wasn't the intended target. I was."

There was radio silence on the other end. She couldn't even hear him breathing.

Celine pulled the phone away from her ear and looked at the screen. They were still connected.

She was about to utter his name when he spoke: "And you think it was me?"

"I beg your pardon?"

"Your first question when you called was: *Did you send your mother a box of chocolates?* You think I'd kill you? You think I'd be dumb enough to send you poisoned chocolates knowing that my mother can't keep her hands off them?"

"Bryan, that's not what I—"

"Yes, it is. That's exactly what you meant. You think I'm some lowlife murderer? You think I want your winery and bar so badly, I'd kill for it?"

Dear God, she hadn't intended for this conversation to go this far south.

"Bryan, listen, please—"

"Don't bother with the explanations." His voice was cold. "I'm not interested." He asked for and took down Annabelle's room number and the hospital phone number, and hung up.

Celine winced as she heard the abrupt click. *Damn! That had gone well.*

He does share some culpability, you know, Sister Mary Catherine said.

But Celine was too tired to figure out what her guardian angel meant. If Bryan hadn't sent the chocolates—and she believed him when he said he hadn't—how could he bear any responsibility for what had happened?

❧

"Anthony Reynolds?"

The voice that came out of Celine's throat was surprisingly deep and masculine. But before she had time to analyze the change, the sculptor turned to face her. His eyebrows were raised in the expression of surprised anticipation a celebrity might have when hailed by a fan.

The surprise turned to bemusement as Reynolds glanced down at her hands.

The next thing Celine knew she was following him past the counter in the Mechelen's Tasting Room, down a narrow corridor, toward the office in the back.

"Hey, you can't go in there!"

Her voice was back to sounding normal. But Reynolds either hadn't heard her or had chosen to ignore her.

He swept past the door, approached her desk, and looked around. His eyes searched the room, skating past her as though she didn't exist.

"You shouldn't be here," she repeated.

Shouldn't be here. Shouldn't be here. Shouldn't be here.

❧

The words were still echoing in Celine's mind when her consciousness surfaced. Although her eyes remained closed, she was aware of the bright sunlight streaming in through the peach organza silk curtains hanging at her windows.

Memories of the night before were crowding back into her mind, shuffling out the dream images of Reynolds in the Mechelen's office.

Eyes shut, she focused on the images, fixing the few fragments that remained on her mental screen. A premonition of things to come? Or a vision of what had already taken place?

She felt the touch of a finger on her brain as the second option passed through it.

That meant Reynolds had been inside her office. But why?

The question, insistent as a fire alarm, forced her eyes open. Her gaze drifted to the clock on her nightstand.

Alarmed, she bolted upright. How could she have slept so long? It was nearly nine.

Her phone rang, chimes of Vivaldi's *Summer* cutting through her guilt.

"Celine, it's Jonah. I just heard. Are you okay?"

"I'm fine. It's been a long night."

She kept her response short, hoping he'd get the message.

That she was in no mood to carry on a long conversation about the incident.

"Listen, I had no idea. The police were here." Jonah was rambling now. "Is Annabelle okay?"

An image of Jonah's face—white as a sheet—when she'd snapped out of her trance yesterday pressed into her mind. It seemed an eon since she'd had her premonition about the General's decision to eliminate her.

"Annabelle's going to be fine," she assured him, although she found herself questioning the genuineness of his concern. He was calling for some other reason; she was sure of it.

"I am so sorry," Jonah bleated into her ear. "I had no idea."

She cut his apologies short. "Jonah, I have to go. It's been a long night. I hope you understand—" She was finding it increasingly hard to be civil to him.

"Sure, sure. Ah . . . you didn't taste any of the chocolates yourself, did you? I mean, you're fine, right?"

Irritation intensified into anger, the emotion pulsing hot through her. He was angling for a story. It was typical Jonah. Self-centered, ambitious to the point of ruthlessness. Annabelle had nearly died, but all that *There's-Nobody-But-Me-Jonah-McGee* could think about were the headlines the story would make.

"Jonah, let me make one thing clear. If the *Gazette* publishes so much as one word of what happened last night, you lose the right to any exclusives on this case. Capiche?"

"Of course. But you misunderstand. I wasn't at all trying to suggest—"

"Not one word," Celine reiterated. She hung up.

The encounter had been so distasteful, she closed her eyes, invoking the psychic defense shield her psychic cop friend Keith Elliot had taught her. "You need to protect yourself from other people's negative energy and intentions. They can sap you of vitality," he'd told her. "When that happens, you'll feel raw, exposed, and chafed."

Just the way she was feeling now. She focused her mind, imagining herself standing under a shower that poured a dazzling white light onto her, irradiating her entire being.

I surround myself with the wisdom, love, and healing light of the Universe.

Celine uttered the mantra several times. She'd nearly calmed down when she heard her guardian angel's soft whisper.

Don't forget your dream, Celine. It's important.

Her dream. Celine's eyes flew open. Something Reynolds had said before he left reverberated in her memory.

I've done what I set out to do.

The memory made her stomach heave.

Chapter Eighteen

Special-Agent-in-Charge James Patrick Walsh pursed his lips. "This surveillance on Reynolds."

He flipped through the surveillance photos of the sculptor.

Blake had no idea how they'd found their way to his superior's desk or why Walsh had chosen to concern himself with the nitty-gritty of an operation in its early stages.

"A waste of time, wouldn't you say?" Walsh glanced up, craning his head forward questioningly.

Blake remained silent, forcing his superior to explain himself. Walsh knew as well as he did that the better part of any surveillance consisted of snapshots like the ones captured in the eight-by-eights on his desk.

"Nothing going on." Walsh frowned, visibly annoyed at having to spell out his concerns. "This looks like a waste of budget, Markham. Not to mention a potential lawsuit in the making." He jabbed at the photos. "What's this guy done?"

Blake shifted his position in one of the two uncomfortable chairs Walsh reserved for visitors.

"We began surveillance because Ms. Skye sensed a connection between Reynolds and the individual known as the General."

"The man who supposedly masterminded the Gardner theft?"

"Possibly one of two men, according to Ms. Skye's insights."

"So we think following this guy around is going to lead us to the loot?" Walsh's pained expression was akin to that of a professional skeptic asked to put his faith in the afterlife. "On the say-so of a *psychic*?" Walsh pronounced the word as though it were an expletive.

"A psychic who helped recover the most valuable of the Gardner's stolen works," Blake pointed out.

Walsh waved an irate hand in dismissal of this argument. "Because she had it in her backyard, so to speak. Who knows what else she might have had?"

So they were back to that, were they?

The surprise raid on the Mechelen had been about as necessary as the tactical force used in the pre-dawn arrest of Roger Stone. A simple knock on the door would've yielded the same results.

But try explaining that to an SAC with little to no field experience— a man who was essentially an unelected bureaucrat. Walsh had thought the headlines the raid inspired would be worth it. A nice show of force indicative of the FBI doing something about a thirty-year-old cold case instead of simply spinning its wheels.

"And so we're following Reynolds?" Walsh returned to the matter at hand.

"We're following him, sir, because Ms. Skye received a premonition of an attempt on her life. By the General. That attempt was made last night —with a box of poisoned chocolates. Cyanide."

Walsh's eyebrows shot up.

"She didn't touch the chocolates, fortunately," Blake assured the SAC before he could ask. "But her friend Annabelle Curtis did."

"Duarte's sister." Walsh's tone suggested that an attempt made on the relative of someone with even minor ties to the Gardner heist was excusable.

Blake didn't bother pointing out the obvious. Duarte had been a minor cog in the wheel, compelled against his will to participate.

"Anthony Reynolds, whom Ms. Skye believes could be associated with the General, was at the Mechelen yesterday. About the time the chocolates were delivered."

Walsh's frown deepened, the connections beginning to make sense.

"Do we have enough to question Reynolds?"

"Ella"—he was referring to his personal assistant—"is getting all the information from Rick Mailand. He's the Sheriff's Office detective assigned to the case."

Walsh sat back. "Well get on with it, then, man. No need to waste time here."

"No sir, no need at all." Blake resisted the urge to roll his eyes. As though it had been his idea to waste his morning in the SAC's office.

❧

"Julia?"

Showered and dressed and armed with a soothing cup of Chamomile tea, Celine clutched her phone to her ear.

"I was just about to call you," the former fed replied. "Everything okay?"

Celine hesitated. Was everything okay?

Other than the fact that she'd spent the past several minutes crouched over her toilet bowl, heaving the contents of her stomach into it, she supposed it was.

She nibbled on a piece of dry toast.

"Celine?" Julia's voice sounded urgent.

"Still here. Listen, I think I know how those chocolates got here."

"We're surmising it was Reynolds," Julia said.

"And you know that . . . how exactly?" So much for her psychic insights.

"It's the only explanation that fits." Julia's voice was matter-of-fact. "The box had no postmark. The mailwoman assigned to the area is adamant that she only delivered a stack of envelopes. No packages.

"Mailand confirmed that with the post office as well. There were no packages scheduled for delivery to the Mechelen."

Celine swallowed the piece of toast she'd been chewing. "I'm guessing Andrea was too busy to even go into the office."

"You're absolutely right. But when Jonah went in there at closing time, he found the box sitting next to the stack of envelopes in the tray."

The Mechelen's mail slot was on the side of the Tasting Room, set into the wall by a door that opened into the office.

Celine pictured the mail tray—a black enamel affair with a floral pattern in bright red. It was set on a low table, strategically positioned to catch the envelopes that fell through the mail slot.

She'd bought it several months back, hating the idea of mail littering the office floor.

The slot wasn't large enough for packages, though.

Those were left on the stoop, the mailwoman pressing the buzzer on the wall to alert staff to the fact.

"I saw Reynolds going into the office," she told Julia. "In a dream." Strangely, she hadn't seen anything in his hands.

She turned her attention back to Julia's voice.

"That confirms it, then," the former fed was saying.

"It does," Celine agreed. "We should ask Blake—"

"Already on it. Mailand's on the horn with Blake as we speak. It ties in with our case, and given that the prime suspect is in Boston, it makes sense to ask for FBI collaboration."

There was a pause.

"You should probably take the day," Julia suggested. "Wanda's quite capable of handling things at the bar herself. I'll help out as much as I can and also be on hand if Annabelle needs anything." Another pause. "Bryan should be here in a few hours. So we won't be stretched too thin."

So Bryan had gotten in touch. Celine wondered if he'd mentioned their conversation to Julia. The former fed hadn't said anything. And Celine wasn't about to ask.

An unpleasant sensation stirred in her stomach. She owed Bryan an apology. Big time. She knew that, but she wasn't looking forward to having to abase herself.

"Sounds good," was all she said. "Keep me posted."

Celine had just about finished her tea when Andrea called.

"You are well, *cara*?"

"I'm fine, Andrea."

The note of fatherly concern in his voice brought a smile to her face. Her parents' untimely death had left her with no surviving relatives. But she had found a family here—in Andrea, Wanda, Julia, and Annabelle.

"And Annabelle will be, too," she went on before he could ask.

But Andrea's worries weren't so easily allayed.

"The chocolates were for you, *cara*? It is what the police say."

"I . . . uhmm . . . yes, they were." What else could she say?

"You knew of this?" Andrea pressed her. "You sensed it, as you put it."

Celine knew why he wanted to know. She'd asked him to be her partner, told him she was settling her affairs, but she hadn't explained why. She'd intentionally left the details out, although she'd insisted they were a team.

He would never say it, but Andrea Giordano was hurt.

"I had a premonition. I didn't want to say anything. I deliberately didn't. I didn't want to get you alarmed."

"I understand, *cara*. You do not need to defend yourself."

But something was eating at him, Celine could tell.

"Had I known, I might have been more careful."

"Oh, Andrea, there's nothing you could've done. It's not your fault. How could you have known?"

"I should've suspected, *cara*. Your work is dangerous. And your insistence, yesterday, that I partner with you . . . Well, it was telling."

"But, Andrea, seriously, how could you have prevented any of this?"

"*Cara*, I should've personally checked your mail, inspected postmarks on every envelope and package that was brought in. Instead, I let Jonah take your mail."

Celine understood what he was saying. The box of chocolates placed beside the mail tray would've stood out like a sore thumb. Andrea would've known the mail lady hadn't left it there. She left packages on the stoop.

The door by the mail slot was locked. Meaning that only an intruder—someone who had no business in the office—could have left the box for her.

"Don't beat yourself up over it, Andrea. Besides, the police and Julia have already figured out who it could be." She told him Mailand and Julia suspected Anthony Reynolds of having brought in the doctored choco-lates. "It's all under control."

"By God's grace, it is, *cara*," he replied fervently.

"But now you understand why I want—need—you to be my partner? If anything were to happen—"

He stopped her before she could finish.

"Do not say it, *cara*. Yes, of course, I understand, and I am happy to oblige. But let us pray nothing happens to you. You are much too young to let thoughts of death overshadow your life."

Chapter Nineteen

Blake took a cautious sip of his coffee and instantly regretted not ordering it iced. The brew, hot enough to almost burn his tongue, was the worst thing he could've asked for on a muggy July day.

He set the medium-sized paper cup down and stared at the tall, muscular figure sitting across from him.

"You were at the Mechelen yesterday, Mr. Reynolds." He didn't bother phrasing it as a question.

The sculptor stared back at him, hands interlaced around his large latte.

"I've already told you I was, agent."

Blake regarded him for a moment, trying to interpret his body language. Reynolds sat before him, taut as a newly tuned guitar string.

He'd seemed cagey when he answered Blake's knock on his apartment door, scanning the empty hallway for imaginary intruders before suggesting they meet at the Starbucks down the road.

Now as they sat here at a black metal table on the nearly empty Starbucks patio, Blake detected a subtle difference.

The wariness had gone, replaced by a watchful, expectant attitude that Blake couldn't quite decipher.

He made his move. "Any reason for wandering into the Tasting Room office?"

He pushed his weight against his chair, making it rock backward onto its rear legs. He'd decided to go with Mailand and Julia's theory. It was the only explanation that fit.

Reynolds' pupils—a brilliant green—briefly dilated before resuming their normal size.

"There were cameras?" The sculptor's voice was quiet, as though the significance of that possibility had just begun to sink in. "They picked up on my presence?"

There had been no cameras, but Blake chose not to correct the impression. Reynolds had already given him what he wanted: an admission of his presence in the Tasting Room. Blake remained silent, hoping for more.

Reynolds attempted a grin. "I didn't take anything, if that's what you're asking."

Blake regarded him. "It's not what you took that concerns me, Mr. Reynolds." He paused. "It's what you left there."

That got the sculptor's attention. He went rigid.

Excitement pulsed through the agent. They were getting somewhere. Finally.

"What I . . . left there?" Reynolds repeated, picking his way around the statement as though he were walking through shards of glass. He stared at his latte, his hands still wrapped around it as though it were some kind of talisman.

The tan had faded, leaving the sculptor's features an unhealthy shade of gray.

"I'm not so sure I understand, agent?" Reynolds looked up, his eyes watchful, his stance wary—like a gladiator bracing himself for a vicious attack. "Penny Hoskins didn't send you, did she?"

"No." Blake allowed his gaze to bore into the other man's eyes.

"Then who did?" Reynolds surveyed the patio, eyes alighting on the portly guy hammering away at his laptop two tables away. Guy Shepherd, the agent on surveillance duty. Reynolds' gaze returned to Blake. "What is this about?"

"A box," Blake informed him. "About yea big." He spread his hands wide to indicate its dimensions. "It contained chocolates."

Reynolds gaped at him. Then, oddly enough, he relaxed.

"Yes, I remember that." He seemed mildly surprised they were discussing it. "It was for Celine—a gift from Penny."

"A gift from Penny?" Blake's voice rose despite himself. "Penny Hoskins?"

"Yes." An Oscar-winning actor couldn't have injected more bewilderment into that one syllable. "I meant to tell Celine. I forgot. But she found them, no problem, I take it."

"She did." Blake decided to break the news. "They were poisoned."

Reynolds stared. "That's not possible. Why would—?"

"That's what we want to know. The chocolates were poisoned. You're admitting to placing them in Ms. Skye's office—"

"Hey!" Reynolds leaned across the table, visibly outraged. "I had nothing to do with this. I didn't poison any chocolates."

"You're suggesting Penny Hoskins did?"

"No, of course not." Reynolds shook his head vehemently. "That's ridiculous." He wiped his hand across his face.

Blake considered the sculptor. He couldn't detect any signs of deception. Either Reynolds was a grade-A psychopath or he was telling the truth. He didn't know the chocolates had been poisoned and he genuinely believed Penny had sent them.

"How did the chocolates come into your possession, Mr. Reynolds?"

Reynolds glanced up. "It was yesterday, at the winery. This USPS guy approached me. He musta thought I was an employee." The sculptor frowned, remembering something. "Wonder how he—?"

Blake interrupted him. "When you say USPS guy, you mean a mailman?" Mailand had mentioned a mailwoman being on the route.

"Yep." The sculptor's thoughts seemed elsewhere. His eyes roved past the only other occupied table toward the dull-blue patch of sky visible behind the buildings on Grove Avenue.

"A man?" Blake pressed him. Was Reynolds making this up? "Not a woman? You're quite sure?"

"Absolutely." Reynolds met his gaze. "Thin guy, medium height. Definitely not a broad." The sculptor smiled, genuinely amused now. "Trust me, agent, I can tell the difference."

I bet you can, buddy, Blake thought. He wondered again if the sculptor was lying. It didn't look like it.

"You'd recognize him if you saw him again?" Mailand would need to re-interview the other postal employees. One of them must have made an unauthorized stop at the Mechelen.

Would the SLO County Sheriff's detective be able to put together a photo lineup at such short notice? If so, they had a chance of nipping this thing in the bud.

Reynolds shrugged, responding to Blake's question. "I guess."

Blake rocked forward, bringing his chair back to the ground with a thunk. He had one more question.

"So a mailman hands you a box of chocolates. And you assume it's from Ms. Hoskins because . . .?"

"There was a note."

"A note? Which you opened?"

"Why wouldn't I? It was addressed to me."

Chapter Twenty

"You think he's telling the truth?" Ella Rawlins searched Blake's features.

He'd returned to FBI headquarters fifteen minutes ago and had just finished filling his personal assistant in. After the sweltering heat outside, the cold air blowing from the vent above his chair felt damned good. He relished in it as he weighed his impressions.

The sculptor had clearly not been expecting to be questioned. He'd been nervous during the interview—cagey even. But on the subject of the box of chocolates, Reynolds had been astonishingly forthcoming. He hadn't denied entering the Tasting Room or leaving the candy box in there.

His outrage, when Blake had mentioned the candy was poisoned, had been genuine.

But there were aspects of his story that didn't add up.

And when Blake had asked whether the message Reynolds claimed to have received from Penny Hoskins had been postmarked, the sculptor's pupils had dilated. Without warning, he'd thrust his chair back.

"I'm sorry, agent, I have to leave. I don't have much time."

Either Reynolds had realized he'd been caught in a lie or—

Blake caught Ella staring at him, her head tilted to one side. The light glancing off her glasses rendered her expression inscrutable.

"I'm not sure, Ella," he answered her question. "But it shouldn't be too hard to find out."

He pulled the phone toward himself.

❧

"It's not here." He heard Celine rummaging through the stack of mail Julia had left on her kitchen countertop. "No note from Penny."

A whoosh of air burst from his pent-up lungs like a dam being released.

"Damn," Blake swore softly. He'd believed Reynolds. More or less.

"Any kind of corroborating evidence would've been good," he said.

He drummed his fingers on his desk. He'd hoped Sheriff's Detective Rick Mailand had somehow omitted to tell him about the note. Understandable, given that Celine hadn't had time to sort through her mail. But this wasn't looking good.

He said as much.

"No, it's not," Celine agreed.

"I can go check in the Pilot," she offered.

Blake heard the soft, rhythmic sound of her breath and her bare feet slapping on the floor as she padded out to her car. More sounds of rummaging.

"Not here either," she reported. "Where exactly did Reynolds say he left it?"

"With the chocolates. He wasn't any more specific than that."

"Could've been next to the box instead of on it," she mused. "In which case, it might still be in the Tasting Room office."

"Would you mind . . .?" He hated making the request after what she'd been through.

"No, of course not. Call you back in a few."

❧

Back in her kitchen, Celine took a hurried sip of her rapidly cooling tea —a fruit-flavored black Annabelle had recommended to her. She'd just finished brewing it when Blake had called.

The fragrant fluid rolled over her tongue and down her throat. She savored the taste, then reluctantly set her blue ceramic mug down. This was a tea meant to be enjoyed, not gulped down. She'd reheat it when she returned from the Tasting Room.

Killing two birds with one stone. The words she'd heard over and over in her head during Blake's call repeated themselves in her mind. What did they mean?

She didn't know.

She dropped her keys into her blue shoulder bag and set out.

The warm July sun caressed her bare shoulders and arms, a cool breeze making the heat bearable. Visitors wandered through the Mechelen's ornamental gardens, admiring the flowering plants and the fountain.

Celine walked briskly past, tossing a quick smile here, a greeting there, until she reached the Tasting Room. She sprinted up the steps and through the double doors of the Tasting Room. Julia was inside, chatting with a couple, when Celine came in.

"Thought you were resting." Julia's broad face was wreathed in concern as she approached Celine. She flicked her ponytail—a bush of silvery-white hair—back. "What brings you here? Annabelle's doing fine, by the way. Bryan's with her."

Celine smiled a greeting at the couple Julia had been entertaining, then drew her friend toward the office.

"Blake called." She recounted the details as they walked in.

The thick drapes of floral-patterned silk that hung over the floor-to-ceiling window shielded the room from sunlight. A stack of mail was in the mail tray—payments, invoices, wine orders, and applications to the Mechelen wine club.

Celine dropped them on the desk—she'd sort through them later—and began searching for the note Reynolds had claimed to have received. There was nothing on the desk, under it, or in the wastebasket that was placed on its right.

"It's not here." Celine searched under the keyboard, the mouse, the leather notebook, and the stacks of paper and mail on the desk.

"Were you expecting it to be?" Julia asked, watching her closely.

"Based on my dream last night, yes." She looked up at her friend. "It was odd." She recounted it.

"You heard yourself calling him?" Julia frowned.

"What if it wasn't me in the dream? I might have been inhabiting the consciousness of whoever it was who approached Reynolds."

Psychic visions of a crime were always partial—experienced either from the perspective of the victim or of the criminal.

Celine tended to view crime scenes from the criminal's perspective. It gave her an insight into the emotions and motives of the perpetrator but denied her a glimpse of the criminal's features.

"And the male voice you heard—that would fit with Reynolds' claim of being approached by a man." Julia leaned against the desk—a sturdy figure in a knee-length navy skirt and a pink blouse that brought out the intense blue of her eyes and suffused her cheeks with radiance.

"Anything else?"

"*Killing two birds with one stone.* I keep hearing those words."

"Meaning what?" Julia straightened up. "That Reynolds had another motive for coming in here?"

⌘

"Could he have planted something? A bug?" Blake asked when he heard. "I thought I hit a nerve when I mentioned that we knew what he'd left there. I was sure we had him."

"We've searched the place thoroughly," Celine informed him, exchanging a glance with Julia. She'd put Blake on speaker so the former fed could hear as well. "There's nothing here. Nothing that shouldn't be or that wasn't here before."

Julia bent her head toward the phone. "But you didn't get a reaction when you mentioned chocolates or poison?"

"Nope. And I think I would have if he'd known anything about it. He doesn't seem to be a brazen liar."

"But you say he was cagey throughout?"

"Paranoid."

"Could someone be framing him?" Julia asked. They were still standing by the desk in the office.

"He doesn't have much time left," Celine murmured, repeating the words that passed across her mental screen.

"That's exactly what he said," Blake replied. "Before he abruptly ended the interview and left. Now I understand his show opens this evening—"

"There's something he needs to do; he doesn't have much time left," Celine said again.

"What does he need to do, Celine?" Julia's voice seemed to come from a great distance.

"What the General wants him to do."

"Jesus Christ! Sounds like he's going to make another attempt." Blake sounded agitated. "Don't let her out of your sight, Julia."

He hung up, glanced at his watch, and gathered up his car keys. He wasn't due to relieve Guy Shepherd for another couple of hours, but he was going to do it anyway.

"And I need another agent out there in Guy's position," he called to Ella as he left.

Chapter Twenty-One

Outside Anthony Reynolds' apartment, Blake marked his patience in a steady rhythm on his brake pedal and wheel. The tap-tap-tap of his foot and forefinger kept at bay a growing sense that something was off.

He'd stationed himself on a short stretch of private road between Grove Avenue and Waverly Street. It was well over an hour now that he'd sat —window down, air conditioner off—waiting for Reynolds to make an appearance.

Blake shifted his butt, his tailbone beginning to feel sore, his legs cramped and stiff.

"Any sign of him?" he inquired quietly into his mouthpiece.

The sculptor's exhibition at the Gardner was due to open in twenty minutes, but Reynolds had yet to emerge from his building. The silver Ford pickup he drove—an F-250—stood in its parking space in front of 60 Grove.

"Nope," Ted Ridgeway, the agent who'd pulled surveillance duty along with Blake, responded. "Just walked the perimeter. No sign of anybody."

Not one to leave anything to chance, Ridgeway had been circling the block—from Allston where he was parked to Sidney, to Putnam, and back to Grove—every fifteen minutes. It had been his idea—just in case Blake, sitting with a clear view of 60 Grove Avenue, missed the guy.

"Just spoke with the doorman. He confirms our guy's still at home."

Blake appreciated the agent going the extra mile. More so given that technically Ridgeway was still on leave. He'd just got into town and still had about twelve hours of his week-long vacation left. Nevertheless, the man had made no bones about coming out tonight.

"No visitors?" Blake had seen none. Every single person he'd watched entering the building had possessed a key—meaning they were residents.

"Nope."

Damn. What was Reynolds doing up there? Jerking off? Entertaining some hottie—Blake had seen at least two go into that building. God, he hoped it was nothing more than that.

"Wanna go in?"

Blake hesitated. Something was wrong. He could feel it in his bones. But other than that, they had no reason to go thundering up to Reynolds' third-floor apartment.

"Let's give it another ten," he decided. "Then we go up."

He was staring at his phone, counting the minutes, when it rang.

"Penny?"

"Blake, I'm worried. Tony Reynolds isn't here"—

No shit, he thought. The guy hadn't budged—

"He was supposed to be at the museum forty minutes ago. The show starts in twenty."

"Couldn't he be running late?"

It was a lame excuse, and he knew it. But he wanted to give it an entire ten minutes. It had only been five since he and Ridgeway had spoken.

"No, Blake, he could not," Penny snapped.

Something in her voice snagged his attention.

"This isn't just about the show, is it, Penny?"

He could almost see her lips pressed tightly against each other, determined not to talk.

"Is it?" he asked again.

He remembered Guy Shepherd's report from the morning. Reynolds had been out just the one time that day.

"He saw you this morning, right?"

"No, he didn't, Blake. I missed him. There's been so much to do. I haven't been in my office all day." She sounded frazzled.

"But you had an appointment with him?"

"Yes . . . no. He knew I'd be available an hour before the show. My assistant told him that. But, Blake, I've been trying to call him since I returned to my office. He isn't picking up. Something's happened to him, I'm sure of it."

"Because he wanted to speak with you?" The subtext of Penny's remarks wasn't lost on Blake. "Why?"

He pushed the car door open, phone clamped to his ear.

He sensed her hesitation. "Penny, what did Reynolds want to speak with you about?"

She exhaled heavily.

"He said he had information. Something he felt I needed to know . . ."

She hesitated again, reluctant to speak. But Blake had already guessed the truth.

Goddammit. He drove his fist into his palm. *Godf—indammit.* He slammed the door shut.

"Stay put. I'll call you back in a few." He hung up and spoke into his mouthpiece. "Ted? We're going in now. Circle the block one more time, then meet me upstairs. Got it?"

His feet clattered on the marble steps as he sprinted up, sounding alarmingly loud. Huffing and puffing, the doorman, a grizzled, unshaven guy with a beer belly, followed on his heels.

Reynolds' was the only apartment on the third floor. The hallway was clear, the terrace at the end of it, accessible through glass double doors, reassuringly empty.

Blake returned to the apartment door. He raised his hand and glanced over his shoulder. "If he doesn't respond, I'm going in," he informed the doorman.

But the door fell open with the first blow his fist rained upon it.

"Stay behind me," he said tersely. He pulled his gun out, carefully pushed open the door, keeping an eye out for armed intruders. Or an armed sculptor.

"Reynolds?" he called. "It's Special Agent Blake—*Jesus F-in' Christ!*"

Blake stepped back, not wanting the doorman to see the dead body splayed on the living room floor.

"Call 911."—

"But . . .?"—

"Do it now!" Blake snapped. Ridgeway sprinted up just as the doorman began to retreat, his eyes wide with fear.

Too late Blake realized he hadn't told the doorman why 911 needed to be called. Dispatch would want to know. He gave Ridgeway the information, instructing him to follow the doorman, and pulled out his cell phone.

Visiting hours at the Twin Cities Community Hospital in Templeton were officially over. But the head nurse was willing to make an exception for Celine and Julia.

"I wasn't going to intrude with her family there, Gloria," Celine explained over the phone. "But I have a feeling this'll be the last opportunity we'll get before—"

"Mrs. Curtis is doing remarkably well," Gloria interjected. "But if you feel you need to see her, I won't stand in your way." Word about Celine's psychic abilities had spread.

Once she'd been able to talk, Annabelle had attributed her own remarkable comeback from cyanide poisoning to Celine's gifts.

The head nurse hesitated. "And just to set your mind at rest, her son isn't here at the moment." The comment made Celine smile; Gloria in her own way was an intuitive as well. "He returned to his hotel. Bit of an abrasive fellow, but his heart's in the right place."

⁓

The visitor parking lot on Las Tablas Road was empty when Celine—Julia seated beside her—pulled into it. They'd just parked when Julia's phone rang.

"It's Blake." Julia's voice sounded ominous in the subdued illumination provided by the Pilot's dome light.

"Reynolds?" Celine turned to her, one hand still on the wheel, foot dangling out of the half-open driver's side door.

He's gone, Celine. Sister Mary Catherine's voice was soft. *His time was up.*

Julia confirmed the fact. "Murdered," she mouthed, putting Blake on speaker so Celine could hear.

"Looks like the General got to him." Blake paused. "Wonder if Reynolds knew the General was after him, that his time was up."

Meaning that they—*she*—had misinterpreted the message she'd received earlier: *he doesn't have much time left.*

Celine winced, biting down on her lower lip. Blake had too much class to point out that she'd dropped the ball on this one. And grateful as she was for that, she was acutely aware she didn't deserve his consideration.

She was the psychic. If she'd gotten it right, Reynolds wouldn't be dead.

No, Celine, Sister Mary Catherine countered her thoughts. *His time had come. You weren't told,* the nun whispered, *because it wasn't for you to know or to prevent what was meant to be.*

"He was trying to get a message to Penny," Blake went on.

"About?" Julia asked.

"What else?" Blake released a pent-up sigh of frustration. "The Gardner heist."

The connection to the General, Celine thought. *Of course, Reynolds had information about the heist.* But she hadn't realized he'd been willing to share it.

"Unfortunately, he wasn't any more specific than that. He was supposed to meet with Penny this evening, but"—Blake's tone was resigned—"obviously he never made it."

Thoughts and sensations flashed through Celine's mind followed by a characteristic knowing.

"There was something the General wanted him to do." She sorted through her impressions. "Reynolds didn't want to go along. He had a decision to make. He could either do what he was asked to and live . . . or not. I guess he made his choice."

"Any idea what he wanted Penny to know?" Blake asked when Julia had relayed her message to him.

He's already given it to you, Celine. Sister Mary Catherine's voice again.

But what information had Reynolds given her? During his brief time at the winery, he'd closed his mind to her entirely. "You're psychic, aren't you?" he'd thought more than once.

If he'd expected her to read his mind, he hadn't made it easy.

"I don't know. But whatever it is, the General's had no success getting it out of Reynolds." Celine brushed back her long red hair. "That means I'm not a target anymore."

Until she discovered Reynolds' secret.

Then she'd have outlived her usefulness.

She left that part out, however. Blake and Julia were stressed out enough with this development. She didn't want to get them any more strung out than they already were. Her psychic defense shield would have to suffice.

I encircle myself in the white light of God's love and divine protection.

Chapter Twenty-Two

His call ended, Blake re-entered the apartment. He made sure there was no one lurking in any part of the single-bedroom unit, then he returned to the living room.

Reynolds lay on the floor, face swollen and red. The hemorrhaging in the whites of his eyes was visible from where Blake stood. *Petechial hemorrhaging.* The sculptor's green irises were glazed and had rolled back.

Blake's gaze moved down. A closer look confirmed his initial impressions. A jagged red gash encircled Reynolds' neck. He'd been garroted —just like Dirck Thins a few months back in Paso Robles. This was the General's work, no doubt about it.

He bent down and checked Reynolds' pulse. More out of force of habit than any expectation that the sculptor had survived the attack. Even as a member of the FBI's art squad, Blake had seen enough corpses to recognize death when he saw it.

When he straightened up, he turned his attention to his surroundings. The apartment was in disarray. Either Reynolds had struggled with his killer. Or, more likely, someone had ransacked the apartment.

Blake slid his phone out of its holster and snapped a few quick pictures. Cambridge Police would be taking over the crime scene. Not that he had any objection to their taking care of the routine drudgework.

But if Reynolds' death had anything to do with what he knew about the heist—which Blake was almost certain it did—having detailed photos of the crime scene as he'd found it would be enormously helpful.

He walked through the apartment once more, pointing his phone camera and clicking. The bedroom and studio had been searched as well, albeit not as haphazardly as the living room.

What bothered Blake was that someone had managed to get into the building despite the doorman's presence and the two FBI vehicles stationed outside. Despite Ridgeway's rounds around the block. How was that possible?

Unless—

His stomach sank at the thought.

Unless Reynolds had been killed while Guy was still on duty.

Guy hadn't been asked to do anything more than keep an eye on the sculptor's car and his comings and goings. They'd been more worried about Reynolds leaving the place than about anyone entering it.

Shortsighted, in view of the current situation.

❧

He found Ridgeway and the doorman waiting for him behind the reception desk.

"Hey," Blake asked the doorman, "did anyone visit Reynolds today?"

"Except for you, no."

"No visitors, you're sure?"

"Yup. I've been here all day. Doing a double shift today."

The two agents exchanged a glance.

"Any other entrance to this place?" Ridgeway asked. There had to be—unless either the doorman or one of Reynolds' neighbors had killed him.

"Just the side door off of Putnam." The doorman pointed. "Can't picture visitors coming through there, though. It leads into a stairwell. Only people who use that door are repairmen, plumbers, people like that."

"But if someone came in through that side door, you wouldn't know, would you?" Ridgeway pressed.

"Sure I would." The doorman was offended. "I always know when somethin' needs fixin.'"

Sure you do, Blake thought.

"You have keys to that door?" Ridgeway continued to grill the guy. "You lock it?"

"Yes, sir." The doorman nodded his grizzly head. "Every night."

Every night. Great.

"Was Reynolds expecting any repairmen today?" Blake wanted to know.

"Nope. And before you ask, no one was."

The doorman scrutinized his face. "What the heck is goin' on? You have me call 911; your friend here grabs the phone and walks away before I can say a word."

Blake looked at him. "Looks like someone came in through that side door—you know, the one that's only locked at night—and broke into Reynolds' apartment. He's dead."

The doorman paled; his jaw dropped.

"Oh, Christ!"

❧

Annabelle was awake when Celine and Julia made it up to her room. Gloria, the head nurse, a slim woman in her late forties with tight red curls streaked with gray, ushered them into the room.

"You're in luck. I just finished checking her vitals, so she's still awake," Gloria greeted them with a smile.

"I was beginning to think you'd forgotten me." Annabelle pushed herself up against the bank of pillows behind her. Seeing the stricken look on Celine's face, she smiled. "I was just teasing." She patted the rocking chair near her bed. "Come, sit beside me."

A bronze bust of Dirck stood on the plain white nightstand next to the hospital bed—one of the models Reynolds had left behind. It reminded Celine of the call they'd just received.

It was hard to believe Reynolds was gone—his life cut short by the General's men.

Annabelle followed her gaze. "When's he coming back?" she asked. "Have we decided where exactly we're installing the works?"

The eager, yearning expression on her features brought a lump to Celine's throat. She glanced at Julia. How were they going to break the awful news to Annabelle?

"Reynolds won't be coming back, Annabelle." Julia reached out and clasped the other woman's slender palm.

Annabelle frowned, about to ask a question. Julia continued hurriedly, "I'm afraid he's gone. Dead. We just heard the news."

"He was murdered," Celine said, seeing Annabelle struggling to take in the facts. "By the General, we think."

"Why?" Annabelle's lovely blue eyes crinkled. She lifted her face up to look at Julia. "I thought you told Bryan that Reynolds might have been working for the General."

Julia had given Bryan a brief rundown of the poisoning attempt and their theory of why it had taken place. Celine hadn't been sure of the wisdom of that course of action; Julia had agreed with her. But neither of them could deny Bryan was owed some kind of explanation.

"He was." It was Celine who responded. "Tony Reynolds was working for the General. But apparently Tony was also willing to divulge what he knew about the theft to Penny. Who knows why?"

The sculptor had clearly risked his life trying to defy the General; Celine couldn't understand why he'd done it. For the reward money? And how had the General found out?

Annabelle fell back against her pillows, weary. "I was really looking forward to seeing his pieces." She closed her eyes. "Now that won't happen."

She sounded so crushed, Celine couldn't bear it. She vowed to herself she'd do everything in her power to make sure Reynolds' ideas for their winery came to fruition.

Placing her palm gently over Annabelle's hand, she said: "We'll find someone else. I promise you we will. We're going to Boston tomorrow—Julia and I." Blake had asked if they could come; figure out exactly what it was that Reynolds knew. And Penny had called shortly after urging the same thing.

Annabelle nodded feebly.

"We'd better go," Julia said. "She looks tired. And we need to pack."

Chapter Twenty-Three

A refreshing blanket of climate-controlled air enveloped Blake as he stepped into the FBI's headquarters in Chelsea. After the blazing heat outside, the temperate air was soothing, further easing the mild throbbing that still pulsed just behind his veins.

He'd managed to ward off a full-blown headache with an early morning shower, but its dull residue—the after-effect of finding Anthony Reynolds' murdered body—still remained.

Blake's mind had been churning since then, trying to understand the fatal turn of events that had blindsided him into losing the prime suspect in an attempted murder case. He'd entertained some doubts about the extent of Reynolds' involvement in the affair. But that was beside the point.

How—*in the hell*—had he gotten it so wrong?

He strode across discreetly patterned marble floors and muted carpet into the elevator, punching the button before anyone else could join him. The turmoil of potential answers that offered themselves to his mind only made his gut clench in sickening dismay.

The elevator carried him, swiftly and silently, to his domain.

Ella glanced up as he opened the door, intelligent brown eyes gleaming behind her round spectacles. The sight of her was for once reassuring.

"Can we talk?" he asked, shutting the door to the anteroom.

"Breaking up with me?" she asked, her voice light, an eyebrow raised quizzically.

"What?"

Too late, Blake saw the amused smile that tugged at the corners of her mouth. She was messing with him—at a time like this? An expression of sympathy replaced the twitch of humor the instant she saw his expression.

She pushed back her chair, coming around from behind her desk to touch his arm.

"I heard about Reynolds. I'm really sorry."

"I can't help feeling our conversation led to his demise." He'd been unable to shake off the conviction that he was in some way responsible. "That meeting him provoked a deadly chain of events."

It was the single thought that had emerged free from the tangle of ideas struggling for his attention.

"It could just be a coincidence, nothing more than that," Ella reminded him, her hand still on his arm. "Reynolds was a womanizer, he could have offended a client, a former paramour. And if he had information about the heist—"

"Then the General killed him. But"—he looked down at Ella—"how could the General possibly have known about that? Reynolds left a message on Penny's answering machine. No one knew about that. Not even Penny until practically the eleventh hour."

Blake shook his head. Why had Reynolds been killed last evening? The timing of it bothered him.

He looked down at Ella again. "Mind if we continue this"—he tipped his head toward his office door, about to continue when she interrupted him.

"No, Blake." The curling ends of her bob slapped her cheeks as she shook her head. "I'd love to toss ideas with you, but we don't have time for that now."

"Why not?" He glanced up at the clock on the wall above his office door, puzzled. "We have three hours until Celine and Julia get here."

"I know." Ella released her hold on his arm and returned to her desk. "But you need to head over to Cambridge." She shuffled a few pieces of paper on her desk, found the one she was looking for and handed it to him. "Got a call from the Middlesex DA's office."

"Mariah Campari?" Blake read the name scrawled in the middle of the sheet in Ella's characteristic large, round cursive.

"Assistant DA in charge of the case," Ella explained. "She's working with Cambridge PD and wants your statement. ASAP."

Because he'd been the one to find Reynolds' body and report it dead. The Massachusetts State Police detectives on the scene—called in by Cambridge PD—had let him go without comment last night, a courtesy to his status as a fellow law enforcement officer.

But Blake had known the request for a formal statement wouldn't be long in coming. The questions about his presence there—as a special agent on the FBI's prestigious art team—were inevitable.

He swiveled wordlessly around.

"Take the armored car," Ella called after him as his hand reached for the doorknob.

Now why in hell would he do that? He twisted his head around, hand still on the knob, and regarded her, waiting for an answer.

"You have to go to the airport as well, remember?" His personal assistant peered at him, like an anxious wife trying to get through to a thickheaded spouse. Maybe he was being thickheaded, but he had no idea why a routine meeting with an ADA required the use of an armored car.

"We don't know how long this will take," Ella urged again, face pulled into an earnest expression. "You may not have time to get back here and then drive to the airport, Blake."

"Fine." He accepted her reasoning without argument.

Turning back around, he twisted the doorknob and strode out the door.

Chapter Twenty-Four

Vince Soldi, Deputy Superintendent of the Cambridge Police Department's Criminal Investigations Unit, rocked back on his chair and fixed a pair of dark baleful eyes on Blake, who sat across the cluttered, battle-scarred table in Soldi's office.

Soldi, Blake had learned, would be overseeing the detectives on the case.

Mariah Campari, the Assistant DA in charge of the case, was conspicuous by her absence.

"Running late," Soldi had informed Blake unapologetically when the special agent had shown up. He was a beefy, solidly built person with a balding egg-shaped head and a taut, full gut that spilled over his belt.

"How late are we talking?" Blake had glanced pointedly at his wristwatch. "I'm due at Boston-Logan in a couple of hours."

Soldi smirked, revealing a set of perfectly shaped incisors. "Going somewhere, Special Agent."

"Nope." Blake settled into the uncomfortably hard and tiny seat of the chair Soldi's office reserved for visitors. "Picking up a couple of colleagues."

He figured that was an accurate description of the two women.

A few minutes of silence elapsed. Then Soldi rocked forward.

"I guess we can get this started," he offered grudgingly. "I'll fill Ms. Campari in when she decides to show up."

Blake got the distinct impression that Ms. Campari was a high-and-mighty individual who enjoyed keeping people off-kilter. A die-hard feminist with a chip on her shoulder—the sort of person who, despite her achievements, saw male oppression lurking at every corner.

If that was the case, he was glad she wasn't here. He didn't have much patience with people like that. Much easier dealing with a beefy old curmudgeon like Soldi.

The Deputy Superintendent fished out a notebook from under the stack of papers on his desk, moistened a forefinger, and flipped page after page until he found one that was pristine.

"You found the body?" Soldi asked, making it seem like an accusation.

"Yup. I was in the vicinity." Blake saw no reason to offer any more details until he was asked to.

"Any reason why?"

"Why?" Blake deliberately stalled. He was conducting an internal debate on how much to share.

"Why you happened to be in the vicinity, Special Agent?"

Soldi glared at him from under bushy gray-black eyebrows.

"You're a member of the art team, Special Agent Markham. The victim was a sculptor. Is there a connection we should be aware of?"

In other words, was Reynolds a CI or involved in some hanky-panky the art team was investigating?

"No." Blake decided to play it safe. "Mr. Reynolds was due at the Gardner Museum for an exhibition. When he didn't arrive at the appointed hour, Ms. Hoskins, the Director of the museum, asked me to check in on him."

Soldi accepted his response without comment. He flipped a few leaves on his notebook, found the page he was searching for, and studied the illegible notations on it.

"Doorman says you were there that afternoon." Soldi looked up, his fleshy features impassive. "That have something to do with the Gardner exhibition as well?"

So Soldi was aware of that. Damn! Blake scrambled to put together a response that would pacify Soldi without necessitating the sharing of any more details than he was prepared to provide.

"No, it did not. Mr. Reynolds might have been a material witness in an attempted murder on the west coast. We received a request to follow up."

Soldi nodded as if to indicate he understood. These things happened; all in a day's work for a law enforcement agent. But his next words, casually uttered, pulled Blake up short. "And then shortly after you make contact with him, Mr. Reynolds turns up dead."

"That's been bothering me as well," Blake confessed, drumming his fingers on the tiny section of Soldi's desk that was available for the purpose. What exactly had he said to Reynolds that had made him take off the way he had?

Something he'd said must have compelled Reynolds to put in an urgent call to the Gardner. And then, before Reynolds could divulge the information he claimed to have, he'd been offed.

Why? To prevent him from blabbing to Penny?

Soldi's gruff bass interrupted his musings.

"You say you questioned Reynolds about an attempted murder, Special Agent."

Blake nodded, waiting for the question Soldi was attempting to frame.

"Did he say anything that suggested he might be more than a material witness? That he might be involved?"

"No, actually, based on what he said, it was fairly obvious he'd been—"

Blake's train of thought jolted to a stop as abruptly as a car hitting a speed bump. His eyes widened involuntarily.

Framed.

He'd been about to say "framed."

"Special Agent Markham?"

He turned to the older man. "I got the impression someone wanted Reynolds out of the way. That an innocent gesture was being made to look like something much worse."

He pressed forward, shoulders hunched over Soldi's cluttered desk, arms digging into the stack of papers and odds and ends on it.

"You interview a lot of guys, you begin to get a sense of when they're lying, when they're not, you know."

"You sure do," Soldi agreed.

"Reynolds seemed sincere, but"—Blake pushed himself back, exhaling heavily—"the pieces of evidence that could've backed up his story are missing. Didn't know it at the time, of course. I asked him a simple question, and, based on his response, I gather he drew the same conclusion I'm forced to right now.

"Someone must've decided to kill two birds with one stone"—he was quoting Celine now, beginning to understand what the words meant—"Get rid of our victim in California and frame Reynolds for the act."

Soldi stroked his fleshy chin thoughtfully.

"Special Agent Markham," he rumbled after a moment's silence. "I think you owe us a few more details. How about you start at the beginning and explain what this is about?"

Chapter Twenty-Five

The enormous gray-and-black sign welcoming them to Logan International Airport loomed up ahead. The bumper-to-bumper line of cars trickling under it on the single lane looping around to Arrivals offered a surreal view of the typical American cityscape—a sterile combination of concrete, metal, and glass devoid of either humans or nature.

Pretty creepy, if you allowed yourself to think about it, Blake reflected, looking through the windshield. Feeling a pair of eyes on him, he shifted his gaze to the left.

The agent chauffeuring the armored vehicle was looking inquiringly at him. Meeting Blake's eyes, he tipped his chin at the sign. Under the welcome message, large letters inscribed within painted rectangles offered visitors a choice of four terminals.

"Terminal A," Blake tersely informed the guy as they crawled toward the sign.

He glanced at his watch; Celine's flight was landing just about now. With any luck, they'd make it before the women retrieved their luggage.

His meeting with Vince Soldi had taken longer than he'd expected and he'd divulged way more information to the Deputy Superintendent than he'd originally intended to. Blake wasn't entirely happy about that development.

But he had to admit, as they finally passed under the sign, that voicing the tenuous theories snaking through his mind had helped to crystallize the primary facts of the case.

Someone—Blake hadn't referred to him as the General; strictly speaking that was just a moniker for an individual who remained an unsub—was hell-bent on preventing the Gardner's stolen artworks from surfacing.

He—*or she*, as Soldi had stolidly reminded Blake, making a vain attempt to be politically correct—was ready and willing to eliminate anyone who stood in the way.

The memory of the Deputy Superintendent's solemn correction of his use of the masculine pronoun made Blake's mouth twitch in amusement.

Was it Assistant DA Mariah Campari who'd persuaded Soldi to the view that crime was an equal-opportunity, inclusive field?

But the evidence—Blake had felt compelled to point out—suggested a man at the helm. Not a woman.

And *he* appeared to have wanted to get rid of Reynolds all along.

"Looks like what sealed the victim's fate is that a federal agent spoke with him but failed to arrest him," Soldi had succinctly summarized the situation.

"That it does," Blake agreed. But that had led to an even more troubling conclusion. Reynolds' killer—and by extension, Celine's—had been trolling the area, watching for law enforcement to make contact with the sculptor and haul him off to jail.

"Find anything interesting in the apartment?" Blake had asked.

"Depends on what you mean by interesting," Soldi replied. "Books— a ton of them—and shards of ceramic and plaster. Whoever killed him wasn't too impressed with his art."

Or they'd been searching the place—looking for whatever it was that Reynolds knew about the Gardner heist.

"You think he had a line on one of the stolen works?" Soldi asked.

"Seems like it," Blake had conceded unhappily. Soldi was a little too quick on the uptake for his taste.

"Terminal A," the chauffeur announced, head swiveling to the right. They were in the third of four lanes—each one jammed with cars.

Blake glanced at his watch. There was no way they'd be able to change lanes in time to let him out at the curb.

"Keep circling," he instructed the driver as he unlocked his door and peered to the right and left. "And try to get over to the right as you do it." He took one last look around and then slid out the door.

❧

With a small grunt of effort Blake hoisted Julia's blue rolling duffel bag into the cargo area of the Suburban. He pushed it against Celine's red-and-gold case and stepped back.

"You can put your stuff in there," he told Jonah, jerking his thumb in the direction of the open tailgate. He'd helped Celine and Julia with their luggage; it was the gentlemanly thing to do. Damned if he was going to provide Jonah—*douchebag*—Hibbert with the same service.

Blake walked around to the curb and opened the rear passenger door for the two women. He couldn't understand why they'd allowed the reporter to accompany them. Hibbert had already given him attitude about having to ride in an armored vehicle.

"You're free to arrange your own transport, then," Blake had coldly in-formed him, quickly bringing the bozo back in line.

Julia gave Hibbert—struggling to lift his suitcase to tailgate-level—a wry glance, turned to Blake, a sympathetic expression on her face, and mouthed an apology.

"Couldn't think of a good enough reason not to bring him with," Julia said quietly once they were all seated in the car.

"How about that we're going to a crime scene and reporters aren't wel-come," Blake grumbled. He kept his eyes peeled on the rearview mirror. Hibbert was still struggling with his case. What a sorry excuse for a man!

"Want I should go help him?" the agent beside him spoke up.

"We'll be here all day if you don't," Celine said with a smile that eased Blake's stormy mood.

The agent—a muscular fellow—got out of the car, casually strolled around to the back, and effortlessly lifted Hibbert's scarred brown suit-case into the cargo area. Much to Blake's annoyance, he also opened the door for the guy.

But his murmured explanation—"Force of habit, boss; I always hold open doors for women."— when he returned behind the wheel soothed Blake's irritation, making him grin.

With a quick glance behind him, the agent pulled away from the curb, easing the Suburban's massive bulk into traffic.

Chapter Twenty-Six

"Mind if we go straight to Reynolds' apartment?"

Blake turned, his gaze focused on the women. As far as he was concerned, Jonah's opinion didn't count.

But the reporter wasn't one to take a hint.

"Seriously?" he exclaimed. "Hello, we just landed!"

Blake was about to explode, but Julia fortunately intervened.

"We're not here on a pleasure trip, Jonah." His former colleague leaned across Celine to glare at the reporter.

"I'm sure we can drop you off somewhere if you don't want to come with," Celine added. "But I thought you wanted to see how we work—for your article?"

"What article?" Blake growled, his temper getting the better of him. "This is a crime scene, dammit. He's not writing anything."

"Relax." Julia turned to face him. "She's referring to the exclusive Jonah gets to write once this is all over."

Blake forced himself to cool down.

"Listen"—he re-focused on the women—"I know it's been a long flight. But I need you both to see the crime scene while it's still intact. Before Soldi—the guy in charge of Cambridge PD's Criminal Investigations Unit —releases it. He has an officer posted at the door of Reynolds' apartment. But not for long."

Soldi in fact had promised him no more than a few hours. "Budget shortage. Don't have a lot of men. An officer posted in front of the apartment is one less officer on the ground, you know what I mean, Special Agent?"

Blake had known exactly what Soldi meant. He didn't have much time. He looked at his former colleague.

Julia seemed to understand the message in his eyes.

"You think there's something of interest there?"

She leaned forward, straining against her seatbelt to do so. Her blue eyes had sharpened—a hunting dog that had caught the scent of prey.

"Bound to be."

He elaborated the theory that he and Soldi had surmised best fit the situation. The General wanted Reynolds out of the way. Framing him for a murder—successful or not—in Paso Robles had been a convenient solution.

"Except it didn't work," Celine softly said. "*Killing two birds with one stone.* That must've been what Sister Mary Catherine meant. I can't believe I didn't catch that either."

She sounded . . . lost? . . . dejected? Blake didn't have the words to express what he saw in her face and attitude. He'd seen firsthand how she'd reacted to Grayson's murder—once she'd recovered from the trauma of being kidnapped and had time to reflect on—make that *brood over*—the incident.

She'd begun to question her abilities and every failure to get it right dented her confidence even further.

The low hum of speeding traffic thrummed in his ears.

"We all make mistakes," he said gruffly, not knowing what else to say.

"Are you guys sure about this theory?" Jonah piped up in his annoying nasal voice. "I mean yesterday you were certain he'd poisoned Celine and was out to get her again. Granted his murder comes as quite the twist, but . . ."

Blake twisted around, fixing his gray eyes on the reporter. "There were aspects of his story that we never had a chance to check out. Who handed Reynolds the poisoned chocolates?"

"Someone handed them to him?" Jonah bleated.

"How do you think they got there?"

Jonah shrugged. "He could've brought them with, right?"

He turned to Celine for confirmation.

She shook her head. "No, Blake's right. Someone was waiting for Reynolds at the winery.

"I saw it," she added when Jonah still looked stubbornly unconvinced.

"The mailman," Blake murmured. They'd had no time to pursue that angle.

"*A mailman?*" Jonah repeated, his eyes cutting away from Celine. "How do you know?"

"Doesn't matter." Blake shrugged. "Bottom line is someone wanted Reynolds out of the way right from the start."

In the rearview mirror, Blake could see Julia's brow wrinkling as she considered the ideas he'd laid out.

"Because of what he has?" she asked. "What he knows?"

She didn't have to add *about the Gardner heist.* It was clear to them all what she meant.

"Something like that," he replied. "An arrest would've been a low-key affair—"

"Leaving his apartment open to be searched," Julia finished his thought. "But that's not the case anymore."

⸙

The roar of the Ted Williams Tunnel—named for the Boston Red Sox baseball legend—filled Celine's ears. She sat, wedged between Julia's squat, solid form and Jonah's bony elbow.

He nudged her with it just then.

"We're traveling under the harbor," he said—brown eyes round and owl-like behind his spectacles. "Underwater in a car. Can you believe it?"

Celine looked over at him.

"Yes." She ejected the word through tightly clenched teeth. Her arms pressed into her midriff, fingers tightly interlaced.

It wasn't just that Jonah's presence and his whiny attitude toward Blake had begun to chafe her. (She ought to have insisted he stay behind—but Boston was Jonah's home. Who was she to tell the reporter he couldn't return?)

What was infinitely worse was the knowledge that Anthony Reynolds had known—without a shadow of a doubt—that he was going to die. Known it, and been unable to do a thing about it—as though he was inside a plane in free fall.

The realization was sobering. No one deserved to go through an experience like that. What must those last few hours have been like for him?

If it helps, he was angry and betrayed, Sister Mary Catherine interrupted her thoughts. *To the very end, that's how he felt, not terrified.*

"He felt he'd been backed into a corner," Celine uttered her impressions out loud. "He was determined to put up a fight. That's why he called Penny when he figured he'd been a target all along."

The General's decision may have been made long before she'd met the sculptor, but Reynolds had only recognized the threat in the final hours of his life.

Blake's gaze met and held hers in the rearview mirror. "I can tell you exactly when Reynolds made up his mind. When he scraped his chair back in the middle of our conversation." He exhaled heavily. "I'll never understand why he didn't confide in me. He had a federal agent before him—someone ready to listen and—"

"He wouldn't have known whom to trust," Celine said. "In his state of mind, paranoid, fearful, he—"

"Would've taken you for a corrupt agent, on the General's take," Julia finished the sentence, a wry expression on her face.

Because the General had made it clear he had law enforcement in his corner, Celine thought. A name accompanied the thought as Julia continued to speak—"And with good reason. God knows, we've had plenty of corruption within the ranks."—*A Polish name.*

"Aha!" Jonah slapped his thigh—so loudly and suddenly, Celine nearly jumped out of her skin. "The truth comes out at last." He leaned over to grin at Julia. "Can I quote you on that?"

"Not unless you want to be booted out of the car." It was Blake who responded, his eyes grim, his voice quiet.

"And speaking of corruption"—Julia smiled sweetly at the reporter— "isn't it a violation of journalistic ethics to publish unverified content?"

Jonah subsided back into his seat. "That's diff—" he began to huff.

"No, it's not, Jonah," Celine immediately contradicted him, her long-suppressed outrage bubbling over. "It's no different at all. You have a responsibility to check your facts before presenting them to the public as incontrovertible truths. Doing anything less is pandering to sensationalism at best, dishonest and dishonorable at worst."

Done scolding the reporter, she leaned back, exhausted, and closed her eyes. The Polish name pealed in her ears again.

"Wozniak," she said, her eyes still closed. "Who is Wozniak?"

"What's Wozniak got to do with anything?" Jonah asked.

Celine's eyes jolted open.

"You know who this Wozniak is?" Blake and Julia voiced the question in Celine's mind.

Jonah blinked, startled, as all three of them stared at him, then he swallowed. "Well, no, not personally. But who doesn't know of him? I mean, hello, Steve Wozniak, co-founder of Apple?" His tone turned sarcastic. "Are you seriously telling us the Apple guy is involved in this?"

"Of course not," Celine snapped. "It's a name I keep hearing. If it referred to the Apple guy, I'd have seen an image of an apple as I heard the name."

Julia squeezed her hand, an unspoken suggestion to calm down. "What exactly are you seeing?" she probed gently.

"A key," Celine replied. "A big golden key. That signifies Wozniak is the key to everything."

"Wozniak," Julia repeated the name as she exchanged a glance with Blake. "Could be a client of Reynolds, right? Or a friend?"

"Or his killer," Blake agreed. "We'll have to check it out."

Chapter Twenty-Seven

Twenty minutes later, the armored FBI vehicle left the freeway and cruised down a narrow tree-lined street.

Brookline, Celine read the name on the green street sign at the corner.

"We're in Cambridge now," Julia announced as Celine sat forward, scanning the street. "Reynolds' neighborhood."

"I know," Celine said softly. She swiveled her head from side to side, straining to see out the windows on either side of her. "I can feel it." The tugging sensation in her solar plexus had been growing stronger since they'd exited the freeway.

She felt like a dog on a leash, pulled by a power she didn't fully comprehend.

Had she been walking, she'd have been propelled forward—from Brookline onto Allston, where the trees grew sparser and two- and three-story clapboard houses rose skyward from constricted lots on either side of the street. Past the Starbucks on the left.

The coffee shop caught her attention, she didn't know why. Her gaze trailed back to it as the car made a smooth right onto Grove Avenue.

Wozniak. Wozniak.

The name rang ever louder in her head—like the insistent peal of a bell summoning the faithful to prayer.

It was accompanied by a sudden, inexplicable craving for coffee. A thick, frothy, mint-chocolaty concoction. She could taste it on her tongue. *Peppermint mocha.*

The craving subsided as unexpectedly as it had arisen.

And before Celine could question it, the Suburban rolled to a stop in front of an imposing structure of red brick and gray clapboard. Sixty Grove Avenue—Reynolds' apartment building—took up an entire block along Allston Street, stretching from Grove Avenue to Sidney Street.

"This is it," Blake said.

He climbed out and held Julia's door open for her, keeping his hand on the door until Celine stepped out. Then he released his hold on it.

The door swung back.

"Hey!" Jonah yelped. He slid toward the door, thrusting it open to clamber out. But a second later, setting foot on the sidewalk and craning his neck up, he emitted a low whistle of admiration.

"Wow, this is some place!"

Gazing up at the brick-and-clapboard structure, Celine found herself agreeing with him. The combination of warm red on the first story with dark gray above it was quite elegant. Wide marble steps, between freshly painted black railings, led up to glass double doors.

Beyond the doors, she spotted gold-framed paintings hanging on the foyer walls and potted plants adorning the floor.

Jonah whistled again—enviously. "Reynolds must have been doing well for himself."

"Looks like it," Julia commented, taking stock of the place. "It must cost a pretty packet to live here."

"That it does." Blake led the way up the short flight of stairs. "Reynolds was paying about five grand a month for his apartment." At the entrance, he pushed against the double doors, holding them wide open.

"It's not particularly large, but he did have the entire floor to himself."

The doorman acknowledged them with a nod as they entered the foyer.

"Definitely doing well," Julia murmured as they took the stairs—also marble—up to Reynolds' apartment. "Who knew sculpting was such a lucrative profession?"

"He was a fine sculptor," Celine reminded them, the rebuke coming out tarter than she'd intended "He'd paid his dues and earned his reputation."

Her tone caused Blake to turn around, and she bit her lip, mortified, as his intense gray eyes bore into her.

Why she'd felt obliged to defend Reynolds, she didn't know. Was it because he was dead and no longer able to stand up for himself? Whatever the case, something close to anger had lashed out inside of her, stinging through her veins when she'd heard the others commenting on the murdered man's financial status.

It wasn't as though he didn't deserve his success.

She clenched her fists, grateful when Blake deftly changed the subject.

"Cambridge Police, as I mentioned, has charge of the crime scene. One of their guys will be posted up there. Didn't want them releasing the scene before you two had a chance to look at it. You, however"—he turned to Jonah—"will be waiting outside. I'm not letting you into a crime scene."

Celine caught the grimace on Jonah's face, but the reporter accepted the stricture without argument.

Thank goodness! She'd had about as much as she could take of his complaints and snide remarks.

❧

Clutching the banisters, she followed close on Blake's heels—edgy, apprehensive, bracing herself for the awful sensations that would surely assail her when she stepped into the crime scene.

She hadn't stumbled upon the dead body—thank heavens—but the residual energy from the brutal murder would linger weeks and months after the event.

As it had long after Dirck had been killed. Long after he'd gone into the light.

Energy as dark as that—fraught with trauma—takes time to dissipate, Celine, Sister Mary Catherine had explained. *Be prepared for it—*

Dear God! A dark figure suddenly swam into view, shattering the brittle hold Celine had upon herself.

Gripping the smooth black railing, she forced herself to look.

Through the ringing in her ears, she made out a woman—a slender, jeans-clad woman, her dark brown hair pulled back into a bun. Celine pressed herself closer to the railing as the woman whisked past, taking them in with a quick, harried smile.

Celine caught the strong whiff that emanated from the large Starbucks cup in her hand—*peppermint mocha?*

The same flavor she'd been craving. A mere coincidence, or—?

Before she could ponder its significance, her eyes were drawn back up to the second-floor landing. A male figure stood above her, his eyes boring into the woman who'd just flown past. He moved adroitly aside as Blake barreled toward him.

God, what was Blake doing? Hadn't he seen the guy?

Celine was about to call out a warning when she recognized the tall, muscular figure looming over them.

Reynolds.

Chapter Twenty-Eight

He stood, feet riveted to the landing, shaking his fist, his mouth open in a ferocious scream, the words so loud they could wake the dead. Celine pressed her hands to her ears, envying the others for their ability to ignore the ruckus.

You bitch! You coldhearted, f—in' bitch!

His cold, green eyes landed on Celine's face.

Don't just stand there like an idiot. Do something! he bellowed.

Do what? she asked, struggling to understand.

Follow that woman. She's stealing from me.

Follow her yourself, she was tempted to say, but she bit back the words, asking instead: "What's she stolen?"

She must have spoken aloud because Julia grabbed her arm. "What's going on, Celine?"

"Celine?" Blake pivoted around, alarmed.

"Shhh," she hissed, trying to concentrate her psychic hearing on Reynolds's voice. "It's Reynolds."

His shoulders sagged, his energy apparently ebbing away.

Nothing yet, but that's not the point. It's the intent. You need to follow her.

Follow her.

His voice reverberated in her ear even as his form faded away.

"You can *see* Reynolds?" Jonah's squeak startled her. He was staring at her slack-jawed. "You've gotta be kidding me."

"I wish I were." She turned to Blake and Julia. "We need to go after that woman. She was in Reynolds' apartment."

"That's not possible." Blake was instantly dismissive. "There's an officer stationed outside his door. Has been this entire time. You're telling me she got past him?"

Follow her. Follow her. Follow her.

Reynolds' nervous energy was beginning to infect her.

"She managed to get in." Celine turned to Julia, desperate. "I don't know how. But we need to go after her. He's insisting we do."

Blake briefly twisted his head. Reynolds' apartment was on the third floor; they had a couple more flights to climb. Celine saw him wavering, irresolute. A range of emotions flickered across his face—irritation mingling with reluctant belief and skepticism—as he stared at her.

Eventually confusion won out.

"I need something more than a dead guy's word, Celine." His eyes sought Julia's. "I have nothing close to resembling reasonable suspicion. I can't just follow her; stop her—that's—"

"I'm afraid he's right." Julia made a wry face at Celine. "Isn't there anything more concrete you can give us?"

Nothing more concrete than the sound of Reynolds' voice echoing in her head.

Your thinking cap, Celine, Sister Mary Catherine said softly. *Did you leave it on the airplane?*

No, dammit. Why couldn't anything be easy?

"We need a pretext." Celine was thinking out loud.

Her gaze swept over Blake and Julia and then came to rest upon Jonah.

"You're a reporter," she murmured. "For a major art newspaper."

Wispy impressions shot through her mind, coalescing into an idea.

"A feature about the life of our dead sculptor might be in order."

Jonah's eyes narrowed. "What are you talking about?"

"Have you noticed how it's never harassment when a reporter badgers you with questions—however nosy or inappropriate?"

The penny dropped. "You want *me* to go after *her*?" He emphasized the pronouns, drawing them out to showcase his utter incredulity.

"Yes, why don't you?" Julia urged, face wreathed in smiles. With her white hair and the crinkles around her blue eyes, she looked like a mildly pushy grandma urging her grandson to go on a date. "She could be a neighbor for all we know. Here's your chance to be a part of the story, to find out a little more than Blake here might be willing to let out."

"Sounds like a fantastic idea!" Blake was positively beaming at the reporter.

Jonah's eyes narrowed even further behind his round, wire-rimmed spectacles. "I know what you guys are up to. You're just trying to get rid of me."

"No, Jonah," Blake said. "We're giving you a chance to be part of the team, trusting you to do a little detective work on your own."

Jonah studied Blake's features like a merchant inspecting a potentially counterfeit bill. "Fine," he eventually said. "But if I scratch your back, you have to scratch mine."

It wasn't an analogy Blake appreciated, Celine could see that. But he got the message. "You help us, and I'll share whatever information I can without compromising the case."

"You'd better hurry." Celine pressed her palm flat against Jonah's skinny chest, giving him a little shove, as the faint echoes of Reynolds' voice resonated in her head again.

"Thanks," she added as he began sprinting down.

"No worries." He looked over his shoulder, giving her a wolfish grin. "I'll say this for her—she was goddamned hot for an older woman."

He disappeared from view, Blake craning his neck after him to make sure the reporter was headed down.

"Alright, looks like we're finally rid of nosy Nancy." His smile widened as he looked over at Celine. "That was good thinking on your part."

"Just using my thinking cap," she responded as they resumed the trek upward. "What I don't understand is why Reynolds couldn't have followed her himself."

"He must've realized there'd be no point. The man's dead, after all," Julia reminded Celine, effortlessly overtaking her on their way up. "Not much he can do stalking her."

"Yes, I know, but"—Celine splayed her fingers through her hair; the long flight had made it sticky and lank—"he was just standing there, as though he'd taken root."

His anger's chaining him down, Celine, Sister Mary Catherine told her. *He'll be tied to the scene of his death until he grants himself permission to move on.*

Chapter Twenty-Nine

Reaching the third-floor landing, Blake rounded the corner—and stopped short.

An officer was guarding Reynolds' door—just as Soldi had promised. But he was planted on a wooden seat, his mouth open, head lolling back, sawing logs.

Un-f—in'-believable!

"I thought caffeine helped you stay awake."

Blake turned to see the corners of Julia's blue eyes crinkling in amusement as she surveyed the scene: the chubby, young Cambridge Department patrol officer slumped at his post outside Reynolds' third-floor apartment. A Starbucks cup of coffee tilting limply from his hands, its contents sloshing out onto his uniform.

The air reeked of coffee. For some reason he couldn't fathom, Celine was sniffing at the aroma, brow wrinkled, nose upturned.

"Peppermint mocha," she murmured. "Again. It's connected. But how?"

Blake had no idea what she was talking about. Why was the flavor of coffee significant? Biting back an irritable retort, he turned to the young officer. And, beyond furious by now, prodded him in the ribs.

"Cowan!" he trumpeted, using the name on the man's nametag. "Wake up, man!"

Had he been alone, he would've added a few choice four-letter words. But acutely aware of the two women present, he restrained himself.

Cowan's only response was a series of stuttering gasps that ended in a low snort. His head lolled forward, chin rolling from his shoulder to his chest.

Blake grabbed his shoulder and shook him forcefully.

Godf—indammit! What was the matter with the pimply-faced bozo? Shit-for-brains! Asleep on the job—

Dear God, had he been venting out loud?

Celine was looking at him as though he'd just walloped her with a baseball bat. He'd seen the same expression on a girlfriend of his—the relationship had been short-lived—when he'd let forth a stream of foul language in her presence.

Nothing to do with her; he'd been angry about something else, but apparently venting your fury in your own home was uncalled for. A torrent of expletives was as unacceptable as raining blows on a harmless object.

But he'd learned his lesson. Women overreacted to that kind of thing. Nothing you could do about it but apologize. He did so now.

"Sorry," he mumbled, wishing Celine would stop staring at him like that. She looked totally shell-shocked.

"What're you apologizing for?" Julia's eyes swiveled from his face to Celine's. She was clearly more used to profanity than her young friend if she had no idea why he was apologizing.

He was about to explain when Celine's mouth widened into the kind of smile—accepting, compassionate, and forgiving—that he'd only seen on images of the Virgin Mary.

"There's no need to apologize for your *thoughts*," she said. She emphasized the word, confirming that he'd kept his ravings to himself. "They're in your head; no one can hear them."

Thank God for small mercies. He was embarrassed enough as it stood.

"The only reason I heard them was because of the energy with which your mind expelled them. I've never seen you this angry before."

"Sorry," he said again. He didn't want her intimidated by him.

"No, it's okay. Really. But"—she turned back to the sleeping beauty in uniform—"it's not Cowan's fault." She pointed to the Starbucks cup in the cop's hands. It was tilting forward now.

She plucked it from Cowan's sluggish hold before he could slosh any more of its contents. "I think he might've been drugged."

"Drugged?" Blake had no idea what she was talking about. But apparently Julia—quicker on the uptake—did.

"By our mystery woman?" she asked, her tone somber. She shot him a worried glance.

The look on his former colleague's face alarmed Blake. *Mystery woman?* Did she mean the woman who'd passed them on the stairs? God, he hoped not!

Pinpricks of tension pierced the back of his neck; his collar felt unusually constricting. He looked toward Celine, hoping she'd deny the link. But this clearly wasn't his day.

"I'm afraid so," Celine said.

Jesus Christ! Blake slapped his hand against his forehead. It was yet another thing he hadn't foreseen. SAC Walsh would have a field day with that.

"It's hard to believe, I know." Celine was sympathetic. "She seemed harmless enough. I can't say I detected any strong negative energy as she passed us. No malevolent vibes, nothing sinister."

Her words didn't ease his sense of culpability. As an investigator, Blake was trained to be suspicious, to look out for—if not to expect—the worst. And he'd failed to anticipate this. Just as he'd failed to anticipate Grayson Pike's murder four months ago. *Damn!*

"She didn't even act nervous or guilty," Celine went on.

"Hardened criminals rarely do," Julia pointed out dryly.

A fact Blake should've remembered when he'd first caught sight of the woman. Instead, he'd balked at following her. Cursing himself, he pulled out his phone.

They needed to get a handle on this thing.

"Let's hope Hibbert's managed to catch up to her." He punched a few buttons on his iPhone and pressed the device to his ear. Hibbert answered on the first ring.

"Any luck?"

Blake listened intently. "Damn." She'd left. That wasn't good news.

His gaze shifted to the cup in Celine's hand. "Listen—"

But Jonah was way ahead of him. Good for him!

"You're headed to the Starbucks on Allston? Great!"

Maybe one of the baristas would remember serving the woman. If nothing else, they had a chance of getting her name—assuming she'd been careless enough to provide it.

That coupled with her appearance—which they'd all noted—and the silver Mercedes Benz Jonah had seen her driving off in could be all they needed to track her down.

He disconnected, still clutching the phone in his hands.

"Gone, I take it," Julia guessed.

He nodded.

"At least, she didn't take anything. Right?" He heard her ask Celine. The younger woman's murmured assent was reassuring.

He scrolled through his contacts. Cambridge PD and Soldi were his next calls.

"Sorry, this needs to be handled before we can go in," he said as Julia turned toward him.

He wanted Cowan sent to Urgent Care and crime scene techs to take charge of the coffee cup. They needed to confirm it had been drugged.

They also needed a better plan to secure the place. The initial walk-through of the apartment had yielded nothing of interest. Blake had surmised the killer had found what he was looking for.

Clearly that wasn't the case.

❧

As Blake had expected, Vince Soldi was far from pleased.

109

"I can't keep a permanent guard posted there," he expostulated. "Cambridge may be a small town compared with Boston, but I assure you, Special Agent, this isn't the only case we've got. It's definitely not the only homicide we're working."

"I understand," Blake said in as reasonable a tone as he could manage. Phone clutched to his ear, he paced the hallway floor. From the double doors leading out to the terrace, past the snoring Cowan, all the way to the door—painted to blend in with the neutral beige walls—Reynolds' killer had used to gain access to the third floor.

Celine was studying the side entrance as he walked past. "I don't think our interloper lives in the building," she told Julia. He stopped to listen; Soldi was still grumbling. "She came in through a side door like this one —but not this one."

She looked up at the ceiling.

"There's a door like it on every floor—on the floor above as well," Blake told her. He covered the mouthpiece on his phone, but Soldi heard him nevertheless.

"What?" he asked gruffly.

"Looks like our trespasser came in the same way the killer did. From the floor above, however." That was how she'd made herself appear to be a resident of the apartment, on her way out.

"Hmmpf," Soldi grunted. "And you know this how exactly, Special Agent? Tarot cards? Some other psychic mumbo jumbo?"

Blake was ready for that. "Doorman didn't see her come in," he explained smoothly. He'd taken the time to check this out. "Visitors have to sign themselves in."

Soldi would know that to be fact. The Massachusetts State Police Detectives had questioned the doorman last night.

"And listen," he continued as Soldi digested the information, "about guarding the door, I'm sure the FBI can figure something out."

"You better not think of posting your men there," Soldi warned. "We don't release the apartment in time, and it's our department that gets to hear an earful. Media talking about civilian rights being encroached and all that crap. I can do without that."

Damn. No men.

"Can't Assistant DA Campari handle the media?"

"She can handle anyone, Special Agent. The point is, she's a special kind of something. She sees a bus barreling toward her, and she shoves the first person she can toward it. Helps her preserve her social justice credentials."

"Even though it potentially compromises her case?" *Jesus,* what kind of ass was this woman? Blake had suspected all along that ADA Mariah

Campari was a piece of work—years of experience working on the job gave you an insight into people. Even those you had yet to meet.

But even the most hard-assed district attorneys he'd met had the sense to try to win—not lose—cases they were assigned to.

"What's she care? She gets paid, regardless," Soldi growled cynically. "Bottom line, no men."

The Deputy Superintendent sounded as likely to budge on the subject as a bullet lodged in a murder victim's cranium.

"Fine, no men," Blake agreed. "How about something more subtle?"

"What do you have in mind?"

"Concealed cameras," Blake informed him bluntly. That was *his* last word on the subject. "If you think the ADA is going to have a problem with it, don't tell her."

Chapter Thirty

Blake had been tempted to sneak Celine into Reynolds' place before the crime scene techs got there, but he held off. If there was any evidence in there—anything that could lead them to the killer and whatever information Reynolds had possessed—Blake wanted it discovered.

Not just by the book, but uncontaminated by any material that could steer them off-course.

The wait as it turned out wasn't that long. Soldi sending his men, as promised, in under ten minutes.

"You'll need to fingerprint the place," Blake informed the three techs. Out of the corner of his eye, he was aware of Cowan being lifted onto a gurney and wheeled to the elevator. It was fortunately large enough to accommodate a stretcher.

Cowan was a big guy, and muscular as the two paramedics appeared to be, Blake didn't want to bet on their chances of carrying the heavyset officer three floors down.

"We've already fingerprinted the goddamn place," one of the three techies—a redheaded guy—grumbled.

"And you'll do it again." Blake looked him squarely in the eyes. "We've had an intruder. Doesn't look like she was wearing gloves. That means her prints are all over the place."

"Maybe concentrate on the bedroom," Celine softly added. She and Julia were standing on the outskirts of the small group, patiently waiting until they were given the all clear.

"The *bedroom*? Why?" The redheaded guy and his two companions pivoted toward her in unison.

"It's the only room that didn't seem to have been as thoroughly searched as the other two," Blake explained, a little too hastily perhaps. "By the killer, that's to say."

The assertion wasn't entirely truthful. Even Carrothead, who'd been there the evening before, looked justifiably skeptical.

When Blake had entered the apartment the previous evening, every room in it had looked as though it had been thoroughly ransacked. It had seemed mostly a chaotic, haphazard effort, but thinking back Blake was beginning to think the search had been more systematic than that.

In his experience, random searchers didn't pull open every drawer and peek behind every cabinet door. No effort had been made to put anything back in its place, but that's precisely how he'd known every nook and cranny in Reynolds' apartment had been scrutinized.

If the woman who'd just whizzed past them was the killer's accomplice, there was no reason to believe she'd been any less thorough.

Still if Celine thought the tech guys' efforts should focus on Reynolds' bedroom, given her track record, Blake for one was willing to go along. And he'd do anything to ward off the inevitable discomfiting questions.

"Seems likely that the killer or his gal would focus on the bedroom the second time around," he pressed home the point.

"If you say so," Carrothead muttered. He picked up his case, gestured to his colleagues, and entered the apartment.

A few minutes later, Carrothead poked his head out the apartment door. "You sure you had an intruder here?" He paused, then receiving no reply continued, "Looks more like a cleaning lady came through."

That caught Blake's attention. "What do you mean?"

Carrothead shrugged. "Place looks considerably more tidied up than it was last I saw it. I'm not saying she did a bang-up job, but . . ." He held his palms up, spreading them apart, and shrugged again.

✎

"Think she was sent to contaminate the scene?" Julia mused aloud when the redheaded technician slid his head back inside Reynolds' apartment.

Celine considered this. A dullness settled like a stone within her. A sign that Julia's hypothesis didn't jive with reality. The shapely hands she saw straightening knick-knacks, closing cabinet doors, pulling out and shoving drawers in suggested a different interpretation.

"No, I think she was a neat freak in search of something."

"A burglar with OCD," Blake said with a harsh laugh.

The prospect of their intruder having potentially destroyed evidence didn't seem to bother him—surprisingly enough.

"Either way, doesn't really matter," he said now in response to Celine's unvoiced question. "The place has already been processed, and we're reprocessing it. Hope Carrothead has the sense to take some more photographs."

He strode to the door and barked out the order. His edginess—while understandable—was making Celine feel unsettled. She closed her eyes, taking a few calming breaths. Whatever awaited her inside would likely drain her of her energy. She needed to prepare for it.

A few deep breaths later, her now lulled mind began to wander. Where was Jonah? He'd been gone a long time.

She opened her eyes, about to ask the question, when the techs emerged from Reynolds' apartment. "It's all yours," they said to Blake.

"You should probably fingerprint us," Julia reminded the redheaded guy who seemed to be in charge.

Blake nodded. "We didn't go in, but it's not a bad idea. You'll want to eliminate our prints from any that were found."

Let's not give your stupid ADA any reason to wriggle out of doing what needs to be done. Celine heard the thought as clearly as though Blake had spoken aloud. She wondered if it was the ADA—a female, Celine sensed —who was the reason for Blake's jumpy energy.

Or was it sleep deprivation? One of the crime scene techs brought out a fingerprinting kit—the action punctuating her speculations.

She'd noticed the dark shades under Blake's eyes when he'd met them at the airport. They were even more prominent now. He clearly hadn't gotten much sleep. And it was wreaking havoc on his temper.

"Mine are on file," Blake said when the tech approached him. But he held out both hands, nevertheless.

A few moments later when they'd all been fingerprinted, he turned to her.

"Ready to go in?"

"Sure." She nodded, nervous now. The energy that assailed her in places where death and violence had occurred was so traumatic she had no words to describe the experience. The only thing worse was the shock that had slammed into her when she'd realized she'd never see her parents again.

The incident was seventeen years in the past, but it was a memory time had no power to fade.

Reaching out for Julia's hand, she stepped toward the threshold.

Chapter Thirty-One

She walked across the threshold. The redheaded tech was right. The place didn't look nearly as torn apart as it had in the crime scene photos Blake had shared on the ride over.

Her gaze moved past the mantelpiece, the broken sculptures, the colorful abstracts on the walls—*were they prints?*—to the dust-streaked wooden floor. She took two steps, lifted her foot to take a third, and stopped.

Oh my God! Was that Reynolds?

She hadn't expected to see his body still here, splayed out like that.

She'd known Reynolds was dead. She'd been aware she was seeing an apparition when he'd appeared above them on the second-floor landing. But none of that was sufficient preparation for the shock of stumbling, almost literally, upon his corpse.

Oh my God! This was just as bad as when she'd discovered Dirck's dead body.

"I thought he'd been taken away." She pointed, finger trembling.

Why hadn't they removed the body? They'd come twice—*and hadn't considered removing the body?*

Wasn't that standard protocol? Or had someone thought the presence of a corpse would enhance her visions?

Reynolds was wearing the same clothes she'd seen him in a few minutes ago—blue denim jeans and a white dress shirt, rolled up at the sleeves, open at the collar. It would've been a sexy look but for the angry red gash that sliced through the skin on his neck.

"Thought who'd been taken away?" She heard Julia's voice but couldn't locate her. Where was she?

"Him." Celine pointed.

Why was Julia sounding so puzzled? Couldn't she see Reynolds lying lifeless on the floor? His head was turned toward them—green eyes, flat and emotionless, staring accusingly at them.

At her.

"*Reynolds?*" It was Blake asking the question now. Celine couldn't see him either. Her eyes seemed incapable of taking in anything but Reynolds.

"Yes, Reynolds." Celine was getting impatient now. Who else but Reynolds? Why did they keep asking these stupid questions?

She stretched her hand out as far as it would go, forefinger pointing.

"He's dead." She tried to drive home the point.

"Yes, Celine, that's why we're here." Julia's tone irritated Celine. She sounded like she was talking to someone mentally impaired.

"Why is he still there?" The sculptor's tall frame was twisted, his face contorted into a grimace.

"Where?" Blake sounded mystified. "Shhh!" Julia hissed. "I think she sees him."

Of course, she saw him. How could she not? There he lay—not a person, not even a threat, but a twisted, broken mannequin.

The light had gone out of those vivid green eyes, like a candle snuffed out. One moment, the eyeballs had been dancing, rolling in their sockets in agony. The next—

Oh, f—what a mess!

"I didn't mean to kill him." Her voice sounded like the anguished cry of an injured animal. "Didn't want to."

"No?" Julia asked.

Celine shook her head. "I was just trying to talk some sense into him." With a piano wire? Sure, the cops would buy that! She could feel the thin wire in her palms—trying to escape her slick, sweaty grasp.

She shook her head again, the sense of desperation rising.

"He didn't know what he was getting into. What he was getting us into. He wouldn't listen."

"What happened?"

Celine looked down at her hands—compact, beautifully tanned hands, the nails manicured and buffed. Hands that had never had any dirt on them.

Bits of skin and blood glistened on the wire clutched in them.

She grimaced. "Don't want to get that stuff on myself."

"What stuff?"

"The stuff on the wire. His blood, his skin . . . Oh God, I'm going to be sick." She bent over, stomach heaving.

What had she done? She'd never killed anybody. Never lifted a finger against . . .

"Jesus Christ, get me out of here," she moaned.

Julia guided her out of the apartment. The sensations subsided, the nausea loosened its grip on her.

Still bent at the waist, Celine stared at the marble floor. This wasn't working. How was she expected to get any useful impressions with a corpse staring her in the face?

She raised her head and eyed Julia and Blake.

"You need to get that body out of here. I'm not going back in with it still there."

Blake was staring at her as though she'd lost her mind. "There's no body in there, Celine."

"Yes, there is." She straightened up. Why was he lying to her? "I saw it."

"No, Celine." It was Julia who replied, her arm still around Celine's shoulder. "There's no body. You were just . . ."

"Seeing things?" It had felt like a waking nightmare.

"Having a vision," Julia explained. "You were talking about not wanting to kill Reynolds. You saw a piano wire in your hands."

Okay, so she'd occupied the killer's mind. That made sense.

"I hate to ask, but you think you can go back in there?" Blake looked distinctly uncomfortable making the request. "Tell us more?"

Celine hesitated. She knew her response ought to be an unequivocal yes. After all, that's why she'd been brought here. But she simply could not bring herself to encounter Reynolds' stiff body again or his dull accusing eyes. It was just too horrible.

"Is there a way of not seeing his body?" Celine turned to Julia. "I don't think I can get anything useful with my attention riveted on his corpse. How do I get past it?"

Her friend reached into her voluminous handbag. "I might have an idea. Don't know if it'll work, but it's worth a try."

∿

Julia had just wrapped the navy bandana around Celine's eyes when Jonah Hibbert bounded up the stairs. It wasn't an interruption Blake relished. Sure, he'd wondered what was taking the guy so long. But Hibbert's presence was about as welcome as a taser to the ribs, and Blake had been grateful for the brief respite.

As always, the reporter had something to whine about.

"Hey, why did those CSI guys wanna fingerprint me? Am I a suspect now?"

"We've all been fingerprinted," Julia informed him dryly, although the question had been meant for Blake. "Standard procedure."

Blake suppressed a smile. Figuring Jonah was less trouble downstairs and out of their hair, he'd asked the techs to corner the reporter and get his prints as well—buying them a few more precious minutes of peace. But here the reporter was, back in their midst, like the proverbial bad penny.

Jonah turned to Julia, took in the bandana around Celine's eyes, and stared at them, bemused. "Playing blindman's bluff?"

Blake ignored the question, as did the others. "Any luck at Starbucks?"

"I got a name." Jonah flipped pages in his tiny notebook. "Sofia, spelt with an f."

"Would she have used her real name?" Julia wondered. She adjusted the bandana around Celine's eyes.

Blake considered the question.

"No reason not to," he said finally. "I don't think she figured on being intercepted. As it stands, if it weren't for Celine, we wouldn't have found her out. Besides, without a last name—"

He turned to Hibbert with another question.

"You get the impression she's a regular?" If she was, she might live in the area.

"Nope. The baristas have never seen her before."

"So we have a first name and the make and model of her car," Celine spoke for the first time since Jonah had returned. She pushed the bandana up from her eyes. "That's not too bad, I guess."

"Reynolds recognized her, didn't he?" Julia asked her. "She could be a client."

"Or somehow connected to whoever killed him," Celine said.

She sounded hesitant, as though doubting the impressions she was receiving. Or her interpretation of them. Blake wondered why. He was no psychic, but as an investigator, he thought she was on the mark.

Sofia wasn't a client.

"Employee of or girlfriend." Blake ran through the options in his mind.

She had to be fairly close to the killer. Why else had she come? And why else had Reynolds staged a hissy fit when he'd seen her—not that Blake had heard any of it, fortunately?

That indicated some connection—however tenuous—to the General. Celine had picked up no such thing when Sofia had run past them. But their interaction had been so fleeting, how much could she have psychically picked up?

Based on what Celine had shared before Hibbert showed up, the killer—a white-collar individual, judging by her impressions—had no prior criminal record. Obviously someone Reynolds had known.

A client, maybe?

Blake would need to get a list of Reynolds' clients from Soldi. Hopefully the old fool wouldn't balk at providing the information. His mind returned to the killer.

The guy might have stayed squeaky clean until now. But his choice of weapon linked him to the mob. No doubt about it. An associate of the General; Blake was willing to wager every penny of his Federal TSP on that. An underling, perhaps. Or his business partner in the still-to-be-solved Gardner heist—the man Ella had dubbed the Boston Brahmin.

Blake had no idea where or how his personal assistant had come up with that moniker. But it seemed to fit. And he liked it.

Chapter Thirty-Two

"I'll bet DMV could help us track down the gorgeous Sofia."

Jonah's light tenor interrupted Blake's train of thoughts—the words chafing his raw nerves like a steel wool pad.

"With just her name and the color of her car?" Blake gave up on trying to mask his disgust.

How was it that the same idiots who complained about federal intrusion into people's private lives could—in the same breath—enthusiastically expect that a few odd details about an individual would call up an entire file of personal facts?

"We don't exactly live in a police state, you know. There isn't a vast file in some centralized location on every person living within the United States."

Heck, if they'd had something like that, he wouldn't have had to go through the process of being fingerprinted just to volunteer at his niece's elementary school. As though as a federal agent, he hadn't been fingerprinted enough.

"*What?*"

Jonah was staring at him, a pained expression on his face.

"I have a partial license plate."

"You do?" It wasn't much, but it would certainly do.

"Yes, didn't I mention it, the lovely Sofia almost got a ticket."

"And the meter maid"—Blake was aware of Julia wincing at the term, but heck, what else could you call those guys?—"remembered bits of her plate?"

"No, but it was seeing the officer that gave me the idea of taking down her license plate. I didn't get all of it, but—"

Hibbert flipped through a few more pages of his notebook, found what he was looking for, and glanced up.

"Z39," he proudly proclaimed. "There was a letter before the Z. I can't remember what it was."

"Which part of the plate is that, Jonah—the first or the last?" Celine voiced the question in Blake's mind.

"The last part"—Jonah looked at Blake, wide-eyed, eager, apparently trying to seek his approval—"I figured that was more important." He turned back to Celine. "You see, the last digit on a Massachusetts plate tells when the car's registration is up for renewal. So a plate ending in Z39 means—"

"We're looking for a car with a registration coming up in September," Blake mused. "It's not much, but it does help to narrow things down. Let's go down, give Ella a call."

It was a nice excuse to get the journalist away from the scene of the crime, and he took it eagerly. He didn't need Jonah broadcasting the few details Celine had gleaned to the public. You could never trust a journalist not to blab.

He turned to Julia and Celine.

"Why don't you guys finish up here and join us downstairs?"

❧

"DMV will be able to figure it out, right?" Jonah sounded breathless as he followed Blake past the heavy glass doors of 60 Grove Avenue.

"Yeah, sure," Blake mumbled as he emerged into the afternoon sun. It was a bit more complicated than that—especially when all you had was a partial plate. But he was okay with Jonah thinking law enforcement could work magic. "We'll let Ella take care of it."

He noticed the sky as he pulled his phone out of its holster. It was a serene blue, not a cloud in sight. Strange, how the oddest things caught your eye in moments of stress.

His personal assistant picked up on the first ring.

"I have a license plate I need you to run," Blake informed her. "It's a partial," he continued apologetically.

"Story of my life." Ella's tone was matter-of-fact. He could picture her sitting upright at her desk, pen poised over a legal pad. "Give it to me."

Blake read the numbers. "There's a first name to go with that, assuming she was driving her own car."

"Any reason she wouldn't be?"

"It's a possibility—given that she broke into a crime scene, drugging the officer on duty to do so."

Ella came as close to whistling as she ever had in all the time he'd known her.

"*My, oh my!* Quite the determined little thing, isn't she?"

Blake murmured noncommittally. Jonah was staring at him avidly, like a scavenger eagerly watching for crumbs to drop from a feasting lion's jaws.

"Did she get anything out of Reynolds' apartment?"

"No idea. I sure as hell hope not."

But several minutes after the call had ended, he was still mulling over Ella's question, his foot tapping a relentless beat on the cracked concrete of the sidewalk.

Thanks to Celine, only eleven of the Gardner's stolen works were outstanding. Except for one, they were all too large to be tucked into a jeans pocket. And he doubted anyone with any sense would risk putting the eleventh item into their pockets.

No, Sofia Without-a-Last-Name had probably not taken anything at all.

The question was: had the killer? Had Sofia been sent to pick up whatever the killer had failed to find?

Or had she been asked to clean up after him?

After all, Mr. Clean Record hadn't meant to kill Reynolds. The murder had been a spur-of-the-moment, desperate move. The work of a nervous Nellie rather than a cold-blooded iceman.

Either way, Blake was betting Sofia was an employee. Not a girlfriend. Efficient, capable. Someone the white-collar douche who'd killed Reynolds could trust implicitly.

Someone like Ella. A personal assistant.

If DMV was unable—or unwilling—to help, Blake figured he had a way of tracking the mysterious Sofia down. It would be tedious, time-consuming work, but Blake had never had a problem with that aspect of detective work.

He discovered Jonah studying his face again, reading it like an ancient scholar poring over the Old Testament.

He raised his eyebrows. "What?"

"Shouldn't we go back up?"

Blake glanced over his shoulder at the entrance to Reynolds' apartment building, then shrugged. "Nah. We can wait for them down here."

Chapter Thirty-Three

Back in Reynolds' apartment, Celine allowed Julia to guide her into the middle of the living room. Lightly gripping the former fed's hand, Celine twirled around the room, head tilted back. The gesture was as much to orient herself as to avoid any possibility of seeing Reynolds' dead form on the floor.

Open my eyes, Sister Mary Catherine, she whispered to her guardian angel.

Clouds of energy swirled before her mind's eye, gradually resolving into impressions.

Reynolds stood before her—arms bent at the elbow, hands clenched into fists, a fighting stance. To her growing frustration, he vehemently shook his hand.

"No, no, no!"

They'd been arguing for some time. This was going nowhere.

She reached for him. "You've gotta listen to me, Tony."

"No way." Reynolds turned his back on her.

The movement enraged her. "Just listen, dammit!"

The muscular form, the broad shoulders, the long neck—turned resolutely away from her—made her feel like a pipsqueak. A helpless pipsqueak. She was only an inch shy of six feet. But he loomed over her.

A figure she was powerless against. Or so he believed.

"You think you can ignore me? Bastard! You think you can mess with me?"

Her arm swung forward. A glint of steel and glass flashed in her hand as it plunged through the air and made contact with Reynolds' neck. She felt the resistance of muscle as she pushed the syringe in.

"What's going on?" Julia asked. The sound of her voice—perturbed, troubled—caused Celine's consciousness to distance itself from Reynolds' killer.

"Horse tranquilizer," Celine said. "He used horse tranquilizer to subdue Reynolds."

The distinction between her personality and the killer's dissolved again.

The force of her arm had caused the entire contents of the syringe to empty into Reynolds' veins. Damn, he'd be out before he could reveal where he'd secreted her art.

"Where is it, Tony?" she hissed as he fell back against her arms.

The sculptor's eyes were beginning to glaze over. "You'll never find it." He grinned. "Fussy Phil."

"Tell me where it is," she snarled. The wire was around his neck, the smirk on his face turning into a grimace of pain.

She squeezed hard as she repeated her question. "Where is it, you arrogant sonovabitch?"

Reynolds opened his mouth—but refused to answer her question.

"Where is it?" she growled and squeezed harder. And harder.

She could see the thin veins in his eyes bursting, his neck bulging. He struggled, writhing in her arms, too stupefied to fight back.

Then it was over.

A moaning filled the room.

It was her voice.

"Celine?" Julia squeezed her hand. "Are you okay? What's going on?"

"I need some air," Celine gasped. "Is there a balcony?"

"Just beyond the living room." She felt Julia draw her gently forward. "A few steps forward and we're there."

She tore the bandana off her eyes as they stepped onto the tiny balcony. The air was still and sultry, but it helped to clear her mind. She took a deep breath, filling her lungs with the warm, stultifying air.

It was like trying to quench your thirst with lukewarm water on a sweltering hot day.

"God!" She shuddered, gazing out at the vista of low buildings and skylines spread out before her. "I'd do anything to unsee what I just saw."

"What did you see?" Julia peered up at her anxiously. "You don't have to give me a blow-by-blow," she hastened to add. "Just the broad details will suffice."

Celine leaned against the wrought iron balcony railing, trying to marshal her thoughts. What were the pertinent facts?

"We're looking for a man. Five inches shorter than Reynolds. Someone with an interest in art."

"The General's partner? The Boston Brahmin?" Julia was using the moniker Ella Rawlins had conferred on the man.

Celine frowned, searching her mind.

"I don't think so. His personality feels different. Not quite as powerful. He lost control of himself in there. He couldn't get Reynolds to take him seriously and he lost it."

"Sounds like he has self-esteem issues." The wrinkles at the corners of Julia's eyes deepened. "That should make it easier to catch him. What did he want?"

"A work of art. Something he owned that was in Reynolds' hands for some reason."

"One of the Gardner's stolen works?" Julia surmised. "And Reynolds discovered what it was and refused to give it back?"

"I can't say for sure, but that's probably the case." She'd sensed the killer's frustration and anger, but she hadn't been able to penetrate his mind deeply enough to gauge the precise work of art he was after.

And Reynolds' reasons for not complying with Fussy Phil's request had been equally obscure.

Fussy Phil? Had she been lucky enough to catch a name? She mentioned it to Julia.

"Sounds like a nickname," Julia said.

"Well, he was absolutely infuriated when Reynolds called him that."

"I wonder," Julia mused. "Fussy as in fusspot, fastidious? That tells us a little more about his personality. And is Phil his first name?"

"They seemed to be on first-name terms." The killer had repeatedly used Reynolds' first name.

When she shared that detail with Julia, the former fed nodded. "Sounds like it could be his name, then." She rubbed her hands together and smiled. "We're making good progress. Well done, Celine!

"But now"—she turned back to face the living room—"the most important thing is to figure out which work of art it is that we're dealing with and to find out where Reynolds hid it. I'm guessing Fussy Phil didn't find it."

"Nope."

Celine slipped her bandana back on.

"Take me to his bedroom and his studio. Maybe we'll be able to pick up something there. The energy imprint of his murder is so strong, it's all I can get in the living room."

Chapter Thirty-Four

"Bedroom," Julia said.

Celine heard her push open a door and felt the former fed's arm gently pulling her in.

Her shoes pressed into a softer, textured surface.

"*Carpet?*"

"Yup. It's the only room with wall-to-wall carpeting." Julia stayed put while Celine slipped her left foot out of its shoe and let it sink into the thick carpet fibers.

"Sofia did a pretty good job straightening up this room," the former fed continued.

"Did she?"

Celine's head automatically pivoted around the room, although with Julia's bandana covering her eyes, the state of the room was lost on her.

"Oh, yes." Julia tugged her arm, towing her half-across the room.

Celine's shoe, catching on her toe, dragged along the wide curve after Julia.

"Remember the photos Blake showed us? The bedroom was a complete mess."

"Sure."

Celine had given the photos a very cursory glance, but she recalled the bedspread had been dragged off the queen-sized bed onto the floor. The closet doors thrown wide open. Coats still on their hangers piled up on the floor.

She felt Julia come to a stop and hastily slipped her shoe back on.

"Fussy Phil did quite a number on this room," Julia said. "But look at the bed now, all tidied up. Exactly what you'd expect considering Reynolds didn't have an opportunity to use it last night."

"I get the sense he had no use for it most days."

Celine bent down to touch the thick satiny bedspread. From Blake's photos, she knew it was patterned in a blue-and-orange abstract design. Reynolds had been a fan of bright colors.

"I think he spent most nights in his studio," she continued softly, describing the images filling her head. "Falling asleep as he worked."

"Aha! So this room was just for his lady friends." Julia sounded amused, cynical. "Figures. It's full of knick-knacks. Along the headboard. Bright floral paintings on the wall. Definitely a room to entertain women."

"I'm sure you're right," Celine said lightly. "But I doubt this bed saw much action these past few days."

She straightened up, opening her senses. She'd intuited women all right—more than one—but no intimacy. That was odd.

Withdrawing her hand from Julia's, she slowly turned around, breathing deeply, stretching out to feel the air. A strong feminine energy enveloped her—pushy, predatory, even.

Sofia?

Celine bent down to touch the bed again, feeling under the mattresses, along the headboard. Her fingers touched smooth glass and ceramic—miniature figurines and other decorative items.

Sofia had touched these. Made sure the miniature sculptures were upright, facing the right way.

She'd shaken the dust off the bedspread and neatly covered the bed with it. But the energy emanating from these objects felt softer and more subtle than the other energy that billowed around the room, threatening to overpower Celine.

Celine stood up, turning to where she thought Julia might be.

"I think there were two women here—Sofia and someone else."

"WHAT?"

The explosive bellow startled Celine.

"Sorry." Julia pushed her volume down several notches. "Didn't mean to bark at you. But you're saying Sofia had . . . someone else with her?"

"Not with her, no." Celine shook her head. "The other woman was here hours before Sofia arrived. I'm sensing a different personality. Stronger, more powerful—more threatening, I'd say. It's the same presence I felt in the living room."

She'd mistakenly attributed the undercurrent of rapacious energy to Fussy Phil. He'd been desperate, had gotten violent. It had seemed to fit. Now she realized she was wrong.

The determination and cunning Celine was sensing were quite distinct from the nervous desperation that characterized Phil. A nervous energy that was markedly absent from this room.

"It's not the killer?" Julia's voice intruded into her thoughts. "Not Fussy Phil? You're sure?"

"Absolutely." Celine's conviction was growing. "I don't think Fussy Phil was in here at all, Julia. He was too distraught to consider searching the apartment of a man he'd just killed."

"You're saying someone else searched the apartment." Julia's voice was flat. "Before Blake discovered the body?"

Her voice rose as the implications of this seeped in.

"Jesus Christ!"

❧

"The door was open when I got there." Blake's voice sounded tinny over Julia's speakerphone.

Celine had a vision of the special agent standing on the sidewalk, his eye trained on Jonah, making sure the reporter stayed out of earshot in the armored vehicle.

Julia had called to break the news that someone other than Fussy Phil had rifled through the apartment sometime between Reynolds' murder and the discovery of his dead body.

"Anyone could've gone in," Blake continued. "A curious bystander, someone with an ulterior motive."

Left unsaid was the notion that the woman could either have entered surreptitiously through the side door or brazenly through the front entrance. There was no way of knowing.

"But what you've told me just confirms my belief that Sofia must've been sent by our killer—a white-collar individual with no stomach for crime."

"The question is," Julia said, "was the other woman sent by the killer as well? Or by someone else?"

"I'd say she has a direct connection to the General," Celine found herself responding.

She adjusted her bandana as further questions buzzed in her head. Why had it been necessary to send two women? Incensed as Reynolds had been about Sofia's presence, he'd said nothing about the other woman. Wasn't that strange?

When you've suffered a violent demise, you want your body discovered, Sister Mary Catherine said. *It's the first step toward justice.*

Meaning what? That Reynolds didn't know the woman at all?

Or that he'd seen the woman and had no reason to suspect her motive in entering his apartment? Either way, her guardian angel's words had provided her with the glimmer of an insight.

"If she didn't know him well enough," Celine voiced the thought out loud, "she wouldn't know where to look. She could trash the place. Make it look like a burglary gone wrong."

There was a sharp intake of breath—the sound of Blake's breath snagging painfully in his throat. Something she'd said had struck a discordant chord.

"That's exactly what it looked like. Are you saying that's all this other woman was trying to do?"

"I think she was doing both," Celine spoke quickly, hoping to capture the half-formed thought before it dissipated. "Ransacking the place, in too much of a hurry to be careful about it, but realizing at the same time that her haste could disguise the motive for Reynolds' murder."

"Except this place has fairly strict protocols for visitors," Julia reminded them dryly.

"Yet the killer managed to get in," Blake pointed out. "Through a side entrance no one bothers to monitor."

"And Sofia and Fussy Phil would've been aware of the fact," Julia said. "Although I guess a simple reconnaissance mission could have told them that as well."

"The killing was a spur-of-the-moment thing," Celine interposed quietly. "So there was no reconnaissance. We're looking for people who've visited Reynolds often enough to know the quirks of the building's security system."

"Soldi has the visitor's book. Shouldn't be too difficult to find what we're looking for," Blake said. "The thing is, Reynolds had no visitors yesterday apart from me. So our second mystery woman must've come in by the side entrance as well."

"Unless she lives here." The possibility had just entered Celine's mind.

But Blake rejected the idea out of hand.

"Nope, not likely. If that were the case, the General would've had no reason to frame Reynolds. A plant—assuming the General had one—could access Reynolds' apartment any time. A woman especially would've had no problem getting in, given Reynolds' proclivities. No, I'm willing to bet she was sent here."

"But that would mean Fussy Phil confided in the General—let him know things got out of hand."

Would a panicking Phil have been willing to admit his mistake? To a cutthroat mobster?

Blake seemed to think so.

"If he was the General's lackey and had a screw-up of that magnitude, his best bet would be to get it off his chest. Give the boss a chance to rectify the situation. Anything less, and he'd have a target on his back for the rest of his life. Of course, he still might."

All true, *if* Phil had been in any condition to make the best choice. Somehow Celine doubted that was the case. But with no tangible insights to offer, she opted to set her doubts aside.

And Julia had accepted Blake's premise without much question either.

"So Fussy Phil gets word to the General that the situation has gone pear-shaped and the General sends this other woman to clean things up," Julia summarized the key idea. "Why send a woman, though?"

"Why not?" Blake asked. "It's the perfect solution. The dead guy has a reputation as a skirt-chaser. A woman snooping around his place looks a little more natural, wouldn't you say, than a tough guy?"

Pushing her bandana up, she saw Julia bobbing her head in agreement. But Celine didn't think Reynolds' reputation as a lady's man had factored very much into the General's calculations, if at all.

"I have a feeling he had a better reason for thinking her presence at a crime scene would go unnoticed—or unremarked, at any rate," she repeated the thought floating into her mind, although she had no idea what it meant.

What reason could there be for accepting a stranger's presence at a crime scene?

But the words must have meant something to her listeners. A moment of stunned silence followed—as though she'd dropped a bomb.

Then Julia responded, her voice troubled: "I don't like where you're going with this, Celine."

Followed a half-beat later by Blake's fervent, "God, I hope you're wrong about that."

Chapter Thirty-Five

Celine fingered the bandana that was sliding down the bridge of her nose and peered anxiously at her friend.

Julia looked tightlipped, stern. What exactly had she said to bring on that expression?

"You don't get the implications of what you said, do you?" Julia asked, responding to Celine's unspoken question.

"I'm afraid I don't." Celine shook her head. "A woman who'd go unnoticed at a crime scene—" Then it hit her. "Oh!"

"Exactly." Julia's smile was tight, her blue eyes weary. "You're opening up a can of worms—ones that probably should be opened. But we have no idea now whom to trust. It's worrisome."

She put her hands on her hips, bracing her shoulders back.

"But the General's always had corrupt agents and officials in his back pocket. So what's new?"

"Like Bill McCormick?" Celine's voice was quiet. They'd never talked about this.

Seven years ago the FBI, in the person of Special Agent Bill McCormick, had marched into the New England museum where Celine worked and upturned her life. The intrusion had coincided with the apparently accidental death of a museum intern.

Celine had been able to persuade then Durham PD detective Keith Elliot that Laurie's fall was no accident; it was a well-staged murder. But the killer had eluded capture.

"I had my suspicions," Julia said. "McCormick was too smooth, too slick. But there was never anything concrete. Then back in March, Penny said—" Julia pressed her lips tightly together, a flurry of emotions—anger, outrage, betrayal—warring for control on her face.

She took a deep breath. "Penny said McCormick called the Gardner asking about the tip Laurie had called in. Not the other way around."

Laurie Robbes, the flaky intern under Celine, had made a career of blackmailing the museum's wealthiest patrons, accusing them of possessing stolen art. In Hugh Norton, she thought she'd hit the jackpot.

"I always thought Hugh Norton should've been investigated," Celine now said. "Laurie tries to blackmail him, just like she does several other museum patrons, and she gets murdered for her troubles? Somehow that never washed. And it was cyanide that killed her."

The same toxin used to poison the box of chocolates left in the winery.

"Yup." Julia nodded. "It was the General. That's obvious now. But"—her blue eyes penetrated Celine's—"there was never anything on Norton. And when we went to his place—well you know; Keith would've told you, I'm sure—the Gardner's Shang dynasty gu turned out to be an imitation. Very well done, but an imitation nonetheless."

"Forged by a clever sculptor," Celine said. "Someone like Reynolds." She wasn't sure why the thought had occurred to her. "He was talented enough to pull off something like that."

"What could I have forged?"

The slurring male voice behind them caught her by surprise. She spun around.

Reynolds stood, leaning unsteadily, against the doorjamb. His green eyes were dark with hostility.

"You're back?" Celine managed.

"Why wouldn't I be?" Reynolds swayed across the room. "I live here."

❧

"Who is it, Celine?" Julia gripped her arm.

"It's Reynolds." Celine kept her eyes fixed on the sculptor's swaying back. "He's here." And he looked drunk, wobbling unsteadily across the room to his closet.

The aftereffects of the horse tranquilizer, Celine, Sister Mary Catherine breathed into her ear. *He's confused.*

Of course! Reynolds' connection to his body—still strong despite the severance of the silver cord—was causing a memory imprint of its physical state to seep into his energy.

That coupled with the aftermath of a violent death was enough to make him disoriented and woozy.

"Can you get anything out of him?" Julia's fingers dug into her flesh.

"I can try." Celine shrugged off Julia's arm and followed the sculptor to the closet.

"Tony?" She kept her voice quiet, gentle, not wanting to alarm him.

"She was in here." His voice was loud, belligerent.

"Who, Tony?"

"Sofia."

She bit her lip, disappointed. They already knew that.

He suddenly whirled around, making her jump back.

"Why are you here, anyway? Checking up on me?" He jerked his chin toward Julia. "Who's the older broad?"

"Julia, my friend. She used to be an FBI agent."

Reynolds' face shut down, his expression stony. He turned his back on her.

"Don't want to talk with any FBI agents. They're all in the tank . . ." his voice faded to a mumble.

Celine crept closer to him. "You can trust Julia, Tony. She's an honest cop. She helped me figure out who killed Dirck. She can help bring your killer to justice." She paused. "If you'll just talk to us."

But Reynolds was ignoring her. "My key," he mumbled. "She got my key. The bitch!"

"Who got your key?"

"Sofia, who else?"

"Was it in your closet?" She had a vision of a slim hand, its nails painted a deep magenta, closing over something.

"Don't be an idiot," he scolded her. "It was in my pocket. She filched it."

"But Sofia couldn't. . ." Celine looked back at Julia, and lowered her voice. "He had a key in his pocket. Someone took it."

"Couldn't have been Sofia." Julia shook her head. "The body was long gone by the time she arrived. Must've been Fussy Phil. Or the other woman. Ask him who she was?"

"Tony?" Celine crept a little closer to him. "There was another woman here, remember? She came after Fussy Phil left."

"I asked her to call 911. I don't know if she heard me." His face—greenish-white now, drained of energy—wore an expression of bewilderment. "She barely gave me a glance. I was on the floor. It wasn't that dark."

"A police officer?" Celine asked. He must have already been dead; she wasn't surprised the woman hadn't heard him. But not to have afforded him so much as a look—that was callous.

Reynolds shook his head. "Don't think so. She was in a business suit. I may have seen her around. I don't know." He clutched the back of his head. "My neck feels weird. My head hurts. Don't know what Fussy Phil stuck me with."

Go easy on him, Celine, Sister Mary Catherine whispered.

Celine nodded. She was losing him, but she needed to ask him one last question.

"Tony, who is Sofia? Why was she here?"

He looked up at her, a half-bitter, weary smile on his face. "She's a Daddy's little girl I should never have bothered with. She dumped me." He indicated the shelves in the closet. "There's a picture of her somewhere in there."

Reynolds headed for the door. "I'll be in the studio if you need me. Have an exhibition at the Gardner. There's your commission to complete." At the door, he turned back to her. "You ought to check out my installation at the Gardner. I think you'll like it."

"Where'd he go?" Julia asked, seeing Celine staring at the door.

"To his studio." Celine turned to face her. "I don't think he realizes he's dead. But he's missing a key—to what exactly, I don't know. And it turns out he and Sofia were an item. She broke it off."

"Wow! I never would have guessed. And you have no idea why Reynolds thinks she'd turn against him, steal from him?"

"Nope." Celine turned toward the closet. "But there's a picture of her in his closet."

She reached toward the shelves the sculptor had indicated. The magenta-painted nails swam onto her mental screen again. She saw the slender white hand crushing something. A photograph?

She searched the shelves. Nothing.

"The photograph's gone," she gasped out loud. "Sofia must have taken it."

"She risked being charged with criminal recklessness for the sake of a photograph?" Julia voiced the question in Celine's mind. "She hated the guy that much?"

Julia's words triggered a series of impressions.

Celine stood before Reynolds, body slightly bent, fists shaking. "You're a fraud, a phony. You disgust me!" she heard herself scream at him. The sense of anger and betrayal she felt were overwhelming.

"Sofia, please." Reynolds moved toward her, pleading. "That was all in the past. It's over, I swear."

"Get away from me," she shrieked. She whipped something off her finger and flung it at him. A glint of gold caught her eye as the object struck Reynolds on the side of his face.

"We're done, you understand. Done!"

"They were more than just an item," Celine said as the images receded. "They were engaged. She broke it off."

"How recently? If she's a respectably married socialite now, I can see why she'd want her picture back. A liaison with a playboy, however distant, is not the kind of gossip you'd want the media getting their claws into."

"I can't tell how long ago. But whenever it happened, she was livid."

Why had Sofia been so infuriated? There'd been such contempt in her voice. As though she'd caught Reynolds cheating on her. Somehow Celine didn't think that was the case.

There are other reasons for a woman to hate a man, Celine, her guardian angel said. *To lose respect for him.*

Such as what?

"She called him a fraud and a phony," Celine said, thinking out loud. "She felt betrayed."

"Well, he's always been quite the womanizer," Julia replied.

"No, that wasn't it. This was something to do with his past. He swore he'd put it behind him."

Forger.

The word entered her brain. It was followed by an image of gold-framed canvases stacked one in front of the other.

She described the images to Julia.

"Wow, some girlfriend. She was ready to believe the worst of Reynolds —based on what? Gossip, rumors?"

"Sounds like it. Although he didn't exactly deny it."

Chapter Thirty-Six

Sofia Wozniak picked up the phone and punched in the number she'd memorized. She was using the landline in a hole-in-the-wall restaurant she'd discovered as she hightailed it out of Tony Reynolds' neighborhood.

Former neighborhood. He was dead. Good riddance!

But a pang of doubt—sadness even—welled up within her as the phone at the other end began to ring. She hadn't spoken to Tony since they'd broken up.

Not one word.

Tony hadn't bothered to reach out either. Not to her. There'd been plenty of *other* women.

Oh yes, she'd heard all the rumors.

Now he was dead. Murdered?

She pushed back the deep, aching hurt that threatened to bring tears to her eyes.

That's what happens to criminals, Sofia, she told herself. *If he'd given it all up, like he told you, he wouldn't be dead now, would he?*

"Hello?" The voice at the other end of the line was soft, cautious.

"It's me," Sofia said, equally cautious.

She'd intentionally decided against using her iPhone. Too easily traced. Ditto, the landline in her apartment.

"You found it?"

Sofia's slender fingers gripped the receiver tightly. "No." Her tone was apologetic, regretful. "I found nothing." But Tony's place had been trashed. Should she mention it?

"It's gotta be there, Sofia. I don't know where else—"

"I know." Her cheeks were flushed—the bitter acid of long-held certainty and resentment making her skin burn. Only someone like Tony—a criminal and a two-bit crook—would be willing to hide a hot item.

Where else could it be? Who else could have it?

"Sofia"—the voice sounded hesitant—"would . . . do you think . . .?"

"No!" Sofia's tone was sharp. "We don't need help."

It had stung when Tony had called her a Daddy's little girl all those years ago. She wasn't going to prove him right in death.

If things didn't work out, she'd ask for help. But until then . . .

"We handle this ourselves. Trust me. I'll figure something out."

&

"Tony?" Celine pushed open the door to Reynolds' studio. He was sitting at a workbench, staring at a clay bust that looked remarkably like Dirck. The smell of drying clay and plaster dust permeated the air.

"It looks like Sofia took her photograph." She crossed the room, Julia close upon her heels.

"Why are you telling me this?" Reynolds didn't bother to turn around. "It's a curious thing," he continued, his tone casual. "I can't pick up a thing. My arms just go through anything I try to touch."

He demonstrated his point. He reached for the bust. His arm penetrated the clay torso, fingers wiggling out from between the bust's shoulder blades.

"What's he saying?" Julia hissed into her ear.

"Just that he can't touch anything" she whispered back. "His arms slice through solids."

"Oh, for Pete's sake! He's dead. What does he expect?"

"I know, I know. But he doesn't seem to realize that. And I can't tell him that he is."

"Why not?"

Celine sighed, exasperated. "Because," she hissed, "you can't just break that kind of news to people. I may be psychic, but it isn't my job to inform people of their demise. It's the kind of realization that needs to come on its own."

It was the sort of thing Sister Mary Catherine had frequently said—in life and in death. But now her guardian angel was changing her tune.

Julia's right, Celine, she said. *You should break the news to him. He needs to realize he's free of his physical body. He's been in denial long enough.*

Oh, for heavens' sake! But she did as Sister Mary Catherine asked.

"Tony." Celine walked around the workbench until she was facing him. When he looked up, green eyes puzzled, she continued, "What's happening to you is perfectly normal, Tony. You don't have a body. That's why you can't touch anything."

He stared at her. "No body?" His eyes roved the length of his arms. "No body?" he repeated. "Are you kidding me?"

"I wish I were. Fussy Phil destroyed your body. He killed you. The question is why?"

"Why?"

Celine nodded. "Why did Fussy Phil want to kill you?"

"You should know why. You're psychic, aren't you?"

"Yes, but—"

"I didn't want to lie anymore. I wanted to give it back."

"Give what back? One of the stolen items from the Gardner?"

"What else?"

"All right." Celine ran her fingers through her hair, exasperated. Extracting information from the dead man was like trying to wring water from a rock. "Which one?"

"I thought you were psychic," he said again.

"I am," Celine ground out. "That's how I know Sofia and you were engaged. It's how I know Sofia took the photograph you had of her. But was she after anything else?"

"Frankly, I find it hard to believe she was desperate enough to assault an officer of the law just for the sake of a photograph," Julia added. Celine could have communicated with Reynolds telepathically, but with Julia around, she figured the former fed should at least have the opportunity to hear part of the conversation.

Reynolds swiveled around on his seat to look at Julia. "You're right, Sofia wasn't here just for a photograph. She came here for the key."

"She can't hear you," Celine informed him. To Julia she said, "He still thinks Sofia was after his key."

"What does it open?" Julia asked immediately.

"My warehouse studio."

"Your warehouse studio?" Celine repeated for Julia's benefit. "Where you work on larger pieces? Why would Sofia want to go there?" She scanned the walls, a sudden insight striking her. "She didn't come in here, did she? Why not?"

"She's allergic to plaster dust. It affects her sinuses."

"And she went to the warehouse because . . .?" Julia spoke over the sculptor's voice.

Reynolds grinned. "She thinks it's hidden there."

"Thinks *what* is hidden there?" Celine snapped, at the edge of her tether. She'd had just about enough of Reynolds' cryptic answers.

"You're telling me you don't know what it is? Or where it is? You haven't found it yet? Some psychic!" Reynolds rolled his eyes.

Celine clenched her fists. The man was impossible! "Could you please just tell me what you're talking about?"

"Take a look at my installation in the Gardner," Reynolds suggested. "Maybe it'll give you some ideas."

She turned to Julia, frustrated. "He won't tell me anything. Apparently, there's some clue in his installation at the Gardner."

He's learned not to trust people, Celine, Sister Mary Catherine explained. *It's hard to break a habit like that. You'll have to be patient.*

I am being patient, Celine thought resentfully. *As patient as any human could possibly be.*

She must have spoken the words aloud because Julia responded with a sympathetic smile: "You've been great, my dear. I had no idea dead people could be so hard to work with." The crinkles at the corners of her eyes deepened and an amused smile tugged at her lips.

She walked around to where Celine stood and put a reassuring arm around her.

"Listen, don't worry. We'll figure it out. Don't we always?"

Reynolds regarded them, bemused.

"Must be nice to have a friend you can count on," he said wistfully. "I never had anything like that."

Yes, he did. Remind him that he did, Sister Mary Catherine urged Celine.

Celine didn't have to ask who the nun was referring to. An image had accompanied the words.

She turned to Reynolds. "What about Sofia?" At Sister Mary Catherine's prompting, she added: "She never stopped loving you, you know."

"Oh yeah?" Reynolds' smile was cynical. "Why is she working with my killer then?"

Chapter Thirty-Seven

Celine stood up, chair scraping back across the copper-hued tiles of the restaurant floor to accommodate her rising motion.

"If you'll excuse me, I'd like to go wash up."

She caught Julia's eye as she spoke.

"Absolutely. Take your time." The former fed smiled sympathetically at her. "It's been a long day. I'll place your order for you if you're not back in time to do it yourself."

Celine smiled her thanks and set off for the restroom, weaving her way past the crowded lunch tables, the plexiglass-enclosed cashier's desk, and the oil paintings of the Boston coastline hanging on the restaurant's wine-red walls.

Stopping at the Copper Plate Grill & Restaurant had been Blake's idea. The name, when he'd mentioned it, had tugged at Celine's mind as though it held some kind of significance. Something to do with what Reynolds knew, but she still hadn't worked out what.

But Blake had made it clear it was the Turkish restaurant's location—rather than its Michelin-starred cuisine—that was its main draw that afternoon. It was en route to Cambridge Police Headquarters where Deputy Superintendent Vince Soldi was expecting them.

"He wants an official statement," Blake had informed them apologetically. "As well as our help generating a composite for Sofia. We can get a bite to eat on our way," he'd added before Jonah, who was about to protest, could say a word.

Celine felt the corners of her mouth twitching at the memory. With his large wire-rimmed glasses and his mouth hanging open, then abruptly closing, Jonah had looked exactly like a startled goldfish.

The restaurant floor narrowed into a hallway. The restroom doors were blue, the copper female figure on the door in the left wall facing her male counterpart on the door across the hallway.

She placed her palm on the hand-lettered *Women's* inscribed within the copper sign plate, giving the door a tentative push. It yielded to her touch, revealing an exquisitely appointed square powder room.

White tile rose from the floor to a height of four feet; a marble countertop with an oval mirror above the sink was on the left; a gold-framed still life—half-open red tulips in a crystal vase—decorated the wall across from it.

It was charming—and restful, Celine thought as she turned the long-handled brass faucet in the sink. A gush of cold water gurgled out. She splashed her eyes and her face, feeling the tension drain out of her.

Julia was right. It had been a long day. The two hours they'd spent inside Reynolds' apartment had been especially exhausting. Not to mention, futile.

She was no closer to knowing what information Tony Reynolds had about the Gardner theft now than she'd been last night when she'd heard he'd been murdered.

She glanced up at the oval mirror; a white frame bordered it. Within its shiny surface, her face looked paler than usual, starkly white against the red-gold strands of her long hair. There were shadows under her eyes—the same shade of green as Reynolds'.

A sudden movement caught her eyes. Startled, she was about to snap her head around when the sculptor's familiar figure materialized behind her. His tall frame shimmered into and out of focus within the mirror's polished surface.

"Do you remember what you saw when we met?" he asked.

"When we met in your apartment?" she faltered. Somehow he'd found a way to get out of his apartment. She'd thought his energy was bound to it.

"No." Reynolds sounded impatient. "At the winery."

Celine cast her mind back, struggling to remember. Hard to believe it was only two days ago that he'd come out to Paso Robles.

"You read my mind, didn't you?" he continued when she remained silent. "When we shook hands? I could tell from the shell-shocked look on your face."

Oh! Memory returned—bringing with it the shock of images that had raced into her mind. Green wallpaper. A gold-framed portrait. A hairy tarantula.

"You're remembering." A smile of relief eased the tension in Reynolds' mouth. "Now you know where it is. Keep it safe."

"Wait!" She turned frantically around. "Keep—" He disappeared before she could complete her question: *keep what safe?*

She remained frozen, eyes fixed on the stretch of empty marble between herself and the powder room door.

The jiggling door handle and a sotto voce "Hello! Anyone in there?" yanked her consciousness back to the present—and to the whoosh of water raining into the marble sink.

Waste not, want not, Celine, her guardian angel said at the same time as the significance of the sound rushing through her eardrums sunk in.

Dear God! The faucet was still running.

She turned in time to avert a crisis.

Jonah was gone when she returned to their table.

"He got a call from the nursing home. He needs to check on his mother," Julia explained as Celine sat down. The former fed took a sip of her coke. "I can't say I'm sorry he's gone."

Celine nodded. "We should go to the Gardner when we're done at Cambridge PD," she reminded her friends again. Maybe Reynolds' installation would hold some clues to what he'd known in life. If nothing else, they'd be able to share what little they'd learned with Penny.

Chapter Thirty-Eight

"You think one of his clients did him in?" Vince Soldi asked.

Blake was aware of the Deputy Superintendent watching him as he flipped through the pages of the Moleskine pocket notebook in which Reynolds stored his clients' contact information.

"That's what it looks like." He heard Soldi's door open and the muted tap-tap of high heels enter the office. ADA Mariah Campari, he guessed.

"Anthony Reynolds had a roster of clients that included some of the wealthiest families in Boston, Special Agent," the newcomer said. "Are you really going to accuse one of them of murder?"

He glanced over his shoulder. A slim woman with long legs, a haughty posture, and hair cut shorter than his stared back at him—the glint of challenge hardening her brown eyes.

With longer hair framing her features, ADA Mariah Campari might have been a reasonably good-looking woman. But the severe haircut exposed the broad planes of her face, and with her flaring nostrils, she was about as appealing as a man in a skirt.

Ordinarily, he would have risen to greet her. But a diehard feminist like Campari would probably feel the heat of male oppression if he behaved like a gentleman, so Blake kept his rear glued to the chair.

"ADA Mariah Campari, I presume," he said with a smile. "Blake Markham, FBI. I'm not planning to accuse anyone. I'm merely exploring a possible avenue of investigation."

"That a burglary gone wrong was perpetrated by one of Reynolds' clients?" Campari strode the few steps toward Soldi's desk and dumped her leather case on it.

Blake turned to Soldi. "Don't tell me you're buying the burglary angle. Reynolds wasn't surprised by a burglar. He left his apartment only once that morning to oversee the installation of his works at the Gardner."

"He left it a second time with you, special agent," Campari countered before the Deputy Superintendent could respond. "The killer entered the building through a side door. So could a burglar."

It was an idiotic theory and Blake relished pointing out the gaping hole in it.

"You think our burglar thoughtfully waited until Reynolds completed his call to the Director of the Gardner Museum before killing him?" Blake exchanged a glance with Soldi.

He sure hoped Campari was playing devil's advocate. If not, she was just the type of airhead who gave blondes a bad name.

But, Jesus Christ, she wasn't kidding.

"The place was trashed," she insisted, leaning across the table aggressively. "I've seen the crime scene photos."

"Ma'am, I was at the crime scene. The killer—or someone else who came afterward—ransacked the place, looking for whatever work of stolen art Reynolds had stashed away."

"You think he had the art?" Soldi cleared his throat. "Not just information about one of the stolen items—but the item itself?"

"It seems to be what the killer was looking for. By the way," Blake continued, recalling Celine's insights, "how many sets of unknown fingerprints did your guys find in their initial walkthrough?"

Soldi looked as though he was suffering from a bout of indigestion. "Two. We haven't identified them yet, but neither of them matched the victim. You think the killer had an accomplice?"

"I didn't know you'd picked up two sets of fingerprints." Campari spoke through clenched lips. Blake got the idea the second set of prints was off-putting.

Why, he wondered. Was a burglar with an accomplice harder to accept than a lone operator?

"Three, if you count Sofia's."

He had a strong suspicion she hadn't been informed of that either.

"Sofia?"

"The woman Special Agent Markham and his friends caught breaking into the apartment today," Soldi explained.

"You know her name?" The ADA's eyes glittered with barely concealed suspicion—like a cobra preparing to strike. She tossed her head, flicking a straggling lock of hair off her forehead.

Blake shrugged. "She used it at the Starbucks when she placed her order. Got a cup for herself and the one she drugged Cowan with. Jonah Hibbert, the reporter who was with us, did some asking around. Found out her name and that she was Reynolds' ex."

He was deliberately fudging the details, not wanting to reveal the source of his information. Casually attributing them to Hibbert was the best way to do it. Blake was guessing neither Campari nor Soldi would think to question the reporter too closely, if at all, about these mundane facts.

Campari swallowed the explanation.

"If this Sofia was a former girlfriend"—she shrugged—"couldn't she have been there for personal reasons? To retrieve her effects, a photograph, letters—things like that."

"Seems a little strange to wait until after a man's murdered to do that," Soldi replied, revealing he did possess a backbone, and it wasn't entirely made of jello.

"Not to mention that they'd broken up sometime back." Blake didn't feel the need to attribute this tidbit to Hibbert. Logic had led him to that conclusion. Reynolds had a long reputation as a skirt-chaser.

Based on Celine's insights, that must have started when Sofia dumped him.

But even without it, it was well known that none of Reynolds' affairs lasted long enough for any woman to consider herself his girlfriend. Clearly any woman who could legitimately claim that status was long in the past.

"And you know this how, Special Agent?" Campari placed her hands on her hips. Standing like that, she appeared menacing, like an Amazon. Her slenderness, Blake realized, was deceptive. She was quite powerfully built, muscular.

Undeterred, he explained his reasoning.

"Okay," she grudgingly conceded. "I see what you mean. Doesn't mean she was working with the killer."

"Would be quite the coincidence if she wasn't," Soldi said, exhibiting more gumption. "But," he scratched his chin. "I still don't see why the killer has to be one of his clients."

Campari favored the Deputy Superintendent with a smile, keeping it plastered on her face as she turned to face Blake.

"I have to say I don't either, Special Agent."

Her arguments were so easily refuted Blake wondered where—and how—she'd managed to get her law degree.

"I didn't say the killer was a client. But logic leads me to believe that's where we should be looking. Reynolds claimed to have information about the Gardner heist. Most likely he'd discovered the location of one of the stolen works. A recent revelation, I imagine. Which means the information could only have come through a client."

The sour expression on Campari's face intensified as he spoke. But Soldi, at least, was buying the theory. They were looking for a white-collar individual, likely with no priors.

The Deputy Superintendent rubbed his protruding belly. "And the client kills Reynolds to stop him getting the word out? Makes sense."

"Or," Blake decided to share the other hypothesis Celine's insights had given them, "Reynolds' client gives him the object for safekeeping. When Reynolds realizes he's holding a hot item, he gets nervous—"

"Yes, but why would anyone give a sculptor he patronized a stolen item to hold onto?" Campari interrupted.

Blake noted the use of the masculine pronoun. "You're assuming the killer was a man?"

"I don't think a woman would have the strength to pull off a murder like that, do you?" she snapped back. "And my question still stands: why would any man ask someone else to hold onto a supposedly valuable possession?"

"Well now, Ms. Campari," Soldi rumbled, "there are several reasons for a man to hide his assets. With the kind of divorce laws we have, you can hardly blame a guy for trying. . ." He spread his hands out, gaze sliding to Blake for support.

"Divorce!" A light bulb blazed in Blake's head. He hadn't thought of that.

He'd figured the killer—a white-collar individual associated with a mobster—could only be a moneyman. Some kind of accountant, perhaps.

A man like that could come under financial scrutiny for a variety of reasons.

But divorce made just as much sense—more, perhaps.

"You're definitely onto something, Soldi." Blake tapped the Moleskine notebook. "We need to pay special attention to anyone going through a divorce."

Chapter Thirty-Nine

How'd it go?" Julia asked Blake as the revolving glass door conveyed them out of Cambridge Police headquarters. "Did they swallow our line of thinking?"

Celine was only half-listening as she stepped out after them, squinting at the late afternoon sun that suffused the narrow street.

"I think they bought it. Listen!" Blake scanned both ends of the street lined with parked police cars, fished out a small notebook from his jacket pocket, and slipped it into Julia's hand. "Do me a favor. When we get in the car, take pictures of every page in that notebook before I realize I accidentally walked off the premises with a piece of evidence."

"You filched evidence?" It wasn't the kind of thing Celine would have expected from a by-the-book kind of guy like Blake Markham. "Couldn't Soldi have made you a copy?"

"The problem is"—Blake prodded her elbow, nudging her toward Rogers Street where their armored vehicle was parked—"this is Cambridge PD's murder, and they—or at any rate, the Assistant DA on the case—don't want anyone butting in."

At five-eight, Celine was only four inches shorter than Blake, but she found herself scurrying to keep up with his long strides.

They turned the corner onto Rogers, Blake's watchful eyes continually sweeping their surroundings. "Between you and me, I don't think Soldi would mind a helping hand. The link to the Gardner theft is a complication he doesn't need."

Reynolds' murder was a complication she could've done without as well, Celine thought ruefully as Blake propelled her to their parked car.

Once inside, Blake directed the driver to back out of their parking space and circle the block. Julia, seated beside Celine, flipped the pages of the slim notebook, briskly snapping photos with her iPhone.

"Getting everything?" Blake tossed the question over his shoulder.

"Yup."

"Is there a Wozniak in there?" Celine leaned over to take a look at the tiny white pages filled with Reynolds' sprawling writing. The Polish name she'd sensed earlier had begun echoing in her head again while they were at Cambridge PD headquarters.

There, working with the sketch artist—a police officer who operated the SketchCop software—she'd heard the name as clearly as though someone in the room had voiced it.

"Doesn't look like it." Julia kept her head bent over the notebook. "I'll let you know if I see it."

Sofia Wozniak. The two names had passed fleetingly across Celine's mental screen as though she were picking up on a thought that had briefly surfaced in the minds of one of the people in the room.

Apart from herself and Julia, there'd been Vince Soldi, ADA Mariah Campari, the sketch artist, and a couple of other officers.

"I wonder if Sofia's last name is Wozniak," Celine said.

"What makes you say that?" Blake snapped around to face her. Even Julia looked up.

"You think that's the reason you heard the name as we passed the Starbucks near Reynolds' place?" Julia probed. "You had that strange craving for a peppermint mocha about the same time, didn't you?"

She'd told Julia about that while waiting for the crime scene technicians to finish up at Reynolds' apartment. It had obviously been a psychic message; she'd never been the coffee-guzzling type. The single cup she drank in the morning was all she needed of the stuff.

"That's not the reason, I'm afraid. Although it should be." Celine's eyes narrowed, following the rabbit hole her hunch was leading her down.

Outside the tinted car window, traffic streamed slowly past the armored vehicle. They passed a couple of brick buildings, then a nearly empty parking lot.

She watched, barely registering the world outside. Twisting her mouth, chewing at her lip.

The SketchCop program had developed an exceptional likeness to the woman they'd seen coming down the stairs in Reynolds' apartment building. Had someone at Cambridge PD recognized it?

Had Celine telepathically picked up on that?

But Julia's explanation of why she'd put the two names together made more sense. So why hadn't Celine immediately linked the name Wozniak to the woman they'd seen hurrying down?

"I heard the two names together," she said cautiously, "when the sketch we approved was being shown to Soldi, the ADA, and those other officers."

"Heard them?" Julia pressed. "You didn't put it together. You actually heard the name—as though someone in the room had thought it aloud?"

Celine nodded hesitantly. "I think so. But I still don't understand why I didn't instantly think Wozniak when I saw her."

"You didn't sense her first name either," Blake reminded her.

"True," Celine admitted, staring out the window. "I guess I didn't."

Some psychic. Reynolds' words echoed in her mind. She was losing her touch. Barely four months after accepting her talent, she was losing it.

You can only listen to one radio station at a time, Celine. Sister Mary Catherine startled her with the non-sequitur.

"I can only listen to one station at a time?" Celine repeated aloud. "What does that even mean?"

"I beg your pardon?" Blake was gaping at her as though she'd lost her marbles.

"Sorry, just something my guardian angel said. She speaks in riddles sometimes."

She'd meant it as a playful jab. But an audibly exasperated sigh filled her ears.

It means, Celine, the nun said, sounding as though she were speaking through clenched teeth, *that you can only tune into one source of information at a time. You were attuned to Reynolds' energy. Nothing else could penetrate.*

Okay, so what exactly was I attuned to at the police station? The thoughts of one of the people present or did Sofia Wozniak's name come from some other source?

Does it matter, when you know her name?

Chapter Forty

"You think whatever it is might be in Tony's warehouse?" Penny Hoskins, a slim, elegantly dressed woman in her fifties, anxiously surveyed her visitors. Hope flickered and wavered in her blue eyes, warring with tense apprehension.

It wasn't the easiest question to answer. Celine was glad it hadn't been directed at her.

The Director of the Gardner had been eagerly awaiting their arrival. That had been evident in the way they were whisked up to her office when they entered the museum lobby.

"I'm so glad you could come." Penny had hugged Celine and asked after Annabelle. "I can't believe we almost lost her!" She shuddered.

Then, the business of exchanging greetings over, she turned expectantly to Blake and Julia, silently agitating to know the latest.

By tacit consent, Blake had done most of the talking, bringing Penny up to speed.

But now he was naturally balking at offering any sureties. Psychically, Celine had received no indication that the item was in Reynolds' warehouse. Logically, though, it made sense to search any property the sculptor had owned.

Celine caught Blake's gray eyes sliding over to Julia's, mutely seeking her help in navigating a potential minefield.

"We don't know that for a fact." The former fed chose her words carefully. "But it's worth a shot. Reynolds' apartment was thoroughly ransacked."

"Not once, but twice," Blake added. "A strong indication that the killer didn't find what he was looking for. But the key to the warehouse is missing. It wasn't on Reynolds' person. Cambridge PD didn't find it. There must have been some reason for taking it."

"But Cambridge PD can take a look?" Penny clasped her hands together as though praying for a miracle. "They can get a search warrant, figure out a way to get in?"

"They were planning on doing it even before I suggested it," Blake informed her.

"And they'll let us—let you—know if they find anything?"

"They will," Blake assured her.

"But we don't know what exactly Reynolds had information about?" Penny's inquiring blue eyes moved toward Celine.

"All I can pick up," Celine replied with a rueful smile, "is that there's a clue hidden in his exhibit at the Gardner. If we could see it . . ."

"Oh yes, of course, you can." Penny smiled, nervous anxiety fading away at the prospect of enticing a viewer into enjoying one of the museum's many treasures on display. "In fact, I was hoping you'd want to. It's simply amazing!"

Her head pivoted, including Julia and Blake in the conversation. "I'm thinking of keeping the works displayed for an additional week. It could be a memorial of sorts."

"Sounds like a wonderful idea." Julia smiled back. "You might want to promote it."

Celine knew what the former fed was thinking. A memorial service could attract people from the sculptor's past as well as present-day associates and clients.

She hadn't got the impression that Reynolds had been particularly close to anyone in recent years. She could still hear the loneliness in his voice when he'd commented on the close friendship she and Julia shared.

The gold-framed paintings stacked against the wall and the image she'd seen in the restaurant washroom at lunch returned to her mind. A wisp of an idea occurred to her.

"It's called *Lines of Authenticity*, isn't it?" Celine met Penny's eyes. "Tony Reynolds' installation, I mean."

"Yes." Penny nodded. "He was going to explain what it meant, but . . ." She made a wry face as she spread her hands wide. "I'm afraid it wasn't meant to be."

She shuffled a stack of papers around on her desk, then looked up.

"Why, is there some significance to that title? It is pretty telling, I suppose."

"I'm wondering if . . ."

The idea, too tenuous to be captured, dissipated, like a bubble fizzling out of existence. Celine shook her head.

"I don't know. I guess we'll know more when we see it."

✺

"Well, what do you think?" Penny finally burst out.

Celine had been aware of her gaze boring into her back while she circled around the vast Hostetter Gallery where Tony Reynolds' sculptures were on display.

The Museum Director had cleared the gallery, closing it off to outsiders, before taking her visitors in. "I'd like some privacy," she'd explained, "in case you discover any important clues."

The only problem was, Celine hadn't found a thing. Nothing that related to the heist or the stolen works at any event.

"I'm not sure what to think," she replied.

Sunlight from the wall of north-facing windows hit Celine's eyes as she turned to face Penny, making her squint. She gave the exhibit a sweeping glance over her shoulder. The works were more abstract than she'd come to expect of Reynolds' usual style.

But what they symbolized, she had absolutely no idea.

"Well, he's talking about artists, clearly." Penny indicated the white-cloth-covered table at one end of the semi-circular display. Large brushes protruded from glass jars and metal tools were neatly arranged beside it.

"And sculptors, I guess." Julia fingered one of the tools on display—a long shaft extending from a wooden doorknob-type handle. A set of similarly shaped tools lay nearby, some with bent shafts.

Sculptors' chisels, perhaps, Celine thought. A wooden pencil-holder held a thin needle—a representation of the kind of mechanical pencil some watercolor artists preferred? Or something else? She didn't know.

"I'm a little disappointed, to tell you the truth." She'd made the decision to dispense with tact. "This"—she gestured at the first table—"is such an unimaginative way of representing anyone who creates art. All he's done is display a collection of art supplies easily available at any art supply store. It's lazy."

"*Lazy!*" Penny's penciled eyebrows arched up so high, they looked like inverted u's. "I disagree. I think it's very contemporary. Very now."

"Could be what he was going for." Blake was leaning near the window, arms folded. He hadn't shown a whit of interest in the works—not that Celine could blame him—leaving her and Julia to examine them. "Who doesn't want to be hip and trendy, right?"

Blake wasn't aware of it, but the Lady—Belle Gardner—was standing next to him. Her presence hadn't bothered Celine. Belle was simply admiring the meandering paths that curved around what had once been her private garden.

Still called the Monk's Garden, the area where Belle had walked her dogs in life had been completely redesigned six years ago. It was altogether different and yet managed to encapsulate the original contemplative spirit of Belle's museum. In a word, it was beautiful.

Not something you could say of the pieces exhibited in the room, unfortunately.

Now Belle turned around and gave Celine a sympathetic grimace as she
took in Reynolds' works.

"It seems uncharacteristically unsubtle," Celine said, Belle's reaction
buoying her confidence.

She didn't think Reynolds was the kind of person to just assemble a
motley collection of tools and call it a sculpture. Some sculptors might
think nothing of doing something as cheesy as that. Not Reynolds—unless
she'd completely misread him.

She said as much.

"Oh, Celine"—Penny was regarding her as though she were a philistine
—"that's just one piece! Look at the next work. He fashioned that."

So he had. Reynolds had created three plaster of Paris globes, given
them a smooth finish, and then stacked them to form a triangle. A miniature version of the same thing balanced atop a metal cross was the third
piece.

"He might be talking about artists who create abstract pieces," Julia suggested. "That piece is about as abstract as it gets."

"Or it could suggest the many possibilities inherent in the raw material
of paper, plaster, and clay," Penny said with a grateful smile at Julia. "If you
look closely, you can see triangular indentations in the surface of those
plaster of Paris globes. Very reminiscent of jack-o'-lanterns."

"Nice! He's suggesting we're all sculptors."

Celine knew Blake was being sarcastic, but Penny gushed over his remark as though he were the art critic of the century. "Exactly. Whether
you're carving a jack-o'-lantern or marble, it's the same creative process
that's involved."

"But none of this has anything to do with the theft," Celine pointed out.

In fact, nothing about the installation made sense. None of the pieces
connected up with the images she'd seen earlier. She scanned the works
again, her eye catching on one particular piece.

The profile view of a head with its long nose, seven-pointed jester's cap,
and five-pointed collar with beads.

Does it remind you of anything? Sister Mary Catherine asked.

It took Celine a few minutes to remember, and it was only when the nun
began to direct her to put on her thinking cap that it came to Celine.

"It's Feste," Celine exclaimed as she recalled the costume the nuns at
Notre Dame had designed for a student production of *Twelfth Night*.

"What!" Julia and Blake erupted in unison.

"Yes, it's a fool—a seventeenth-century figure," Penny said, head oscillating between Julia and Blake. "Quite well done, I think. But why is it important? Artists comment on society just as jesters did—subverting norms and expectations."

"Or conning their audiences," Blake muttered, although Penny fortunately showed no sign of having heard him.

Celine wished they'd stop talking. Something Penny had said had triggered an association, but it was gone now. She tried to pursue the thought, then gave up.

"I'm still not sure what this has to do with the painting Reynolds has been showing me since we first met," Celine said.

"He's been showing you paintings?" Julia demanded. "Why didn't you say so?"

"Because what I'm seeing isn't one of the works stolen. I don't understand why he keeps showing it to me."

"What exactly are you seeing?" Blake asked.

"A portrait within a gold frame," she said as the image filled her mind again. "A three-quarter view of a young man—face partially in shadow—in a greenish cape. He's wearing a gauzy scarf and a black hat with a long, curling plume in it."

"Oh my goodness!" Penny gasped, hand rising to cover her mouth.

"You know what this means?" Julia's head snapped sharply toward the Museum Director.

"Yes!" Penny's head bobbed in stunned excitement. "It's a work from the seventeenth century. A self-portrait. I think I know where Reynolds was going with this."

Chapter Forty-One

"There it is!" With a dramatic flourish, Penny pointed to the portrait Celine had been seeing in her mind's eye. "The painting that started the Gardner Museum."

She turned toward Celine, giving her a quick smile. "And the one Reynolds wanted you to see."

They were on the second floor of the historic building. In the gallery that had received the worst of the thieves' attention.

The large empty frames on the Dutch Room's south wall were hard to miss. They stared you in the face like ghostly carcasses the moment you stepped in. Penny, Celine had noticed, had been unable to conceal her grimace as they walked in, pivoting swiftly to the left and coming to a stop before the portrait.

It hung above a Flemish oak cabinet built in seventeenth-century Dutch style.

"Rembrandt." Celine breathed the name. So that's what Reynolds had wanted her to know. He had information about one of the Rembrandts stolen from the Gardner. If only he'd come right out and said so.

She gazed at the painting, into the young Rembrandt's lustrous eyes, studying his earnest, hopeful features. She ought to have recognized him.

The Dutch master had created countless self-portraits throughout his life. He looked just a little bit different in each one, but the wiry curls of his hair—scratched into the paint with his brush handle—and something about the nose were so characteristic of Rembrandt Harmenszoon van Rijn as to be unmistakable.

"Painted when he was twenty-three." Penny stood before the self-portrait, hands clasped to her chest in a reverent attitude. "He was still in Leiden at the time, sharing a studio with Jan Lievens."

"If I'm not mistaken, this was Mrs. Gardner's first important find." Julia stared at the green-brown RHL inscribed on the lower right of the portrait.

"It was," Penny confirmed with a nod. "Bernard Berenson, the man who acted as the agent for most of Mrs. Gardner's acquisitions, wrote to her about the self-portrait when it came up for sale in 1896. It would be hanging in the National Gallery in London now if Mrs. Gardner hadn't bought it. It was even then an extremely valuable treasure."

"Strange the thieves didn't take it," Blake remarked.

"They thought about it." Glimpses of the night of the theft flashed into Celine's brain. George Reissfelder hefting the Rembrandt self-portrait down with a grunt, stumbling back under its awkward weight, and then forward to stand it against the Flemish cabinet.

He stood up peeved. "You coulda helped, Lenny. No need to let a fella do all the work himself."

DiMuzio shone his flashlight over the painting. "You sure that's the one?"

"Sure I'm sure. It's a portrait, ain't it?" Reissfelder jabbed at the air around him. "Hangin' just where we were informed, by the door."

DiMuzio coldly appraised the painting. "Too big," he finally said. "Won't fit in the hatchback."

"Hey, we can't just—"

"Shut the f— up, George. If I say it's too big, it's too big, okay? We'll take something else." DiMuzio turned toward Celine, eyes flashing dangerously behind his spectacles. "Alright, kid, where's the rest of the stuff?"

Grayson Pike had been in the Dutch Room with the thieves. The thought blazed through Celine's brain just as her consciousness retreated from the scene. He'd shown DiMuzio and Reissfelder where the artworks were. They must have come with a list.

"DiMuzio said it was too big," she told the rest of the group. Her eyes felt wide as though someone were pulling at the skin around them. "That's probably why they left it."

"Too big!" Penny's voice rose, assuming its characteristic shrill tone when her emotions were aroused. "It's quite a bit smaller than the Rembrandts they did steal. The size of those didn't deter them."

"Well, they had a moving truck for those," Celine began to explain. But Penny wasn't listening.

She spun around, flinging her arm out at the two empty frames on the south wall.

"I can't believe those two incredible works are gone," she moaned as Blake shook his head. He'd probably heard her reproaches a thousand times. "Still gone. All these years later. Do you know Mrs. Gardner deliberately positioned the self-portrait directly across from those works—a double portrait of a couple and one of Rembrandt's most arresting narrative paintings."

"Yes," Celine said softly. She knew why Belle had positioned the paintings the way she had. "She wanted the young Rembrandt to look out onto his future greatness, the things he'd achieve in a few short years in Amsterdam."

The Rembrandts were clustered around the entrance, the self-portrait to the left as you entered, the other two diagonally across, because they'd been the most important of Belle's collection—the foundation of the museum she would institute.

After she bought that painting, Belle realized she could only pursue first-rate works of art for her collection, Sister Mary Catherine told her.

"But the good news"—the forced brightness of Julia's voice brought Celine back to the living—"is that now we know what Reynolds wanted to discuss with you. He'd obviously located one—maybe both—of those works. So, now in addition to the Vermeer we brought back in March, you'll get your Rembrandts back."

"Yes, that is good news." Penny smiled. "I shouldn't complain." She squeezed Celine's arm and gave Julia and Blake a wry smile. "I know you're doing your best. And you're getting results. Finally."

But Belle who was standing behind the long tables at the center of the gallery shook her head. Her eyes bore into the self-portrait behind them.

Belle says you're missing the mark, Sister Mary Catherine warned her. *You're off-target.*

Celine turned around. *Lines of Authenticity*. The title of Reynolds' exhibition hovered on her metal screen.

Was there something wrong with the self-portrait? What were they missing?

✦

Blake noticed Celine's eyes shift toward the Rembrandt self-portrait. Was there a problem with the work? The question entered his mind for no reason he could fathom.

Maybe it was the wrinkle of concern creasing Celine's forehead. And the fog of bewilderment shrouding her green eyes.

"Is that authentic?" he asked Penny—the question coming out a little more brusquely than he'd intended. She was offended; he could see that by the way her lips pursed tightly together in response.

"Of course it is. Why wouldn't it be?"

Blake shrugged. "It was nearly stolen. It seems, I don't know"—he spread his hands wide—"too much of a lucky break that it was left behind. Why not steal all the Rembrandts in the room? Why leave one behind?"

"Wonder if that says something about the person who organized the theft," Celine mused quietly. Penny's outraged gaze ping-ponged from his face to Celine's like a tennis ball tossing from racquet to racquet. "It would be such a low blow to steal that self-portrait, knowing how much it meant to Belle."

"Belle?" Penny's eyebrows rose, motivated by what emotion Blake couldn't tell.

Either the Museum Director really had no idea who Belle was. Or she knew perfectly well whom Celine was referring to, and considered the young woman's use of the nickname over-familiar and presumptuous.

"She's talking about Mrs. Gardner—Belle Gardner," Julia calmly explained. How his former colleague could remain so unfazed no matter what the circumstance, Blake had no idea. His own feelings inevitably spilled over into his expression and his words.

And Penny Hoskins was no different.

"Oh, for heaven's sake!" She expostulated. "It's that insider job business again, isn't it?" Her lips compressed into a thin line of irritation. "Mrs. Gardner died long before the theft took place in 1990. Anyone who knew her well enough to care whether or not she'd be hurt by the theft of that portrait was long dead as well."

"But," Blake persisted, deeply curious now and unwilling to give up, "the painting was taken down and almost stolen. You didn't have a psychic back then to tell you why that happened. Did no one wonder whether a fake had been substituted? Wouldn't it have been natural to have it examined?"

"No, it wouldn't, Blake," Penny snapped. "The entire staff was in shock —understandably—when the theft was discovered. We—they—were all just grateful that this one painting had been left behind."

Blake suppressed a groan of frustration. He'd done it again—put his big foot in it.

His eyes sought Celine's. She seemed to understand the thread he was pursuing.

"But, Penny," she began, "can we be sure this painting is a Rembrandt? I'm wondering why Reynolds keeps showing it to me in conjunction with his exhibition. *Lines of Authenticity?* How does that refer to Rembrandt?"

Yes! Blake clenched his fist, resisting the urge to punch the air with it. That was precisely his point.

But Penny didn't seem to understand. She closed her eyes wearily and let fall a sigh so loud, Blake was convinced it was audible in the courtyard below.

"Listen, people. The panel has been cleaned since then. Several times, in fact. We schedule cleanings at regular intervals. Trust me, if there'd been the slightest problem with the painting, our restorers would've picked up on it instantly."

"Well, that's a relief, isn't it?" Julia boomed cheerily making Blake wince. From where he stood, there was nothing cheerful about the situation. It seemed that either Celine had lost her touch or that Reynolds was giving them the runaround.

Why not indicate the specific work he had information about? Why go to such lengths to provide clues in such a roundabout manner?

"I still don't understand why Reynolds thought it was important for you to see the self-portrait," he griped to Celine. "Wouldn't it have been easier to just show you the work of art he had in mind?"

He could see from Celine's face that the question had resonated with her. But Julia responded instead. "I think it was a shorthand way of referring to Rembrandt. There was more than one of his works stolen, you know."

Sure, he knew that. He'd seen the file. But he let it go.

"Okay. And the sculptures in the Hofstetter Gallery. How do those relate?"

"Oh, I can answer that." Penny's lips stretched into a beatific smile.

She was in her element—pontificating on the art world, the old masters and their works.

"You see Rembrandt was quite an unusual artist. We know him for his oil paintings. But he also left behind a huge collection of drawings and sketches. In his own day, he was well known for his etchings. They were enormously popular at the time."

"I guess that makes sense," Celine said slowly, as though some aspects of Penny's explanation fit whatever she was seeing in her mind, while others didn't. Her next remark made it clear she was thinking about the very first sculpture on display—the collection of art equipment. "Rembrandt did experiment in different media."

"Quite successfully, as I understand it," Julia put in.

"Oh yes." Penny nodded.

All right, Blake thought. That still didn't explain the rest of the pieces on display. The plaster of Paris jack-o'-lanterns, for instance. Blake was no art connoisseur, but he didn't think Rembrandt had painted any jack-o'-lanterns.

He decided against pursuing it, however. The women were satisfied Reynolds was leading them to a Rembrandt. Blake expected they'd find out soon enough which one.

He felt the subtle vibration of his phone against his hip and pulled the instrument out of its holster.

Ella.

Chapter Forty-Two

Hurriedly excusing himself, Blake stepped out onto the balcony overlooking the museum's courtyard.

"Hello." He held the phone firmly to his ear as he stood by the parapet looking down at the clusters of blue and white hydrangea surrounding the stone-and-glass Roman mosaic below him.

"Blake, it's Ella," his personal assistant began, rather unnecessarily, he thought. He knew exactly who it was. "Listen, I ran the partial you read out to me, got quite a few names, but no Sofia."

He digested this. So Sofia had driven someone else's car to Cambridge. That wasn't a surprise.

"Blake?" Ella's voice rose, anxious.

"Still here." He angled the mouthpiece up as he spoke. "Listen, so none of these cars are rentals, right? She was driving a car registered to someone else?"

"None of the plates I'm looking at are reported stolen. Meaning—"

"Meaning, she may have been driving the killer's car." A surge of excitement pulsed through Blake. They were getting closer.

"Or whoever ordered the killing," Ella said. "Some of the vehicles on the list are registered to women."

"Or whoever searched the place a second time," Blake mused. Was Sofia working for the woman who'd slipped into the apartment shortly after Reynolds had been killed and torn the place apart?

"Searched the place a second time?" Ella's strident tones pierced his ear. "What do you mean *searched the place a second time*?"

"I thought I'd mentioned it to you." He explained what Celine had discovered.

"If you want my opinion, whoever it was had to be in league with Reynolds' killer as well," Ella provided a deft analysis of the situation. "Who else would have a motive to go in there?"

"Anyone who wanted to make a quick buck on a Rembrandt."

"Rembrandt? You've gotta be kidding me."

"Nope, Reynolds had the goods on a Rembrandt." He gave her the details. "If only we knew which one."

"Looks like you've made good progress." Ella hesitated.

That gave Blake pause. His personal assistant had cut herself off so abruptly, it was obvious. That usually meant he'd overlooked something.

"Anything else you want to tell me?" he asked after hearing crickets for several seconds.

"You know that partial you had me track down?"

"Yup. What about it?"

"It may or may not mean anything, Blake, but the SAC wanted me to track down the same plate. He had the tag end of it just like you did."

"I see." Blake frowned. He didn't see at all. And he didn't like it either. But he needed to probe a little further. "Walsh give you a reason?"

"Just that his golfing partner had caught a suspicious vehicle hanging around his neighborhood and wanted it checked out."

"Today?"

"Around noon. That caught my attention. It's highly unlikely given when you guys saw her vehicle. Walsh tried to check it out himself but didn't know the DMV codes to access the data." She giggled. "He was really upset about that."

"I'll bet he was." Blake's lips twitched as he pictured Walsh, red-faced and irate, bursting into the anteroom where Ella was stationed.

He made a quick decision.

"Do me a favor. Don't give Walsh any information until I've had a chance to look over what you've found."

"Sure. Anything else?"

"See if you can find out who Walsh's golfing partner is—assuming that isn't just a cockamamie ruse he came up with. If the guy exists, he could be a man named Wozniak.

"Wozniak?" The faint scratching of Ella's pen scribbling his instructions ceased. "How do you figure that?"

"Just a hunch. Based on the fact that it might be Sofia's last name as well. At least that's what Celine thinks. Check it out, would you?"

Ella was still puzzled. Blake could tell because her pen hadn't resumed its scribbling.

"So you think Sofia somehow managed to find out you guys are onto her and got who—*Dad or her hubby*?—to press the SAC for information?"

Put like that, Blake had to admit, it seemed far-fetched. Not to mention troubling. How could Sofia have known she'd been found out? But who else could've informed SAC James Patrick Walsh—or his golfing partner —about the partial they were looking into?

Blake gripped the cold parapet. It all came back to the one thing he'd been worried about right from the start. There was a leak within the FBI —a leak that could cost him this investigation.

"Just find out what you can, Ella. And be discreet," he warned tersely before ending the call. "Looks like someone's watching us."

Chapter Forty-Three

Slipping her feet free of her sandals, Celine stretched her legs out with a grateful sigh. Four months ago when she and Julia had visited Boston, they'd stayed at the Revere Garden Inn, a small, comfortable family-owned establishment in Brookline.

This time the FBI had made all the arrangements, and judging by the opulence that surrounded them, the agency had stinted no expense.

The executive suite Ella Rawlins had booked for them in the Boston Plaza Hotel was nothing short of exquisite. Queen-sized rooms faced each other across a large living room furnished in what appeared to be a French rococo style.

Dirck and John would've known, Celine thought, quietly taking in the beautiful room.

She was seated in a fauteuil—a Louis XVI-style open armchair upholstered in blue. Julia had commandeered the white-and-blue chaise lounge, and they'd left the more plush armchair—a bergère, if Celine knew her furniture—for Blake.

He was still on his cell phone, talking in a low voice with Ella as he paced the carpeted floor by the window.

The hotel had brought up a light dinner—fluffy omelets, a green salad, and a basket of hot dinner rolls—which waited for them on the mahogany trolley room service had wheeled up. A pot of coffee and another of tea sat on a tray painted with poppies on the gilded glass-topped coffee table.

With another barely stifled sigh, Celine picked up the coffeepot. If only she could sneak in a hot bath. But that indulgence would have to wait until Blake left their suite.

She eyed the special agent as she pushed the cup of coffee she'd poured across the table to Julia. She lifted the teapot and poured herself a cup of tea—white Oolong. At nearly seven o'clock, it was too late for caffeine of any kind.

But it had been such a long day and she was so beat, Celine felt she needed it.

Especially if they were planning to pull an all-nighter on this case.

Taking a sip of her tea, she cast another glance at Blake. If only he'd go. All she wanted to do right now was to slip out of her clothes, into a warm bath, and then into bed.

When she finally turned her head, she caught Julia watching her with an amused smile.

"Don't worry," the former fed said with a grin, "rest is definitely on the cards tonight." She gestured toward Blake with her cup. "If he isn't out of here in an hour, I'll shove him out myself. There's just so much I can take."

Julia's eyes—Celine realized with a guilty start—were red-rimmed and swollen with exhaustion. The wrinkles on her weather-beaten face had deepened. Silvery tufts of her hair had escaped their ponytail and framed her face like stiff, matted strands of hay.

But the former fed was as stoically cheerful as ever.

"Any news?" she asked as Blake finally ended his call and joined them at the coffee table.

"I'm not sure." The special agent sank into the bergère. Wearily, he rubbed his forefinger and thumb over his eyes. "Ella managed to squeeze out the name of Walsh's golfing partner. It's not Wozniak, so that's a dead end."

"What is it, did she say?" Julia took a dinner plate off the trolley, handed it to Celine, and took a second plate for herself. "Don't mind me," she excused herself to her former colleague. "My stomach's growling. Want to eat?"

"Sure." Blake dumped a dinner roll and a generous serving of salad onto the remaining plate and pulled it toward himself. He shoveled a bite of omelet into his mouth before responding to Julia's question.

"It's Norton." He took another bite and chewed. "Not exactly the kind of name anyone would be likely to make up. If Walsh wasn't lying about the man's name, it's unlikely he'd be lying about Norton's interest in the same partial we're trying to run down."

He stuck his fork in another piece of omelet. "Makes one wonder if this isn't all just a simple coincidence."

"Norton," Celine repeated. The omelet—stuffed with ham and oozing with cheese—suddenly felt overly rich. She put her plate down, appetite gone. "Did you say, Norton?"

"Yup," Blake mumbled through a mouthful of salad. "Norton. Hugh Norton."

Celine sought Julia's eyes, troubled. Did Walsh have any idea who he was consorting with? Worse still, why wasn't Blake more worried?

"It was never officially in the FBI books," Julia quietly explained. "Bill McCormick made sure of that. I wondered about it at the time. But we'd been chasing so many cock-and-bull theories by that time, I figured he'd decided there was no point adding one more to the file."

The clink of Blake's plate as it settled on the glass-topped coffee table startled Celine.

"What are you talking about?" he demanded. "What isn't in the files? What did Bill McCormick make sure of?"

"You've never heard of Hugh Norton?" Julia countered.

"No." Blake frowned. "Who is he?"

"A wealthy art collector—" Celine began.

"He's in the art insurance business," Julia interrupted her. "We discovered that seven years ago when we were looking into a dicey tip about the Gardner's gu turning up."

"Supposedly at his house," Celine added.

Between herself and Julia, they managed to bring Blake up to speed in about five minutes. Blake listened thoughtfully, asking a few questions here and there.

"Let me get this straight. You never found the gu."

"What Norton had in his home was clearly an imitation," Julia responded crisply. "Very well done, but an imitation nonetheless."

"So . . ." Blake frowned. Hunched in his chair until now, he sat up, eyes narrowed, struggling to understand.

He didn't agree with their reasoning. That much was clear.

Celine leaned forward.

"If it weren't for Laurie's murder—cleverly staged to look like an accidental fall," she explained, "there wouldn't have been any reason for suspicion. Why kill Laurie if it could be so easily proven she was mistaken? Why not let the law take its course? Prove her guilty, ruin her reputation in the art world."

Just like they'd ruined hers, Celine thought.

She couldn't help feeling bitter and disenchanted about that time of her life. A part of her had died then just as surely as it had several years before when her parents had been killed—and their murderer allowed to go free.

Justice is still worth fighting for Celine, Sister Mary Catherine whispered. *You know that, don't you, my dear?*

"And Bill McCormick was one of the most corrupt agents the bureau had at the time," Julia's voice threaded in with the nun's.

Blake smiled. "So we're looking at guilt by association?"

Celine knew what he was referring to. Julia had been on the team of agents that had taken down Boston mafia underboss Gennaro Anguilo. A rival gangster, Whitey Bulger, had helped in the takedown. But years later it had come out that some of the very agents involved in the Anguilo case had forged a nefarious alliance with Bulger.

Bulger had been allowed to commit the most vicious crimes in return for supplying the FBI with information against Anguilo. Problem was none of the information he'd given them had been worth what Blake would've referred to as a "squirt of piss."

John Connolly, Bulger's FBI handler, had been prosecuted. John Morris, the weak FBI agent who'd overseen their relationship, had admitted to turning a blind eye to it. Several of their colleagues on the Anguilo-takedown team had been tainted.

But not Julia Hood.

The former fed flushed a deep angry crimson. "Hugh Norton was the only person with a motive for killing Laurie," she snapped. "The poison used was cyanide."

"Maybe the General thought she was onto something and decided to eliminate her," Blake suggested.

"Professional hitmen don't kill for the heck of it, Blake," Celine found herself saying. "Every kill is a job and needs to be worth it—financially—for them to undertake."

"He's been trying to kill you," Blake countered.

"And I'm sure he was paid to do it."

Celine was aware of Julia's eyes on her, agape.

"Is that your guardian angel speaking or logic?" Blake asked pointedly. The implication being that if it was logic, she—as the only civilian in the room—wasn't allowed to have it.

That was how she interpreted it, at any rate.

"A bit of both," she shot back. "I can lead the General to the loot that slipped out of his hands. I'm not worth killing—unless someone wants me dead and is willing to pay for it."

"That someone being . . .?" Blake prompted, his gray eyes flashing a challenge at her.

Celine took a deep breath, aware of her rising anger. She'd never crossed swords with the special agent—not like this. And she didn't like it. Not one bit. Her psychic senses tended to shut down when people grew confrontational with her.

And with her growing fatigue, it was even harder to keep her senses from clouding over.

The shrill ringing of the phone filled the room—a fortunate interruption.

"I can get that," Julia offered, but Celine was on her feet and by the sleek blue instrument the Boston Plaza Hotel furnished its guests before her friend could hoist herself out of the chaise lounge.

"No, let me," she said as she picked up the receiver. She glowered at Blake, green eyes blazing. "I'm done with this conversation."

Chapter Forty-Four

It took an effort of will to step into the study, but Sofia steeled herself to do it.

Clutching the after-dinner cup of espresso and dessert plate that Aria—Sofia might have had to accept Dom as her dad, but Aria would never be "Mom"—had pressed upon her, she reluctantly followed the hulking six-four frame that loomed before her toward the thick plank of butcher-block oak that served as a desk.

Resistance was futile. No one had ever defied Dom Wozniak—not with any success at any rate.

Her heart muscles clenched tightly and her chest constricted as though it were in the grip of an icy vise. Why had she been summoned here? Into this room that had always been out of bounds to the rest of the family. Where even Aria was not allowed.

What did Dom want with her?

"We need to talk," he'd informed her—in a voice so quiet it had sounded all the more menacing—while Aria bustled in and out of the kitchen, bearing platters of roast chicken, fingerling potatoes, and the salads and wines that would accompany their meal.

That was all he'd said. Until dessert was served, when he'd fastened his dark eyes upon her, flicked his glance to his study door and back again to her face.

The time had come.

"Sit." Dom indicated the leather chair placed across from where he sat —legs spread wide—like a potentate ready to receive an emissary from a troublesome enemy.

Sofia set her cup and plate on the desk—Dom had never bothered with coasters—and lowered herself gracefully into the leather chair. Light splashed from the green desk lamp—the only source of it in the room— into a middling-sized pool that encompassed her own chair and the area of carpet between it and Dom's.

It was like being snared in a harsh spotlight. Dom's eyes—dark and inscrutable—studied her face minutely. The scrutiny made Sofia nervous.

Why had she been summoned here? But with her hands decorously placed in her lap, she squared her shoulders and met his gaze without flinching.

"Find anything of interest?" he eventually asked.

"For the shop you mean?" Were they going to be talking business after all? Sofia allowed herself to relax.

Dom stared at her.

"In Tony Reynolds' apartment."

The clarification uttered in Dom's low rumble caused her nerves to explode as though a bomb had gone off under her chair.

"You were there today, weren't you?"

My God! Her hands fell away from her lap. How in the world had he found out about that?

Denial would be futile, she knew. Dom never confronted you without marshaling all his facts.

But she wasn't a child anymore. Sofia pressed her lips together. She wasn't going to be browbeaten into a defense.

"What if I was?" she replied tightlipped. "What of it?"

He gently stroked his gray beard. Under the thick, scratchy mustache, his lips twitched. The small gesture of amusement—the calm before a storm—made her flinch as though she'd been struck. Her hands felt cold and clammy.

"What did you take?"

"I d-didn't," she stammered, startled by the question. What was he getting at? Sofia struggled to understand. "I took nothing."

"A key is missing. Tony's warehouse key."

Her eyes widened. Of course, he'd have a warehouse. How dumb of her not to consider it. Or to remember that an artist like Tony needed a space far larger than the tiny studio in his apartment to mold the large-scale pieces he sculpted.

Back when they'd been engaged, he'd mentioned the warehouse. But she'd never been all that interested in his work. Never asked where the warehouse was. Never asked to visit it.

"Missing?" she repeated.

"Stolen from the scene of a crime."

She was only half-listening, barely registering the fact that Dom had learned of her whereabouts through official channels.

If Tony's warehouse key was missing, Sofia suspected she knew who'd wanted it and why. But that would mean . . .

She felt sick to the core of her stomach.

"His warehouse must've had something worth stealing," she said, cursing herself for not thinking of it.

"Only if we take the word of a forger at face value, my dear."

"But it wasn't just his word," she muttered.

And it was likely gone now. They'd never find it.

Chapter Forty-Five

"Celine? It's Jonah."

"I know." Celine clutched the receiver to her ear. She'd have recognized the journalist's whiny, nasal tenor anywhere. "How's your mother? Everything okay, I hope."

"Oh, yes. She wandered off"—Jonah's mother had Alzheimer's—"Fortunately, she didn't get too far before the attendants realized she was gone. They brought her back, a little dazed, somewhat confused, but otherwise more or less in one piece. But you don't want to hear about my mother."

"No?" Celine smiled.

Jonah was calling for information. Not to chat about his mother's well-being. In a way, she understood his eagerness. It probably took every cent of his journalist's salary and more to pay for his mother's bills at the care facility where she was housed. Celine couldn't even begin to imagine how Jonah afforded it.

The inexplicable anger that had arisen earlier began to subside. Probably a side-effect of her extreme weariness, she thought, dismissing any residual sense of guilt she felt about the emotion.

"Well, you know what I mean." Jonah was unabashed. "I want to know what the scoop is."

"Well, so far all we've been able to ascertain is that Reynolds had information on one of the stolen Rembrandts."

He emitted a low whistle, but listened quietly while she talked.

"So chances are it's in his warehouse, which Soldi will be searching tomorrow, right?"

"That is right," Celine confirmed. "I certainly hope the painting's there. But if it's not, I have no idea where we'll look." A telltale flutter in her stomach told her Soldi would have disappointing news for them the next day.

It seemed almost too good to be true that the lost Rembrandt should be so easily found. And with Reynolds' key missing, it was almost inevitable that when it came to searching the warehouse his killer would've beaten them to the punch.

"If it's not," Jonah said, bringing her thoughts back, "we might want to consider that Reynolds entrusted the painting or information about it to someone he trusted."

"Such as whom?" Celine pressed the receiver closer to her ear. Jonah's idea was a good one. But from the little she'd learned of Reynolds, he was a lone wolf who trusted no one.

"I don't know. A friend. Someone like you, perhaps."

"Me!" She was astounded. "Why would he entrust anything to me? We were barely nodding acquaintances, if that."

But as she voiced the question, Reynolds' words to her when they'd first met began ringing in her ear.

You're psychic, aren't you? You're psychic, aren't you? You're psychic, aren't you?

Over and over again. It was maddening.

She jammed the receiver closer to her ear, plugging her other ear with her left forefinger. She was having a hard time hearing Jonah over the din.

"Well, you're clearly a person of integrity," the journalist was saying. "And you helped recover the Gardner's Vermeer. Everyone knows that."

Thanks to you, she thought. She'd never wanted her role in the recovery to be so publicly disclosed.

And as for integrity, Jonah's article at the time had implied that the rest of the Gardner art was stashed away somewhere in the Mechelen. The subsequent FBI raid had been both unpleasant and humiliating.

The news that the Mechelen had none of the Gardner art never seemed to have been broadcast quite as widely as the rumor that she was privy to its location and reluctant to give up the details.

"What?" she asked, realizing he was asking her something.

"Could Reynolds have passed along some information to you when he visited the Mechelen?" Jonah repeated himself.

"No," she began to say.

"It's something we should consider, you know."

Celine shook her head, beginning to lose patience again. "Jonah, there was nothing he gave me except for his plans for the installations I'd commissioned for the grounds. And a few miniature pieces—replicas of what he'd planned."

Reynolds' chant was still buzzing in her ears. It was accompanied by a phrase that didn't make any sense. *Don't trust the mailman.*

Her senses overwrought and overwhelmed, Celine struggled to tune the sculptor's voice out, focusing on Jonah instead.

She could barely hear what Jonah was saying. Something about plans and replicas. He was probably repeating what she'd just told him. But his next words came through loud and clear.

"Could he have slipped something else to you, unnoticed, as it were?"

"Of course not. Don't be ridiculous."

Chapter Forty-Six

The Dutch Room was empty. Celine wasn't sure how she'd made it back to the historic building of the Gardner Museum. But here she was, at the doorway, peering in. She stepped inside, the icy atmosphere of the gallery making her shudder.

It was cold enough to raise goose bumps on her bare arms. Vaguely aware of the flimsy, sleeveless nightdress she had on, she huddled her arms around herself. The rash of goose pimples on her chilled skin felt rough against her palms.

Her gaze alighted on the empty frame of Rembrandt's seascape, *Christ in the Storm on the Sea of Galilee,* hanging just across the doorway on the south wall. Celine moved farther in.

Was this the painting Reynolds had discovered?

Or was it the double portrait he had information about? Her glance moved a few feet to the left to the empty frame of *A Lady and Gentleman in Black.*

You're missing something, Belle had informed her through her guardian angel. But Celine didn't understand. What was she missing?

"You're looking in the wrong direction."

Celine heard the deep voice before she felt a warm, masculine presence next to her.

She recognized him before she turned to meet his gaze.

Tony Reynolds.

The gash on his neck was healing. His clothes looked less disheveled and bloodied.

He's getting used to his circumstances, Sister Mary Catherine told her. *He's coming to terms with what happened.*

"Looking in the wrong direction?" Celine asked the dead sculptor. They were conversing normally, she realized. Not communicating telepathically the way she usually did with the dead.

"You're looking at the south wall." Tony placed his warm, strong hands on her shoulders and firmly swiveled her around. "Look at the north wall, instead."

"But the self-portrait wasn't taken," she argued.

"Look down, not up." He propelled her toward the Flemish oak cabinet placed between Rembrandt's self-portrait and another portrait by Albrecht Dürer.

"Look down, Celine."

She felt her head being pushed firmly down.

"No, stop!"

Darkness engulfed her like a fog.

Wake up, Celine. It was Reynolds' voice, so faint, so far.

Wake up. Louder now. *Wake up.*

Her eyes opened and she gazed straight up. The ceiling above her supine form was pristine and white, its ornate crown molding very familiar. Beneath her, the mattress felt soft.

She was back in her hotel bed.

It took a second to realize the covers had blown off her, leaving her cold and shivering in the air-conditioned room.

What had Reynolds been trying to do back there? Kill her? She pushed herself up, slowly surveying the room.

Celine?

At the sound of his voice, her head turned sharply to the left.

Reynolds was in the white cane armchair with its powder blue cushion by her bed.

What are you doing here? She pulled the covers back up, aware of the sheer nature of her chemise. The action, once she'd performed it, seemed ridiculous. The man was dead, after all.

He fixed his eyes on her, oblivious to her concerns. *Now do you understand?*

Understand what?

What you need to see? You've been looking in the wrong direction.

And the right direction would be . . . the cabinet?

He smiled. *Now you're getting it.* Then the smile faded, and a puzzled expression settled over Reynolds' features.

But why do you still trust the mailman?

The mailman?

You can't trust him, Celine. Beware the mailman.

But . . .?

He was gone. Darkness engulfed her again.

❦

Morning sun poured through the lacy curtains at her window. Instinctively Celine's glance cut to the armchair by her bed.

It was empty.

She sat up, rubbing her eyes. Had Reynolds really been here? Or had that been another dream?

Beware the mailman. She recalled the warning Reynolds had issued before his form dissipated. But what mailman was he warning her against?

He's referring to the mailman who accosted him in Paso Robles, Sister Mary Catherine told her. *As you get closer to the truth, beware who you share it with.*

The nun's words were accompanied by two quick flashes of insight. Something had gone down at the Mechelen. Celine's heart twisted—a painful clenching of her muscles that was followed by a rush of apprehension flooding her being.

Oh, God! Annabelle. They'd been betrayed.

Her hand reached for the phone, then stopped.

The oak cabinet in the Dutch Room. What had Reynolds been trying to tell her? Who was she not supposed to trust?

Blake? She'd been about to call him, but . . .

The FBI agent had grown wary of her insights. And he'd outright dismissed their suspicions about Hugh Norton . . . Why?

The strident ringing of the phone curtailed the trend of her thoughts. "Hello?"

Chapter Forty-Seven

"Celine?"

Annabelle's voice sounded tremulous, quavering as though she were on the verge of tears.

Celine was instantly alarmed.

"Annabelle? I was about to call you." She swung her legs off the bed and stood up. "Is everything all right?"

"Yes . . . no."

Celine heard a gulping sound followed by a loud sniffle.

"Are you okay?" She opened the door of her room and peered out into the living room. Julia's door was closed; the former fed was still asleep. "You're not still at the hospital, are you?"

Another gulp. "Oh no. They discharged me yesterday. I was hoping you'd have time to call . . ."

Celine knew her failure to call wasn't the cause of Annabelle's agitation. But Annabelle seemed so distressed, she felt a twinge of regret for not making more of an effort to stay in touch.

Leaving the door ajar, she turned back into her room. "I'm so sorry, I—"

"That's not why I'm upset, Celine." Annabelle's voice sounded firmer. She'd obviously regained control of her emotions. "I know you and Julia must've been busy. It's just . . . We had a break-in last night—at least, I think we did."

"Another break-in?" They'd had one four months back when the Mechelen's handyman-slash-guard, Bob Massie, had foolishly given a couple of the General's men access to Celine's cottage.

She'd instituted fairly stringent security protocols since then, but obviously that hadn't deterred the intruders.

"But how is that possible? I don't understand. Is anyone hurt? Anything missing?"

"Yes, that's why I'm so sure we weren't imagining it. Do you remember that lovely miniature sculpture you let me have?"

"A bust of Dirck in a Sherlock Holmes-like cape and a soft hat with a paintbrush stuck in it?"

Celine hadn't seen the resemblance at the time, but now that she thought about it, the bust Reynolds had molded looked remarkably like the Rembrandt self-portrait in the Dutch Room.

The one he'd shown her yet again last night.

Recalling the dream, she wondered if the likeness had been a conscious decision on Reynolds' part—a message to her. (*You're psychic, aren't you?*) Or a subconscious one.

"It's gone." Annabelle's voice quavered again. "Last night Bryan heard a noise in our cottage. There was no one around when he went to check. But this morning I noticed the bust was gone. I'd displayed it in the living room."

Don't trust the mailman. Reynolds' warning returned to Celine's mind as Annabelle continued to speak.

It wasn't the mailman this time, Sister Mary Catherine informed her.

Then who? Celine thought as she directed her attention back to Annabelle.

At his mother's urging, Bryan Curtis had questioned Bob Massie and learned that the second guard on duty that evening had called in sick. Bob had been alone when a man pulled up, asking if he could come in and search for his wallet, which he claimed to have misplaced during one of the morning's wine tours.

"And Bob let him in?" Celine was appalled. This was in direct violation of the Mechelen's security protocol.

No visitors were allowed into the winery after the last tour of the day.

"No." Annabelle sighed. "It wasn't really Bob's fault. He allowed the man to wait in the guard's room while he checked the facilities for his wallet. You know how he hangs his master key on the hook, in full view of everyone."

Celine did know. It should've occurred to her that this was a security hazard as well. But with two guards taking every shift, who would've guessed a stranger would find themselves alone in the guard room? Or that Bob Massie would carelessly leave his master key where anyone could take it?

It was her turn to sigh.

"It wouldn't have been hard to make a wax impression of the key, have a duplicate made, and to return later at night, would it?"

"That's what we figure."

"Have you called Mailand?" Celine wasn't sure what, if anything, the Sheriff's detective could do about the break-in and the missing bust. But she'd feel safer knowing that he'd been alerted to potential trouble at the winery.

"He's on his way, although other than taking a report, I don't see what he can do."

"One thing he *can* do is to check up on the guard who didn't show up for work. And I wonder if the cameras at the gate picked up anything. I just hope whoever it was didn't manage to disable them."

"I'd forgotten about the cameras," Annabelle confessed. "But I just don't understand why *anyone*"—her voice quivered with a shrill, intense outrage —"would've wanted to steal Dirck's bust."

Blake was at the office earlier than usual the next morning.

He scanned the pages of information Ella had laid out on his desk. His personal assistant had managed to obtain the VIN of every silver Mercedes Benz license ending in the sequence Jonah had noticed on Sofia's car.

It was an impressive array of data—complete with the name, photograph, driver's license, and mailing address of the title owners—but ultimately useless.

There was not a single Sofia in the bunch. And no one with the last name Wozniak.

He leaned back and sighed.

"God, this is such a bust!" His hand moved up to his chin, feeling the scratchy beginnings of stubble. Damn!

He'd been so eager to get out of his apartment after the restless night he'd spent, he'd forgotten to shave. Not that anyone had noticed as far as he could tell. Ella certainly hadn't. She hadn't looked at him askance or made any other kind of disapproving comment.

And knowing her, she would've. His personal assistant didn't miss a thing. Or an opportunity to let her opinion be known.

Blake raised his eyes toward her. Ella's bespectacled eyes were trained upon the documents spread out on his desk.

"Do any of the women look familiar, at least?" she asked.

"Nope. I'd have told you if they did."

Her lips were pinched together, her face looked strained. She'd been to a lot of trouble to track down the partial he'd given her. He knew that— and he felt bad telling her it was all to no avail.

"So I gather there's no objection to letting the SAC have this?" She waved a hand over the desk bristling with papers.

Blake shouldn't have had any objection, and yet . . .

"Let me take another look." He sat up. "I was thinking you could—"

"Cross-check this list with Reynolds' client list and eliminate any names not on it?"

"You read my mind." He glanced up at her with a smile. "Good thinking, Ella."

She returned the smile, eyes twinkling brightly behind her round lenses. "I thought you might like that idea. Glad you appreciate it."

"I do." He meant it, too.

He glanced down, eyes roving over the documents one last time.

"And let's make sure the SAC doesn't get hold of any name included in Reynolds' list of clients."

"The golfing partner story still bothering you?"

"Yup."

Blake hadn't thought much of Celine and Julia's theory about Hugh Norton. But Walsh's story had struck him as suspicious. Were Walsh and Norton really golfing partners? Even if they were, why would Norton be interested in the same partial they were looking into?

Judging by what he'd learned from his parents, Norton was on the up-and-up.

The Markhams didn't move in the same elevated circles as Norton, but they'd heard of him. Norton was a well-known and well-respected patron of the arts—a donor on the list of countless museums, the Gardner included.

There was no way he was involved in the Gardner Museum theft. For one thing, Norton had the moolah to buy any artwork he set his eyes on. And he had too much respect for art to steal it.

Blake ignored the quiet voice nudging him: *But nothing in the Gardner was for sale.*

Yes, I know that, he thought irritably.

"Any word on Sofia?" he asked Ella, more to distract himself than to press her for an update on an assignment she may not have gotten to yet.

"I haven't had much time to look into it. All I've been able to find out is that there are two Sofia Wozniaks."

"Oh!" He looked up.

She nodded. "An older woman, who's been dead for over two decades."

"And the other one?"

"A woman in her late thirties. If your Sofia was engaged to Reynolds, this could be her."

Blake cast his mind back to the woman they'd seen sprinting down the stairs. A slender, attractive woman, he'd judged her to be in her early thirties. But he supposed she could be older than that.

"Follow up on it, would you?"

"Sure thing." Ella tipped her chin at the papers. "Done with those?"

"Give me another minute." He bent his head, taking one last look.

His gaze traveled over his paper-strewn desk. The uppercase beginning of a name snagged his attention. He swept his gaze over it again.

Jesus Christ!

If this was happenstance, it was one helluva coincidence.

He pulled the paper out.

Chapter Forty-Eight

Annabelle's question was still reverberating in Celine's mind when she broke the news of the break-in to Julia. Why had the bust portraying Dirck been stolen? What had anyone expected to find?

"I don't think there's any question it was the General," Julia said thoughtfully.

"No, I guess not."

"So the General must believe Tony concealed some clue about the Rembrandt's location in one of those miniatures. There's nothing in his apartment; where else could it be?"

The former fed had emerged from her room just as Celine was getting off the phone.

"Who was that—Blake?" she'd asked, rubbing her eyes sleepily.

"No, Annabelle." Celine had been glad to get the news off her chest. Dealing with a situation like this, being unable to do anything to help, was frustrating.

Now as Julia voiced her surmise, Celine interlaced her fingers around her coffee mug and frowned. They were sitting in the living room of their suite where room service had delivered a pot of coffee and a plate of croissants.

"But no one knew Reynolds had given me those pieces other than the three of us—And Blake," she added.

Not to mention that she'd detected nothing in Reynolds' manner to indicate the miniature pieces had any significance other than as a model of his artistic vision.

But Julia didn't agree. "He was obviously trying to tell you something. He still is. The problem is, he communicates in such a cryptic fashion, it's hard to understand what he's trying to get at."

Celine bit her lip, unable to counter that point.

"As for who else might've known about those pieces, Annabelle could've mentioned it to someone at the hospital—" Julia hesitated. "Or to Wanda or anyone else at the winery."

Or Byran, Celine silently added, although she didn't at all care for what Julia was hinting at. And even if the former fed was right, something wasn't adding up.

"Then why wait until last night to make an attempt?"

Don't trust the mailman.

"But it wasn't the mailman, this time," she murmured to herself.

And he doesn't work for you. Sister Mary Catherine's words flitted through her mind, making Celine smile. *The mailman didn't work for her.* She'd known that, but her guardian angel's reminder was reassuring all the same.

"I beg your pardon?" Julia lowered the mug of coffee she'd brought to her lips, her weathered face puzzled.

"The mailman," Celine repeated. "Reynolds has been warning me about him." She recounted the dead man's warning and her guardian angel's whispered information.

Julia took a sip of her coffee and swallowed thoughtfully.

"This is the mailman he met in Paso Robles, right?" She went on before Celine could confirm the fact, "Reynolds is dead. I guess he has no reason to lie now."

"Someone did approach him at the winery. I saw it." The dream—how long ago had she had it?—was still vivid in Celine's mind. "Reynolds was telling the truth."

"That means the General has a direct line to someone in Paso Robles." Julia leaned forward, hands clasped around her coffee mug, blue eyes shrouded in thought. "That's worrisome, but we can use it against him. If we follow the mailman angle, it could lead us straight to the General."

Her gaze, piercing and intense, bore into Celine's. "Have you had a chance to call Blake? We need to get Mailand on this ASAP."

Celine broke eye contact.

"Why don't you call him?" she suggested, unable to keep the edge out of her voice. She'd found Blake's mule-headed pooh-poohing of her suspicions last night highhanded and extremely offensive. Blake had dismissed everything they'd had to say about Hugh Norton without even weighing the evidence.

It wasn't something she could easily forget. Or forgive.

She looked back at Julia. "I'd like to ask Penny about that Flemish oak cabinet they have standing under Rembrandt's self-portrait. I still don't understand what Reynolds was trying to tell me."

"Maybe that he concealed some kind of clue in there? He must've frequented the museum often enough in the weeks preceding the exhibition."

"Maybe." Celine's mug clinked softly as she set it on the glass-topped coffee table and got to her feet.

Blake slid the document across the table to Ella.

"Don't know if you noticed, but there's a Norton listed here. A Hugh Norton."

"The SAC's golfing partner?" Ella leaned over for a closer look. "Wow, he wasn't lying about that!" She looked up, eyes wide. "Think it was Norton's car Sofia was driving?"

"I don't know." His mind was still reeling.

But Norton's interest in the partial was starting to make sense. And, in light of what he'd discovered, the suspicions Celine and Julia had shared seemed even more plausible.

It was too much of a coincidence that Norton's name had come up—not once, but twice—in connection to a murder with a peripheral tie-in to the Gardner theft. Blake would've been willing to dismiss the first incident as mere coincidence.

But twice in under a decade, what were the odds?

The two homicides were startlingly similar in other respects as well. Like Laurie, Tony Reynolds had been willing to capitalize on the information he'd obtained about the Gardner theft. Why else had he called Penny?

And like her, Reynolds had been murdered for what he knew.

But there was yet another realization that struck Blake with sickening force. Hugh Norton, patron of the arts and prime suspect—in two cases, now, connected to the Gardner heist—was also SAC James Patrick Walsh's golfing partner.

Blake had long suspected a leak in the department. If this was it, it obviously went all the way to the top. *Jesus F—in' Christ.*

"I need you to find out whether Norton was on Reynolds' roster of clients. And regardless of whether he was or not, his is the only information you pass on to the SAC, got it?"

"Blake, I don't understand." Ella's eyes, wide with anxiety, peered through her large glasses.

"I don't have time for explanations," he growled. "Just trust me, okay?"

He shoved his chair back and got to his feet. Memories flooded into his mind as he turned blindly to the window.

It had been the SAC's golfing partner who'd recommended Mary, the General's mole in the FBI. She'd vanished without a trace before they'd cottoned on to her true identity.

The SAC had brushed aside his concerns, focusing instead on Grayson's murder and Blake's negligence in allowing it to happen. *Oh God!*

He turned around. Ella was still sitting in her chair, staring earnestly at him.

"Ella, for God's sake," he began when the phone shrilled.

He glanced at the caller ID. Soldi from Cambridge PD.

Jesus Christ, what now?

Chapter Forty-Nine

Penny seemed distracted when Celine called.

"You were in the Dutch Room, looking at the south wall, when Reynolds spun you around?" She was repeating Celine's words mechanically, as though reiterating the details would help her better understand the facts.

"Yes." Celine hoped her dream was making sense to Penny—although she doubted it.

"He said I was looking in the wrong direction," she offered.

"And you think *I* might know what he meant by that?"

"Yes." Celine winced, moving the phone away from her ear. Penny's voice tended to get ear-piercingly high when she was in the throes of any kind of negative emotion. It was a mixture of frustration, impatience, and outrage this time.

"My dear, I hardly knew the man. I'm sorry but I don't have the faintest clue what he was trying to tell you."

You need to ask the right questions, Celine, Sister Mary Catherine whispered. *It's the only way you'll get the answers you need.*

Ask the right questions. That had been another one of the nun's favorite sayings in life. Right along with: "Put on your thinking cap."

Ask the right questions, Celine repeated to herself. What were the right questions?

"Celine, I really need to—"

Penny was in a hurry; she wouldn't be able to keep her much longer.

What did Tony want you to see, Celine? Her guardian angel jogged her memory.

"Celine," Penny began again. "Listen, I need to—"

"What is it about that Flemish oak cabinet that's so special?" Celine rushed the words out.

"It's a nineteenth-century copy of a seventeenth-century style. There's no connection with Rembrandt that I can think of. It was fabricated long after he died."

"Is there anything in it? Was there anything in it?"

"No. Like I told you it's just a piece of furniture. If it were a glass case, there'd have been some reason to display items in it. But it's not. There's no reason to open it."

A thought occurred to Celine. Reynolds had turned her toward the north wall and forced her head down. What if he'd wanted her to look inside the cabinet?

There was no reason to open it, Penny had said, unless—

Unless . . .

"Penny, what if Tony did open that cabinet? What if he concealed something in it? Some clue about where the Rembrandt is? It could never fall into the wrong hands. You said yourself, there's no reason to open it."

"I eh-m . . . I—" Penny seemed stunned. "You think that's what he was trying to tell you? Whatever he wanted us to know is right here in the Gardner?"

"How could it not be?" Celine was warming to her interpretation. "He's probably been in and out of the museum for weeks now. What better place to hide whatever information he had?"

"I'll look into it, Celine. But, listen, I've got to run. There's the memorial service to organize. I have tons to do."

"Sure, I understand. Check it out when you have a minute. You can call us if you find something."

"I have a better idea," Penny said. "Why don't you and Julia come over after lunch?"

❧

Ella pushed her short, glossy black hair behind her ear and sucked thoughtfully on a pencil. Hugh Norton wasn't on Reynolds' client list. That issue had been easily answered.

But cross-referencing the list of names she'd obtained from the DMV with Reynolds' client list was proving more daunting than she'd imagined.

They'd been operating on a number of false premises. And while it was one thing for her boss to make anti-feminist assumptions, it was quite another for a diehard feminist like herself to buy into them.

God, how stupid she'd been!

Reynolds' notebook listed primarily male clients. But as she'd run down the list of registered car owners, Ella had noticed a few female names with last names that matched those of Reynolds' male clients.

She'd made a note of the names, then instantly chided herself for assuming that car owner Linda Cottman was married to Reynolds' client Glen Cottman. Or that Beverly Standish had to be connected to Peter Standish.

Ella's pencil had hovered over the sheet of paper she was scribbling on, ready to scratch out the connections she'd presumed existed. Then she'd lifted the tip of her pencil up, letting her notes stand, just in case her initial assumptions had been accurate.

But what she hadn't taken into consideration—and this was making her feel like grabbing fistfuls of her hair and tearing it out—was that some of the women on the DMV list might be associated with Reynolds' clients even if they *did not* share last names.

For all Ella knew, Linda Cottman was married to Peter Standish or Roger Connery while Sofia Wozniak—the woman they were after—was married to Glen Cottman. Women frequently didn't take their husbands' names these days—and good for them. Ella smiled.

There was no reason for a woman to give up her identity just because she was married. Why didn't men give up theirs? Oh, no, you'd never catch a man doing that. That had been the deal-breaker in a couple of Ella's relationships—her refusal to bow down and renounce Rawlins as her last name.

Not gonna happen in a million years, Ella thought. She reined her thoughts in. Better get this done quickly or Blake would have a hissy fit.

She ran her eye down the DMV list.

This car Sofia had borrowed, had it belonged to a girlfriend—Trina DiMaggio (the name appeared on both lists, Ella noted) or Jane Elks? Her eyes, shifting from the DMV list to Reynolds' client list, spied a Dennis Elks on the latter. She circled it.

You're doing it again, Ella, the ultra-critical voice in her head chided.

Well, some women do take their husband's name, she countered, resenting herself for being on the defensive. *It's been known to happen.*

She shook her head. Arguing with herself wasn't going to get the job done. Now where was she? Had Sofia taken a girlfriend's car?

Or had she been driving her husband's or boyfriend's car? Couples did tend to drive each other's cars, she firmly informed her inner feminist critic.

But now that she thought of it, there was yet another option. Ella's head swung over to Reynolds' client list. Sofia could've been working for any of these men—or women?

Roger Connery. That name appeared on both lists. Had she made a note of that? Her head shifted to the other list. Nope. Better do it now.

And here was another that overlapped both lists: Gloria Aldman.

What was really disappointing, though, was that Norton wasn't on Reynolds' client list. He'd been such a promising lead. But he wasn't on the list.

Not on the official client list, Ella reminded herself.

If there'd been shady goings-on between the two men, Reynolds was hardly likely to record it in a notebook easily accessible to anyone who chose to wander into his place and snoop around.

She dropped her pencil on the sheaf of papers on her desk. This assignment could take forever. Maybe it was time to put Blake's plan in action and watch the SAC squirm.

She pushed her chair back, about to get up, when the phone rang.

Ella sighed. It was probably Blake wanting an update. Or—worse still —with more chores to add to her already full to-do list.

Chapter Fifty

Blake cruised past Harvey Street and parked by the curb on Everett Street. It had been a twenty-minute drive—give or take—from the FBI office in Chelsea, but here he was at last. Vince Soldi's call had aroused his curiosity, but Blake kept his excitement in check.

This could turn out to be a dead end. With his luck, it probably would.

Soldi's men had located Reynolds' warehouse and searched it. It was what they'd discovered in it that had caused Soldi to put in an urgent call to Blake.

Blake could see no sign of Soldi, but the warehouse was up ahead where the road curved gently to meet the other Everett, a narrower branch separated from the Everett he'd been driving on by a pony wall.

Eyes narrowed against the glare of the sun, Blake peered through the windshield.

So this was where Reynolds had his workspace—in Allston. A neighborhood in the western part of Boston.

Blake thrust his door open and maneuvered himself out of the sedan. *Makes sense for a man like Reynolds to have his studio here*, he reflected. The neighborhood was named for the nineteenth-century American landscape painter, Washington Allston.

And Reynolds had lived and breathed art. Blake had noticed the Rodin reproductions and prints in his apartment. The books on classical and contemporary artists.

Allston, the painter, was considered the father of American Romanticism. But there was nothing remotely Romantic about the neighborhood named after him.

Fifty Everett Street—Reynolds' warehouse—and the green dumpster in front of it looked like something straight out of an industrial wasteland.

Adjusting his shades, Blake surveyed the area. Nope, the Cambridge Police cars were nowhere in sight. He figured they were in the parking lot attached to the complex he'd just passed—it boasted a Stop & Shop, a Home Goods, a Dollar Tree, and a Citizen's Bank.

He'd noticed the names on the picturesque sign at the entrance to the lot, but not the blue-and-white vehicles of the Cambridge PD fleet. But he resisted the temptation to walk back to the parking lot. Soldi and his guys had to be somewhere here. They'd agreed to meet at the warehouse.

He'd obviously missed the squad cars as he drove past, he told himself. Scanning his environment was second-nature to Blake, and usually very little tended to escape his sharp eyes. But the parking lot had been packed.

It would've been easy to overlook a few white-and-blue sedans.

Arms swinging by his side, Blake strode up to the warehouse—an ugly white brick building with a pale-green roll-up door of corrugated iron.

"You'll want to come check this out, Special Agent. We found something," Soldi had informed him tersely a half-hour back when he'd called. But that was all he'd said.

That and the fact that ADA Mariah Campari had insisted the FBI be called to inspect Reynolds' warehouse.

Check out what, Blake wondered. There'd been an undertone of tense excitement in Soldi's voice that had aroused the agent's curiosity.

Approaching the studio entrance, he noticed the corrugated iron door was rolled halfway up.

Not high enough to see who or what was inside. Or to allow a full-grown man to walk under it erect. He poked his head under the door.

"Soldi?"

A team of police officers swarmed the large, brightly lit area. Gigantic works in marble, bronze, and plaster of Paris lined the walls. A huge worktable stood in the center.

At the sound of his voice, the cluster of uniformed men thinned out, and Soldi emerged from their midst.

"Agent, there you are." Soldi waved him in. "Come on in."

Back bent in a low crouch, Blake entered the warehouse. As he approached Soldi, the crowd of men parted like the Red Sea. Through the thinning ranks, Blake detected a stack of gold-framed paintings standing by the wall.

The Gardner loot?

He caught Soldi's eye; saw the glimmer of excitement in the Deputy Superintendent's gaze, the satisfied expression on his face. *Look at what we uncovered, Special Agent.*

Jesus Christ, had Reynolds had it all along?

Chapter Fifty-One

Muttering under her breath, Ella picked up the receiver. "Hello?" She didn't bother to add her usual message: "Blake Markham's office." It was probably the man himself.

"Ella?" The female voice startled Ella, and it took her a second to place it. But the caller was already identifying herself. "It's Julia. Listen, I've been trying to get through to Blake. Is he available?"

"Oh, Julia, hi." Ella had always admired the older woman. There was a no-nonsense efficiency about the former agent that Ella respected. "Blake's probably got his phone on silent or vibrate. He was called out to Reynolds' warehouse. Cambridge PD may have found something."

"At Reynolds' warehouse, you say?" There was a pregnant pause.

Julia was obviously fishing for information—information she wasn't exactly entitled to. Not that Ella would've minded sharing, if she had anything to share.

"I'm sorry, Julia," she said after the silence had stretched out several seconds. "I don't know much more than that. Soldi wasn't very forthcoming and Blake hasn't phoned in yet. But that isn't why you called, is it? Anything I can do to help?"

She listened carefully, taking notes, as Julia explained what she wanted done.

"You know, I think"—Ella tucked her pencil between her lips and pushed aside some of the papers and files on her desk—"Oh yes," she said, finding her Post-it reminder from a few days back, "Blake did ask me to call Mailand to check out Reynolds' story."

"But you never got around to it?" Julia asked.

A remark like that coming from anybody else would've offended Ella, but Julia's tone hadn't implied she thought Ella had been shirking her work. Just that she—Ella—had been too overwhelmed to get to everything on her to-do list. Which was certainly true, although she had made the call.

"No, it's not that. I haven't had a chance to check back with him. I'm making a note to myself to give Mailand another call. I'm sure he'd have gotten back to us if he'd found anything, but—"

"But now you can also convey Celine's concerns to him . . ." Julia hesitated. "It might be better coming from the FBI."

Ella nodded. "Sure, no problem. I'll get on it ASAP."

Right after she'd cornered the SAC and confronted him about his friend's car being seen under suspicious circumstances.

❧

"Ah, Ella! Come in." SAC James Patrick Walsh waved her in with an expansive gesture and indicated the chair across from his desk.

When Ella had carefully lowered herself into the chair, primly crossing her legs, and smoothing her skirt over her knees, Walsh leaned forward, elbows on the desk.

"Well, what have you got for me, young woman?" He gazed at her with avuncular fondness.

Ella had a feeling Walsh's geniality would be completely eroded once she'd revealed her information.

"There's something I thought you should know about, sir." She fixed her eyes on him.

"Yes, yes, I understand." Walsh was beginning to sound impatient. His eye drifted to the clock on the left wall. Ella could see it out of the corner of her eye as well. "Go on."

"As I was running the partial you gave me, sir, I found something a bit disturbing."

"Yes?"

"I'm sure there's a reasonable explanation, but I thought you should know before we go any further with this."

"Ella, I'm a busy man. What exactly is it that you want me to know? You ran the partial. I'm assuming you came up with a name, address, that sort of thing?"

"Yes, sir, I did. The system returned a match." She took a deep breath and dropped the paper she'd been clutching in her hand onto Walsh's desk. "The car belongs to your golfing partner, Hugh Norton."

She pushed the paper across the desk and waited until Walsh drew it toward himself and peered down. She saw the question flickering over his features, but before he could raise his eyes, she hurriedly continued.

"It gets worse. This car was found at a crime scene in Cambridge. The sculptor Tony Reynolds' neighborhood. The woman driving it is suspected of having drugged a police officer to gain access to the crime scene. Cambridge Police has a BOLO out on her."

She didn't know this last to be true. But if there wasn't already a BOLO out, there would be soon enough.

Walsh's eyes narrowed. "Ella, all I gave you was a partial. There's got to be more than one car that ends with the same sequence. And they can't all be Mercedes Benzes, can they? In fact, I don't recall telling you we were looking for a Mercedes Benz."

Ella flushed. The old boy had more intelligence than she'd given him credit for. She'd taken him for a clueless bureaucratic nincompoop.

"Yes, sir, but you mentioned a silver car and when Special Agent Markham called in with a request from Cambridge Police to track down a silver Mercedes Benz with the same sequence . . ." She shrugged her shoulders. "I'm sorry, I simply assumed it was the same car."

"I see." Walsh's eyes remained narrowed. He glanced down at her hands, resting on her knees now. "And the rest of the names?" He raised his eyes. "I presume there are more."

"Oh, yes," Ella nodded. "I haven't downloaded them all yet." She resisted the urge to clench her fingers as was her wont when telling a lie. "I just thought you should know about that . . ." She pointed at the piece of paper in his hand.

"I think we can safely eliminate Hugh Norton from Cambridge PD's list of suspects, Ella." As she'd predicted, a hard, cold stare had replaced his earlier amiability. He leaned back, waving his arms expansively again. "Let's be intelligent here. I mean the man's a well-respected entrepreneur, a patron of the arts. How could he possibly be involved in anything shady?"

Ella watched the SAC closely. There was nothing to suggest the SAC did not believe the line he was feeding her. On the other hand, it sounded like such a crock of a certain something that Ella found it hard to believe the SAC was taken in by his own bull.

"Yes, of course, sir." *Let's be intelligent.* Had he just insulted her?

Well, she could play dumb as well as anyone else.

"But don't you think, sir, your friend might want a heads-up about the Cambridge Police calling to ask him questions?"

"Ella!" The SAC threw his eyes up, exasperated. "I thought we'd agreed that it wasn't necessary to let Cambridge PD have Norton's details. It would be an utter waste of their time and resources to go chasing after a man who's clearly not involved."

"Oh, I see." Ella nodded, eyes widening as though the penny had just dropped. "So, withhold Mr. Norton's details from Cambridge PD?" She gave him a bright thumbs-up. "I got it."

Walsh looked annoyed. "What about the other names you were supposed to give me?"

"I'll have them to you ASAP, sir. There are a couple of things Special Agent Markham wanted me to do." That was the truth. And Ella had promised Julia she'd call Mailand.

Walsh frowned. "What exactly does Blake need you to do?"

Ella hesitated. What could she tell the SAC that wouldn't compromise their investigation—if it turned out he was the source of their leak?

Walsh was still looking at her, disgruntled. She'd already ruffled his feathers. How much worse could it get if she deliberately let loose a cat among the pigeons?

"He wants me to research the name Wozniak," she said, enunciating the words carefully. "Sofia Wozniak may have been the woman driving the Mercedes Benz seen outside Cambridge PD's crime scene. Cambridge PD thinks Tony Reynolds was killed for what he knew about the Gardner heist —"

"The Gardner heist?" Walsh bleated the words after her.

"Yes, sir. Someone must've thought Reynolds had a line on the missing art. And Sofia Wozniak and the silver Mercedes Benz she was driving are mixed up in it somehow."

Chapter Fifty-Two

"Enjoying your stay, ma'am?"

The plump, rosy-cheeked receptionist at the Boston Plaza Hotel smiled brightly at Celine as she took their room key.

"Oh, absolutely." Celine returned her smile. "I don't think I've ever stayed in a hotel suite this opulent. And the food and room service have been just marvelous."

The receptionist—the brass nametag pinned to her breast had the name Molly engraved on it—beamed. Her gaze traveled over Celine's shoulders to where Julia stood by a magazine rack browsing one of the glossy publications on display.

"Headed out for some sightseeing?" Molly's eyes returned expectantly to Celine. She had the look of someone eager to provide visitor tips and recommendations to a tourist.

"Not exactly." Celine hesitated. She and Julia did need help. But it wasn't a museum, or restaurant, or public garden they were in search of.

They had a few hours to kill before their appointment with Penny later that afternoon. With nothing much to do until then, she and Julia had decided to see if they could sniff out a sculptor to take Reynolds' place.

Celine had promised Annabelle she'd find someone. And after last night's break-in, she was more than ever determined to keep that promise.

It would also be an opportunity to locate some of Reynolds' friends—assuming the man had any—and learn more about him. But the job was proving more elusive than the sculptor's clues.

Penny, when Celine had asked her advice, had been unable to provide much help.

"I'm sorry, Celine, we don't usually deal with sculptors. Reynolds was a one-off."

With nothing better coming to mind, she and Julia had planned on walking around the Cambridge neighborhood visiting local art galleries. Maybe one of them could recommend someone. Julia was also leafing through the many visitor's guides and directories on display in the hotel reception in preparation.

But perhaps there was a better alternative.

"Molly—may I call you that?" At the other woman's emphatic bob, Celine continued, "I guess you've heard about the sculptor Tony Reynolds' murder."

She'd decided to keep as close to the truth as possible. After all, they'd arrived in an unmarked armored vehicle, accompanied by a man who'd introduced himself as an FBI agent. Everyone at the hotel must've guessed she and Julia were no ordinary tourists.

"Oh, yes." The young woman looked appropriately distressed. "You ladies are helping out the FBI, right?"

"No." Celine shook her head. She didn't want to broadcast their role as unofficial consultants to the FBI. That was a surefire way of attracting trouble. And they'd attracted enough of it already.

The General must have surmised she was involved in the investigation, but at least this time he had no idea where she and Julia were staying.

"No. We're just here to provide our statements. You see I'd commissioned a few pieces from Tony Reynolds for my business. He was in California the day before he died—"

"Oh, my goodness! That's awful." Molly's hand rose to cover her gaping mouth.

"Yes, yes, it is. And now we've lost our sculptor—" Celine hoped she wasn't coming across as completely heartless. But fortunately Molly seemed to understand.

She bobbed her head. "You need another artist to continue the work. Of course."

"It has to be someone of his caliber. Someone with the ability to carry on his vision."

"To be sure." Molly nodded some more. She leaned over the desk. "You know you could try the Cambridge Sculptors' Association. I don't know for a fact that Tony Reynolds was a member. But he must have been."

Celine felt her spirits rise. Excellent! They were getting somewhere at last.

"The Cambridge Sculptors' Association? Is that close to where we are? Walking distance, perhaps?"

Molly wrinkled her nose apologetically. "It's about two miles from here, actually. And it's in Boston. But you know it's only a nine-minute drive—just across the Charles River."

"What's a nine-minute drive?" Julia had come up to the reception desk, armed with brochures and magazines.

"A sculptors' association Reynolds might have been a member of," Celine informed her. "We could go there, see if we can find someone to take over from him."

Left unsaid was the fact that they might also discover someone who could shed light on Reynolds' doings in the weeks before he'd been terminated. Someone that he might have confided in, although Celine sensed that Reynolds tended to play his cards close to his vest.

Still, even a man like that was apt to carelessly let fall a clue or two.

Flushed with her success at rattling the SAC's cage, Ella dialed Mailand's cell number. The Sheriff's detective didn't seem surprised to hear her voice.

"I figured I'd be hearing from either you or Special Agent Markham," he said the moment Ella identified herself. "First an attempted murder. Now a break-in. It doesn't take a brain surgeon to realize the two incidents are connected. I'm guessing the FBI's come to the same conclusion."

Ella smiled. The man was quick on the uptake. She appreciated that.

"You're absolutely right, Detective," she said.

She saw no reason to beat about the bush or to be cagey with local law enforcement. It was that kind of foolish attitude that ensured a case remained unsolved for as long as the Gardner theft had been.

Back in the nineties when the heist had taken place, if the FBI had allowed Boston PD a hand in the case, they might've recovered the art and put, if not the General himself, then at least his henchmen behind bars.

But that was in the past. Nothing to do with her. Ella reined her thoughts in, concentrating on the here and now.

She'd already conveyed Blake's suspicion that Reynolds might have been framed for the attempted murder in her earlier call. Now she quickly filled Mailand in on their latest working theory—that the sculptor had been killed for what he knew about the Gardner heist.

"So either Reynolds passed some information to Ms. Skye during his visit. Or our perp thinks he did," Mailand concluded once she'd finished.

"Exactly."

Ella leaned forward, pen poised in the air, about to explain the reason for her call. But Mailand wasn't done talking.

"I think we have enough evidence to confirm that theory, Ms. Rawlins," he said.

"I beg your pardon?" Ella brought her hand, and the pen grasped within it, down to her desk.

"You see Mrs. Curtis's cottage wasn't the only one broken into."

"It wasn't?" She was being rude, interrupting the man. But Ella was confused. Julia hadn't shared any of this with her. And Julia had gotten her information from Annabelle, hadn't she?

Ella mentioned this to Mailand.

"That's because Mrs. Curtis herself wasn't aware of it until we arrived and began checking out the other buildings," Mailand explained.

"And the other building broken into?" Ella asked, although she had a feeling she knew what Mailand's reply would be.

"Ms. Skye's cottage. The intruder—or intruders, hard to tell how many there were—must've broken into her cottage first. They did a better job concealing their steps there, locking the door when they left. But the place was thoroughly ransacked."

"Obviously, they found nothing there," Ella mused, "so they went on to Annabelle—Mrs. Curtis's—cottage." Where they'd found one of the models Reynolds had given Celine. The only one—judging by the description Julia had provided of it—that had any chance of containing clues to the whereabouts of the Gardner's stolen Rembrandts.

The stream of frustrated air she blew out must have been audible at the other end of the line because Mailand immediately caught on, and responded.

"The piece stolen from Mrs. Curtis's cottage was important, I gather."

It was a delicate albeit unnecessary attempt to fish for information.

The only reason Ella hadn't spelled out the facts was because she'd assumed Mailand had already divined the truth.

"It might have been." Ella explained its significance, suggesting he take charge of the other miniature pieces Reynolds had left with Celine.

"On the off chance," she said, "that they've taken the wrong thing."

It was unlikely. But there was no point leaving any stone unturned.

"No, there's not," Mailand agreed. "Although at this point, our only hope might be to put pressure on the mailman Reynolds likely saw when he visited here. He may not have been our intruder, but he may know something about what went down."

Ella was glad he'd brought up the subject. She'd been wondering how to broach it.

"I think we can safely conclude that whoever hired him, hired our intruder as well." She paused. She'd noticed his use of the definite article: *the mailman*; not *a mailman*.

Did it mean anything? Or had he just misspoken? It was her turn to probe.

"I take it you have some evidence that points to this mailman's involvement in the first incident."

"We've identified one guy who seems more than suspicious. Luckily, he's coming in for a polygraph today."

Chapter Fifty-Three

The Cambridge Sculptors' Association was on Newbury Street, behind Old South Church, a Gothic church Celine and Julia had visited on their last trip to Boston. The cab had just dropped them off when Julia's phone trilled.

"It's Ella," she said, putting the phone on speaker.

"Julia, I'm glad I caught you." Ella's voice emerged in a tinny blare from the former fed's iPhone. "I have troubling news. It turns out the General may have someone in Paso Robles feeding him information."

A twinge of alarm pulsed through Celine's chest, a psychic sign that unwelcome as the news was, Ella was right. Her gaze locked with Julia, her own worry mirrored in the agent's narrowed eyes.

Julia's knuckles whitened as her fingers tightened around her phone. "Someone at the winery?"

Dear God, that couldn't be true. Celine caught sight of her face in the glass gallery door across the street. The color had drained from it, leaving it a ghastly shade of white. A mole in the winery? That was impossible.

Andrea had been with them for years. Wanda had—only been with them a couple of months, but Celine was certain she would never do anything to betray her. And Annabelle—Annabelle was Dirck's sister.

Was it Bryan?

"No, nothing as bad as that." Ella was responding to Julia's question. "It's the mailman Reynolds was warning you about. The one he saw when he visited the winery. Mailand may have tracked down the guy. I called him a while back."

"And?" Julia bent her head over the phone. Celine hunched closer as well. The news that her cottage had also been broken into, she brushed aside. There'd been nothing there for the intruders to find.

"And this guy Mailand ferreted out?" she pushed impatiently.

"I'm getting to that," Ella said, unoffended by Celine's tetchiness. "When we asked Mailand to verify Reynolds' story, he questioned the van drivers and delivery guys again."

Mailand had detected signs of deception in one of the men.

"A scrawny, brown-haired, shifty-eyed, weasel-faced guy—that's in Mailand's words," Ella said. "So he had his guys do a little more digging. Turns out deliveries on this guy's route were delayed on the day Reynolds was in town."

They'd been delayed longer than usual, according to the residents on the mailman's route.

A little more digging had produced camera footage of the mail truck parked for an extended period on one of the residential streets outside downtown Paso Robles.

"You can see a blurry, uniformed figure climbing out of the van. But we have no idea where he went. The camera's across the street from where the van was parked, and didn't capture that. Then about fifteen minutes later, the truck pulls away from the curb—driving not in the direction of, but away from its usual route. It was gone long enough to have made the trip to the Mechelen and back."

"Meaning it was seen returning to this spot—the spot where it was initially parked?" Julia asked.

"Yup. It was parked there for another ten or fifteen minutes before resuming its normal route."

They digested this information. Then the faintest tendril of a thought stirred in Celine's mind.

"You said residents on this guy's route were complaining their mail was delayed longer than usual that day?"

"Yup. That's what they told Mailand's guys."

"Meaning it had happened before. Or was happening on a regular basis," Celine probed, unsure where she was going with this.

"I-uh-well, yes, I suppose that's what they were saying." Ella sounded embarrassed—and a little bewildered. "I guess neither one of us picked up on that."

Julia looked at Celine. "What's your point?"

Celine shrugged, chewing on her lip. "I'm just wondering if this guy made a habit of stopping on this particular street. If so, he might be meeting someone there."—a sharp intake of breath audible through the phone's speakers told Celine her suggestion had resonated with Ella—"Someone who's the General's agent. I don't see a man as cagey as the General making personal contact with a hired hand, so to speak."

"No, no, I guess not," Julia agreed.

"*Oh, God!* If you're right," Ella was sounding distressed, "we need to figure out who the mailman's handler is." They heard the scratching of a pen as she continued, "He's supposed to be coming in for a polygraph today. I'd better get on the horn with Mailand again."

"Thanks," Celine's voice joined with Julia's. But as Julia hung up, another disturbing thought occurred to her.

"I'm sure Mailand's on the right track. But I still don't see how this guy could've known about the sculptures Reynolds left with me."

Don't trust the mailman, the breeze whispered in her ear.

But she hadn't. She didn't even know the guy.

Chapter Fifty-Four

"This is it, I think." Julia stopped in the middle of the sidewalk and craned her neck up.

Forcing her thoughts away from their recent phone call, Celine looked up as well. Although their cab had dropped them almost directly in front of their destination, talking with Ella had taken them nearly a block east to Exeter Street.

They'd retraced their steps and were now standing in front of an unassuming building. A short flight of eight steps led up to a nondescript glass door. The street number painted in an elaborate gold script on the glass was the only sign of embellishment visible.

"Looks like it." Celine read the number. "160 Newbury Street. That's the number the receptionist back at the hotel gave me."

"They're not too big on promoting themselves, are they?" Julia commented dryly. Leaning heavily on the iron railing, she planted her foot on the first step. "No sign, no nothing." She propelled herself up to the next step.

"Probably just the way Reynolds liked it—cryptic, discreet to the point of being invisible." Celine followed Julia up the short flight. The steps were steeper than they looked. "Assuming he was a member."

It occurred to her that Reynolds might have hidden some clue to the whereabouts of the Gardner's Rembrandt here. It was the perfect place. How many people even knew the Cambridge Sculptors' Association existed—let alone that Reynolds might have been a member?

The glass door led into a spacious, brightly lit hall. Rows of frosted-glass light fixtures on the ceiling expertly illuminated gold-framed landscapes and still lifes. A seated bronze figure, contorted beyond belief, was displayed in the center of the room.

It had been ages since Celine had entered a contemporary art gallery. And she felt the familiar sensations of nostalgia mingled with nausea for the world she'd left. Been forced to leave, she reminded herself, breathing in the air-conditioned, sterile atmosphere of the place.

The art world at its condescending worst, she thought sensing Julia's warm presence behind her.

"This place looks dead," the former fed hissed into her ear. "Where is everybody?"

"It's like being in a long-abandoned but well-preserved crypt," Celine agreed in an equally low voice.

She searched the interior for any signs of a reception or lobby.

"You'd think they'd have someone here to greet visitors," Julia grumbled, following her gaze.

"I guess it's appointment-onl—"

"Need any help?"

The greeting bellowed out in a confident young voice was as startling as a loud clap of thunder on a sunny day. Celine pivoted around, following the sound until—

"Oh, good heavens, we didn't see you!" she exclaimed, her gaze colliding into a stout young woman with a side-swept, pixie-cut hairstyle. The desk she sat behind was set against the left wall, so close to the glass door, it was easily missed.

Why on earth hadn't the woman chosen to speak up sooner? The question buzzed insistently in Celine's mind as she and Julia approached the desk. The woman must have read her mind.

"We like to let visitors soak in the atmosphere," she said, lips pressed into a small smirk of self-satisfaction.

Like to let passersby show themselves for who they are, more likely, Celine thought. *Sophisticated patrons to be cultivated. Or ignorant rubes to be shown the door.*

They'd put themselves in the ignorant rube category, she guessed. She'd have to repair the impression or they'd get nowhere here.

Rising, the woman held out her hand. "Trina Kolev, Associate Secretary. What can I do for you?"

Celine shook the proffered hand, her eyes flickering toward Julia. The former fed inclined her head—in a barely visible gesture. They'd agreed earlier to let Celine take the lead at the Cambridge Association, and now Julia was confirming the strategy.

"We were told Tony Reynolds might be a member," Celine began.

Trina nodded. "That's right. One of our most prominent members, in fact, but . . ." She hesitated. "If you want him for a commission, you're out of luck. He's—"

"We know," Celine interjected gracefully. "That's why we're here. I'd commissioned a few pieces from him for my winery. I'd just approved his designs when we heard the news."

"And you're looking for someone else to complete the project." Trina was nothing if not blunt.

Clearly the sculptor's death wasn't regarded as a great loss.

Not giving Celine a chance to respond, Trina went on, "Well, you've come to the right place. We promote representational art—mainly sculpture, but we are making a foray into painting as well, as you can see." She gestured at the walls around them.

Likely because there weren't too many sculptors interested in representational art anymore, Celine guessed. Even Reynolds, judging by his installation in the Gardner, had been transitioning into the abstract.

But Julia, never able to abide glaring contradictions, couldn't help but comment.

"So the Cambridge Sculptors' Association is located in Boston—and promotes painters as well as sculptors?" The former fed's gaze moved pointedly to the small brass sign—engraved with the association's name—on the wall behind Trina.

Trina glanced over her shoulder at the sign. "I know, we should change the name." She turned back to them. "We're not in Cambridge anymore, and we obviously promote artists and sculptors from all over New England. Somehow no one's ever gotten around to it."

She tilted up her chin, inviting some type of response. Celine ignored it—as did Julia, her curiosity exhausted, now that the matter had been explained.

"Now, about our little problem," the former fed deftly brought the subject back to Reynolds.

Celine took the hint. "We're looking for someone willing to work from Reynolds' blueprints," she explained. "Someone familiar enough with his work—his process—to carry on in his spirit, as it were."

It was a roundabout way of asking whether Reynolds had been close to any of his fellow artists. Too subtle for Julia's taste obviously. The former fed went straight to the point.

"*Was* there anyone here he was close to?"

Trina flicked back the silken strands of hair that swept over her right eyebrow and gave them a hard stare, every sign of accommodation gone.

"Okay"—she waved her hands in an emphatic gesture—"I can give you someone willing to work with the guy's blueprints. Anyone here would be able to emulate his style. But if it has to be someone close to the guy, I can't help you."

She sat back down, a belligerent expression on her face. Celine sighed. They'd been relegated to ignorant rube category again. She'd have to resurrect the conversation somehow.

You need to establish a rapport with her, Celine, Sister Mary Catherine advised.

It took a second to understand what she needed to do.

"I guess I'm not surprised," she responded. "I did get the sense he was an intensely private man."

Trina frowned. "Well, no, I wouldn't say that exactly. He was friendly enough. Generous with his time. Ran a couple of workshops here for the neighborhood kids—clay modeling and oil painting—"

"*Oil painting?*" Julia erupted, interrupting the conversation again.

But this time Celine didn't fault her. Reynolds had been an excellent draftsman. That had been evident in the blueprints he'd left with her and in the sketches they'd seen in his apartment.

But a painter—in oil?

Trina smiled—a sly, smug grin of pleasure at the effect her information was having on them.

"Most people find that hard to believe," she said. "But he was pretty good, actually. Well versed in the techniques of just about every artist from Rembrandt to Degas. The kids loved his workshops."

Chapter Fifty-Five

"Well, what d'ya think?" Soldi pressed after a while.

The question made Blake feel like an antiques appraiser at a road show. Aware of Soldi's expectant gaze on him, he kept his eyes on the canvases propped against the wall.

He'd been allowed several minutes to soak in the stash. Now he was expected to deliver an opinion.

Fake—or fortune?

He was inclined to think fake, although he would've been hard put to explain why. The draftsmanship was excellent. The canvases were the right size, lined with the expected craquelure—a fine pattern of hairline cracks that covered the paintings.

Anyone with a glancing familiarity with the works stolen from the Gardner would've assumed they were looking at the three Dutch works still outstanding: *Lady and Gentleman in Black*; *Christ in the Storm on the Sea of Galilee*; and Flinck's *Landscape with an Obelisk*.

But would that assumption be correct?

Blake was inclined to think not. "This may not be quite the find you think it is, Soldi."

"Oh yeah?" Soldi's voice was dripping with skepticism. "How do you figure that?"

That was a much harder question to answer.

Despite poring over the Gardner files from the time he'd been assigned to the case, Blake didn't recall all the minute details that could help identify the stolen works should they show up. But one fact stood out in his memory.

Not every stolen work had been an oil on canvas. Flinck's landscape was an oil on panel.

He pointed to it. "That's supposed to be on oak panel. Not canvas."

"You mean it's a copy—like a forgery!" One of Soldi's men emitted a low whistle of awe. "And you think Reynolds did that? Hey, not bad for a sculptor! Guy must've been talented."

Blake shook his head. Detecting 101: don't make assumptions; ask questions. Sure, he'd made a colossal one himself: if the Flinck was a copy, then so were the other two. But he was confident he was right.

"There's no evidence this is Reynolds' handiwork. But if it is, I want to know why it was created. And for whom?"

Hugh Norton, SAC Walsh's golfing partner? Or the General?

"And if it isn't," he continued aloud, "I'd want to know how he came across these and why he had them stashed away here."

Had the forged stash been one of Fussy Phil's motives for killing Reynolds?

"Well, Markham." Soldi rubbed his hands together. "Sounds like you have your work cut out for you." He jabbed a finger in the direction of the officers behind them. "Want I should have one of the boys carry these to your car? ADA Campari insisted we call you guys the minute she saw this.

"Cambridge PD isn't qualified to deal with art crime and forgery. The murder obviously is our case. But this . . ." Soldi spread his hands wide, lifting his shoulders in an exaggerated shrug.

That drew Blake's gaze toward the man. So that was it. The FBI could shove off as far as Reynolds' murder was concerned. And they could do what they would with this cache of forged works.

Well, that wasn't going to wash.

"Sorry, Soldi. Whether you like it or not, the FBI's involved. Reynolds was murdered for something he knew or something he had." He pointed to the paintings. "How this figures into it, I don't know. But it obviously does. As such the FBI is involved." He gestured with his hand at his throat. "Right up to here."

Soldi's features twisted into a scrunched-up, sour expression, as though he'd inadvertently sunk his teeth into a large lemon.

"ADA Campari isn't going to like that," he mumbled.

"One other thing," Blake added, ignoring the Deputy Superintendent's grumbling. "There's a security camera over the entrance. You guys check it out yet?"

The sour look on Soldi's face deepened. "Yup."

"Find anything interesting?"

Chapter Fifty-Six

Forger.

The word floated unbidden into Celine's mind as she stood before Trina Kolev's desk at the Cambridge Sculptors' Association. It was accompanied by an image—a hoard of gold-framed paintings stacked against a wall.

They've been found, Celine. Sister Mary Catherine's voice sounded in her ear. *But that's not important. It's over. Long over.*

Before she had time to react, Julia's voice asking a question and Trina's response intruded into her consciousness.

"I don't think anyone outside of this place knew. He was so talented. I don't know why he didn't do more with it."

"Did anyone try to find out why?" Julia probed.

Trina shook her head. "It wasn't a subject you could broach with him. Not without having him bite your head off. That's when you realized you couldn't really get close to him. He didn't allow anyone inside. There was a clear line drawn, and you couldn't step beyond."

"He didn't think he was original enough—not in oil, not on canvas." The words spilled out of Celine's mouth before she could stop herself. She stopped short, gasping.

A momentary sense of panic filled her as Trina turned toward her, her dark eyes hard, questioning.

"That's usually the case with artists, she means." Julia rushed to fill in the void of silence that had engulfed them. "The fear that they aren't good enough or original enough to succeed."

"You could say it's almost a cliché," Trina replied with a quick roll of her eyes. "I don't think that was Reynolds' problem, though."

"Well"—Celine was desperate to change the subject—"any suggestions about whom we might approach?"

Trina shrugged. "We have a couple of guys, I guess." She pulled out two cards from the brass holder on her desk. "Try these folks. But the guy you want is Mitch Finlay." She looked up at them. "Can't give you his contact details. He's not a member. But I'm sure he'll be at the memorial—"

"What memorial?" Julia demanded. Not the one Penny had planned, surely, Celine thought. The museum director had barely begun organizing the event.

"For Tony Reynolds—at the Gardner Museum," Trina said. "They're having it over the weekend. Talk about short notice. The program was emailed to us just this morning. I don't know if there'll be much happening tomorrow. But they're setting aside time for personal tributes on Sunday. I'd be surprised if Mitch hadn't been invited to say something."

That piqued Celine's interest. "Because they were close?"

"Because they shared studio space—years ago when they were both starting out."

❧

"Yes, we reuse the tapes," Bill, Reynolds' bespectacled, middle-aged landlord, informed Blake. "No reason not to, right?"

He looked eagerly at Blake, seeking approval of this idiotic decision.

Blake refused to give it to him, and Bill's eyes shuffled away.

The reason for Vince Soldi's gloom was becoming apparent with every passing minute.

The security camera, and any footage it might have captured, was utterly useless for their investigation. Each week's tape was recycled and written over the next week.

Bill had already conveyed this information over the phone to Soldi, but the Deputy Superintendent had summoned him to the warehouse when Blake started asking to see tapes from the weeks and months leading up to the murder.

He'd wanted to know when the three canvases had been transported to the warehouse. In the days prior to Reynolds' murder? Or several weeks or months before? By whom? Reynolds himself or somebody else?

The answers would help Blake figure out the significance of the stash and whether it bore any relevance to Reynolds' murder.

"You see, if there's nothing suspicious on the tape. . ." Bill scratched his ear sheepishly, his voice trailing off.

"Tell Special Agent Markham about the footage from the other night," Soldi commanded, his face flushed and red from the heat.

They were gathered outside the warehouse now, the sun beating down on them. The corrugated entrance to the warehouse had been rolled down and locked, Soldi taking charge of the master key. All but a couple of his men had left—after hefting the forged cache into the trunk of Blake's sedan.

The other night? Soldi meant the night before last—the night of Reynolds' murder.

Bill scratched his ear some more; it was beginning to turn red.

"There's no footage, I'm afraid."

"Why not?" Blake's eyes bore into Bill's face, pinning him like a squirming butterfly.

"I—uh—don't know. Glitch in the camera, perhaps."

"Looks like it was erased," Soldi informed him. "Deliberately. There's a noticeable jump in the video."

"Erased?" Blake turned to face him. "By whom?"

"The dame who was poking around here last night would be my best guess," Soldi replied. "She's the only person recorded approaching the warehouse door this week."

"A woman—you recognize her?"

Soldi shrugged. "The footage is too grainy to make anything out. See for yourself." He waved the two remaining officers over and directed them to play the security camera tape for Blake on their portable player.

Blake crouched down to peer at the screen. Soldi was right, the footage was grainy. And the tiny screen on the player made it hard to see very much.

But the woman's figure and the way she moved were quite distinctive—memorable even.

Chapter Fifty-Seven

"You sensed something in there, didn't you?" Julia said when they were back on the street.

Celine turned to look at the building they'd just left. The image she'd seen was vivid in her mind—gold-framed canvases stacked against a wall.

"I'm not sure it had anything to do with Reynolds' murder." She turned to meet her friend's piercing gaze. "Or what he knew about the Gardner heist."

"But what did you see?"

Julia had planted herself on the sidewalk, oblivious to the stream of approaching shoppers parting to circumnavigate her.

Celine tugged on her elbow. "Let's walk a little, and I'll tell you." She described the image she'd seen and the word that had accompanied it as they headed east toward Exeter Street.

"I think Reynolds was a forger before he turned to sculpting."

It was the only surmise that made sense based on what they'd learned about the sculptor. A talented oil painter who preferred to keep his gifts under wraps.

She felt Julia's eyes on her as she shared it.

"And that's what Sofia found out about him?"

Celine nodded. "That's why she broke up with him. But he'd long given it up by then. I heard him tell her that. Back in his apartment, I mean."

"There must have been far more to it for her to react the way she did." Julia stopped, squinting up at the sun. "Scandalized, disgusted to the point of breaking off her engagement?"

"Sister Mary Catherine told me they'd been found."

"The works Reynolds forged?" Julia turned to her, blue eyes narrowed, suspicious. "Where?"

"I have no idea. Maybe in the warehouse Cambridge PD was supposed to be searching. The point is, it's not relevant. It's a distraction."

"Then why do you keep seeing it?" Julia demanded.

Celine shook her head. "I wish I knew." But there'd been no mistaking her guardian angel's message. The forged paintings were a distraction. "All I can tell you is that they were planted to lead us astray."

"*Planted?*" Julia's eyebrows rose.

I'm not sure why I phrased it that way. I just meant . . ." She stopped, unable to answer Julia's questions. "I don't think Reynolds' past had any bearing on what he discovered about the Gardner heist."

No direct bearing, Sister Mary Catherine corrected her.

What was that supposed to mean?

Before Celine could ponder the question, an invisible force pushed her head back, forcing her to look up. They'd been about to pass under a wine-colored sign that projected out from the brownstone at the corner of Newbury and Exeter.

Rose Antiques.

She turned toward the brownstone. The name was painted in gold letters on the glass pane of the slate-colored door as well.

"Can we go in there?"

Celine started up the short flight of stairs without waiting for an answer.

Why she felt so drawn to the place she didn't know. There were art galleries and antiques stores aplenty on Newbury. But something within her was tugging her toward this antiques store.

As though the answers they needed were stored right here, waiting to be unlocked.

⚘

"That's your woman, Soldi." Blake jabbed a finger at the screen of the portable player as he rose, relieved to stretch out his cramped knees. "The woman who slipped a sleeping potion to your guy yesterday."

It took Soldi some effort to recall the name. Blake could see the gears churning in his brain as he processed the information.

"So-ofia . . .?" He stared at Blake.

"Yup, Sofia Wozniak." Blake uttered the last name without thinking about it, and regretted his indiscretion instantly when he saw the stunned look on Soldi's face.

"You found out her last name? Already?"

"That is Sofia," Bill confirmed, studying the screen. "I remember her."

He turned to them, a goofy smile on his round, soft features.

Jesus F-in' Christ! Blake cursed himself. He'd carelessly dropped sensitive information within earshot of a civilian. What had he been thinking? This was how leaks happened. Not because someone had been bribed. But because someone—Blake himself in this case—had been stupid.

But Bill seemed oblivious to the look of consternation on Blake's face.

"She was Tony's girlfriend. He never brought her here. But he carried a photo of her. He was so taken with her. Pity it didn't last. He was never the same after they broke up."

"Photo?" Soldi demanded. "My men didn't find any photo."

"She must've taken it back when they broke up," Blake said, wanting to deflect from this.

"Or when she broke into his apartment," Soldi pointed out.

"Could be why she broke in," Blake suggested, although he wasn't sure he believed it himself. Not after seeing the footage from the security camera.

"Wonder why she came here," Bill mused.

Blake silently cursed the man for putting that question on Soldi's radar.

"Must've been looking for that photo of herself," Bill went on. "Tony never returned it, you know. Kept it in his wallet for a long time after she dumped him, poor guy." He shook his head.

"She was in search of something, no doubt," Soldi said, his eyes on the video footage replaying on the screen. "She sure didn't bring anything in."

And she hadn't taken the stack of paintings out, Blake added to himself. So what had she been interested in?

The same thing that Reynolds' killer was searching for? Some hint about where the Rembrandt the sculptor had information on was located?

They needed to find Sofia. Pronto.

Chapter Fifty-Eight

A bell chimed as Celine twisted the brass door handle of Rose Antiques.

The place was disconcertingly empty of people, but a woman's vibrant voice called out, "I'll be with you in a second. Make yourself comfortable. Look around."

"Why are we here?" Julia muttered, her footsteps muted on the blue carpeted floor.

"I don't know. Something to do with Reynolds, I think." Out on the street, his presence had been palpable—his hand forcing her head back so she could see the store sign. But why had Reynolds wanted her to come in here? What was she supposed to see?

Celine's eyes swept the store, searching for some kind of clue that could explain why she'd been drawn to this place.

The store had wall-to-wall carpeting, scuffed and somewhat worse for wear. Furniture filled the room they stood in, and she could see more in the room adjoining it. Glass cases were crammed with jewelry. Table lamps and bric-a-brac jostled for space on floating wooden shelves and every inch of wall space was covered in paintings.

A torrent of questions rushed through Celine's brain. Had the Gardner's stolen Rembrandts somehow made it to this antiques store? The slender bronze vases on an end table caught her eye.

Were they authentic Shang dynasty vessels? Or twenty-first-century reproductions?

She picked one up, instinctively turning it upside-down to examine the bottom. If it had ever belonged to the Gardner, a label with the accession number printed or penciled in would be affixed to the bottom.

"I don't think that's what you think it is," Julia said, quietly coming up behind her.

"Those are junk." It was the same voice that had called out to them. "Reproduction Shang dynasty wine vessels that tourists buy. I'm actually not sure why they're even out here."

Celine whirled around. A name reverberated in her head, but her guardian angel's voice was drowned out by the rush of blood draining into her brain.

A slender, attractive woman about her own height—five-eight—stood before her, her dark hair pulled back into a loose bun. She smiled at Celine.

"I have some authentic Chinese bronzes, if you're interested in that kind of thing."

Celine stared at the woman; she was having trouble breathing. She stole a glance at Julia, but her friend appeared to have noticed nothing out of the ordinary.

"You said these were junk," the former fed said, holding up one of the faux Shang dynasty vessels. "Why do you have them displayed so prominently then?"

The woman pursed her lips, lifting her shoulders in a delicate shrug. "I guess my assistant thought they stood a chance of being snapped up now. You see they were made by—"

"Tony Reynolds, your murdered lover," Celine breathed the words out.

"Celine!" Julia expostulated, head pivoting from Celine to the store owner's ashen features.

"You're Sofia, aren't you?" Celine's eyes never left the older woman's face. Her age was beginning to show now—faint lines and wrinkles revealing themselves in the smooth white veneer of her face. "Sofia Wozniak."

"Oh, *Jesus Christ*, it is her." Julia gaped open-mouthed at the woman who'd sprinted past them down Reynolds' stairs the day before.

❧

"I don't understand."

The woman they'd recognized as Sofia backed away. The counter behind her stopped her progress. She reached out, gripping it with white knuckles.

"Who are you two? How do you know my name?"

Tell her, Celine. Reynolds had materialized, arms folded, an expression of pure venom on his face. *Tell her how you know. Tell her you're psychic.*

Celine glanced at him; she had no intention of revealing her abilities to Sofia.

"You passed us by on the stairs yesterday," Julia responded to Sofia. "Do you remember? In Tony Reynolds' apartment?"

"I don't know what you mean." Sofia shook her head. "We were lovers once, Tony and I. But it was over seven years ago. I haven't seen him since."

Seven years ago. When Celine had been cast out from the Montague Museum? When Laurie, her intern, had gotten herself killed? When Hugh Norton—her eyes were drawn toward the faux bronze gus.

That's when I made those, Reynolds told her. *Seven years ago.*

Celine knew instantly without having to be told why he'd copied the bronzes. Before she could confirm her impressions, Julia's words penetrated her senses.

"You may not have kept in touch with Reynolds, but you were in his apartment yesterday, Sofia. You were seen by more than one law enforcement agent—one of them from the FBI. I'm sure the man you drugged remembers you pretty well."

"You're law enforcement?" Sofia's dark eyes were wide—a trapped deer backed into a corner. A vein in her neck pulsed rapidly.

"Julia Hood, FBI." Julia held out her badge, not bothering to preface her identification with the usual and more accurate adjective—*former*. She tucked the badge back into her skirt pocket.

Ask her why she stole from me, Celine, Reynolds demanded, his arms still folded.

"What did you take from his apartment?" Celine turned to Sofia.

Sofia's eyes—wary—turned from Julia to her and then returned to Julia. "I didn't take anything, I swear it."

"Not even a photograph?"

Sofia's gaze snapped toward Celine. "Why would I want any photographs of him?" Tears stained the mascara around her eyes. "I was done with the man—a long time ago."

But the intent was there all along. Ask her why she was in my warehouse.

"Wait, she was in your warehouse?" Celine blurted out aloud.

"Who're you talking to?" Sofia's screech of alarm startled her. Celine turned to face her.

"You were in Tony Reynolds' warehouse last night. What were you doing there?"

She heard the door swing open as she spoke, heard muffled footsteps on the carpet.

"Answer the question, Ms. Wozniak"—it was Blake's voice, colder and harder than carbon steel; how had *he* tracked them down?—"What *were* you doing in Tony Reynolds' warehouse?"

Celine assumed he'd held out his badge, identified himself as an FBI agent. But her eyes remained glued on Sofia, who shrank farther back against the onslaught of their questions.

Chapter Fifty-Nine

"Don't bother denying it." Blake strode across the carpeted floor. "We know you were at Reynolds' warehouse. The security camera he'd installed picked you up clear as day."

Sofia flinched as though she'd been struck, but her lips remained tightly clamped together. If they were hoping for an admission of guilt, they weren't going to get it.

She's a stubborn woman, that one, Reynolds said. *Always been that way.*

What was she looking for? Celine pressed him, but Reynolds just shook his head. *Ask her*, he persisted. He crossed his arms, staring at the back of Blake's close-cropped head.

"What were you looking for?" the FBI agent demanded again.

Sofia gripped the corner of the counter, her knuckles white.

"What did you take, Sofia?" Julia's tone was gentler than it had been before.

"Nothing." Sofia's gaze swept past Blake toward Julia; her face was wreathed in a desperate uncertainty. "I didn't take anything. I didn't fi—" She stopped herself abruptly and glanced away.

Spit it out, Sofia, Reynolds urged, although it was doubtful she heard him *What were you trying to steal from me?*

In an instant, he was at her side, so close to her, he could've reached out to touch her. So close that had he been alive, she would've felt his warm breath on her neck. She may not have been psychic, but Celine wondered if Sofia could sense Reynolds' presence all the same.

What were you trying to steal from me?

"Tony thinks you were working with his killer," Celine said. The remark acted, as she'd intended, like a jolt of electricity on Sofia's nerves.

Her head shot up. "I have no idea how he got himself killed. Or who killed him." Her back stiffened, her eyes blazed. "I don't know because I'm not a criminal. I don't associate with criminals."

"Not a criminal." Blake laughed. "You could've fooled me. Drugging a police officer, breaking and entering—not once, but twice. Those don't seem like the actions of an upstanding citizen."

Sofia flinched again, as though she'd been slapped, and looked down. She was struggling with herself, Celine sensed, wondering how much to reveal to them. What Celine couldn't understand was why.

"It would be easier to just tell us the truth," she urged.

"And if you work with us, we won't have to arrest you," Julia reminded her. "I don't think Daddy would take too kindly to that, do you?"

That evidently got Sofia's attention. She was close to forty, yet her father's approval—or lack thereof—still served as a strong incentive. That was Julia's guess—Celine picked up the thought passing through her friend's mind.

But it wasn't a desire for approval that kept Sofia tethered to her father. It was something else. Celine focused on Sofia, struggling to interpret the waves of sensations washing toward her.

But the other woman must have tamped down her emotions; the tenuous impressions subsided as abruptly as they'd begun.

Sofia raised her head, facing them squarely. "All right. I did break into Tony's warehouse. There was something I needed to find. Something that isn't his to keep."

Her words had whipped Reynolds' face into a perfect storm of fury.

It isn't her pal's to keep, either, he spat out. *Tell her that.*

"Tony says it isn't your friend's to keep either," Celine informed the other woman.

Sofia's face crumpled. "I know. I'm just trying to help her get away from her husband. This is all the leverage we have."

I don't buy that, Reynolds scoffed. *Her friend's just a gold-digging whore.*

Celine ignored the dead man. She didn't think Sofia was lying. She stole a glance at the others. Both Julia and Blake seemed convinced as well.

"His possession of stolen goods, you mean?" Blake inched closer to Sofia. "Stolen artworks?"

Sofia nodded. "He showed it to her once. That's how she knows what he has."

"One item. Definitely stolen. Have you seen it?" Blake pressed.

Sofia shook her head. "No. But I believe her, Agent. She wouldn't lie to me."

"And this has what to do with Tony Reynolds now?"

Julia's question was a brusque reminder that Sofia was still a wanted woman with questions to answer, although it was clear to Celine how the sculptor had been involved.

Sofia seemed to welcome the question, however, turning eagerly to the former fed.

"He must've asked Tony to keep the item for him"—She was going to great lengths to avoid naming it, Celine noticed—"It's not in the house my friend shared with her husband. And Tony is the only person we can think of who wouldn't bat an eyelid at something this shady."

Celine gasped, feeling the gut-wrenching pain Sofia's contempt was causing Reynolds as surely as if the woman had physically assaulted her. He'd never stopped loving her; and he'd never stopped hurting from her withdrawal.

Sweet, loving Sofia. Reynolds' features twisted. *Always ready to see the best in me.*

He needs to make peace with her, Celine, Sister Mary Catherine told her. *They need to be at peace with each other before he can leave.*

Celine didn't have to be told twice. Sofia was in agony, too. She'd seen the tears welling up, the gaunt, haunted expression whenever Reynolds' name was mentioned.

"Tony was trying to return the Rembrandt, Sofia," she said. "It was a Rembrandt, wasn't it?"

"How do you know what he was trying to do?" Sofia's head snapped toward her. "Did he tell you so? You were a fool to believe him."

"He made a call to the Gardner on the day he was killed," Celine said quietly. "He tried repeatedly to get in touch with Penny Hoskins."

"We believe he was killed to prevent him from talking," Blake confirmed.

How he'd divined what she was trying to do, Celine didn't know, but she was grateful to him all the same. Blake could be mulish and pigheaded, but when push came to shove, he'd also shown himself to be extremely insightful.

"But—" Sofia was clearly having trouble believing them.

There's no point. She'll never believe you, Reynolds sounded a bitter warning. *It's your word against Daddy's.* He faded away.

But Celine felt compelled to continue.

"He was no forger, either, Sofia. He'd given that up a long time ago."

"That reminds me." Before Sofia could react, Blake twisted abruptly around and headed for the door. The bell chimed again as he pushed the door open.

"There's something I need you ladies to see."

❧

Sofia barely registered Blake's departure. Her lustrous dark eyes remained fixed on Celine's face. She chewed on her lip and swallowed, obviously working up the nerve to ask a question.

"How do you know so much about Tony?" she eventually asked, bringing each word out as though it were a hard pebble she'd swallowed. She paused. "Were you his latest?"

"His latest client," Celine clarified. She stepped closer to Sofia, taking her cold, bloodless palm in hers. "Listen to me, Sofia. I'm psychic. That's how I know Tony never stopped loving you. That's how I know he was striving not to fall back into his old life."

Sensing Sofia was opening up to her, Celine continued. "Did Tony know a man called Hugh Norton?"

A harsh laugh erupted from Sofia, breaking the spell Celine had woven. "Are you kidding me? It was Hugh Norton who helped nurture Tony's talents, turning him from forgery to a legitimate career in art."

"I don't think Hugh Norton is quite the noble gentleman you take him for, Sofia," Celine began. But she'd clearly lost Sofia.

Sofia pulled her hand away from Celine's. "I have no idea who you are, but you're no psychic if you're suggesting Hugh Norton had anything to do with Tony's foray into criminality."

Great! With her characteristic bluntness, she'd managed to shatter the fragile connection she'd forged with the other woman. *Nice going, Celine*, she chided herself.

Fortunately, Julia was quick to step in.

"Tell us more about Hugh Norton," she invited Sofia with a smile. "How did he and Tony get to know each other?"

"Tony was fifteen when he came to Rose Antiques. He'd brought a Degas sketch with him. It was so good, it fooled my mother into believing it was authentic. She purchased it, and immediately contacted Hugh Norton."

"Because Norton has a taste for Impressionists," Julia surmised. They already knew that to be the case, but Celine knew Julia was simply trying to keep Sofia talking.

"Yes." Sofia nodded. "True art lovers are as much fascinated by an artist's sketches and preparatory work as by their finished paintings. Hugh Norton was no different."

Just like the General's partner. The thought surfaced unbidden into Celine's mind, but she kept it to herself.

"And it was Norton who discovered the Degas wasn't authentic?" She heard Julia asking.

"It was the signature." Sofia smiled. "Degas never signed anything he wasn't planning to sell or exhibit. After his death, his estate stamped all of his remaining works. Many of his sketches and drawings carry that red stamped impression of his signature. But Tony had used red ink to recreate it."

"He thought Degas had signed his works in red," Celine voiced the thought as it entered her mind.

"Yes. He was looking at images in his books. It's hard to tell it's a stamped, not a handwritten, signature. And the watermark was all wrong.

Norton had the money to have an expert examine the paper. He's always been careful like that about his acquisitions."

"I take it he didn't press charges," Julia said.

"Because Tony was just a boy—but clearly a very talented one. Norton thought his talent should be developed."

So he could become an art forger. Celine was quite sure that was the reason for Norton's interest in the young Reynolds.

Her face must have mirrored her skepticism because Sofia turned to her.

"You can talk to Tony's teacher if you like. He'll confirm what I'm telling you."

"His teacher?"

"Frank van Mieris. He's retired now, but he was a BU art professor at the time."

"Yes." Celine's eyes flickered toward Julia. They exchanged a glance. "Yes, we know who he is."

Van Mieris had taught Simon Underwood and her former employers, Dirck Thins and John Mechelen, as well.

With his interest in understanding the techniques of classical painters, van Mieris's influence would've ensured that Reynolds developed an expertise in the precise techniques used by any painter from the Dutch masters to the impressionists.

The perfect skill for an art forger to possess.

Chapter Sixty

Things were falling into place, Blake thought. Sofia had been telling Julia and Celine about Hugh Norton's connection with Reynolds when he'd re-entered the store, lugging the canvases in with him.

He stole a glance at Celine. Damn! He should never have mistrusted her intuition. She'd been right about Hugh Norton; right to suspect a connection between the art patron and their murder victim.

And she'd somehow known—before he'd even had a chance to reveal the canvases he'd discovered—that Reynolds was a forger. The van Mieris connection Sofia had revealed just sealed the deal.

But his hopes deflated as soon as they'd crested. They didn't have a prayer in hell of proving Norton was connected to the Gardner theft. Norton wasn't the only art collector with a passion for Impressionist works and sketches. Heck, Isabella Gardner had possessed the same passion herself.

Blake cleared his throat, announcing his return. When the women looked his way, he hefted the canvases across the room and onto the wooden counter.

"Found these at his warehouse," he said. "I take it you saw them when you went in."

Sofia dipped her chin, her lips pursed. "Those are Tony's works, if that's what you're asking."

Julia and Celine lowered their heads, studying the works intently. "They're remarkably good," Julia said after a while. "But if he copied these, he must've had access to the originals."

"That's what I thought, too," Sofia said. "Or someone he knew did. He refused to tell me anything about it, though. That's why we broke up. I just couldn't live with his lies."

"He didn't want to hurt you," Celine said.

It was clear to Blake she had no idea what the words meant. She was merely repeating a message—from her guardian angel, he supposed. And Sofia, judging by the hard expression on her face, was having a hard time believing Celine. What could possibly make the truth—whatever it was—more painful than Reynolds' lies?

"So you recognize these?" Blake probed. "He showed them to you?"

"No. Hugh Norton discovered that Tony had gone back to forgery. He was absolutely distraught. He knew we were engaged, so he felt honor-bound to tell my father—"

"Who insisted you break it off with your fiancé," Julia guessed.

Catching movement out of the corner of his eyes, Blake swiveled around in time to see Celine approaching an end table. She snatched up a bronze gu-like vessel.

"That would've been around the time Tony made these, right? One for your mother, too?"

"My aunt," Sofia explained.

Celine frowned as though the explanation didn't make sense. "Your father's wife is—"

"My aunt," Sofia said firmly. "My mother died a few years after Tony showed up here."

"But he is your father?"

"He would like to be," Sofia said.

"But—?"

Sofia shook her head. "I don't want to discuss my family, okay? It isn't relevant."

Time to take back the reins of conversation, Blake decided. "There's just one thing I want to ascertain: These were not in Tony's possession when you broke up with him, were they?"

"No, I told you. Hugh Norton found them."

"And took them away." Things were beginning to fall into place. "The question is"—he looked at Julia and Celine—"how did they get back into his warehouse?"

"They were planted," Celine said immediately. Was she reading his mind? Or had she worked that out?

"Nonsense!" Sofia scoffed. "Why would anyone do such a thing?"

"To confuse the issue," Blake said. He was about to continue when Julia interrupted.

"How do you even know they were planted? Does the security camera footage show that? Are you saying Sofia here brought them in?"

"The footage from the night he was killed is missing," he told her. "There's a clear jump in the video—evidence it was tampered with."

"By whoever killed him?"

"Who else?" he asked.

"Couldn't they have been looking for whatever it was Sofia was in search of?"

"His killer found it," Sofia gasped. But Blake ignored her, responding to Julia instead.

"They could have, but clearly they didn't find it. Why break into Annabelle's cottage and Celine's?" He turned to Celine. "Ella filled me in."

He was letting her know that he was aware she'd avoided calling him; she had his cell phone number. She'd chosen not to call. Not that he could blame her after his behavior last evening.

But he didn't have to like it.

Color rushed into Celine's pale cheeks. Her eyes darted away. Was he still unforgiven?

Had they been alone, he'd have pressed her for an answer. But now—now there were other matters to deal with. He forced his mind back to Sofia Wozniak.

"What exactly was it you were looking for?"

She bit her lip, uncertain. "I'll need to talk with my friend before I discuss this with you. It's a question of her divorce. The alimony she's owed." She spread her hands wide, begging him to understand.

"Can you give us her name? Persuade her to talk to us?" Blake didn't think anything he could do or say would make Sofia budge. And the problem was he understood her reluctance all too well.

"I can't. Please, you've got to understand. I can't risk having her husband find out where she is."

"If she comes forward," Celine suddenly said, "can you protect her?" Her eyes were on him—vividly green. They were both remembering the shots that had killed Grayson Pike four months back. She'd asked if they could protect him. And he'd said yes.

And then failed miserably. Failed to protect Grayson. Failed to protect her. She was still staring at him, eager, hopeful.

Blake wished he could be as confident as he'd been back then. Wished he could provide the reassurance she wanted. But he couldn't lie to her.

"I can't provide any guarantees. You know that, Celine."

She didn't answer, turning to Sofia instead. "You're right to fear for your friend, Sofia. She is in danger. I just think it might be far worse if she remains hidden instead of coming forward. They will find her. No matter how careful you are, they will find her."

Chapter Sixty-One

Penny was not available to meet when they arrived at the Gardner Museum.

"I'm afraid Ms. Hoskins is still at a meeting," the woman behind the reception desk in the lobby informed Celine. "It's running late, and she sends her apologies." The receptionist's gaze—appropriately regretful—swept past Celine to encompass Julia and Blake as well.

It was obviously an act, but one that Celine appreciated, nevertheless. The woman had deliberately adopted a tone and manner calculated to assuage any feelings of resentment the prospect of a long wait might induce.

It was soothing.

Just what you needed in someone hired to greet visitors. And just what Celine herself needed. She smiled gratefully at the woman.

"But you're welcome to wait in the living room." With a graceful hand, the receptionist pointed westward. "It's back that way, and to your right."

The session in the Richard E. Floor living room was coming to an end—the host for the week and the visitors who'd shared his collection preparing to head out for lunch. But the buttery aroma of freshly baked shortbread and steaming Brazilian coffee drew Celine in.

She lifted the pot and turned, about to offer a cup to Julia, when she realized—with a sinking sensation of dismay—that it was Blake who'd followed her to the refreshments table.

Her eyes searched the room, locating Julia amidst the departing throng. The former fed had gone up to the host, engaging him in conversation about what looked like an eclectic collection of meteorites, stamps, and Russian nested dolls.

Celine couldn't imagine coming up with the words to discuss a collection like the one showcased here. But Julia had never wanted for words and never seemed to have any compunctions about engaging perfect strangers in conversation. An excellent trait for anyone in law enforcement to have.

If only she hadn't chosen to exercise it at that precise moment. Celine didn't want to be left alone with Blake.

She forced herself to meet his eyes. "Like some coffee?" she offered, giving the pot a slight wiggle.

"Sure thing." To her astonishment, he stepped forward, took the pot from her in one easy motion, poured out a cup, handed it to her, and then poured himself one.

"Listen, about last evening," he began after he'd taken a sip from his Styrofoam cup.

"It's fine." She cut short his apology. "You don't always have to agree with me."

"I know." He smiled warmly at her. "But I don't always have to be an ass about it."

His eyes rested on her face, intent, serious, expressing a need she wasn't ready to deal with.

She looked down, chewing on her lip.

"I shouldn't resent questions," she said, wanting to deflect them both onto a safer path. "They force me to think and see more clearly. I'm no use to you if I can't answer the specific questions you have."

He remained silent for a while, then he took the hint, retreating to more mundane matters.

"You were right about Hugh Norton. I'm beginning to realize that."

She listened carefully as he filled her in.

"It's a funny kind of coincidence, isn't it," she said, "that the partial Jonah got from Sofia's car matches Hugh Norton's car as well."

"Down to the make and model," Blake agreed. "But I don't think Sofia was driving his car."

"No, she'd have told us if she was. I'm guessing, it's more likely that the car belongs to her friend—the one she's helping."

"I should ask Ella to concentrate on the women on that DMV list," Blake said.

They sipped their coffee companionably, watching Julia making her way around the room, animatedly chatting with the few visitors who lingered in the room.

"Wish I had that woman's ability to schmooze," Blake said.

Celine laughed. "You and me both."

He turned abruptly to her. "How in the world did you figure out Reynolds had been a forger? And how did you two manage to locate Sofia?"

She shrugged. "I just put together the images I'd been seeing with what we learned about him at the Cambridge Sculptors' Association. He was an extraordinarily talented painter, but he chose to keep that side of him shrouded. It wasn't hard to understand why."

"I guess not." Blake downed his coffee and tossed the cup into a nearby trashcan. "Those unsigned paintings of his Sofia's store sold—they'll be worth several thousand now."

"If they ever come to light, yes—now that he's dead." She shuddered. "I hate that aspect of the art world. It takes a good story to sell a work of art. Not the art itself or any intrinsic merit it has. His paintings—good or not—will be valuable just because of who they're by and the way he was murdered."

She'd realized when Sofia had been telling them about it that Hugh Norton had ensured the paintings were left unsigned so no one could ever find the artist, tell him how much they'd appreciated his work, and commission more. Norton would use that fact to convince Reynolds he had no future in painting.

That his only contribution to the art world would be as a forger. It was a cruel deception.

She clenched her fists, fingernails digging into her palms.

"We've got to take Hugh Norton down, Blake. We've just got to do it."

"We will, Celine." His fingers closed over her wrist. "Trust me, we will."

She appreciated the words but sensed Blake was providing a reassurance he didn't feel himself.

After a pause, he continued. "Did Reynolds guide you to Sofia?"

She nodded. "Yup. He needs her to know the truth." Celine shook her head. "She's so convinced he's a criminal, though."

"You can't blame her," Blake said gently. "She saw the forgeries—the paint still fresh. What was she supposed to think?"

"He was touching them up for a deal they'd struck—stolen art as collateral for a loan to buy drugs. Reynolds had probably raised Cain about doing it, so Norton and the General got back at him in the only way they knew how. By destroying his relationship with Sofia."

Something stirred in her brain. A wisp of a clue. She tried to home in on it, but Blake's grip tightening around her wrist distracted her.

"That was a low blow," he murmured.

What was a low blow, she wondered. Then she remembered. *Oh, yes.* The way Hugh Norton had eliminated Sofia from Reynolds' life. Twisting their love, turning it into hatred.

Chapter Sixty-Two

"Ah, there you are." Penny hurried into the Richard E. Floor living room. "Renata over at reception said I'd find you here. I'm so sorry I'm late."

She included Celine and Julia in her smile, but her eyes were on Blake. She looked hopefully at him now. "Anything at the warehouse?"

"A couple of forged Rembrandts and a forged Flinck."

"Copies of our stolen works?"

"Afraid so."

He hated to admit that. It was an admission not just of failure, but of a lead that had brought them tantalizingly close to recovering the museum's lost art only to fizzle away.

Penny was taking it remarkably well, though. "Don't tell me they were Reynolds' creations."

"Planted in his warehouse. But yes, they were his works. He'd been forced into it."

Penny's eyebrows rose as he added this last bit. "By?" she asked.

Blake shot a warning glance at Celine and Julia before he responded. Mentioning Hugh Norton's name before they had any solid proof of his involvement would be a mistake. They seemed to understand.

His gaze reverted back to Penny's curious features.

"By the men responsible for his death."

She frowned, turning to Celine. "Then I don't understand his message to you. The Flemish oak cabinet in the Dutch room. That wasn't the only item stolen."

Blake had no idea what Penny was talking about. But a single arrow of understanding pierced through the fog of uncertainty that enshrouded him—what stolen item? What oak cabinet?—and jolted him into a painful awareness.

Reynolds had conveyed a message to Celine—one that she'd shared with Penny and Julia. But not him.

It was small comfort to see that Celine and Julia seemed as nonplussed as he.

"What stolen item, Penny?" Celine managed at last. She turned to him. "I had a dream last night. I was looking at the south wall, at the empty frames of the stolen Rembrandts, when Reynolds spun me around and told me I was looking in the wrong direction."

All right, that made sense. He felt the hot turbulence that had welled up within himself easing away.

"I thought Penny might know what he meant," Celine continued.

She turned from him to Penny.

"I do" Penny's eyes sought his, puzzled. "Or at least I thought I did. But if Reynolds had access to the Rembrandt oils and the Flinck panel, why would he focus on the least valuable item stolen?"

He had no answer to that. But Celine fortunately did.

"He didn't have access to the originals, Penny. All he had were photographs. I imagine that's all the General had as well."

Penny's face cleared. "Okay, I guess I understand why he was pointing you to the Flemish oak cabinet, then."

Chapter Sixty-Three

"I'm sorry I was so short with you this morning," Penny looked over her shoulder at Celine as she led the way into the Dutch Room. She'd managed to have the gallery cleared of its visitors before taking them in.

"I understand," Celine brushed aside the apology. "You had a lot on your plate. The memorial—"

"Oh my goodness, yes!" Penny gasped, stopping abruptly just inside the threshold and turning around. Her hand rushed up to cover her mouth. "I meant to mention it to you. You're invited—all three of you, of course." Her eyes glided swiftly over the three of them. "It's tomorrow and Sunday, with the main events scheduled for Sunday."

"We'll be there," Julia assured her. "Yup." Blake nodded his assent as well.

"It's a good thing you're psychic, Celine." Penny spun around and headed left. "My memory's an absolute sieve these days. I wouldn't have remembered to tell you about the memorial until it was too late."

"Actually, we heard about it at the Cambridge Sculptors' Association," Celine found herself saying. *Damn. Why had she opened her big mouth? And after she'd decided not to say anything, too.*

Just as she'd expected, Penny was instantly distracted.

She turned to face Celine. "Were they able to recommend someone?"

"Mitch Finlay." Celine contained her rising impatience. Penny had evidently deciphered Reynolds' message to her; Celine could hardly wait to discover the significance of the oak cabinet. But here they were talking about Mitch Finlay.

"Is he going to be here?" Julia asked.

"Oh, yes. I expect you know they were quite close at one time, sharing a studio." She turned to Blake. "It might be useful for your investigation to speak with Mitch."

"Absolutely," Blake agreed readily enough. Then much to Celine's relief, he turned the conversation back to the all-important matter at hand. "But why don't you tell us what you wanted to show us."

Penny grinned. "I can't believe you haven't guessed yet." Her heels tapped sharply on the floor as she strode toward the oak cabinet and stood before it. "Although I have to admit it took me a while to figure it out my-self. But I still don't understand how Tony Reynolds could be so sure—"

Celine couldn't help herself, interrupting Penny midstream. "What exactly did you find out, Penny? Did Reynolds leave something in the cab-inet?" It was a more logical conclusion than to suppose he'd handed over clues when they'd met—it seemed eons ago—back at the Mechelen.

It had been Tuesday, she realized with a shock, that they'd met. Just three days ago. Tony had still been alive then. She'd seen the Lady—Belle Gardner—drifting in and out of her vision, and mistakenly assumed Reynolds would cause her demise.

How wrong she'd been.

There was a death connection between them all right. But Reynolds wasn't meant to be her agent of death. He'd merely shared the misfortune of being in the sights of the same hunter.

The thoughts faded and Penny's chatter filtered back into her conscious-ness.

"I'd just about given up and was about to leave when my skirt brushed against this frame." Penny moved to the side of the cabinet beneath the large self-portrait the thieves had omitted to take. "Do you see it?"

She looked over at them, a slender, well-manicured forefinger pointing to a thick gold frame.

"We keep forgetting that was the third Rembrandt stolen. Not the most valuable one. But a Rembrandt nevertheless."

Compared to the self-portrait that hung above the cabinet, the empty frame on the side of the cabinet was tiny.

"You mean he was referring to the etching?" Celine stared at the gold frame, stunned. "Reynolds had information about the self-portrait Rem-brandt etched?"

"Created in roughly the same period as the self-portrait in oil, yes," Penny said. "They were also coincidentally the first two Rembrandts Mrs. Gardner acquired. That's why they were placed together."

"So that's the connection between that portrait"—Julia raised her eyes toward it—"and the stolen Rembrandt Reynolds discovered."

Her gaze shifted to Celine. "That must be why he kept showing it to you."

The same realization had darted through Celine's mind a mere fraction of a second earlier. She nodded wordlessly.

It was the perfect clue. She'd seen it the first time she and Reynolds had met.

You're psychic, aren't you?

"It was a gentler way of showing me what he knew. I was already apprehensive of him—sensing his connection to the General minutes after I'd sensed—"

She stopped, unable to pronounce the words. It had been shortly after she'd sensed her own death. But she also understood it hadn't been Reynolds' decision to convey his message in such a cryptic fashion.

Her own guardians—Sister Mary Catherine, Belle, and the countless other watchers gathered around her—had intercepted his message and presented it to her in the only way she'd find palatable. But after his death, her own preconceptions had shaped what she'd seen.

Her lips twisted into a wry smile. "Isn't it weird not one of us realized he had information about the etching?"

"Not really." Blake was quick to dismiss her misgivings. "We were all hoping he had something more substantial."

"Not that this isn't a good start," Penny hastened to reassure them. She looked wistfully at the empty frame. "I just wonder how he was so sure it was our print." She turned back to them. "I mean this is a print we're talking about. There are hundreds of impressions. There's one right across the street from us at the MFA for heavens' sake. There are two or three in the Rijksmuseum."

"That's why it took him so long to come forward." The light of perception was beginning to dawn in Celine's mind. "He wanted to make sure it was your stolen print."

Her eyes sought Julia's. The same thought must have occurred to them, for they both said, "Lines of authenticity!"

Julia's eyes widened. "That's what his installation is about, isn't it?"

"Yup," Celine confirmed her friend's insight. "And it's intentionally abstract."

"Wait," Blake broke in. "You're saying he managed to establish it was a genuine Rembrandt print that belonged to the Gardner?"

"Yes." Celine turned to him, mind racing. "And whoever gave it to him is—or has access to—the General." It was all becoming clearer to her now.

Of the thirteen works the General and his partner had stolen, only the gu, the etching, the five Degas sketches, and possibly the Manet had made their way to their intended recipients. Recovering any of these would lead them directly to the perpetrators of the biggest heist in contemporary history.

"Blake," she continued breathlessly, "we really need to get Sofia to persuade her friend to come forward. It's the only way we'll get to the bottom of this."

Chapter Sixty-Four

Jonah called as they were leaving the Gardner. Celine allowed Julia and Blake to walk ahead, staying by the sidewalk to take the call.

"Any news?" the reporter asked the moment she answered her phone. "I've been busy with my mom," he explained before she could get around to asking him where he'd been all morning.

Jonah's absence had been a Godsend, but they'd all known he'd get in touch eventually and want to know more about the investigation. What she was to tell him had already been decided.

"There was nothing in the warehouse, if that's what you're asking," Celine informed him once she'd made the usual inquiries after his mother— questions Jonah brushed aside. More curtly than usual, Celine noted.

Her eyes traced the pattern of shadows the museum threw on the gray sidewalk.

"Nothing?" Jonah's voice rose, reflecting his skepticism. "Absolutely nothing?"

The shadows on the ground flickered and wavered.

She wondered what—if anything—he'd uncovered to question her veracity. Had he spoken with Cambridge Police? He was a reporter after all, and being nosy—and resourceful—went with the territory.

But she stayed firm.

"Nothing of interest in the Gardner theft," she told him, her voice emphatic. There was no way of knowing for certain that Reynolds had forged the works they'd found in his warehouse. And they'd so clearly been planted there that to now attribute them to the dead man seemed an injustice.

Reynolds had worked hard to outlive his past as a forger. A past that Hugh Norton hadn't allowed him to forget. Celine was damned if she was going to allow anyone—in particular a journalist with a penchant for unsavory scuttlebutt—to sully his reputation now that he was dead.

Before Jonah could pursue the question any further she continued. "But we've discovered which Rembrandt he had information about. It was the etching."

To her surprise, Jonah didn't ask how they'd found out—through psychic channels or more usual investigative routes. He simply accepted her word for it.

Why, she idly wondered as her foot outlined the shadows. But she didn't have time to pursue the question for too long.

"The etching," Jonah echoed. "It was a stamp-sized print as I recall."

"You're right. It was tiny. Less than two inches long and across."

"Are we thinking someone gave it to Reynolds—a client perhaps? For safekeeping. Or that he stole it?"

An unexpected note of alarm sounded in Celine's head. But its significance eluded her. It couldn't have been due to the possibilities Jonah had named. Neither one was unreasonable. How else could the etching have fallen into Reynolds' hands? But . . .

Uneasily she suppressed the twinge of unease that had snaked up within her. There'd be time enough to make sense of it later.

"Gave it would be more appropriate," she said, squelching the urge to snap. The dead man hadn't been a thief—that much she was sure of. "Remember, he *was* trying to return it to the Gardner."

"Alright. So someone gave it to him. He recognizes it for what it is, keeps it in the hope of getting the reward."

"Or because it was the right thing to do," Celine pointed out dryly. "I know you need a good story, Jonah. But you can't embellish the facts like that. The man was rich enough not to need the paltry reward he'd get for returning a tiny, not particularly valuable Rembrandt etching."

"You're right, you're right." He laughed, a small nervous bark of amusement. "But listen, so he has this thing. It's tiny. If it's not in his warehouse or apartment, isn't it possible he concealed it somewhere? Maybe one of those miniature models he made for his clients."

"Someone must have thought so." She told him about the break-in at the Mechelen. "I don't see how they could've come to the conclusion it was in the one thing they stole rather than in the other items they were unable to lay their hands on."

"Well, if the etching was given to him for safekeeping—that's the theory we're working on, isn't it?—then—"

She swept on, ignoring Jonah's attempt to speak. "If that's the case, then whoever gave him the etching commissioned a specific piece to hide the print in. Wouldn't you think?"

Her words must have carried because Blake and Julia pivoted around instantly. It was a consideration that hadn't occurred to either of them before, although now Celine could see the gears spinning inside their minds.

Jonah was speaking again. She pressed her phone closer to her ear.

"But think, Celine, if Reynolds had no intention of returning the etching, would he have carried out the commission? No, of course not. So what does he do instead? He gives it to you—hiding it in the one piece that would carry the most significance for you."

Another twinge of alarm sounded, but she stifled it, considering instead the implications of what he'd just said. Had the General's men—who else could've been responsible for the break-in—succeeded in recovering the stamp-sized Rembrandt print?

It's safe, Celine. It's still with you.

"It's safe," she said, repeating the words she'd heard—from whom? Sister Mary Catherine or Reynolds?

"Safe?" Jonah's voice was like an explosion in her ear making Celine start like a nervous horse. "What do you mean?"

"I mean that wherever Reynolds hid it, it's safe. We'll find it, Jonah," she said with more confidence than she felt. "Not to worry."

It's still with you, Celine. It's still with you.

Still with her? But how? She'd never had it to begin with.

"How?" Jonah echoed the question reverberating in her brain. "How are you going to get the etching back, Celine?"

His skepticism chafed her. True, she still had no idea where the etching was. That didn't mean her intuition wouldn't lead her to it—eventually.

"I don't know. But—"

An image surfaced—a figure in a mail carrier's uniform. A large red "X" crossed it out. What did that mean? That the mailman wasn't relevant?

She pushed aside the image and the questions it elicited, determined to show Jonah the bigger picture. They were onto something larger than just the one, tiny, stamp-sized etching stolen thirty years ago.

"Listen, Jonah, we're very close to finding out who killed Reynolds. And that'll bring us right on the General's heels. We could end up recovering more than just the one stolen piece."

"B-b-ut how?"

She'd never heard Jonah stammer like this. She was giving him the story of a lifetime.

"We found Sofia."

"Sofia can lead you back to the General?"

"Not Sofia, her friend. If we can persuade her to come forward."

Chapter Sixty-Five

Blake wasn't happy about being summoned to the SAC's office. They were in the middle of an investigation—on the brink of solving a cold case that had long eluded them. He didn't have time for this.

Walsh leaned back in his chair and steepled his fingers. A man with all the time in the world.

Utterly oblivious to the countless pieces of the case that still littered Blake's plate, waiting to be put together.

Blake suppressed a sigh and resigned himself to the inevitable.

"This inexplicable, bullheaded decision of yours to pursue Hugh Norton as a suspect," Walsh began. "Where is it coming from?"

Ah, so that was it. Ella had needled and prodded the old boy, and Blake was left to pick up the pieces. *Goddammit!*

He was in no mood to argue, however.

"We're simply pursuing all avenues of investigation, sir. Looking into Reynolds' social circle—trying to ascertain what he knew about the Gardner theft. How? From whom? That kind of thing."

Walsh stared at him—eyes fixed on Blake's features, stone-faced, silent. Blake recognized the tactic, having used it on suspects himself. But this was his boss. He couldn't afford to antagonize the old man.

Hating himself for it, Blake caved.

"We're looking into Reynolds' clients, his known associates," he elaborated.

Walsh rocked his chair farther back—a little more and it would be in danger of tipping over. Not that the SAC seemed to care.

"And is Hugh Norton on Anthony Reynolds' client list?"

"No."

"No?" Walsh's eyebrows flew up. He rocked back down, chair legs landing with a decided thud on the carpeted floor.

"Then what is the reason for looking into him, Agent?"

Oh, there was more than one. A psychic's unerring instincts. Unresolved suspicions from an unsolved murder seven years ago.

But not one of them could be offered as a solid reason for prying into the life of an otherwise upstanding citizen—not that they'd done much prying so far.

Still, the little they'd uncovered had more than rattled the SAC's cage, it looked like.

"And this Wozniak business"—the man was on a roll now—"What's that all about?"

He frowned—the ill-tempered, annoyed frown of a man under pressure, Blake thought. Or of a stooge being paid extremely well to stall any effort to encroach upon Norton's private affairs.

Walsh clasped his hands and looked sternly at him. "Well?"

"Sofia Wozniak." Blake enunciated the name slowly. "She's the woman who broke into Reynolds' apartment. They used to be an item."

Walsh took the explanation better than Blake expected.

"She's being charged, I presume." Walsh's sanctimonious tone as he uttered the query was nauseating.

Blake shook his head.

"I've asked Cambridge PD to hold off." Soldi hadn't been particularly happy about this, but DA Campari had been surprisingly amenable to Blake's plan. "Sofia Wozniak's testimony has been remarkably helpful to us."

"How so?" Walsh seemed genuinely taken aback.

"Well, for one thing, sir,"—a surge of triumph coursed through Blake's veins as the thought flashed serendipitously into his brain—"she's established a connection between Reynolds and your friend Hugh Norton. Seems Norton was responsible for taking Reynolds in hand and directing his talents."

He happily provided the details.

"Everything she's told us can be easily verified." Thanks to Sofia Sr.'s propensity for keeping a detailed account book.

The purchase of Reynolds' forged Degas sketch and its subsequent sale to Norton had been dutifully noted. The unsigned oil paintings Reynolds had sold through Rose Antiques had been noted as well.

Along with the fact that they'd been placed on consignment by Hugh Norton.

"My mother kept excellent records," Sofia had explained. "I saw no reason to toss anything out when I took over the store. Everything's here— every note; every entry; every book."

Amen to that!

"It's pretty clear it was Norton who tried to exploit Reynolds' skills as a forger, sir. Norton who tried to keep him in that line of business. Norton who insisted that Reynolds leave his paintings unsigned."—That had been

Celine's insight, not Sofia's. But why give the SAC any ammunition?— "Reynolds was determined to break free."

"None of this amounts to proof, Blake."

"But it does give rise to reasonable suspicion."

Walsh tapped his slender, tapering fingers on the desk—a nervous, fluttering rap. Was he on the take? Or just unwilling to believe he'd been deceived by someone he thought he knew?

Blake couldn't tell.

"And the information Reynolds claimed to have about the Gardner theft," Walsh said. "Where are we on that?"

"Sofia and the friend she's helping can lead us back—directly back"— Blake struck the desk with the flat of his palm for emphasis—"to the mastermind behind the theft."

One of whom was most likely Hugh Norton. The man had a passion for Degas sketches and drawings, was expert enough to recognize when they were forged. Moreover, of the thirteen works stolen from the Gardner, a full five had been Degas sketches.

Coincidence? Not f—in' likely.

But Blake kept his suspicions to himself.

"We're close to solving this thing, sir. An infamous heist, unsolved for three decades. And we solve it—under your aegis. Recover the stolen art. Consider the headlines."

As he'd expected, Walsh preened, his mouth twitching in anticipation of the gleeful moment of reflected glory. *Typical bureaucrat!*

"Okay." The old man nodded his graying patrician head. "But Blake, I want to be in the loop every step of the way. Every step of the way, you understand."

Blake hesitated, then agreed.

"Fine." It was no different than the arrangement Soldi had insisted upon. The sole difference being that Blake trusted Soldi as a fellow lawman. Walsh, he wasn't so sure about.

His voice must've reflected his unhappiness with this covenant, his acquiescence tentative, for Walsh's gaze bore into his, and he continued sharply.

"Every detail, Blake. When and where your meeting with Sofia's friend takes place. Precautions you'll take. Everything. From this moment on, I directly oversee this case. Capiche?"

"Sure." Blake pushed his chair back, eager to get out of the SAC's claustrophobic, airless office. He was beginning to feel like a hapless quarry caught in the vicious grip of an anaconda's embrace.

He'd find a way out of this Faustian bargain, he told himself as he walked out the door. He'd figure something out. He had to.

Chapter Sixty-Six

"This isn't good, Blake." Ella peered anxiously at him through her large, round spectacles.

"No shit, Sherlock," he snapped. "I know it isn't good."

"Language, Blake. There's no need to get like that with me."

He looked up, instantly contrite.

"I'm sorry. I'm just"—he rubbed his eyes; they were feeling dry again—"I'm just beat, totally exhausted."

They were at his desk, poring over the names Ella wanted him to consider. And he'd made the mistake of confiding in her. What else was he supposed to do?

Call Celine? At least Ella would think no worse of him than she already did. But he was beginning to regret saying anything.

He passed his hand over his face, feeling the light stubble covering his cheeks.

"We're this close"—his forefinger and thumb moved to within a fraction of an inch apart—"to solving this thing, and I worry we could mess it up. Yet again."

Ella crossed her arms, tilted her head, and regarded him quietly.

"Worrying about it won't get you anywhere, Blake," she said matter-of-factly.

She was right. But it didn't solve his problem.

"How do we ensure nothing important gets into Walsh's hands?" he asked, looking at her despairingly.

"We tell him the truth," Ella said. "Some aspects of the investigation have to be on a need-to-know basis to protect the civilians involved. Tell him it would be a PR disaster if things went pear-shaped."

"It would." Blake found himself breaking into a smile. "You're right, it really would. And boy, is the old guy sensitive to negative PR." He beamed at his personal assistant. "You're a Godsend, Ella."

"Glad to have solved that problem," she replied dryly. "Now, let's get back to this business.

"There are potentially four couples we can look at—that's assuming a connection between the folks with matching last names. And it's also assuming there's no connection between those without."

Blake suppressed a grin. This was quintessential Ella. She made the average, run-of-the-mill assumption any investigator would make, then compounded the issue by overthinking it.

He cast his eyes over the names on the sheet of paper between them. Linda and Glen Cottman. Jane and Dennis Elks. Beverly and Peter Standish. Bonnie and Dale Benson.

Four couples. Potentially married. Hopefully—for the health of this case—going through a divorce. The women with silver Mercedes Benzes that matched the one Sofia had been driving; the men all clients of the victim.

"We know whoever gave Reynolds the etching was a client," he said, raising his eyes. "Doesn't have to be a client, but it's the most likely assumption."

Ella nodded earnestly. "So if one of those four couples don't work out, we concentrate on the male clients on Reynolds' list."

"Yup. His killer was a man. Someone who knew him."

"That makes sense."

She glanced down, scrutinizing the paper as though it might yield some secret wisdom.

"By the way, forgot to mention Mailand called."

"Yeah? What did he say?"

"Reynolds' story checks out. A Paso mailman, who was in the habit of stopping at a certain neighborhood to get with his married chick, was bribed into letting some guy borrow his vehicle on the day Reynolds arrived in town."

"He get a name, description?"

"Nope," Ella said. "No name and the description's too generic to be of much use. But he has persuaded the guy to come back and meet with their sketch artist."

"Fine." Blake wasn't much interested in this aspect of the investigation. It was probably some Boston guy—one of the many enforcers the General employed for this kind of thing.

Bugger probably couldn't, Blake figured, *do much further damage. Celine's concerns notwithstanding.*

He tapped the sheet of paper between them. "You good with this plan?"

"Yes, but"—sunlight hit her round glasses making them gleam when Ella lifted her head—"it would be easier if you could get Sofia to tell us which one of these people it is that we're looking at."

"I know. I've tried talking to her." He had—just before he'd returned to the office. "She won't budge. I don't blame her. Her friend's life is in danger."

"All the more reason to come forward." Ella's lips tightened into an obdurate line. Emotion seemed to play no part in her calculations. She was all logic.

At least that was how she came across to Blake. Did she really not get how much was at stake for someone in Sofia's position? How impossible it might be to make a careless decision that could betray her friend and cost the woman her life?

Ella was staring at him, waiting for a decision. He resisted her silent goading.

"Maybe, maybe not. But it's Sofia's call to make. Not mine."

But there was another reason for his reluctance. He'd never been able to forget what had happened to Grayson Pike. The man had been a washed-up loser of a guy, but he hadn't deserved to be brutally murdered in broad daylight—a few yards away from an FBI agent.

Blake's gut tightened. He already had blood on his hands. He didn't want anymore.

He met Ella's gaze squarely, daring her to keep goading. To his surprise, she let the matter drop.

Instead, she lobbed a grenade at him.

"What does Celine think?"

Damn. Celine wanted him to get Sofia to cooperate. Had specifically asked him to persuade her.

Blake glared at Ella. He picked up the phone and dialed.

"I guess I'll find out. But she better be willing to put her money where her mouth is."

The tinny sound of Vivaldi's Summer was quickly curtailed. "Hello?"

"Blake here. You still think Sofia and her friend need to come forward?"

Chapter Sixty-Seven

Sofia was closing up Rose Antiques when Celine and Julia returned to Newbury Street. Her head jerked, twisting around at the sound of her name when Celine called out to her.

It was clear Sofia hadn't expected them back. Her dark eyes fell on them, wide with alarm and despair.

"I've made my decision," she said. "I'm not going to ask her to do this. I can't do it."

She returned to the business of locking the store entrance, shoulders hunched, head bent. As though ignoring them would will them away.

Julia followed her up the steps.

"Isn't that her decision to make?" she asked. The former fed glanced around at Celine, tilting her head to indicate Celine should come up as well.

But Celine found herself unable to move.

Sofia's misery was palpable—a little more prodding and she'd cave. There was no doubt about that. The insight gave Celine pause.

Was she right to insist Sofia's friend come forward? If anything happened to the woman, the responsibility would lie squarely with Celine. Not with Blake—who hadn't had the stomach to force Sofia to go against her will—but with her. Not that Celine could blame Blake.

It had been her idea, after all. Not his. And he'd been only too eager to wash his hands off it.

"Celine," Julia muttered fiercely, tilting her head in the direction of Sofia's back again.

She had to do something. But what? Her hand remained glued to the wrought-iron parapet, her feet planted firmly on the sidewalk.

Sister Mary Catherine, help me, she begged.

There's danger, Celine. It swirls around her friend.

"Your friend is in danger," Celine repeated the nun's warning to Sofia.

"I know." Sofia clutched the door handle, leaned against it, and closed her eyes. "I can't risk her life."

There's no saving her, Celine, Sister Mary Catherine said.

Like Grayson? Celine's heart tightened. *But how can I tell Sofia that?*

You must play your part, Celine. What is meant to be will be no matter what you do.

Jesus Christ! Celine forced herself up the steps. When she was nearly at the top, she reached out a tentative hand and touched Sofia.

"Your friend is in grave danger, Sofia. From the same man who killed Tony."

"What do you mean?" Sofia turned, her face streaked with mascara-stained tears. A puzzled frown creased her forehead. "What do you see?"

"Only that the man who killed Tony—the same man who gave him the etching to hide—will kill your friend."

Sofia gasped—an audible explosion of stunned disbelief. Her knuckles turned deathly white.

Celine could envision what was going on in her mind. Pieces Sofia had never put together were falling into place—being reshuffled like a deck of cards into order.

"It's her husband, isn't it?" Celine pressed. "Her husband who killed Tony."

Sofia closed her eyes, wordless. But the tightening of her lips was all the response Celine needed.

"He's a dangerous man," she continued softly. "He'll stop at nothing to protect himself from the wrath of those above him."

Sofia opened her eyes.

"If we can stop him," Celine went on, "we can bring the men above him, the men he fears, to justice."

"Those men have killed before," Julia added.

Sofia turned mutely toward her.

"They killed Celine's employer in Paso Robles as well as a painter and a potential eyewitness we'd located. It was because of them that your friend's husband felt he had no choice but to kill Tony. And because of them that he'll strike out at his wife."

Sofia straightened up.

"Fine," she choked out the word, the acquiescence wrung out of her. Turning, she fumbled with the key in the lock. "Fine, I'll call her. But it's her choice, okay?" She looked over her shoulder. "Her decision to speak with you or not."

She managed to get the door open.

"I'll give you a call when I'm done."

She was about to close the door when Celine wedged her hand between it and the doorjamb.

"Sofia, you knew Tony well. Where would he have hidden the etching? If he'd realized he couldn't let B—" The name on the tip of Celine's tongue evaporated. "Your friend's husband," she amended, "have it back?"

Sofia's mouth stretched into a wan smile. "If he had time to think about it, it would've been somewhere of significance to him."

"A sculpture?"

"Sure. Either a piece with a hidden compartment or a piece he wouldn't mind breaking open."

Chapter Sixty-Eight

"I hear you had a visit from the feds."

Sofia closed her eyes. She wished she hadn't answered the call. She'd been about to dial the number of the shelter in Quincy when Dom called. And not having caller ID, she'd made the mistake of picking up the receiver. God, what a drastic error that had been!

She wasn't ready to deal with Dom.

His voice, tight with anger, sapped her body of energy, made her back hurt as though she had the flu. No, she definitely wasn't ready to deal with him.

"Yes, Dad," she whispered into the receiver, bracing herself for the onslaught that would surely follow.

"I can't hear you, Sofia."

"Yes," she said a little more firmly. She opened her eyes. "Yes, I did."

"What about?" Dom demanded harshly. "Are you in trouble?"

"No, Dad."

Dom didn't seem to believe her.

"No?" His voice barely rose, but had she been lying, the strong note of skepticism she heard would've made her quail. "You sure about that?"

"Yes, I'm sure." Sofia's patience was wearing thin, her temper rising. "They asked about breaking into Tony's apartment. I admitted to it. They aren't pressing charges."

"So, they're okay with you breaking into a crime scene?"

She didn't bother to respond. She'd copped to it, explained her side of the story, and they'd seemed to understand. At least the young girl—the psychic—seemed to get it.

"What about Tony's warehouse? They okay with you breaking in there as well, Sofia?"

God, how did he know about that? She noticed the slip in his syntax as well—a sure sign of wrath so uncontrollable, he couldn't be bothered to speak correctly.

She pressed a hand to her stomach, forcing herself to calm down.

"It wasn't my presence there that bothered them, Dad. It was what they found there."

She felt him relax—even over the phone, she was aware of that, she had no idea how. He emitted a chuckle—a throaty chortle of amusement.

"So they've discovered your lover was a forger. The whole world will know his shame now."

"No, Dad." She straightened up, incensed now. "What they've deduced is that someone planted those works there—most likely whoever killed him."

"Nonsense!"

"I'm surprised your contacts didn't break that news to you. It would be obvious even if they didn't have other evidence to hang their theory on."

"What evidence?"

It was a simple question—she had no reason to believe he was mocking her—but it irritated her, nonetheless.

"How should I know? They didn't give me specifics. But I've been wondering—and they are, too—why Hugh Norton didn't destroy those works. All those years ago when he discovered them and thought Tony had betrayed his trust, why didn't he destroy them?"

"Sofia—"

"You told me Norton took them away from Tony, didn't you? That's what you said. You still trust the guy?"

"I have no reason not to, Sofia. And this cockamamie theory of yours —"

"It's not my theory, Dad, it's what they believe." That wasn't entirely true, she knew. But the feds did have their suspicions. At least the young girl did. "They have a psychic—"

"Who came to you fishing for information? My child, that's how these charlatans work. You're thirty-eight, Sofia. You can't be that naïve."

She resented that comment. He'd always treated her like a child—a stupid, brain-dead infant.

"You know what else they believe? They think Hugh Norton's accountant—that stand-up guy you call the Rock?—they think he murdered Tony. Are you going to support our mutual friend if it turns out he's a murderer?"

She'd managed to silence Dom. Apart from his labored breathing, there was no sound.

"Does this have anything to do with your friend?"

"You're damn right, it does. Her life's in danger. Because of what she knows, what she's seen. If you weren't such a misogynist, Dad, if you didn't believe that all women are over-emotional, overwrought toddlers given to mindless temper tantrums, you'd have taken her plight more seriously.

"And if you weren't blinded by your hatred of Tony, you'd realize there was good in him. He wasn't a bad man, he wasn't a criminal. He died trying to return the Gardner's art."

Hot tears spilled out of her eyes. Why had she judged Tony so harshly? Why hadn't she listened to him? Now he was dead.

She felt a hand stroking her head. She could've sworn it was Tony's. It was just her imagination, she knew, recreating his presence. Tony was gone.

Fresh tears welled up.

"What have you decided to do?" Dom's voice was quiet, resigned. "What do you want to do for your friend?"

"She's coming forward, Dad. She's going to talk to the feds. It's the only way to keep her safe."

Chapter Sixty-Nine

Celine plucked her phone out of her shoulder bag. The screen sprang to life, portraying an image of the Delft, the moment she touched the home button.

"No calls, no messages," Julia commented, looking down at Celine's phone.

They'd returned to the Boston Plaza Hotel and were riding up the elevator to their room. But there was still no word from Sofia.

Yet, Celine reminded herself. *No word yet.*

"She'll get in touch," she said more firmly than she felt as the elevator doors slid open, revealing the carpeted hallway that led to their suite.

It's not safe. The message beeped urgently in her mind as she dropped into the living room couch. *It's not safe.*

She was about to repeat the message to Julia when the phone trilled, interrupting the din in her brain.

Celine grabbed it, putting it on speaker. "Sofia?"

"She'll meet you." Sofia's voice sounded tense, strained. "But only you and your friend."

"Julia?" Celine softly asked.

"Yes. Please—I beg of you—please don't involve the police. Not just yet."

Julia bent forward. "We understand, Sofia. And you have my word, it'll just be the two of us—Celine and me."

It's not safe. The message played itself over and over in Celine's head. *It's not safe.*

"Where are we meeting?" she asked out loud. "Is it safe?"

Safe for whom? Herself? Sofia and her friend?

It's not safe.

But Sister Mary Catherine had told her there was nothing she could do. She had a role to play, and she must play it, come what may. She ignored the warning beeping incessantly in her mind.

"Sorry, what?" She'd missed Sofia's words.

"Don't worry, I know the place," Julia mouthed, nodding at her.

"The Prudential Mall," Sofia said a little louder, obviously repeating herself. "It's a four-minute walk from my store. You take Newbury, heading toward Exeter, go up to Gloucester. Turn left and then take another left onto Boylston."

"Okay," Julia leaned into the mouthpiece. "Then what?"

"Take the elevator up to Dunkin Donuts. That's where we meet."

"Is it safe?" Celine asked again. "Is this safe for your friend?"

Her gut was twisting, wrenching inside of her in pain. There was something wrong with this plan. But she couldn't figure out what.

"It's the safest place I can think of," Sofia replied. "Why? What do you see?"

Celine shook her head helplessly. "Nothing. I don't see a thing. I was just confirming that it is safe."

"There's a church in the building—St. Francis Chapel."

"They're sheltering your friend," Celine read Sofia's mind. "She feels safe meeting close by, but she doesn't want to involve them."

"Yes." Sofia hesitated. "There's one other thing. If what she tells you gives you cause to investigate her husband, could you . . ." Her voice trailed off.

"Keep it discreet?" Julia guessed.

"Yes. Yes, just in case—" Sofia broke off again.

"Just in case you've misjudged her husband?" Celine asked. She sensed the thoughts running through Sofia's mind. And she understood why.

"Just in case there's an innocent explanation for all this," Sofia said, more firmly this time. "They were deeply in love at one time—like Tony and me. Maybe she's—"

"She's not mistaken about this, Sofia," Celine said. "He'll sacrifice her to protect himself if he has to. Tony would never do that to you. You know that now, don't you?"

"Y-yes." Her voice was thick with tears. Celine could barely understand her.

Tell her about Tony, Sister Mary Catherine directed her.

"Tony thanks you for believing in him, Sofia."

"What?"

"In the store," Celine explained, "when you felt his presence, it wasn't your imagination. He was stroking your hair, just like he used to."

"Oh, God!" Sofia sobbed.

Celine let her quietly weep for a few seconds.

"Fussy Phil killed Tony, Sofia. Your friend's doing the right thing."

She forced herself to utter the words, even though her brain kept on screaming: *It's not safe.*

"Fussy Phil?" Sofia sounded surprised.

"Your friend's husband."

"I know." Sofia emitted a sound somewhere between choking and laughter. "That was Tony's nickname for him. He was the only one who called him that."

There was a pause.

Then, "You really are psychic, aren't you?"

Some psychic!

It wasn't a remark she could acknowledge.

"We'll see you tomorrow, Sofia. Be careful, okay? And keep the details of our meeting to yourself."

Chapter Seventy

The meeting was set. The decision had been taken out of his hands; Sofia's friend was coming forward. But Blake wasn't invited.

"It would only spook her," Celine had said. "And we promised her there'd be no law enforcement presence."

"What about security?" he wanted to know.

Celine had sighed. "Probably not a good idea." And Julia had agreed. "It's a public place. No one knows about the meeting. It's just us. Let's keep it that way."

"Fine," he'd reluctantly agreed.

There'd be no police presence—no plainclothesmen staking out the scene. No armed FBI agents keeping cautious watch upon the place.

"That's going to attract attention, Blake," Julia had said. "Exactly what we don't want."

And Blake understood. He understood, too, that the matter was entirely out of his control. Whether Sofia's friend survived the meeting or not would have nothing to do with him.

But he didn't know whether he was relieved or not.

"It's just an informal meeting," he told himself as he pushed his chair back. Walsh would want to know the latest. He'd already called Soldi.

"And this meeting, where is it taking place exactly?" Soldi had inquired.

"No idea, Vince."

"A public place?"

The man was sharp, Blake had to give him that.

"It would be the safest option, wouldn't it?" had been Blake's noncommittal response. From a civilian's point of view. From the perspective of someone afraid of law enforcement.

A criminal wouldn't hesitate to fire into a crowd. Collateral damage meant nothing to a mobster.

He entered Walsh's office. The SAC's eyes lit up when he came in.

"Come on in, son."

It was about as expansive a greeting as Blake had ever gotten out of the old man.

But Walsh's expression soon soured.

"You have no idea where this meeting is taking place."

"Nope."

"And you agreed to this?" Walsh looked at him in growing disbelief, as though Blake had just offered to take a bullet to the head. "You actually agreed to this plan?"

Blake nodded.

"No security?"

"It doesn't seem to be required."

Seeing Walsh about to argue, he continued: "Besides, we'll lose our quarry if we deviate in any way from what Celine's agreed to."

"I'm not happy about this," Walsh informed him emphatically.

"No, sir."

Blake sat, hands resting on his thighs, and stared impassively at the older man.

Walsh drummed his fingers on his desk—a nervous, irritable rapping.

"So what now?"

"We sit tight and wait for the operation to go through."

"Damn!" Walsh cursed, then wagged his fingers at the door. A gesture of dismissal.

⁓

The Brahmin's ring glowed in the amber light, the facets of the orange sapphire flashing fiery flames into his eyes. *Let the investigation play out,* his informant had advised him.

Well, he wasn't about to do that.

"She needs to go," he growled into the phone. "She's becoming a liability."

"Dead women talk, my friend," the man on the other end reminded him. "Dead men don't."

"What's that supposed to mean?" the Brahmin snapped.

"The trail doesn't end with her, as you well know."

"Damn right, it doesn't. It leads straight back to you and me."

He heard a throaty chuckle.

"I hear some people are already interested in you, my friend."

"Listen to me, this affects you as much as it does me. Don't think I'm going down alone. You make that bitch stop. Fix it, you hear. Fix it!"

A soft click told him the phone had been disconnected.

He'd been dismissed.

Goddammit! He slammed the receiver down. His throat was fiery hoarse from screaming. He picked up the glass of whiskey on his desk and downed the liquid.

Dead men don't talk, his friend had said. He'd been too irritated to understand the significance of the remark, but now he did.

He'd have to fend for himself.

But at least his partner had supplied him with a solution.

Dead men don't talk. Neither do dead women, no matter what his friend thought.

Damn bitch should've been reined in a long time ago.

He lifted the receiver again and dialed a number.

"Exactly how much does she know?" he demanded.

Chapter Seventy-One

The knock on the door of their hotel suite startled Celine and roused Julia out of her nap.

"Is that room service?" Julia straightened up. She glanced at the door, and then back at Celine. "Or are you expecting someone?"

"Neither." Celine shook her head. She walked quickly to the door and yanked it open.

"Jonah?"

She stepped back to allow the lanky reporter in.

"What are you doing here?"

She followed him into the living room.

"Well, now that my mom's fine"—Jonah sank into the couch—"I thought I'd see how things were going with you guys."

His gaze shifted from her face to Julia's.

"What's the plan for tomorrow? Are you guys attending Reynolds' memorial?"

Celine stiffened. Logically, that would've been the best place to be. But —

"There's something else we need to do tomorrow," Julia said easily. "But it might be a good idea for you to go. See what you can find out."

"But what are you two going to be doing?" Jonah's eyes narrowed suspiciously. A lock of dark hair fell over his eyes as his head swung up to face Celine and then back down toward Julia.

"Sofia's friend *might* be willing to come forward," Celine said. Best to give him some sort of explanation, she thought, rather than let his curiosity fester.

"*Might?*" Jonah's eyebrows lifted.

"Nothing's certain," Julia informed him. "And if she sees anyone else but Celine and me, it'll only unnerve her into leaving."

"Will Blake be with you?"

"No," Celine assured him. "Just the two of us. That's what we've agreed to."

"Where? Sofia's store?"

He was still fishing for information. For some reason that annoyed Celine.

"If you're thinking of going anywhere near her store tomorrow, Jonah, don't." The words came out harsher than she intended, but she couldn't help herself. He had to be deterred from being anywhere in the vicinity of Newbury Street. "We won't be there."

"Be patient, Jonah." Julia leaned forward and fixed her blue eyes on him. "If you ruin this for us, you ruin an entire investigation. And your chances of getting that story you were counting on."

"But you'll let me know when you have more, right?" Jonah looked anxiously up at them.

"Absolutely." Celine inhaled deeply.

She'd decided to throw him a crumb.

"Listen, we are getting closer to finding that etching. And that's why it might be a good idea for you to go to the Gardner tomorrow. Talk to some of Reynolds' colleagues, anyone who might be there."

"Oh?" Jonah's eyebrows lifted again. A show of interest, although it didn't seem he was buying what she had to sell.

"Sofia thinks Reynolds would've hidden the etching either in a sculpture that was significant to him. Or in a piece that he'd be okay with destroying. And"—she glanced back at Julia—"we both think it might be in one of the pieces he created for his Gardner exhibit."

She seemed to have piqued the reporter's interest at last. He considered what she'd said, chewing his lip thoughtfully.

"I guess that makes sense," he admitted at last. "No one would think to look there."

"We certainly didn't until Sofia mentioned it," Celine said. "But it makes sense. I mean what else was he working on at the time?"

"And, trust me," Julia added, "some of those abstract pieces look exactly like the kind of thing no one would miss if they were shattered into a thousand pieces."

❧

Tony Reynolds was in the room—a dark silhouette against the window —when Celine opened her eyes the next morning. The sliver of gray light that entered the hotel bedroom through a crack in the drawn curtains told her it was too early to wake up.

"You won't be able to see her," he informed Celine regretfully.

See whom? Celine pressed her palms down on the soft mattress, trying to push herself up. But her arms felt leaden and listless, unable to support her weight.

She stared helplessly up at Tony. What was he talking about? She wished he'd reach out a hand, help her sit up.

But Tony seemed unaware of her struggles. He stood by the bed, looking down at her, his features cast in shadow.

"You're meeting her today. Remember?" His voice had taken on a quality of urgency.

The meeting? Celine frowned. *What meeting? With Penny?*

Oh, the meeting. *That meeting.* Her eyes widened as she remembered. She tried again to sit up, but her arms were like jelly, slipping into the mattress when she tried to brace herself against it.

"You won't be able to see her."

"Why not?" she asked him. Her heart muscles contracted painfully, the spasm sending wave after wave of agony through her chest.

Behind the sculptor, she made out a hazy figure. The familiar dark dress with its plunging neckline, cinched in at the waist. The Lady. A sign of death.

But whose? Hers?

Tony smiled. "No, not you. Your time hasn't come yet."

Another spasm shot through her chest.

"Tell Sofia I'll take care of her. I'll be there."

"Take care of whom, Tony?" This time she managed to sit up.

"I'll be waiting for her. Tell her. Tell Sofia I'll be there."

"Tony, wait." Celine reached out toward him, but a thick fog separated her from him.

She was still moaning, crying out his name when consciousness returned.

Her senses moved up her body. They detected the bedsheets tangled around her contorted form; felt her chest heaving with each ragged breath that entered her lungs; and collided finally with her eyelids, pressed shut, long eyelashes feathering her cheeks.

As her breathing slowed, the details of the dream returned.

Tell Sofia, I'll be waiting. Tell her I'll be there.

Dear God! Understanding filtered through at last.

She was out of her bed in an instant, in front of Julia's room, pounding upon the door.

The words were pouring out of her mouth before Julia had wrenched the door fully open.

"It's Sofia, Julia. Sofia's in danger. She's not going to make it out of there. He's going to kill her. Not his wife. Sofia!"

"*Jesus Christ!*"

Julia reached out as Celine collapsed into her arms.

Chapter Seventy-Two

Changing the venue was not an option. Celine had considered Julia's idea and dismissed it.

It was one of two suggestions the former fed had made. Axe the meeting or change the venue.

Neither one seemed appropriate at this juncture. Calling off the meeting wouldn't avert the danger. If someone had Sofia in their sights, she'd be dead. Sooner or later, they'd take her out.

And as for making a last-minute change to the meeting place . . .

Heat from the cup of Oolong room service had brought up seeped into her fingers, burning her skin. "Remember when I sensed Grayson was in danger?"

"He was," Julia bolstered her spirits. "You were right." The former fed reached out and gently squeezed her hand.

Celine knew what Julia was trying to do. She needed to trust herself, trust her instincts. And Celine appreciated the impulse. But . . .

Her fingers tightened around her cup, oblivious to the searing heat. Things had gone horribly wrong when she'd intervened in Grayson's situation. She gazed blankly at the blue wall ahead of her, remembering.

"Bringing Grayson out of that church was a mistake. We led him straight to his killers."

She shook her head, turning to face her friend. "No, let's not change anything. We'll only make matters worse."

Besides the mall was as public a place as you could get. They'd be in full view of people. There'd be security cameras all around. Hard to kill someone and get away with it under those circumstances.

"Can't argue with that," Julia agreed when she pointed this out.

There was a slight pause, then Julia continued, "So we go ahead as planned?"

"Yup." Celine put the cup down. The Oolong had calmed her down, but the caffeine had also sent her adrenaline pumping. "I need to warn Sofia, though. I don't want her going into this unprepared."

Her phone was on the coffee table. She pulled it toward herself. Her fingers stiff and tense, she rapped out Sofia's number. The phone rang, seemingly endlessly.

Pick up, pick up, pick up, she urged.

"Celine?" Sofia sounded calm, at peace—almost happy. The way Martin Luther King, Jr. had felt on the day he'd been assassinated, Celine thought, recalling Sister Mary Catherine's history lesson on the civil rights leader's life.

"He must have known," the nun had said, "that death was nigh. That his work here on earth was done, his time had come."

Had Sofia come by the same knowledge?

Celine's fingers gripped the edge of the table as an intense pain shot through her body.

"Sofia," she managed to pronounce the name. "Is your store open on Saturdays? Were you planning on going in this morning?"

"Actually, yes, I was. Need anything?"

Celine cleared her throat. How was she going to break the news to her? How in the world did you tell someone they were going to die? Was there time enough to beat around the bush?

"Think you can take the day off—just for today? Don't go in, head to where we're meeting instead?"

"Why?" Sofia's voice had lost some of its brightness. "It's Bev, isn't it? She's in danger?"

"No, Sofia, it's you." It was a relief to bring the words out. "You need to be careful. Go to the mall, please. And when you're there, make sure you're in view of a security camera at all times. Okay?"

She got off the phone and turned to Julia. Her face felt haggard and drawn.

"There's just one other thing we need to do," she said.

❧

"What now?" Ted Ridgeway, the agent driving the unmarked car they were in, turned to Blake.

They'd completed their third circle around the Prudential Center mall and cruised to a halt a few yards past the Boylston Street entrance.

"We wait." Blake squinted out the window.

The streets were narrow, crowded with retail stores. The hot summer sun reflected off the tall stone-and-glass buildings on either side, too strong for the shades that tried vainly to shield his eyes.

"Then we go around again."

He'd been on high alert since Celine had called. But her premonition had been too vague to accurately determine where the threat was coming from.

"From outside," she'd said. "I see an infiltration from outside."

That meant he could rule out the security guards, the cleaning crew, and the store clerks. But it also meant surveilling the streets outside for any sign of suspicious activity and keeping their eyes peeled on the many entrances to the mall.

He didn't think the streets themselves posed any danger. They were way too crowded and this wasn't a residential area. Getting access to the roof to put a sniper up there would be tough. But he wasn't sure how anyone could pull anything off inside the Prudential Center either.

Mall security was as tight as one could expect. Blake had been reassured on that point by the head of Tevah Security. There were cameras at strategic locations, two shifts of four guards each provided security during mall hours with an additional overnight shift of two guards.

Blake and Ridgeway had seen the morning shift guys enter the Dalton Street parking garage at eight.

They'd witnessed a cleaning crew—three stocky, middle-aged women accompanied by a slimmer brunette of medium build—enter the Huntington Avenue parking lot near Five Napkin Burger.

Each time, Blake had gotten out of the car, walked into the parking lot to get a closer look at the individuals entering the building. And he'd called security both times to confirm both the number and the description of the people entering.

Chapter Seventy-Three

A few minutes after eight a priest sprinted up to the main entrance of the Sheraton Hotel on Dalton Street.

Blake had tensed at the sight until Ridgeway reminded him that the St. Francis Chapel was located inside the mall.

"Chapel opens at eight on Saturdays," Ridgeway informed him. "Mass is at 8:45."

Then there'd been a van with Quincy plates. An assorted group of men and women had tumbled out of it.

"Nothing to worry about," the head guard from Tevah Security had assured Blake when he'd called. "They're headed for the chapel."

There'd been little to no foot traffic on the glass bridge over Huntington Avenue leading from the Marriot Copley Hotel into the mall. But Blake had kept an eye on that as well.

He'd seen Sofia walk in through the Boylston Street entrance followed about ten to fifteen minutes later by Celine and Julia.

Julia had caught sight of their car and discreetly acknowledged their presence. Sofia hadn't noticed a thing. And no one else seemed to have paid them any mind either.

∽

Catching sight of Blake on their way into the Prudential Center went a long way toward calming Celine's wire-taut nerves. If anyone suspicious tried to enter the mall, he'd notice.

Although the fact that he had a lone car circling the block made her uneasy.

"It's better this way," Julia explained, seeing her gaze lingering upon the car. "It's easier to surveil undetected when it's just the one car. We don't want to risk unnerving Sofia and her friend, remember."

Celine looked at her. "Or whoever has his sights on them, right?"

She wasn't naïve. She knew both Julia and Blake viewed the meeting as an opportunity to draw out the killer. If they could catch him red-handed, it would be the chance of a lifetime to crack open a case that had eluded them for thirty years.

"We're not using her as bait," Julia reminded her sharply, thick white ponytail whipping around as she turned to face Celine. "You know that. Blake's here to prevent the danger you've sensed.

"If Fussy Phil or his agent are here, frightening them away will only postpone the inevitable. If they can't execute their plan here, they'll do it someplace else."

"I know. I know." Celine bunched her hands into fists. *It'll be all right,* she reassured herself. *Everything's gonna be fine.*

"What we want to do," Julia said as they approached the Boylston Street entrance to the mall, "is squash the plan completely and at the same time nail Fussy or his guy."

"I know," Celine said again.

She craned her neck up, her gaze drawn to the rooftops of the buildings that hemmed in the narrow street. Grayson's killer had located himself at a window in a third-story apartment.

But it was unlikely that either rooftops or upper-level windows would be accessible for a last-minute assassination attempt in this area.

"Plenty of security cameras," Julia pointed out as they entered the glass portico and headed for the elevators.

Logic told Celine nothing could possibly go wrong. Yet alarm bells were screeching in her mind as soon as they got off the elevator. A man brushed past her to go into the Microsoft store, startling her. Her senses blared out at her, screaming danger.

Every detail of her surroundings—the people at a nearby coffee shop, the yellow sign outside the restroom, the cleaning cart being wheeled inside its door—assailed her vision, a fresh cause for panic.

By the time she and Julia strode into Dunkin Donuts, her heart muscles were clenching, sending spasm after painful spasm through her body. She gripped Julia's elbow, an attempt to steady herself.

A lone woman—her slender back turned to them—stood by the display case of donuts. Where were they—Sofia and her friend?

She bent her head toward Julia, her panic rising.

"Where's S—?"

"She'll be back in a minute."

A wave of relief washed over Celine as Sofia turned to greet them. The spasms ceased.

"Where is she?" she asked, calmer now. "Your friend? Has she arrived?"

"Yup. She just went to powder her nose."

The restroom—she was in the restroom?

"She should be back any minute now." Sofia glanced at her phone.

No, Celine, Sister Mary Catherine whispered. *She's gone.*

The woman had bailed? She must've done, if she was gone. But why?

"Stay here," Celine told the women. She held Julia's gaze. "Stay here, don't leave. I'll be back."

❧

Outside, an empty cab passed by.

"Let's do one more round," Blake said.

They followed the cab, cruising slowly from Boylston to Dalton to Belvidere and then to Huntington. The cab turned into the parking lot, and Ridgeway picked up speed.

"One more time," Blake said when they were back on Boylston.

"Sure." Ridgeway had pulled into a parking spot, but he merged into traffic again, slowly circling around.

Chapter Seventy-Four

The retail stores at the Pru were all located on a single level. The main restroom near a group of businesses at the Huntington Avenue entrance was closed off for cleaning.

So which restroom was Bev—Celine had no idea how she knew the woman's name—using?

"The Hynes Convention Center has restrooms on every level, miss," a young guard told her when Celine frantically hailed him. She couldn't find her friend, she'd confided. "There's one in the South Lobby. Another right across from Lost & Found, past the main lobby. And several more upstairs."

She's gone, Celine. She's gone.

She headed into the convention center, ignoring the voice chanting in her head.

The plaza-level restrooms were empty. *She's gone, Celine.* She headed upstairs. There were five restrooms on the second level. Celine scoured them all.

She was walking past the exhibit halls to return to the stairway when she heard a muffled moan from the supply closet door on her right.

She pressed her ear against the door. The moans and thumps seemed to get louder. Was that a woman? Sofia's friend?

Her heart lifted. Bev was still here.

"Hello? Anyone in there?"

Had they heard her? Celine couldn't tell. She tried the door handle. Locked.

She stepped back to stare at the gray metal door, taking stock of the situation. A couple of phrases blitzed through her mind.

Supply closet. Cleaning staff.

She didn't need to hear Sister Mary Catherine's urgently whispered, "Go back down, Celine," to race down the stairs back into the mall. With any luck the cleaning woman would still be in the main restroom when Celine arrived.

❧

Blake and Ridgeway were about to approach the Huntington Avenue parking lot when a cab pulled out. Same vehicle as the one they'd followed on their last go-around, Blake idly noted. Although this time, the cab had a passenger.

"Kinda dumb to have a cab pick you up inside a mall parking lot, no?" Ridgeway commented as they waited for the cab to pull out of the lot. "It's a frickin' fifteen-dollar fee whether you're in there five minutes or five hours. And you can bet the cabbie isn't taking the hit."

"Nope, that he's not," Blake agreed. They were bumper-to-bumper now, the cab's license plate filling his vision. Traffic opened up just past the intersection.

He watched the taxi pick up speed along Huntington, while Ridgeway maneuvered them onto Exeter Street and then back on Boylston.

"So far so good," he said to no one in particular.

"Wait here, then?" Ridgeway turned to him.

"Let's do one more round."

❧

Celine's lungs were bursting by the time she came in sight of the restroom. The yellow cleaning sign was still outside the door. She barreled through the door—and slid to a halt on the slippery floor.

Oh my God! Oh God!Oh good God!Blood. Blood everywhere.

She bent over, clutching her stomach; the spreading red pool and the pretty white face in the midst of it filled her vision, making her sick.

Gone meant dead. How had she failed to understand that? Gone meant dead. Oh God!

Get a grip on yourself, Celine, Sister Mary Catherine's voice cut through the keening that filled her ears. *She's gone. There's nothing you can do about it. Call Julia. Call her before it's too late.*

Too late for what, Celine wondered. *She's already dead.*

But she obediently straightened up, pulled open the restroom door, and headed back to Dunkin Donuts.

❧

Traffic was moving a little faster this time. Blake was beginning to relax, about to ask Ridgeway to go around a fourth time when his phone rang.

"You'd better come up here."

Tension laced Julia's voice, giving it an uncharacteristic warble; the disturbance over the phone wasn't loud enough to obliterate the high-pitched screams and commotion in the background.

Something had gone down. Something bad.

Jesus F—in' Christ!

Chapter Seventy-Five

An audacious killing.

That was Blake's first conscious thought as he stared at the auburn-haired woman sprawled at his feet. One leg was extended, the other bent at the knee. A small hole with ragged edges disfigured her smooth, perfectly tanned brow.

How the f— had this happened?

A glistening pool of blood extended around her head on the travertine floor. Streaky rivulets of it ran under the low granite countertop with its rows of white sinks and gleaming chrome faucets.

This was a slap in the face. *His face, dammit!* And on his watch.

The untold audacity of the act staggered him. To be taken out in a mall restroom. Executed swiftly, quietly while thousands milled around, unsuspecting, just beyond the door.

They hadn't foreseen that.

The woman hadn't either. He could tell from the wide-eyed look of disbelief that her glazed eyes still wore. She'd recognized her killer. That much was evident as well. Her eyebrows were arched, her facial muscles locked into the final expression of stupefaction molded upon her features.

Jesus Christ, he hadn't seen this coming.

His gaze tracked a course beyond the rugged head guard of Tevah Security's day shift who stood shell-shocked beside him and caught on the yellow plastic sign still outside the restroom.

DO NOT ENTER. RESTROOM CLOSED FOR CLEANING.

Blake turned to the head guard—a broad-shouldered, muscular guy in his forties.

"The cleaning crew," he demanded hoarsely. "The four women who came in this morning. Where are they?"

He still remembered them. Three stubby, portly women accompanied by a fourth—a lean brunette with straggly shoulder-length hair, about five-nine.

Same height as the dead woman.

That was significant. Based on the entry wound, he'd judged the killer to be no taller than the woman lying dead at his feet.

The head guard gaped. "You can't want them to see this?"

The guard's eyes shifted involuntarily to the floor, then jerked away toward Julia and Celine and the two guards posted beyond the yellow restroom sign.

"I don't care what they see. One of them is our killer. I want to know where they are."

But Blake stepped out of the restroom, nevertheless. The guy was right. There was no reason for three innocent cleaning women to be traumatized by this incident.

As for the fourth . . .

All entrances to the mall had been closed off. They'd find her.

He assiduously avoided Celine and his former colleague. He'd relied upon Celine's intuition and ruled out the mall staff. It wasn't her fault.

He was the lawman here. It was his job to trust but verify. But after he'd doubted her about Hugh Norton and been proven wrong, he'd hesitated to question her insights. Clearly a mistake.

It wasn't her fault. He kept telling himself that. But it was hard not to blame her.

The young man the head guard had sent to corral the cleaning crew was back with three portly women.

"The woman with you, where is she?" Blake demanded.

They shrugged.

"This woman," he exploded, completely frustrated. "Your colleague. You have no idea where she is? You've gotta be kidding me!"

"Agent Markham, please," the head guard protested. "There's no need to yell at the staff. They're trusted employees."

"Oh yeah?" Blake glared at the man. "We have a dead woman back there"—he jabbed his finger in the direction of the restroom door—"and you're telling me to cool it. These *trusted* employees are the only folks with access to that restroom."

❧

"Actually, that's not true." It was Celine. "Any female—anyone dressed as a woman could've gone in there."

Blake spun around, irritated. "What're you trying to say?"

She looked green, about to faint. He should've felt some sympathy for her. All he could think of doing, however, was to let his fist crash into her pale features. She'd led him astray. Again.

She'd said Sofia was in danger. But it wasn't Sofia who lay in there, deprived of life. It was her friend. Bev. The name tugged at his consciousness. Blake had no idea why.

His fury was clouding his judgment.

He clenched his fists, held his arms firmly by his side, attempting to rein in his emotions. Anger would do him no good. *And, for the last time, man, it isn't her fault.*

"Sorry, I didn't mean to snap. Go on."

She turned to the head guard. "I went in there to ask the cleaning woman to investigate a noise I'd heard upstairs. It looked like some type of supply closet. I figured she'd have a key. But—" She turned to the restroom and shuddered.

The guard nodded sympathetically. "It's okay, miss. Take it easy. Take your time. This isn't the kind of thing anyone should have to see. Especially a woman as young as yourself."

"You heard a noise?" Blake asked. "Upstairs."

Celine nodded. "I thought it was Bev locked up. That's why I hurried down here." A film of tears misted over her green eyes. "I think that poor cleaning woman—the one who's missing—"

"Her name's Tilda, miss."

"Yes, Tilda. I think she's trussed up in that closet. I must've heard her."

So that's what she'd meant by an infiltration.

"Get someone to check it out," he ordered the head guard.

Blake turned around, mind shuffling through the images he'd scanned and collected during his surveillance of the exterior. One image as it shifted away snagged his attention.

He pulled it back.

The cab. There'd been a passenger. Sitting in the front seat. That was odd.

But it was the passenger's face that caught his attention. The dark hair, the neat features he'd seen in profile. He ran through the other images in his mind, trying to find a match. Dark hair, neat profile. Where had he seen those before?

Holy Mother of God! His eyes widened.

"The priest," he mumbled. "It was the goddamned priest. Jesus—" Just in time he stopped the cuss word from erupting out of his mouth.

He dug his phone out and jabbed Ridgeway's number into the keypad.

"Remember that cab we saw pulling out from the parking lot?"

"Sure. What's the problem?"

"Track it down."

He yanked the license number from the recesses of his memory and called it out.

"Get Boston PD to help you. I need the cabbie and his passenger in custody ASAP."

Chapter Seventy-Six

Celine wrapped her hands around the steaming cup of green tea. They were back in the Dunkin Donuts, seated on plastic chairs that one of the employees had brought out. She stole a glance at Sofia.

The older woman's tea was untouched. She sat, arms huddled around herself, shivering violently, although it wasn't particularly cold inside the mall.

"I'm so sorry," Celine said softly. She'd misinterpreted Reynolds' message. Yet again.

Some psychic!

He'd been talking about Bev, wanting Celine to let Sofia know Bev would be all right. But she'd assumed he was referring to Sofia.

"How did you get it so wrong?" Sofia mumbled, her head still down.

It wasn't an accusation—simply a question.

Celine bit her lip. She wanted to provide an explanation, but she knew anything she said would seem like a cop-out.

Sofia raised her head; her eyes were red-rimmed, desperately seeking some assurance.

"Why didn't you know? Because it was meant to be?"

Or because I'm just not that good. The response came unbidden into Celine's mind.

"Tony told me to tell you he'd be there. *Tell Sofia I'll be waiting.* I thought —" Celine broke off.

Sofia nodded gravely. "You thought I was in danger." She managed a smile. "That's understandable."

She was in danger, Celine, Sister Mary Catherine said. *Getting rid of her was tempting. But the retribution for her murder would have been swift and terrible. He knew that.*

Who? Celine asked silently.

The man you haven't seen, but whose presence you've sensed.

Celine was about to ask whether the nun meant the General when a powerful fragrance filled her nostrils.

Not the General? His partner?

Hugh Norton?

"Did you mention our meeting to anyone, Sofia? I hate to ask, but did you—"

Sofia shook her head. "I told my father I'd decided to ask Bev to come forward. But I didn't mention where we'd be meeting or when."

"Hugh Norton?"

Sofia smiled. "I barely know him. He's my father's associate. When my mother was alive, he'd come by the store. But that was years ago."

Celine caught Julia's eyes. "Will you help me find Blake?"

He'd been avoiding her as though she carried some sort of pestilence. She didn't blame him. This was the second operation she'd botched. First Grayson, now Bev.

But there were questions she needed to ask—and she didn't want to offend him.

❧

"What's up?" Ella demanded after Blake had finished apologizing for calling on a Saturday. "What's the matter? You don't sound too good."

"She's dead," he told her, his voice flat and expressionless. "Murdered. Right in front of our noses. Ella, I have no idea how this happened."

"Sofia?" Ella's voice was tentative, hesitant.

"Nope." He dug his fist into his jacket pocket and walked toward the South Garden. He needed air. "Her friend. Bev."

"Bev?" Ella's voice rose.

He registered the barely suppressed excitement in her tone but didn't understand the reason for it.

In the pause that followed, he heard the rustling of papers.

"Did you say Bev?"

"Yes, why?"

"Bev Standish—that's one of the names on the DMV list. There's a Pete Standish on Reynolds' client list. Assuming they're married—"

"Pete's our killer," Blake's hopes soared. "He's Fussy Phil."

This wasn't such a bust after all. Even if Pete hadn't pulled the trigger on his wife, they could get him for Reynolds' murder. And hopefully also tie him to Hugh Norton and the General.

"Want me to send some agents over? With an arrest warrant?"

"Yes, but let me first verify that last name. I'll call back to confirm. When I do, call Soldi and have him join our guys as well."

❧

Julia walked Celine out of the Dunkin Donuts.

"What's on your mind?"

Celine turned to her, troubled. "Someone must have known we'd be here, Julia. Someone must've guessed. I'm trying to figure out who it could be."

"I agree," Julia nodded. "This smells like an inside job."

Blake was coming their way. He'd been on his phone; he jammed the device into his holster.

"She in there?" he asked tersely. "I need to talk with her."

"Before you do," Julia said, "who else at the FBI knew about this meeting? Did you tell anyone at Cambridge PD or Boston PD?"

"Walsh and Soldi both knew it was today. Nothing more. Why?"

"This killing took some planning, Blake. Knowledge of the security systems, cleaning staff, work routines."

"And no one we've spoken to, Jonah included," Celine said, "knew just where we were meeting. So our killer must've known Sofia and Bev well enough to realize they'd pick the Pru."

"He did," Blake told them. "Pete Standish. If I'm correct he's Bev's husband and Fussy Phil. And you've got to admit he has one helluva motive."

"But how could he possibly have known they'd be here today?"

"Someone had to supply him with that information," Julia said. "Walsh or Soldi? I think we can rule out Jonah. As well as Ella."

"Walsh." The color had drained from Blake's face. "Who else could it be? He must've been on the horn with Norton the minute I left his office. And Norton called Pete."

He drove his fist into the wall. "Goddammit! I shouldn't have agreed to tell Walsh anything. Anything at all."

"Doesn't help to beat yourself over it," Celine said quietly. She knew exactly how he felt, though. "I'm guessing you didn't have much choice."

She peeked in through the glass door. Sofia sat in her chair, chin down, shoulders hunched and heaving.

"You should probably ask her your questions while you still can. She's going into shock."

❧

"You're right," Blake said.

He strode into the tiny coffee shop. Celine and Julia followed him in.

"Sofia?" He deliberately kept his voice gentle, tamped down the fury and the sheer helplessness that threatened to overwhelm him.

She looked up, face stained with tears, mascara running down her cheeks.

"Sofia," he said her name again. "I need to ask you about your friend. Was her last name Standish? Is she married to a Peter Standish?"

"Yes." She frowned. "Why do you ask? You think he killed her, don't you?"

He did, but he wasn't going to admit it—not without concrete proof. And certainly not to a civilian.

"We need to let him know what's happened," he deflected her question. "Is there anyone else we should inform? Any other family?'

Sofia shook her head. "No, she was an orphan—just like me. That's why we got along so well."

He wondered why she'd called herself an orphan. Her mother had passed on, but her father was still alive. Wasn't he? Had she rejected her father? Was she adopted? Daughter of a single mom?

The questions swarmed into his mind. He pushed them aside. Now was not the time.

Chapter Seventy-Seven

Celine had noticed the tall man hovering by the door of Dunkin Donuts, his eyes on Sofia as she spoke with Blake. He wore a well-tailored black suit. A tiny rectangular gold pin with his name inscribed on it was attached to his lapel.

He waited until Blake had left before approaching the small table at which they sat.

"Rick Santana, ma'am," he said, extending his arm out to Sofia. "Head of Tevah Security."

Sofia took his hand limply. Her expression mirrored Celine's surprise. Had Blake summoned Santana? Or had one of the guards sent for him? Whoever had informed him of the incident at the Pru, it hadn't taken Santana very long to get here.

"I don't have the words to express how sorry I am. We at Tevah take security very seriously. And the kind of breach we've had today is simply unpardonable."

"It was," Julia informed him bluntly. "You'll want to talk to the guy who just left"—Julia pointed at the door—"Special Agent Blake Markham. He'll probably have questions for you."

Santana turned toward her and politely inclined his head. "Yes, of course, ma'am. But first, I'd like to express my condolences to Ms. Wozniak." He turned back to Sofia. "I realize, ma'am, there's nothing I can say that will alleviate your grief. But please know we'll do everything we can to get to the bottom of this."

Julia snorted, an expression of derision that Santana much to his credit ignored. He didn't look the type to be easily fazed.

"And when you're ready to leave, there's a car for you."

"She'll need Special Agent Markham's permission before she can leave," Julia put in brusquely.

"We all will, actually," Celine added to soften the remark. Julia wasn't accustomed to being ignored. And Santana—intent on directing the full force of his PR efforts at Sofia—had done just that.

"I understand." Santana inclined his head again, then returned his gaze to Sofia. "The car—"

"What car?" Sofia seemed to have found her voice at last.

Santana smiled. "Your father thought you might need one, given what's happened."

"But how does he know?" The words gushed out of Celine's mouth before she could phrase them more gracefully. She exchanged an anxious glance with Julia. She'd gotten the impression Sofia's father was a well-connected individual.

He had to be to move in the same circles as Hugh Norton. That a man like Norton would think twice about hurting Sofia only bolstered Celine's perception. Even so, Wozniak's knowledge of the murder was inexplicable.

Blake had to be doing what he'd call a "really piss-poor" job of containment if news of the incident had already spilled out.

"Tevah Security must've alerted him," Sofia said wearily. "Dad owns the building."

The news sent an icy tingle of worry through Celine's veins. Hugh Norton had somehow managed to obtain what should've been confidential information about the Pru's security detail and its cleaning crew's schedule. That much had been obvious to both Julia and herself.

But had the question of how just been answered?

Could Sofia's father have been the unwitting source of Norton's information?

"How does he know where you are?" Julia asked unceremoniously, oblivious, Celine noted, to the implications of her question. Sofia had told her father about the meeting, but not much more. How could he have known, unless—?

Sofia didn't seem to have noticed the imputation in Julia's question.

"Most of the guards know who I am." She gave them a wan smile. "I'll bet Dad gets a call anytime I'm here."

She seemed to notice Santana was still holding her outstretched palm.

Her glance brought a tinge of color to Santana's brown cheeks. He quickly withdrew his hand from Sofia's limp grasp.

"The car is downstairs," he repeated. "Please take it. It'll be safer than a cab. The driver has instructions to take you anywhere you want." He glanced at Celine and Julia. "Your friends, too, if they need a ride."

"I think I'd like to leave," Sofia said as Santana left the coffee shop. "If it's okay with Agent Markham, that's to say."

"I'm sure it will be." Julia got to her feet and hauled her black tote off the table. "I'll see where he is and let him know we're leaving." She looked at Celine. "Coming?"

"Stay here," Julia instructed Sofia as Celine stood up. "You might want to accompany us back to our hotel. I have a feeling this is over, but you can never be too careful."

❧

"You'd better have a damn good reason for interrupting my golf game, Markham," Walsh's voice boomed into Blake's ear.

After calling Ella to confirm the victim was Bev Standish, Blake had decided to call the SAC. On his personal cell phone.

"Thought you'd want an update on the operation," Blake said.

He didn't bother to apologize for calling on a weekend. Walsh had insisted on being kept in the loop every step of the way. So, informed he would be.

"Ah, yes, the meeting. How did it go?"

"It never happened. The woman's dead. Murdered."

"What?" Walsh barked. "How did—?"

"That's what I'd like to know, sir." He spoke quietly, struggling to keep his emotions under control. "No one knew about this meeting—other than Julia, Celine, Sofia, her friend, and myself."

"And me," Walsh reminded him helpfully.

"Exactly."

"What's that supposed to mean, Agent?"

"That you have blood on your hands, sir. You called Hugh Norton after I left your office, didn't you? You told him about the meeting." Despite his best efforts, Blake's voice was getting strident. "That's the only way Norton could've known where Sofia and her friend would be."

There was no response. If it hadn't been for Walsh's stertorous breathing, Blake would've figured they'd been disconnected.

Then the SAC exploded.

"This is preposterous! You're forgetting I had no idea where this would play out. I still don't. And as for the individual you're accusing—"

"You're with him, right?"

Walsh was instantly muzzled, subsiding into stupefied silence, his heavy breathing the only sign he was still on the line.

Yup, he'd hit the mark. But Blake felt about as pleased as a woman whose suspicions about a cheating partner have been confirmed.

The SAC hadn't even bothered to deny the accusation.

"You're out of line, Markham," Walsh finally said, but his voice lacked conviction.

"Tell Norton, he may have won this round. But this isn't over. I'll get him. Sooner or later, I'll get him."

"You can't go on some half-assed vendetta, Blake." Walsh sounded like a hostage negotiator trying to reason with a madman. His tone infuriated Blake. "You need proof, solid evidence, something more than just your rage to drive you."

Blake ground his teeth. That the SAC was half-right—he had nothing solid to go upon—only whipped his fury into a boiling rage. He erupted as suddenly and violently as a volcano.

"The man who killed Beverly Standish," he snarled. "That's our victim, by the way, a young woman cut off in her prime. Her killer is the same bozo who killed Tony Reynolds. And get this, he's also your pal Norton's accountant." He'd gotten that little tidbit out of Sofia.

He took a deep breath and drove on.

"Still think we won't be able to find the proof we need?" Taunting Walsh eased the hot turbulence seething within him. "And when Norton goes down, you think he won't drag you into the mud with him?"

"For the last time, Agent, I had nothing to do with this." Blake had the impression Walsh had drawn himself to his full height—the man was six feet, four inches tall. "I understand you're distraught. You need someone to blame. But I'm damned if I'm going to be made into your scapegoat. Get your facts straight. And clean up this mess. Your mess."

The phone clicked in Blake's ear. *Your mess?*

Yes, it *was* his mess. The realization deflated him, driving the last reserve of anger away.

But as his fury ebbed away, spent now, a single clarifying thought emerged.

Walsh had been genuinely surprised at the news of Bev Standish's murder. Was that because he hadn't informed Norton of their plans?

Or because he had, but hadn't realized how far Norton would go to protect himself?

Chapter Seventy-Eight

"Everything all right?"

Hugh Norton looked over at Walsh, an expression of mild concern on his handsome features. He was tall—almost as tall as Walsh himself, but built more powerfully than the lean Special Agent-in-Charge of the Boston FBI.

"Yes." Walsh was curt. He slipped his phone back into the case attached to his belt.

He hadn't taken Blake's accusations seriously. But now—now he was beginning to wonder.

It was Norton who'd recommended the intern whose shenanigans had resulted in disastrous consequences four months ago. Walsh had blamed Blake at the time. Going into a potentially dangerous situation without backup, using a civilian as bait, these were the kind of half-cocked, thoughtless actions you'd expect from a younger, less experienced agent.

Markham should've known better.

But it was Mary's spying, Walsh had to concede, that had allowed things to come to a head.

And Mary had been Norton's—? *Plant*?

Norton had apologized profusely when he'd been told. But the damage had already been done.

Worse still, Walsh had lost his agent's trust. He could command Blake back into line. But he was aware he'd never regain his trust. That was lost forever.

"Sure everything's fine?" Norton asked again. "If there's something bothering you, Walsh, you know I'm always game to listen."

His solicitousness seemed fake. Was he genuinely concerned? Or just trying to probe for information?

Walsh didn't make friends easily. And after his wife had died five years ago, he'd been desperate for companionship. Norton's easygoing manner and his outgoing personality had reminded Walsh of his Trudy. She'd been such a vivacious woman, someone who could draw you out of your shell.

Walsh had allowed himself to confide in Hugh Norton the way he'd confided in Trudy—talking about cases, using Norton as a sounding board.

Now, as he bent over his driver and concentrated on his shot, Walsh wondered if Norton had been taking advantage of him all the while.

"I'm fine," he said, blasting fiercely at the ball. It soared up a short distance, then trickled lamely away. "Just fine."

He lifted his club and took the three steps to where the ball lay.

If Norton was involved in this fiasco, he could get his news from elsewhere. Walsh was damned if he was going to get played into revealing any further details of the case. He'd already warned Norton about Blake's suspicions. That was as far as he was willing to go.

But there was one thing Walsh didn't understand.

If Norton had a hand in this murder, where—and how—had he obtained his information? Despite what Blake thought, Walsh hadn't revealed any of the details Blake had shared—other than the mere fact of his agent's unreasonable suspicions and their source—to Norton.

And he didn't think Blake had either. His agent wasn't devious enough to betray the operation and then turn around and accuse a superior.

There had to be another source. But who?

❧

Blake was just getting off the phone when Celine and Julia caught up with him in the South Garden.

"I don't think it was Walsh," he announced when they were within earshot.

"What?" Celine asked, breaking the promise she'd made to herself to remain as unobtrusive as possible in Blake's presence and let Julia take the lead. Four months ago when she'd gotten Grayson's killed, she'd been kidnapped as well.

This time she hadn't suffered any consequences. That made it easy for Blake to lay the blame at her door. Not that she faulted him. She ought to have seen this coming and been able to prevent it.

You're not God, Celine, Sister Mary Catherine admonished her. *You can only see what is given to you to see.*

Tell him that, Celine thought.

But Blake's anger must have dissipated. He answered her question readily enough.

"I don't think Walsh divulged the details of your meeting to Norton," he explained. "I just spoke with him." He sighed. "He's playing golf with Norton; he may have been indiscreet a time or two. But that's the extent of it, I think."

He gave them a tired smile. "So it's back to square one as far as that's concerned."

"If it wasn't Walsh, it would have to be Soldi," Julia said briskly.

"Or Campari," Celine added, "assuming Soldi told her. And he may well have done."

"Although I'm still inclined to think," Julia went on, "that Norton somehow squeezed the details out of Walsh. If I'm right, he also managed to pry information about the Pru's security from Sofia's dad."

She recounted their conversation with Sofia.

"Seems plausible." Blake nodded. "We still need to prove it, though."

"Any word on Standish?" Julia asked. "He's your best bet. He doesn't seem exactly the type to take a hit for the team."

That brought another smile to Blake's lips. "Nope, that he doesn't. But no, I haven't heard from Ridgeway yet. If Standish isn't in the cab we're chasing, he'll be at home or at work. Our boys and some of Soldi's men are headed there."

He glanced at his phone. "I guess we'll know in a few seconds."

"Sofia wants to leave," Celine said. "She's coming to the hotel with us. Is that okay?"

He nodded. "Sure. I should've told her myself she was free to go. She's not a suspect in this thing."

While they'd been speaking, Reynolds had made an appearance. He stood next to Blake, although the agent didn't seem aware of having a spirit by his side.

Reynolds gave Celine a smile. *Tell Sofia Bev's fine, okay?* He glanced at Blake. *She knows we'll be avenged.*

Was he expressing confidence in Blake's abilities as an investigator? Or predicting the future?

We will be avenged, Celine, Reynolds repeated before fading away.

Her heart lighter, Celine turned to Blake. "You'll find him. You'll find Standish."

He looked at her. "You think so?"

She bobbed her head emphatically. "I know so."

Chapter Seventy-Nine

The car—a sleek black van—had been provided by Tevah Security. The company's name was painted in gold block letters on either side of the van. The windows, which the driver instructed them to keep rolled up, were made of bulletproof glass, the sides reinforced with armor plate.

"Impressive!" Julia emitted a low whistle when they got to the garage.

"Overkill," Sofia said. She slid into one of the bench seats inside the van. "Typical of my father." Celine and Julia climbed in after her, sitting together on the plush leather bench seat facing Sofia.

Thick glass separated the passenger section from the driver's section. Sofia rapped on it, signaling the uniformed driver they were ready to go, when they'd all buckled themselves in.

"Does your father know Hugh Norton well?" Celine asked as they emerged from the cavernous gloom of the parking lot out into the bright sun. She kept her tone easy, conversational.

"They're business associates." Sofia stared blankly out the tinted windows, still in shock. "She was alive this morning. Now she's gone. I can't believe it."

Celine bit her lip. There was nothing to say to that. No words that could assuage the depths of Sofia's grief. Celine reached out and took hold of the older woman's hand.

There's a time for words, Sister Mary Catherine said. *And a time for silence.*

This was a time for silence.

"Is your father in insurance, too?" Julia broke the quiet that enshrouded them. "I understand Hugh Norton is an art insurer."

It seemed more like an attempt at casual conversation than the quest for information it really was. Sofia seemed to appreciate Julia's effort to engage her in distracting conversation.

She turned to face the former fed. "He's in real estate, and a few other things. Mainly real estate. Rose Antiques is his business, too."

Bits and pieces of Sofia's life began to shuffle into Celine's brain—like images from a jigsaw puzzle.

"He gave the store to your mother to run," she said.

"When my father—" Sofia swallowed and glanced quickly away. "She didn't want a handout. She didn't want to be dependent on anyone."

Julia frowned; Celine guessed what was running through her mind. Was Sofia's birth the result of an affair on the side?

She shook her head, warning Julia off from putting the question to Sofia. Besides, it wasn't the truth.

"He's your uncle, isn't he? Your biological father's brother?"

"Yes." Tears spilled down Sofia's face.

An image knocked insistently on Celine's mental screen. A red inhaler —the sign for cyanide—crossed out with a large red X. Then she saw a face —a man with emaciated cheeks and sadness permeating his eyes.

"He didn't do it, Sofia," she said. "Whatever your father was accused of, he didn't do it."

Sofia's face turned sharply toward her.

"He was framed."

And killed.

But Celine kept that fact to herself. Sofia wasn't ready to hear it.

"You see him?" The yearning in Sofia's voice was reflected in her face and the depths of her eyes.

Celine nodded.

"He was such a gentle man. So patient. He'd read to me every day, spend time with me, listen to my ramblings. It was so hard to believe—"

The memory that had drifted into Sofia's mind filtered into Celine's. She saw a child peeping into a living room. A woman—a tired, fragile version of Sofia—wept in the presence of a bear-shaped individual. Sofia's uncle, Dom Wozniak. He'd adopted her, made provisions for her.

"Your father has a message for you, Sofia," Celine said.

Sofia raised her red-rimmed, tear-filled eyes.

"Be careful. Stay away from Hugh Norton. And his friends."

She'd framed the warning as delicately as she could. In time, Sofia would figure it out.

Celine was aware of Julia's gaze on her. The former fed threw her a look of utter incomprehension.

"What was that all about?" she hissed—out of earshot of Sofia—when they were walking into the hotel lobby.

"Her uncle had her father killed—his own brother," Celine hissed back. "She's safe for now. Dom Wozniak brooks no threats to his family. But she may not be for much longer."

"Jesus Christ!"

"If she probes, if she gets too close—"

"Too close to what?"

"I don't know." Celine picked up pace as Sofia turned, looking for them from beyond the elevator doors.

They'd been in their suite for about a half-hour when there was a knock on the door.

"That'll be room service with our lunch," Celine said, although the firm rat-a-tat-tat at the door was far louder and more assertive than they'd come to expect from the hotel staff.

She gave Sofia a reassuring smile before going to the door.

"Jonah!" she exclaimed when she saw who it was. "Weren't you supposed to be at the Gardner?"

She stepped back to let him in.

"I was." Jonah adjusted his glasses as he entered the room, his shoulders stooped from the backpack he was carrying. A ballpoint pen peeked out from the pocket of his red-checked shirt. He clutched a black notebook in his left hand.

"Then I heard about what went down at the Pru." He sat down, acknowledging Julia and Sofia with a brief nod. "My God, that must've been awful. You guys look shaken."

He surveyed them.

"You were with them?" he asked Sofia.

Celine introduced them.

"Rose Antiques?" Jonah wrinkled his nose. "On Newbury, right? You're not far from the Pru."

"You know it?" Celine glanced at Julia, unsure why she found Jonah's knowledge of Rose Antiques and its location so unsettling. He was a Boston native, after all, and the Prudential Center was an important landmark in the area.

Jonah smiled broadly. "Of course I do," he said easily. "I'm on the art beat. Why wouldn't I know the place?" He turned to Sofia. "I'm really sorry about your friend."

Sofia accepted the remark without comment. But Julia's eyes narrowed. She leaned forward, her body tense.

"How did you find out about that?" she demanded.

As far as they knew no journalists had been informed.

Jonah shrugged. "A pal on the crime beat. The mall was closed pretty early in the day. That gets people talking. Then when you hear sirens, see Boston PD rushing in, it's not exactly hard to figure out what's going on."

For some inexplicable reason, an image of Paso Robles entered Celine's mind. The sun bathing the yellow stucco of the Mechelen's buildings in a warm glow. Tony Reynolds standing in front of the Tasting Room, face-to-face with an unknown adversary.

She gripped the padded armrests of the chair she was sitting on. Someone was watching their every move. She felt threatened by it.

She sat frozen in her chair until Sister Mary Catherine's voice shook her out of her stupor.

Tony wants you to know he's been avenged, Celine. He and Bev have been avenged.

"He's dead," Celine announced, looking at Sofia and Julia.

"Who?" It was Jonah who asked the question.

"Pete Standish," Celine replied. "Fussy Phil. He's dead."

Chapter Eighty

"I know," Blake spoke into his phone.

His eyes were riveted on the yellow cab and the passenger whose head lolled back on the seat inside it. To all appearances, the dark-haired man —a little over medium height, with well-formed, almost delicate features —was fast asleep.

It was only when you peered into the vehicle that you saw the bullet holes—one in the head, two in the chest—that told the rest of the tale. Pete Standish, the man in the cab, was a corpse. A gun lay in his lap—the same weapon he'd used to kill his wife.

But the bullets that had killed Standish were of a different caliber.

"Boston PD found the cab with Standish in it in an abandoned parking lot in East Boston."

The lot overlooked the Boston Harbor. Turning his head, he caught a glimpse of the harbor's glittering waters through the wire fence that surrounded the perimeter of the property and the scrubby trees that edged it.

The closest building was a two-story warehouse that hid behind a high brick wall. No one had seen anything. No one had heard anything.

Soldi stood in the confined pocket of shade afforded by one of the trees, conferring with a Boston PD detective. Bev's killing at the Pru fell under Boston PD's jurisdiction. But Standish's prints matched those found in Reynolds' apartment and the key to the sculptor's warehouse had been discovered in the dead man's pocket.

That gave Soldi and ADA Campari dibs on the case as well.

"We're back to square one, Julia," Blake said. "Our best chance of linking this to Norton is dead. We're at a dead end."

"Not really. Standish was working for someone," Julia's voice buzzed indistinctly through the phone. "That much is obvious. This wasn't a guy so hell-bent on avoiding alimony that he was going to kill his ex."

"No, it wasn't." Blake drew a deep breath. "If I had to guess, I'd say he was acting on behalf of a client. Ella has his firm's official client list. She might even be able to dig up information on anyone under the radar . . ." His voice faded into silence.

But would that be enough?

There had to be a way of tying this to Norton.

"There might still be," Julia said when he broached his concerns.

"What do you have in mind?"

He listened carefully, asked a few questions.

"Fine," he said when he was satisfied the plan had a chance of working. "Get the ball rolling."

He hung up.

He was about to walk over to Soldi when his phone rang again. He pulled it out of its holster and glanced at the screen.

Ella.

"Hey," he greeted her.

"Listen, I've found something."

"Oh yeah?"

"A few familiar names who were all using Standish's accounting services."

"Go on."

"Hugh Norton for one."

"That confirms Sofia's statement. They're connected." Didn't prove a damn thing, but they were getting closer. "Who else?"

"Dom Wozniak, Sofia's father."

"Foster father, according to Celine," Blake said. "And murderer."

He briefly recounted what Julia had told him.

"Guy probably had the hots for Sofia's mom." Ella clearly didn't see any significance in the details. Blake wasn't sure he did either. "If Sofia's anything to go by, her mom must have been quite the looker."

"Okay back to Standish's clients. Any other familiar names? Walsh?" Blake lowered his voice. "What about Soldi?"

"Neither one of them is on the list. But you'll never guess who is. Your latest pal, ADA Mariah Campari."

"Oh!" It was all he could think to say. But why, he wondered, would a humble assistant district attorney for the state need the services of a shady accountant?

"I did some digging, and ADA Campari owns works of art that are insured by Morgana Insurance—that's Norton's art insurance company."

"So they know each other." The gears were spinning in Blake's mind. Had Campari been Norton's inside source, supplying him with details of the meeting at the Pru?

It sure seemed that way.

"There's more, Blake," Ella interrupted his speculations. "Campari lives in the same building as Reynolds. She has the apartment above his."

"You sure about this? She never mentioned it. That's odd. Really odd."

"The insurance policy Norton's firm drew up for her and Standish's records both list the same address," Ella said. But Blake wasn't listening.

His mind whirled, recalling bits and pieces of Celine's insights from Reynolds' apartment. There'd been a second woman—someone who'd turned the place upside down searching for what they now knew to be the Gardner's Rembrandt etching.

"She wasn't wearing gloves," he exclaimed.

"Who?"

"The second woman in Reynolds' apartment. She wasn't wearing gloves."

"You're thinking it was Campari?"

Blake didn't bother to confirm. "Get hold of her fingerprints, will you? I'll have Soldi fax over a copy of the prints his guys found in the apartment."

Chapter Eighty-One

The news of Standish's murder didn't seem to provide any comfort to Sofia. Nothing, Celine realized, would. She'd experienced enough death to know that.

"He's escaped justice." Sofia turned from Julia to Celine, lips tightly compressed in a face that was beginning to look gaunt and pale. "What good does that do?"

Raw pain and misery were etched into her face. Celine was close to tears herself. What could anyone say or do to ease that kind of pain?

Julia clicked her phone shut and sat down. Jonah's gaze was riveted on his palms. For once, he had nothing glib to offer.

"You'd have preferred to see him arrested," Celine said gently. "To see human justice served?" She emphasized the words *human justice.*

That hadn't been served, it was true. But a higher justice had. More justice than her parents had received when they'd been murdered, Celine reflected. More than most victims received. She kept that thought to herself; it would've been insensitive to voice it.

Standish had been struck down by a force far greater and more effective than the human hands that wielded the legal justice system.

But Sofia didn't understand. Frowning, she said, "Naturally."

It would've been futile to tell her that Reynolds—and Bev, too—didn't see it that way. Standish had been betrayed by the very people he'd trusted, the ones he'd been working for, the ones whose wrath he'd hoped to avoid by turning on his friend and ex-wife. It was a fitting end.

But arrested and sent to prison, the maximum sentence he'd have served in Massachusetts was life without parole.

All that assuming the prosecution didn't lose the case on some technicality.

He deserved to die, Reynolds said. *A life for a life. Tell her that.*

"Human justice is imperfect," Celine said. "Divine justice is not."

"She's right," Julia added quietly. "You have no idea how long it takes. It doesn't end with an arrest. It can be years before you get your day in court. And even then, a competent defense can get the worst offender off with little more than a slap on the wrist."

She thinks Daddy's contacts would hasten the process, Reynolds scoffed. *It wouldn't. Tell her that.*

"It's better this way," Celine pressed on. "Pete Standish paid for the lives he took with his own."

Sofia turned to her, furious. "Pete was killed by the men he was working for. The ones who hired him to murder Tony and Bev. And you call that divine justice?"

She stood up. "I know you're only trying to help, but . . ." She shook her head. "I'd like to go home now. I need to be alone."

"Of course." Julia nodded. "But it would be best if one of us went with you."

"Allow me." Jonah rose eagerly to his feet and directed what was meant to be a charming, flirtatious grin at Sofia.

Celine winced. The smile and his manner were completely inappropriate, but at least his words were not. Fortunately, it didn't look as though Sofia had noticed.

"I think Celine should go," Julia cut in firmly.

She indicated the couch with her forefinger.

"Sit down, Jonah. You and I have a story to discuss." She glanced up at the reporter, who stood stock-still before her, his expression blank. "Assuming you're still interested in that scoop you've been pestering us about."

"Scoop?" Jonah's eyes glittered. He sank back onto the couch, Sofia forgotten. "Yeah, sure."

Celine suppressed an amused smile. Julia knew exactly how to handle the reporter. And he hadn't even realized he'd been played.

She walked toward the door and opened it.

"Let's go."

✍

Reynolds climbed into the armored van with them, sitting across from Celine and Sofia.

I have to go now, he said. *Tell her it's all right.*

"Tony is here," Celine said to Sofia. "He's at peace. He's leaving now. He wants to say goodbye."

Sofia nodded. Celine saw the glint of barely suppressed tears in her eyes as she turned her face away.

"Is there anything you'd like to say to him?"

"Tell him I'm sorry." Sofia kept her head averted.

"You should tell him yourself. He can hear your voice."

Sofia turned, misery writ large on her features. "Oh, Tony!" Her face crumpled and she began sobbing. "I should've trusted you, stood by you."

Tell her, I understand. There were things I couldn't tell her then. Things that would've helped her understand.

Celine conveyed the message, but there was something Tony was still holding back. She called him on it.

He shook his head, refusing to answer.

They'd nearly reached Sofia's apartment when he spoke again.

Does she remember our last Christmas together?

"He wants you to remember your last Christmas with him," Celine said.

"It was shortly after then that we broke up."

Something had happened at the time to trigger the eventual break-up.

"Do you remember the gift Dom gave your aunt?"

Sofia smiled. "It was a bronze gu—like the one you were admiring in my shop. Dom had Tony make him a replica because he couldn't afford the real thing."

Celine looked over at Reynolds. He was staring intently at Sofia.

Does her aunt still have it? Ask her that?

"Yes, she does," Sofia replied, surprised. "Why?"

"He wants you to look at it. To remember him by. When you turn it over, you'll see a message from him."

"What message?"

Celine turned to Reynolds. But his message this time was for her.

Seven years ago, Celine. Do you remember what happened seven years ago?

She did. She'd lost her job, and a museum intern had lost her life.

It's all connected

Connected? How? Celine's mind was spinning. He'd made the gu for Hugh Norton at the same time, but was there more to it than that?

Reynolds smiled. The edges of his form flickered, like a candle about to be snuffed out. *Don't tell me you haven't figured it out yet.* He tipped his head at Sofia. *Her father knew. That's why he had to die.*

But Sofia's father had . . .

Reynolds interrupted before Celine could follow the thought to the half-formed conclusion that had begun to surface in her consciousness.

I don't have much time. Make sure it gets back.

What? She raised her eyes. A vortex of light had opened up behind him. It was time for him to go.

Make sure it gets back to the Gardner, Celine. He was talking about the etching now. *You know where it is.* He was beginning to fade away.

No, I don't. She leaned forward, desperate to get the answers she was seeking before his form dissolved.

Yes, you do. It's where you couldn't help but see it. I made sure of that.

He was drawn into the light before she could ask him to clarify.

"He's gone," she told Sofia dully.

Chapter Eighty-Two

The Gardner's memorial for Reynolds was being held in the Richard E. Floor living room. Sunlight poured in through the glass windows; the glimpse Celine caught of the pristine blue sky made her nostalgic for home.

It was a warm day—not muggy, but dry and crisp, California-style. The perfect weather to go wine-tasting if you were in Paso Robles.

She scanned the room, searching for familiar faces, but there were few people she knew in Boston.

"Wonder if Hugh Norton is here," she whispered to Julia as they walked toward the refreshment table where large silver urns of coffee and plates of cookies and assorted cupcakes tempted visitors.

Julia, pouring herself a cup of coffee, tilted the urn up long enough to look. "I'd be surprised if he was."

Jonah's article—published with Julia and Blake's blessing—hadn't gone so far as to accuse Hugh Norton of being the mastermind behind Standish's crimes, but the headline had linked the two men.

Renowned Art Collector & Insurer's Accountant Implicated in Double Murder.

A few other of Standish's high-profile clients had been named as well; the fingerprint and ballistic evidence linking him to the two murders had been cited; and Jonah had laid out the FBI's working theory that one of Standish's clients was behind the Gardner theft.

Standish is believed to have been working on behalf of an unknown client when he passed the Gardner's Rembrandt—an etched self-portrait dating back to 1634, stolen during the infamous heist in 1990—to the sculptor. Reynolds was attempting to return the work to the Gardner when he was murdered.

Judging by the snatches of conversation they'd caught as they navigated a course through the teeming room, it was Jonah's article, not the dead sculptor in whose memory they were gathered, that was the reigning topic of conversation.

"Wonder which of his clients was behind the heist," a woman whispered conspiratorially to her friend as she filled her paper plate with cookies. "If the story's even true." She looked up and smiled across the table at Celine.

"It must be." Her companion stretched out a well-manicured hand and selected a cupcake. "Why else would an organization as tightlipped as the FBI be willing to talk to the media about it?"

"I'm telling you, they know far more than they're letting on." A blazer-clad, middle-aged man joined the conversation.

"I only wish that were true," Julia muttered when the group had left. She caught sight of Penny and waved a greeting across the room at her.

Celine took a sip of her coffee and looked around. Jonah was holding court in one corner, surrounded by a group of avid listeners.

"What was the point of running that story?" That she'd been mentioned as someone consulting with the FBI to locate the missing etching had irritated the heck out of her.

She couldn't think of a single good reason to include that tidbit.

"To give Norton and whoever else is involved the heebie-jeebies," Julia replied. "See if we can shake something loose. There's a key piece of information—a small detail not sexy enough to catch anyone's attention but our target's."

❧

"Special Agent Markham?"

"Yes?" Blake had recognized the voice but was damned if he was going to say so. Forcing the caller to identify themselves was a deliberate strategy. It was the kind of thing that threw individuals off-balance.

From the orange-lit button on his phone, he could tell Ella was on the line, listening in—just as he'd instructed her to.

"This is Assistant District Attorney Mariah Campari speaking." She sounded annoyed at having to identify herself.

Blake thrust himself back against his leather chair; it flexed, reclining a little from his weight.

"ADA Campari—yes." He sounded as though it had taken an effort to recall who she was. "What can I do for you?"

"These papers of Pete Standish that the FBI is threatening to take charge of—"

"Whoa, whoa, whoa, hold on! The FBI hasn't made any threats that I'm aware of." Blake injected as much incredulity as he could into his voice. "Where are you getting this?"

"It's in the article by that idiot reporter you've made a pet of, Agent. Or don't you read the papers anymore? The FBI has subpoenaed documents from Standish's accounting firm, hasn't it?"

Blake frowned, struck by Campari's choice of words. As far as he knew Jonah hadn't made specific mention of a subpoena in his article. He scanned the open newspaper on his desk.

The FBI is confident a perusal of Standish's private documents and those from his accounting firm will yield further clues.

He was still puzzling over Campari's words when Ella opened the door, making a rotating motion with her forefinger. *Keep her talking.*

Blake immediately complied, confirming the ADA's assumption. "Yes, it has—"

He was going to add that he didn't see how the subpoena could be construed as a threat when she interjected.

"May I remind you that those documents are material to Cambridge PD and our case against Standish in the Reynolds case? As such, they—and anything the FBI has recovered—needs to be turned over to us."

"No can do, ma'am." Blake smiled. He'd known she'd bite. And if he was lucky, she'd lead him straight back to Norton.

Ella left the room, satisfied he was doing his bit.

"Standish's clients," he continued, "his relations with them, aren't germane to your case. But they are pertinent to the Gardner heist."

"Yes, but you're saying one of his clients hired him to kill Reynolds." Her voice had lost its earlier calm, sounding constricted and tense with fury.

"It's a theory, gives him motive, and we're looking into it. But you don't need that to prosecute Standish for murder." What prosecution, though? The man was dead.

Blake leaned back a little more, propping his legs on his desk.

"Two murders as a matter of fact. Should be an easy case to wrap up. You have everything you need—fingerprints, ballistics, and that parking ticket Soldi's guys found really seals the deal."

Standish had an outstanding ticket from the evening of Reynolds' murder. He'd parked—in violation of the rules—in the alley on the side of Reynolds' apartment building. One of Soldi's detectives had discovered that fact while filing routine paperwork on the accountant as the perp. in Reynolds' murder.

"You don't even have to worry about going head-to-head against a devious defense lawyers. Dead men don't need to be tried."

"You're being unnecessarily obdurate, Agent," she snapped. "I doubt that'll bode well for your career."

"What're you gonna do? Complain to your pal Norton and have him get the SAC to fire me?"

Her labored breathing was the only reply he received.

"You are working for Norton, aren't you? And you were one of Standish's clients."

"As were several others."

"True." He glanced at his watch. About time now. "But you're the only one whose fingerprints are all over the murder victim's apartment."

He heard the pounding on her door.

"You should get that. It'll be Soldi. Trust me, when Norton finds out you were dumb enough to leave evidence of your illicit presence at a crime scene"—he mentally thanked Ella for confirming that—"you'll be a lot safer with Soldi than on your own."

He waited until he heard the door crashing open and the sound of Soldi's voice barking at Campari to put her hands up before he disconnected.

With any luck the woman's cell phone records would yield the evidence they needed to put Norton away for good.

Penny had brought everyone to the Hostetter Gallery to view Tony's sculptures. And for a special announcement. One that Celine and Julia had reluctantly agreed she could make.

With Standish dead and Campari under arrest—Blake had called with the news—there didn't seem much harm in revealing the truth. Although Celine had her doubts, nevertheless.

"As we gather here to remember Anthony Reynolds, sculptor extraordinaire, I'd like to thank law enforcement for bringing his killer to justice. It was a joint effort by the FBI and Cambridge and Boston police."

Cheers greeted the director's statement as the attendees raised their champagne glasses.

Celine stood in the first row, at the edge of the crowd, lightly gripping her nearly untouched champagne flute. Earlier, waiters in red jackets had circulated through the room, passing out champagne for the toast with which Penny had commenced her address.

So far nothing out of the ordinary had been said, but Penny had just gotten started.

"Tony, as you know," Penny continued once the applause died down, "died trying to return one of the Gardner's stolen treasures. A stamp-sized etching, a self-portrait of Rembrandt, that we lost nearly thirty years ago. Once Tony realized what he had in his hands, he made sure to keep it safe. He was killed before he could divulge its secret location to us.

"But he did leave us clues."

Penny paused to survey the room. Then her face broke into an excited smile. Celine closed her eyes, knowing what was to come next. She wished she was anywhere else but here.

"Today, I'm delighted to announce that we've finally managed to decipher the clues he left us"—she gestured toward Celine and Julia—"thanks to our friends here, Celine Skye and Julia Hood."

The crowd turned toward them and burst into loud applause again.

"Open your eyes and smile," Julia muttered with a sharp nudge in her ribs. Celine complied. Her eyes met Jonah's, who glared unsmilingly at her. It was the one detail his report hadn't included. Julia fortunately hadn't considered revealing it a wise move.

Not before the story had run and Norton and his informant had taken the bait. But the story was out now, its goal accomplished.

And Penny—being Penny—had overridden their objections. Julia's about the wisdom of sharing their discovery, and Celine's about the validity of their interpretation. Penny, in fact, had scoffed at Celine's concerns.

"*Where you couldn't help but see it,*" the director had repeated Reynolds' final words to Celine. "What else could he have been referring to? The implications are obvious." She'd turned to Julia, who'd bolstered her stance.

"I have to agree. I can't think of any other interpretation that makes sense."

Now Penny beamed down at her audience as she spoke.

"You could say Tony smuggled our property back to us." The director spread her hands wide, indicating the sculptures that had been moved to an area behind the crowd. "The etching"—her voice rose—"is in one of the pieces he created for us."

"Are you suggesting we shatter them all to find out which one it is?" a white-haired gentleman joked.

Penny grinned. "No, we have a better plan. Massachusetts Imaging Center has offered to do a CT scan of each piece to see which one is contaminated"—her smile grew wider—"with a Rembrandt."

Jonah's gaze shifted from Celine to Penny.

"When are the pieces being transported?" he called.

Celine tried to catch Penny's eyes, wanting to shake her head, no. It was a sensitive piece of information. She still thought they were on the wrong track. But on the off-chance they weren't, Celine didn't think it was wise to give out specifics of their itinerary. But Penny was too euphoric to be contained.

"Tomorrow," she proclaimed jubilantly. "Early tomorrow morning."

Damn. Celine sighed and lowered her head to Julia's ear. "I don't think those sculptures should go to their destination unescorted."

"Me neither."

Chapter Eighty-Three

Celine had never been drawn to abstract art. But as she and Julia walked around the Hostetter Gallery with Mitch Finlay, the sculptor who'd once shared studio space with Reynolds, and Sonia Braeburn, associate curator in charge of prints at the MFA, she found her appreciation for Tony's work growing.

The tools she'd initially mistaken for sculptor's chisels were burins used in the art of engraving.

"You're working directly on the copper plate," Mitch explained.

He was a few years older than Reynolds, with thick brown-gray hair and an easygoing manner—the perfect person to complete the works Celine had commissioned. She'd taken a liking to him from the moment Penny had introduced them.

Mitch raised his eyes, smiling as he went on: "It's not an easy process."

He pointed to a needle protruding from an elongated wooden handle. "Etching provides a more fluid line. You draw on the wax coating laid on the copper plate, then use acid to cut into the metal."

Sonia Braeburn, a petite blond with a stylish bob, followed Mitch around the table, her hands behind her back as she examined the artists' implements on display.

"Many of Rembrandt's prints are a combination of etching enhanced with drypoint—working directly on the etched plate with a drypoint needle." She looked across the table at Celine and Julia. "That combination of techniques is what makes Rembrandt so unusual."

"Tony was showcasing Rembrandt's tools!" Celine was ashamed of her earlier dismissal of the piece. *Lazy art*, she'd called it. When in reality, it was a key to the exhibition's theme—Rembrandt's etching.

A clue she'd been too dumb to read. The same thought must've been going through Julia's mind.

She threw back her head and laughed. "Damn, the clues were all here." She gave Celine a wry grin. "If only we'd recognized them. We'd have realized Reynolds was pointing us to the stolen etching."

"How were you to know?" Sonia gave them a kindly smile. "Only someone familiar with printmaking would've recognized the tools. And you were probably hoping it was one of the paintings. After all, those are rare, one-of-a-kind works of art."

And the etchings were not? The bubble of happiness that had encapsulated Celine's spirit deflated. Sonia's characterization of the stolen print made Reynolds' murder and their efforts to recover the work he'd died for so futile.

Julia wasn't ready to accept the associate curator's assessment. "The etchings aren't exactly dime-a-dozen works, are they? There's more than one impression of each print, but . . ."

"A Rembrandt print—an impression pulled by the artist himself—is certainly valuable. The rarer a print, the more valuable it is. But as I told Tony when he first called about a month ago, there must be about fifteen to twenty impressions of B2, the Gardner's etching. And those are just the ones in known hands."

Celine stared at the associate curator. "Tony called you?" Had he revealed anything about the etching's location? She still found it hard to believe he'd hidden it in one of his sculptures. "What did he say?"

"Something about a friend having bought a Rembrandt etching that he —Tony—thought might have been stolen. Obviously a fabrication, now that we know the truth."

"Obviously," Celine murmured.

"What made him suspect it was the Gardner's print?" Mitch asked as they walked over to the next installation. "It's not easy to tell, is it?"

"Not to the untrained eye," Sonia agreed. "Tony was going by Wilson's catalog—an old, inaccurate catalogue raisonné—that lists only two impressions of B2. He figured since the MFA had one, the other—his friend's —had to belong to the Gardner."

Julia stopped to look at the stacked plaster of Paris globes. Celine followed her gaze. The piece still looked like nothing. But given what they'd discovered, she was sure it held some significance.

Julia turned to Sonia. "So you told him what you've just shared? There's more than one impression of B2."

"He seemed relieved to hear that. But I don't think I allayed his doubts for long. He came back. We talked about paper quality, watermarks, all the usual means of establishing a print is genuine."

"Watermarks?" Mitch pointed to the three globes. "Is this one of them?" He turned to Celine and Julia. "Tony loved research, and he loved to incorporate what he discovered in his work. It's evident in the pieces he designed for you."

He gestured around the room as he went on: "I'm willing to bet he pulled together stuff he got from you"—this to Sonia—"to create these works."

"Absolutely." Sonia nodded emphatically. "The fool's cap was a very common watermark in Rembrandt's time. It's in his etchings and drawings from the 1630s onward." She pointed. "You'll see the seven-pointed collar, the cap, and oftentimes"—her lips stretched into a pleased smile—"under the collar, what looks like a number 4 balancing on three stacked globes. Just like the one here."

"Good heavens, these works are more representational than we realized." Celine shook her head. They'd been wrong about Tony's last works. The abstraction was an illusion.

"Absolutely!" Sonia agreed.

Julia cast an appraising glance at the sculptures. "Based on what you told him, Sonia, which of these pieces would you say has the best chance of containing the etching?"

The curator surveyed the pieces.

"I couldn't say." She pursed her lips. "Really, the best way to establish ownership is to examine the marks on the back. Museums often pencil in an accession number on the back. Certainly, the Gardner must have done so."

"Pencil marks can be erased," Celine pointed out.

"Of course. And Tony asked about that: What if the pencil marks were erased?"

"And you said?" Julia prompted.

"That no mark can be effaced completely. A raking light would immediately pick it up. Those lights illuminate the surface texture, showing indentations in the paper where the pencil has left its mark."

Mitch glanced up. "Did that answer his question? Or did he have more? Tony," he said, addressing Celine and Julia, "had an inveterate curiosity about everything. When something piqued his interest, he'd go down every rabbit hole he could to satisfy his thirst.

"Guess that's what made him such a successful fo—" he cut himself short, turning red.

"A successful sculptor," Celine supplied gracefully; it hadn't been hard to guess what he'd been about to say. "You and Tony must have been close." They'd had to have been for Mitch to be aware of—and okay with—Tony's past.

"We were once." Mitch's eyes saddened. "Then seven or eight years ago, we each got our own studio and parted ways. Kept in touch for a while. But you know how it is, you get busy, time gets away from you."

They contemplated his words in silence until Julia turned to Sonia again.

"Was that the last conversation you had with Tony—when you talked about raking lights?"

The associate curator nodded. "I offered to take a look at his friend's print, examine it more thoroughly. But he didn't seem too keen on that. And I didn't press him. The raking light theory must've allayed his concerns. You see I told him with a print as tiny as B2, it would be hard to find a watermark. Collector's marks would be the way to go."

Celine was about to respond when Penny's girlish voice carried over to her: "First thing tomorrow as I mentioned. Fortunately Massachusetts Imaging Center isn't charging us. There's no money in the budget for this."

❧

"No, this isn't good, but—" Blake released an exhausted sigh. It was clear to Celine that as far as he was concerned this was a burden he could do without.

She and Julia had finished telling him about Penny's ill-advised announcement at the memorial and the sensitive details she'd so cavalierly thrown out later. They'd both feared it could compromise their ongoing efforts to recover the etching.

But to their consternation, Blake didn't agree. Either that or he'd lost his will to fight.

He shifted his position on the armrest he'd perched himself upon. "Look, at the end of the day, I don't think much harm's been done."

Celine wasn't sure she agreed with the sentiment. Julia didn't either.

"Are you sure?" she asked, blue eyes crinkling with worry.

Penny, mingling with her guests in the Hostetter Gallery, had divulged key details of the Gardner's plans to retrieve their etching—the exact time of their appointment with the Massachusetts Imaging Center, the technicians they were scheduled to meet, the time of their departure.

Revelations that were entirely unnecessary, although Penny had vehemently disagreed. She'd been talking with trusted individuals who had every right to be informed. Members of the museum's board.

The problem was her voice had carried all the way to everyone else present. That was how Celine and Julia—walking with Mitch Finlay and Sonia Braeburn—had come to overhear the director's remarks.

Concerned, Celine and Julia had waited for Blake, sweeping him up to Penny's office the moment he arrived.

They'd found the room blessedly empty—Penny's assistant having left for the day.

But Blake seemed unconcerned, and Celine felt the walls closing in on her.

"You don't have Norton. How can you be sure the danger's passed?"

Blake's shoulders slumped, making her instantly regret her words. His triumphs had been minor. He'd caught an informant, but not the mastermind.

His jaw clenched. "I'm confident we've rooted out our informant." ADA Mariah Campari's burner phone had revealed nearly the entire tale. She'd made calls—to the same number—on key occasions.

The night they'd barged into Sofia as she ran down the stairs in Reynolds' apartment building; the Friday night prior to their scheduled meeting with Bev and Sofia; and an hour before Campari had called Blake demanding documents from Standish's firm.

But it was a hollow victory. The number Campari had called had been a burner phone, and it had been discarded shortly after her call that morning.

"I know I don't have Norton," Blake ground out the words, "but we've got his informant. That's got to count for something."

A wily general has more than one spy. Sister Mary Catherine's words evoked an image from long past. A history lesson with the nun at Notre Dame. They'd been talking about General Washington—and his network of spies. There'd been more than one.

There had to be more than one, the nun had explained.

"There's more than one," Celine said. The sense she'd had yesterday of being watched intensified. The room felt claustrophobic. Her chest tightened, making it impossible to breathe. "There's more than one," she said again.

"What!" Both Blake and Julia were staring at her.

"More than one informant. Campari wasn't the only one."

Images zipped through her mind in rapid succession—a mail truck, a mailman, shards of plaster littering a deserted roadside.

The mailman's watching. Make sure he doesn't get away, Celine.

"I can arrange for an armored van, provide agents." Blake spread his hands wide, looking helpless. "I don't know what else I can do."

Make sure he doesn't get away.

Celine met his eyes, her mind made up.

"Let me accompany you. In the van. Let me come with you."

"No," Blake erupted at the same time as Julia bellowed out a horrified, "Absolutely not."

"You've got to let me come with you." She was adamant now. "It's our only chance to weed out this other informant. If we don't, we've compromised the investigation for good."

Chapter Eighty-Four

The van lurched unsteadily over a bump in the road, sending Celine crashing into Jonah's skinny body.

"Sorry," she huffed, grabbing a panel on the back wall to steady herself.

"It's not your fault we have a dipshit driving the vehicle," the reporter griped. "We should've gotten a trained driver for the job. Not some over-paid, paper-pushing law enforcement agent."

Celine saw Blake's jaw clench, but he refused to take the bait.

They'd been enclosed in the windowless van for nearly fifteen minutes. The atmosphere inside was musty and suffocating. Sharing the stale air and constricted space with a team of four agents was bad enough.

But she and Jonah were wedged between the chest-high stack of Reynolds' sculptures and the rear wall—their limbs stiff and cramped. It was an extra layer of protection Blake had insisted upon.

Exposed to such excruciating discomfort, the patience of even the most long-suffering saint might have frayed thin. But Jonah had been whining non-stop from the time they'd congregated, in the early hours of dawn, outside the Gardner Museum on Palace Road.

He'd initially objected to the stifling Kevlar vests Blake had insisted they both wear.

"Seriously?" He'd held the vest up, eying it skeptically.

Museum staff bustled past, carrying neatly wrapped artifacts—each with a hidden tracker—up the rear step of the van into the cargo area.

"I don't want to have to worry about two civilians getting shot on my watch. I don't even know why I agreed to this," Blake had grumbled.

"These vests aren't going to protect our heads or our limbs," Jonah pointed out, looking disdainfully at his.

"Just wear it, okay? Or stay the f—out of my operation?"

Jonah had donned the vest, but the complaints hadn't stopped. The bumpy ride, the cramped conditions, there was a caustic remark for everything. He obviously had no idea when to leave well enough alone.

As the van jolted over another bump in the road, he went on: "I mean seriously, does the guy even know how to drive a cargo van?"

Stung by the comment, Blake spun around.

"No one asked you to come, shitbird. You foisted yourself on the operation, remember?"

"*I want to see this story through,*" Celine replayed the reporter's words to him. "Isn't that what you said?" She'd had about as much as she could stomach of Jonah's never-ending griping, too.

The evening before, when Jonah had found out Celine would be in the cargo van transporting Tony's sculptures, he'd insisted on coming along as well, raising Cain until Blake finally gave in.

"Remember what you said a few days ago?" Jonah had said, pacing the length of Penny's office. "I had the opportunity to be part of the investigation? Well, I still want to be part of it. You guys owe me, and you know it. The progress you've made on this case wouldn't be possible without my contribution."

He'd had the forethought, he reminded them, to jot down the partial license plate that had helped track down Sofia. Had run a story with more innuendo than any reporter should be comfortable with just so they could sniff out Norton's informant.

"I've been a team player, dammit. Every step of the way. You guys owe me."

Now Celine reminded him of his demands.

"You've got what you wanted. Why not be part of the team? Let the agents do their job."

Jonah jutted his chin out, looking belligerent.

"One more crack out of you," Blake warned, at the end of his tether, "and I'm letting you out at the first street corner. Capiche?"

Ka-BLAM!

The force of the impact was deafening. Whether it was the thud of her skull cracking against the panel separating the cargo area from the cab or the thunderous jolt of a powerful vehicle crashing into theirs, Celine wasn't sure.

"Stay back! Back!" Blake yelled as he and his team pushed the doors open, rifles at the ready. The sharp rat-a-tat of gunfire filled the air, blasting through the earplugs Blake had made them wear. Celine pressed herself as far back as she could go, head averted, eyes closed.

Dear God, keep us safe, she prayed.

You'd be dead if they wanted to kill you, Sister Mary Catherine whispered. *But they don't. Not just yet.*

Behind her, she could feel Jonah cowering. Bullets whizzed past, pinging loudly against the interior of the van. A rush of air, stirring the strands of her hair, preceded each ping. Male voices yelling and screaming mingled in a discordant harmony with the gunfire.

Celine squeezed her eyes shut. *Keep us safe.*

Then as suddenly as it began, it was over. The silence as deafening as the gunfire had been. The acrid smell of gunpowder, the only sign they'd been in the midst of battle.

A rough hand tugged at her arm. She opened her eyes.

It was Blake.

"We got them," he announced, cheeks flushed with triumph. "It's over, Celine. We got them."

The mailman? Had they gotten the mailman?

Before she could ask, Blake went on: "I need to take these bozos in. You guys good to continue on by yourselves?" He threw a contemptuous glance at Jonah. Amid the onslaught, the reporter's characteristic bravado had completely evaporated.

"Is it safe?" Celine's voice quavered, and her eyes despite herself were wide with alarm.

Blake nodded. "Ted Ridgeway"—that was the agent behind the wheel —"will be with you all the way. It's fine."

"Yes, but—?" Questions swarmed through Celine's mind, but Blake was already climbing out of the van.

"You can ride up front now," he called, throwing them a grin over his shoulder.

Jonah straightened up and shuddered. "I need a cup of coffee first."

He maneuvered himself out from behind the wall of sculptures.

"Get me one as well," Celine called, wrenching herself out. Near the van door, she paused. "And, Jonah, get a latte or something for Special Agent Ridgeway, too."

He turned to her, lips puckering as though he'd bitten into a lemon.

"We've escaped unscathed, unhurt. And it's because those agents put their lives on the line for us. A cup of coffee for the guy who's staying behind to protect us is the least we can do."

"Whatever you say," Jonah grumbled, but offered no other protest.

☙

By the time Celine climbed into the front of the van with Ted Ridgeway, her head was throbbing violently. The shock of the initial impact had kept the pain at bay. And when the young paramedic had checked her out— his sensitive fingers gently probing her skull before assuring her it wasn't fractured—she'd only felt the slightest twinge.

"It'll get much worse, I'm afraid." He'd handed her a sleeve of painkillers with instructions on how to take them. "Better take these before the pain starts."

Ridgeway turned to her with a wry smile. "How're you feeling?"

"I've been better," she confessed, forcing herself not to grimace. "At least it's not a bullet." Gingerly, she tipped her chin at his bandaged left arm. "Are you sure you're good to drive?"

He grinned. "If it gets too bad, I'll make the journo do it." He glanced at his watch. "Wonder when he'll be back with that coffee."

"Depends where the closest coffee shop is. And how fast he can walk." At least Jonah hadn't made a fuss about that.

She glanced at the brick walls that hemmed them in on either side. They were just outside the Storrow Drive Tunnel, a few yards from where a powerful truck had collided into them, forcing the front edge of the van to graze past the tunnel walls.

The side-view mirror on Ted's side had borne the brunt of the damage —its surface cracked, the handle holding it up twisted out of shape.

The entire length of the tunnel was blocked off. Thankfully. There was a mere eighteen-inch access on either side of them. Not enough room for a skinny person, let alone a car.

It isn't over. Not just yet. Sister Mary Catherine's voice tugged at her mind.

She turned back to Ridgeway. "I'm worried. There's obviously a second informant. Campari wasn't the only one."

"No, she wasn't." Ridgeway looked at her, gray eyes calm. Why wasn't he more worried?

Her head throbbed, tension pricking the back of her neck.

"Are we any closer to finding out who it is? You think one of those men will talk?" One of the three men had been rushed to the hospital; the other two had sustained minor injuries. "We need to find out who it is."

"Could be any one of the folks at the memorial service yesterday. There must have been a thousand people milling around while Ms. Hoskins was blabbing."

Struck by the uncanny accuracy of his description, Celine's gaze jolted up to meet Ridgeway's.

It took her a moment to find her voice. "How do you know?"

Ridgeway shrugged. "I was there. Wanted to see what all the fuss was about." He glanced at his watch again. "We'll be late for that appointment if we don't get a move on. Want to leave your pal here and get going?"

It isn't over yet, Celine.

"No." Celine shook her head. Her palms, gripping the edge of her seat, felt sweaty. "No, let's wait."

Jonah had been gone—for how long now?—fifteen minutes? Twenty? When would he be back?

Chapter Eighty-Five

Blake had returned to the FBI headquarters in Chelsea, flushed with triumph. He and his men had narrowly managed to avert a crisis. And other than the nagging pain in his arm where a bullet had grazed it, he was fine.

He'd reported to Penny, glossing over the events of the morning for her benefit. "Just a mishap," he said. "It's all good. The sculptures are safe and on their way to the imaging center."

The Massachusetts Imaging Center was on Everett Road, not far from FBI headquarters. That was a blessing. If anything further went down, he and his men would be able to respond immediately.

But what could possibly go wrong?

He'd just assured Penny that nothing could and had hung up, when a niggling doubt surfaced into his mind, drumming away at his consciousness. Before he had a chance to explore it, however, the door to his office opened.

Julia stood on the threshold, her face grave, the wrinkles standing out on her sun-weathered features.

"How long have you known Ted Ridgeway?"

"Long enough," he said when he realized it wasn't a casual question. Frowning, he leaned forward, elbows pressing into his desk. "Why do you ask?"

"The van isn't on Storrow Drive anymore."

He didn't ask how she knew. Julia had stationed herself at a laptop early that morning, monitoring both the trackers attached to Reynolds' sculptures as well as the one in Celine's necklace. Blake had been glad to see Celine wearing the jewelry—a gift from her retired psychic cop friend, Keith Elliot—when she'd arrived at the Gardner that morning.

"It seems to have taken an unscheduled detour," Julia continued.

That meant it wasn't heading toward Chelsea and the imaging center anymore. Unwilling to believe there was anything seriously wrong, Blake searched his mind for an explanation.

"Going to a coffee shop, maybe?" he suggested. "When the guys and I left, Jonah was getting ready to head out for the nearest one he could find."

Julia stared at him. "That was how long ago?"

Okay, point taken. "Where are they headed?"

"River Street."

"That's close to where Ridgeway lives," Blake said. "He's on Byron." The question was, why had Ridgeway made an unscheduled stop at his apartment building. "Have you tried calling him?"

"Ella's been trying. No answer." Julia walked toward his desk. "I saw his photograph when Ella called up his contact details on her computer, Blake. He was at the Gardner yesterday. At the memorial service when—"

Julia didn't have to complete the sentence. "When Penny was busy blabbing," he finished for her. "And Ridgeway overheard." The half-formed doubt took shape and grew.

Julia gave it voice. "The ambush was a diversion."

He could see that now. The strike had been nowhere near as deadly as he'd expected. Their attackers had lacked the firepower for a sustained assault. And most of the bullets they'd shot had gone astray, hitting their targets in inconsequential areas.

"That means Celine was right," Julia continued. "There's a second informant. There always was."

"I know. And he's among us." He got to his feet, shoving his chair back.

Ella was at the door now. "Julia, Blake, they're on the road again. On Storrow Drive." She paused, looking at them uncertainly. "At least, Ridgeway is. Jonah and Celine are still on Byron in Ridgeway's apartment."

"Damn!" Blake pushed past her. "Have you tried calling them?"

"I—"

She didn't seem to understand the question.

He turned around. "Have you tried to get in touch with either Celine or Jonah, Ella?"

"No, I—" She hurried out into the anteroom, grabbing the receiver off the phone on her desk.

Blake checked Ella's computer. The trackers on the sculptures showed movement. He switched screens, checking for Ridgeway's tracker. The agent was right where he should be with the sculpture trackers, headed toward Chelsea on Storrow Drive.

But why wasn't the guy answering his phone? What was going on?

Ella turned toward them, frantic. "I can't get through to either Celine or Jonah. They're not answering."

"Julia?" He turned to where she'd stationed herself at a folding table beside Ella's desk.

"Ella's right." Julia's anxious gaze met his. "Celine and Jonah are still on Byron Street. Ridgeway's on his own. I don't like this, Blake. What's going on?"

"I don't know." He was at the door, tugging it open. "But we're damn well going to find out."

He took a step out and turned. "And Ella?" An icy calm had descended upon him, his brain leaping into overdrive. "Find out whether Mailand ever got round to faxing us that composite from the Paso mail guy. See if it's a match for Ridgeway."

The agent had been on leave the week Tony Reynolds traveled to California. A fact Blake had known but not remembered until now.

Grimly he headed out. If he was right, they'd just discovered the mole in their midst. Goddammit!

❧

Ridgeway's apartment was in a four-story brick building on Byron. The street was narrow; Blake had seen alleys that were wider by far. Leaving Julia and the two other agents he'd brought with him to search the area, he stormed up the short flight of steps and in through the front entrance.

"Ted Ridgeway," he bawled to the stooped, gray-haired caretaker who'd shambled out of his office to see what all the fuss was about. "Which floor is he on?" He stuck his badge out, his voice hoarse from yelling.

"Third," the startled old-timer mumbled. "Apartment 3A. But he's . . ."

Blake left his quavering voice behind, thundering up the steps two at a time. He had no time for idle conversation.

Ridgeway's apartment was the first door on the left of the landing.

"Celine, Jonah," he called, fist battering upon the door. There was no answer. But they had to be here.

He thought he heard a moan, but he couldn't be sure.

Were they being held hostage? With or without someone to babysit them?

"Whoever's in there," he hollered. "Open up!"

His bellows had attracted one of the neighbors—a middle-aged woman in a shabby floral bathrobe who poked her head out. He pulled out his badge again, thrusting it forward like a weapon. "Police business, ma'am. Get back in."

Her eyes widened, but she obediently drew her head back in.

"Celine. Jonah," he tried again, then temper rising, he yelled, "Listen, goddammit, whoever you are, you need to open up"

He took a step back, assessing the strength of the door. It was a flimsy piece of wood, easily battered. The question was, was there someone lying in wait on the other side.

Weapon at the ready, he kicked the door, then shoved his shoulder as hard as he could against it. It gave way, falling open, the momentum nearly taking him down. He caught himself just in time, whipping around, arms outstretched, gripping his gun.

The tiny living room was empty—except for the quilt-wrapped form on the couch. Warily he approached it, scanning the dining room to the left and the half-open door on the right.

Heart pounding wildly, he reached for the quilt and with one swift movement, drew it back.

Ridgeway?

It was Ridgeway. Then where—?

Chapter Eighty-Six

"Blake." The sound of Julia's voice was like a gun going off in his ear. He spun around, the adrenaline rushing back into his veins.

His former colleague walked into the room, oblivious to his reaction, her hands full.

"I don't understand what's going on." She held her latex-glove-covered hands out to him.

His gaze fell to the items on her palm. "Their phones?" He raised his head. "Where did you find them? Where are they?"

Julia shook her head. "I have no idea. They aren't anywhere in the vicinity. We've scoured the area. These were dumped in a trash can outside the building."

Blake frowned, his mind trying to catch up with what was going on. Ridgeway's phone was on its way to Chelsea, but Ridgeway—

Remembering the agent, he turned around.

"Check the other rooms, will you?" he told Julia as he bent closer to inspect the agent. He should've checked the apartment out himself, but if there was someone in there, they wouldn't have waited this long to attack.

Ridgeway lay on the couch, eyes closed. His face was a deadly shade of white. Beads of perspiration had formed on his forehead. His lips—a blueish-gray—twitched and grimaced now and again, and every so often a spasm rocked his body.

Other than that he seemed to have fallen into a stupor.

Blake reached out and touched his forehead. It was cold and clammy.

Julia emerged from the bedroom. "They aren't in here. There's no one here." Her eyes fell on the fallen agent. "I thought—?" She frowned, the question unasked.

"We need to get him to a hospital." Blake's hand closed around Ridgeway's wrist. The man's pulse was weak—so weak, Blake could barely feel it. "I think he's been drugged. No idea with what. But it looks bad."

Julia made the call. "I don't understand," she said, hanging up. "What went down here? And Celine and Jonah—?" She surveyed the tiny living room as though expecting the two to emerge from a hidden corner. "And who's in that van?"

Blake didn't respond. She was asking questions he had no answers to. He was about to call Ella to get the current location of the van when his men filled the doorway.

"Found this, sir." The older of the two held out the chain in his hand with a pink jewel dangling from it. It was Celine's necklace.

"They discarded it." Blake's eyes met Julia's. "That means we have no way of finding her."

"I know." The color had left her cheeks. She clenched her fists to her side. Then her eyes widened. "But no one knew—" She stared at him. "Ridgeway couldn't have known about her necklace."

"It's not Ridgeway, Julia. He's not our informant." That should've been obvious given the state in which they'd found the agent. But his former colleague was clearly in shock.

"No, and he didn't know about the tracker. No one did, except . . ." her voice faded, eyes wide with shock. Before he could ask her what she'd remembered, his phone rang.

It was Ella.

"I have two pieces of information. First, Ridgeway isn't on Storrow Drive anymore. He's—"

"I know," Blake interrupted, not bothering to bring her up to speed. There was no time. "What else did you have for me?"

"Mailand faxed the composite. It was transmitted over the weekend. I —"

"Send it to me," he interrupted.

"I have. That's what I was going to tell you. I emailed it—"

"Great, thanks." Blake ended the call. "We have a picture of the mailman Reynolds saw in Paso Robles," he said to Julia.

He opened his email, scrolling through the inbox until he saw Ella's message and the attachment she'd sent.

"Here we go." He held his phone out to Julia, waiting for her to step by his side before he clicked on the JPEG file.

It loaded slowly, pixels filling up his screen with a face that was all too familiar.

"Jesus Christ," Blake whispered. How could he have been so blind? "I don't believe it!"

"Oh God, she's with him, Blake," Julia exclaimed. "We need to find her. How do we find her?"

❧

Celine was lost. There were lights at either end of the tunnel, penetrating its depths, spotlighting the blackness. But she didn't know whether to move forward or to turn back.

Over here, Celine. Sister Mary Catherine's voice came from afar. *Trust your instincts.*

I'm trying, Celine thought, looking first to the left and then to the right, wavering between two hard choices.

"Celine!"

It was a voice she hadn't heard in nearly seventeen years. Her head turned sharply in its direction.

"Mom?"

Vivian Skye stood silhouetted against the brightness at the end of the path on her right. Celine stumbled forward.

"Mom." She was running now, tears streaming down her cheeks, to the arms outstretched toward her.

It was only when she got closer that she saw Vivian's palms were up, motioning her to stop.

"You can't come here, Celine."

"Why not?" Celine's shoulders sagged against the weight of her mother's inexplicable rejection. "Why not, mom? Don't you want us to be together?"

Vivian smiled. "You know I do, sweetheart. But it's not your time yet. You need to go back. Go back, Celine."

Celine stepped forward. "No." She couldn't understand it. Why was Mom sending her away?

"No, Celine."

Vivian disappeared. Puzzled, Celine was about to take another step toward the flickering light, when something—some force like a strong wind —grabbed her and sucked her out of the spinning vortex.

"Wake up, Celine! Wake up."

She heard the words a second before the torrent of water hit her, dousing her face and chest.

"Wake up, dammit!"

A stinging slap followed, to the left cheek, then the right, the force of it sending her face swinging onto the hard concrete that supported her form.

Her eyes opened and her surroundings—the gray, corrugated, sloping ceiling high above, the dim bulb dangling down, the cobwebs—swam into focus. Then she saw eyes—dark, demented eyes—a pale face.

Jonah?

She frowned, trying to sit up.

"Wha—?" The words were clear in her mind, but her voice was too thick to make it past the dryness of her throat. She coughed.

"Wake up." Jonah grabbed her shoulders and pulled her upright. Her head spun, feeling woozy. "Where is it?" he yelled. "You know where it is, don't you?"

A mechanical trill sounded—someone's cell phone. Jonah stopped shaking her long enough to answer it, fury and desperation mingling on his features.

❧

"What do you mean you don't know?" Blake had never felt such a strong desire to wring his personal assistant's neck. The woman had always been infuriating. But he couldn't remember her being this incompetent. "Look at the tracking software on your screen and tell me where that goddamned van is, Ella."

They were out of Ridgeway's apartment. The paramedics had come and gone, taking Ridgeway with them. They'd confirmed the agent had been drugged. "Could be some kind of thienodiazapine," one of the medics had said as he'd helped his colleague lift the stretcher up.

Now Blake was in the hot sun, trying to figure out why Ella was unable to perform the simple task he was asking her to.

"You don't understand, Blake." His assistant sounded flustered, panicky. "You cut me off earlier while I was trying to tell you—"

He released an exasperated breath. "What were you trying to tell me? Get on with it, Ella!"

"Look, the van should've been on the 1-North, headed into Chelsea, right? It should've looped around Millers River. Well, instead, it headed right to the wharf. Ridgeway's phone is on Canal Street. And based on the trackers in the sculptures, the van should be in Burroughs Wharf. Only it isn't. I sent a couple of agents to check it out."

"And there's no sign of it?" He didn't know why he was asking. She'd just told him it wasn't.

"No!" Ella's voice rose, shrill with panic.

If Blake had let himself think about the implications of the situation, he'd have been shitting bricks, too. He'd never had an operation go pear-shaped so rapidly. This was worse than the kidnapping four months ago. This was—

He cut short his thoughts, lest he get himself into a funk. This wasn't the time for that. Definitely not the time for that.

"It's okay." He was calming himself down as much as he was Ella. "It's okay. We'll figure this out."

He hung up, turned to Julia. "I have no idea—" he began, but she shushed him, her head bent intently over the vibrating phone in her palm.

307

"He's getting a call, Blake. Someone's calling Jonah." The vibration ceased. Julia looked up at him. "I think he might have call forwarding enabled."

❧

"No." "No, we don't need it." "No, it's not here." "No—"

Celine heard Jonah barking responses to his caller, too irritated to be polite. He moved away from her, still talking, still arguing. While he spoke, she inspected her surroundings. Captioned images flowed into her mind, making sense of what her eyes saw: Warehouse. Van. Shattered sculptures—

Her gaze snagged on those, and her eyes narrowed. Those were Reynolds' works. They were supposed to be taking them to the Massachusetts Imaging Center. They'd dropped Ridgeway off at his house; he'd taken sick.

"We should call for backup," she'd suggested to Jonah after he'd seen Ridgeway to his apartment.

"Nah," he'd rejected her advice. "I can do this." He'd peered into the side-view mirror and maneuvered the van back onto the narrow street.

That was the last thing Celine remembered. Her memory after that was hazy. She'd sipped her coffee, struggled to fight off a heavy drowsiness that made her eyelids droop. The only thing she could recall after the blackness that followed was—

Her breath caught in her throat. Her mother. She'd seen her mother.

Concentrate, Celine, Sister Mary Catherine warned her. *Stay alert. Don't let your mind drift.*

Chapter Eighty-Seven

Jonah was coming back to Celine, his conversation done.

He stood by her side, his skinny form looming over her. She caught a glimpse of gun-metal gray pressed to his side. *Ridgeway's gun*, she thought. *He's taken Ridgeway's gun.*

"Ready to talk?" Jonah glared down at her. She'd never seen such hatred in his dark eyes.

"Talk about what?" she asked, although she was beginning to figure it out.

"Where that Rembrandt etching is, Celine. I need it, you must understand that."

"It's not where we all thought it was?" She looked past his legs to the shattered fragments strewn on the concrete floor. She was trying to buy time—time to gather her thoughts and process the situation.

"No, it's not." He was pointing the barrel at her now. "So, where is it? If anybody knows, it's you."

She ignored his question, tipping her chin at the weapon he held. "I thought you didn't like guns."

"I like them well enough when it comes to protecting myself," Jonah replied.

"You're not protecting yourself, Jonah." Her fury was rising. Her arms were pinned behind her back. She'd tried to pull them free only to realize he'd tied them. "You're threatening me—an unarmed individual." He was a hypocrite.

He'd argued vehemently against the police carrying weapons; against law-abiding citizens owning them. But here he was, pointing a loaded weapon at her head.

She said as much.

"Call me whatever name you like, Celine. But first tell me where that etching is."

"Why are you doing this?" She stared up at him, pretending to be interested in his answer.

"You really want to know?"

She nodded, bending her head as low as she could to catch a glimpse of —

"Looking for your fancy necklace?" Jonah threw his head back and cackled. "I got rid of that as soon as you went night-night back there. Julia and your buddies at the FBI are never gonna find you."

"I wouldn't be too sure of that," she said, although she couldn't imagine how Julia would find her. Jonah had noticed the necklace when he'd come to their hotel suite that morning and ribbed them about her jewelry.

"It's a tracker," Julia had informed him at last irritably, as she fussed with the necklace and the monitoring software on her laptop.

"They're closer than you think," she was merely repeating Sister Mary Catherine's words—not quite believing it, until she saw his face.

"Chelsea Creek," she said. The name had swum into her mind. "We're on the other side of the Chelsea Creek, right?"

The gun shot out toward her, then regaining control, Jonah pulled his hand back.

"Doesn't matter what you know—or think you know. Your buddies aren't psychic," he gloated. "By the time they find you, you'll be a rotting corpse."

Find a way to tell them, Sister Mary Catherine, Celine intoned silently. But she had no idea how the nun would communicate that to Julia and Blake.

"Time to talk, Celine." Jonah's voice jolted her back to the present. "Where is that etching?"

"I have no idea." It was unfortunately the truth. She'd puzzled over Reynolds' last words to her and still hadn't been able to make sense of them.

"You're lying," Jonah roared. He squatted down beside her, his pale face and matted hair inches from her. "You're the only person who could know. Reynolds must've given it to you. The etching isn't in his apartment. It wasn't in his warehouse. And it damn well isn't in his crappy sculptures. So where the hell is it, if not with you?"

"I don't know."

"Think," he snarled. "He had a leather case with him—"

His words struck her. "How do you know what he had with him?" But the answer had already come to her.

Beware the mailman.

"*You* gave him those poisoned chocolates. It was *you*. The mailman Reynolds said had approached him. Good heavens, you nearly killed Annabelle."

"I didn't know the chocolates were poisoned. How was I to know? I was only—"

"Following orders?" she asked. "Doing what you were told? By whom? Hugh Norton? Why?"

The questions poured out of her, although Celine doubted she'd get any coherent response from him. He'd thought he was helping to get rid of Reynolds, but he'd implicated himself in murder.

"By whoever pays my bills, Celine. Have you any idea how expensive nursing homes are? On a journalist's salary?"

So that's why he'd gone over to the dark side. For his mother. Celine understood his desperation, but that didn't excuse what he'd done. What he was doing.

"You have no idea who he is, do you? He sends you money anonymously."

"Stop asking questions," he screamed, bringing the gun down on her skull. She flinched. A rivulet of blood trickled down her forehead. "Where's that etching? What did Reynolds tell you? Call him here. Talk to him."

"You can't speak with the dead on demand, Jonah. Besides, he's already gone into the light. He's not here."

"You're lying." Jonah's face was white with fury. "He wouldn't have gone without telling you where the etching was. Either he's still here. Or you know where that etching is."

He pointed the gun at her. "You'd better start talking."

❧

Blake was at Burroughs Wharf with Julia when Penny called.

"What is going on?" the Director of the Gardner Museum demanded, her voice clipped. "Massachusetts Imaging Center just called me to say that Jonah and Celine missed their appointment. They tried calling Jonah, and Jonah . . ." Penny paused, clearly too outraged to continue.

"What did he do?" Blake raised his voice, competing with the screeching herring gulls overhead. So Julia had been right. Jonah had enabled call forwarding on his phone. Fortunately, he'd enabled simultaneous ringing as well, or they'd never have figured it out.

They'd checked the settings on Jonah's phone, but Penny's call was further confirmation.

And Jonah was answering his phone. That was a good thing.

Penny huffed. "He canceled the appointment, Blake. That's what he did. Now, will you tell me what's going on or do I have to go over your head and—"

"There's no need to do that," Blake hastily interrupted. "Listen"—he'd have to give Penny some version of the truth, but it didn't have to be the whole truth—"we think they've been taken hostage."

Her gasp was audible. "Good heavens!"

"We're trying to negotiate their release, but this is going to take some time and finesse. And as you can imagine time is of the essence." A polite way of telling her to get off the phone and his back.

"Oh my God!"

"Yes, I know. Talk to you later." He hung up and turned toward Julia.

She was standing on the wooden planks of the tiny dock, inspecting the contents of a large black trash can. A cool breeze whipped her ponytail from side to side. Out on the water, cormorants cruised by the fishing boats.

"Found the trackers," she said. "Jonah dumped them here. Clever."

She looked out over the water. "I don't know why I get the impression they're in Chelsea."

"That would be stupid," Blake remarked. He didn't have to explain why. FBI headquarters was in Chelsea.

"I know." She turned to look at him. "On the other hand, if he wanted to inspect the sculptures"—she shrugged—"there are quite a few warehouses in Chelsea."

Blake looked out across the water.

"He may well have inspected those sculptures," he said. "And found zip." He turned to face Julia. "That was Penny. Jonah responded to a call from Massachusetts Imaging Center. He canceled the appointment, said it wasn't needed."

Julia looked thoughtful. "So he's answering his phone."

"He's not going to respond to a call from either one of us," Blake reminded her. "So that strategy's not going to work."

"No, but there is one call he'll take." Julia turned to him, blue eyes gleaming. "Get Ella on it, Blake. His cell phone company can help us triangulate his location. And"—her gaze turned to the buildings that crowded the waterfront on the other side—"Meanwhile, Chelsea isn't that huge."

No, it wasn't. And the warehouses—the isolated ones at any rate—were clustered around the Chelsea Creek.

"Why don't you—?" he began when Julia interrupted him.

"No, you work with Ella. I'm going to drive around Chelsea, see if I can hunt down that bastard. This was my f—up." Blake knew what she was referring to. It had been Julia who, in a fit of impatience, had let slip to Jonah that Celine's necklace concealed a tracker.

"Retired or not, I can't just sit this one out, Blake." She met his gaze squarely, lips set into a determined line. "I need to be the one to set this right."

❧

Celine stared at the barrel of the gun. "Put the gun down, Jonah."

Jonah's mother had called, the conversation providing a welcome respite. Celine had hoped talking to her would help to calm Jonah down, pull him back from the edge. But it had done nothing of the sort. He was back at her side, his gaze cold and hostile.

She struggled to quell her shaking nerves, but it was hard. "I'm no use to you dead."

"You're no use to me alive," he snarled. "I should kill you right now."

"I don't think whoever you're working for is going to like that." She stared up at him, her arms aching, her legs cramped from being bent at the knee. She felt grimy and exhausted.

Where was Julia?

"Where's the etching, Celine?"

"I don't know." Her eyes closed wearily.

Yes, you do, Celine. It sounded like Reynolds' voice, but she couldn't be sure. *It's where only you could see it.*

In her mind's eye, she saw the office in the tasting room. Reynolds had been in there. She and Julia had searched it and found nothing.

Where only you could see it.

The table in the office came into view. She saw the stacks of mail, the papers, and—

Startled, her eyes flew open.

Jonah read the look in her eyes. "You know where it is." He pointed the gun at her, his finger on the trigger. "Tell me. Now."

"N—"

The gun went off before she could utter the word or finish shaking her head. She closed her eyes, bracing herself for the bullet to enter her brain, but felt nothing.

"Celine?" She felt gentle hands untying the knots that held her wrists behind her back.

She opened her eyes. "Julia!" The former fed was kneeling by her side.

"It's okay." Julia looked up at her and smiled. "He won't be able to hurt you anymore."

Celine turned to where Jonah had been standing. The reporter was on the ground, a bullet in his head. "You killed him," she said, wonderingly.

"I had to." Julia raised her head. "It was either you or him. You know that, don't you?"

Celine nodded.

"I can't believe you found me."

Julia grinned. "He wasn't quite as clever as he thought. The warehouse door was unlocked. And enabling call forwarding doesn't make a phone untraceable." She helped Celine up. "Guess we got lucky."

"We sure did." Celine shuddered, stumbling out of the dim warehouse. Emerging from the warehouse, she shaded her eyes against the bright sunlight.

Remembering something, she turned to her friend. "You need to call Mailand, Julia."

"Why?" Julia gazed up at her, puzzled. "To tell him about Jonah?"

"No." Celine shook her head. "For the Gardner's etching. He needs to fly it out to us. It'll be in his evidence locker."

Chapter Eighty-Eight

"It was where you said it would be." Mailand held out the stamp-sized etching to Celine. He was wearing the white cotton gloves Penny had insisted they all don before handling the Gardner's Rembrandt. "Under the thick candy pad in that box of chocolates Reynolds left in your office."

The Sheriff's detective had flown into Boston along with Annabelle and Bryan about an hour ago. Blake had driven them to the hotel suite Celine was sharing with Julia. Penny had driven over as well. Spacious as the living room was, it was stretched to capacity accommodating seven people.

"To think it was in Paso Robles all this time," Julia remarked to Penny and Blake. The former fed emitted a short, sharp bark of amusement. "Reynolds sent us on quite the wild goose chase, didn't he?"

"That he did." Celine gently plucked the tiny paper from Mailand's hand. Too battered and bruised from her confrontation with Jonah to travel, she'd suggested the gathering take place in their hotel suite.

Room service had brought up a pitcher of iced tea and curried egg salad sandwiches, but both remained untouched on the coffee table.

Celine gazed at the tiny print. The depth of light and shade Rembrandt had forged with his etching needle was quite remarkable. It had all the tonality and detail of a pen-and-ink drawing. The darkness of the artist's eyes, the glimmer of light in the pupils, the detailed crosshatching on his soft cap and on the left side of his face and nose.

"Lost for nearly thirty years," she murmured, "and now it's back with us." She handed it to Penny. "Thanks to Reynolds."

"If only he'd been a little less cryptic," Penny said.

"To be fair, Tony did try to tell me—repeatedly—that it was in my possession," Celine said. "But we'd searched the Tasting Room office pretty thoroughly. And it never occurred to any of us that he might have concealed it in that box of chocolates he left in the office."

"What a weird hiding place," Annabelle commented, squeezing Celine's hand. She'd been appalled when she'd seen Celine's face, black and yellow and blue from the bruises Jonah had inflicted on her. She'd rushed over to hug Celine. "My goodness, are you sure you're all right?"

"Wow, he really did a number on you, didn't he?" Byran had said when he'd walked into the suite after his mother. Celine was glad to see the resentment he'd harbored against her seemed to have all but dissolved.

She looked up at mother and son now. "It wasn't such a weird hiding place. When Jonah handed him that box of chocolates, saying it was for me, Tony figured no one else but I would open it." She smiled wanly. "He didn't realize I'd never had a chance to get into those chocolates.

"He insisted I knew where it was. That it was where I couldn't help but see it. And if any one of us had lifted that candy mat out of the box, we would've seen it."

Celine shook her head ruefully. "It wasn't the only message of his that I misunderstood. He tried—again repeatedly—to warn me about Jonah. *Why do you still trust the mailman? Beware the mailman.* I should've known that pointed to the *mailman* being someone in our midst."

But that hadn't occurred to her. And if it had, she'd have suspected Bryan. She winced, recalling how she'd suspected him of attempting to poison her—and his mother. She owed Bryan an apology.

❧

"Everything all right?" Blake asked Penny, watching as she carefully handled the tiny print, turning it over.

It was Tuesday. He was no closer to tying Hugh Norton to the Gardner theft or of identifying the man known as the General than he'd been on Saturday. And with Jonah's death, any chance he had of resolving the case seemed to have evaporated.

Still, it would be worth it all if Penny could confirm they'd recovered one more bit of the Gardner's stolen property. But her only response to his question had been a curt nod, nothing more.

Mailand had shown him the etching on the drive over. The pencil marks made on the back after Mrs. Gardner had acquired the etching had been erased. There was no telling whether this was indeed the Gardner's Rembrandt. And if it wasn't, all that they'd been through had been for nothing.

"I examined it under a raking light, just as you instructed, Ms. Hoskins," Mailand said when he noticed Penny examining the reverse side of the etching. "The accession number is there, P21n9. And the marks on the mount, Blanc, Bartsch, Claussen. Didn't see any kind of watermark, though."

"There wouldn't be," Penny explained, raising her eyes. "This is such a tiny sheet, cut probably from the edge of a larger sheet. It would be quite remarkable if it did reveal a watermark."

So why didn't Penny seem happier? Julia must've been asking herself the same question because she leaned forward.

"I realize this isn't the biggest recovery, but it's something. We're one step closer to finding out who was behind this. One step closer to finding the rest of the art."

Penny nodded. "I know. It's just that . . ." She paused, swallowing. "So many people have died for this etching, for this tiny piece of art. Tony Reynolds, that poor young woman at the mall, her husband—"

"Who killed her and Reynolds," Blake reminded her.

Penny nodded. "I know, and then Jonah. And all because of what . . .?"

"Pride," Celine said quietly. "And greed and a desire to remain unpunished."

"And so many people have been hurt." Tears had welled up into Penny's eyes. "Reynolds' last sculptures destroyed. And you, Celine, look at you!"

"She's been brave," Annabelle said, hugging Celine affectionately. "So very brave, hasn't she? Simon—Dirck—would've been proud of you, my dear."

⁓

Later when Julia escorted the others down, Annabelle and Bryan remained with Celine.

"Bryan has something to say to you, don't you, Bryan?" Annabelle nudged her son.

Bryan looked sheepish. He stared down at his hands and then up at Celine. "Just wanted to apologize for my boorish behavior. I was acting out my resentment against Simon—for leaving us, for not bothering to stay in touch, and finally for not even remembering us in his will. But none of that's your fault."

"It isn't his either," Celine gently pointed out. "His life was cut short before he could consider reaching out to you in a way that wouldn't put you and Annabelle—or him—in danger."

Bryan nodded. "I get that now."

"And besides, I owe you an apology, too. I knew you felt resentful and I thought I understood why. Nevertheless, the first person I suspected when we realized those chocolates were poisoned was you. I'm sorry about that."

"Well, maybe you shouldn't be," Annabelle said, nudging her son again. "Go on, Bryan. Tell her."

Surprised, Celine looked from mother to son. "You *did* have something to do with that?"

Bryan made a wry face. "Indirectly, I might have. Back in Paso Robles, Jonah and I got drunk and I revealed some details of your psychic visions to him. He persuaded me to call them in to a buddy of his at a rival newspaper. He made the whole thing sound more sensational than it was."

"*Insider involvement in the Gardner heist,*" Celine quoted the newspapers. It had triggered the attempt on her life. Julia had always suspected that.

Bryan nodded.

"I wonder if Jonah knew something we didn't," she said, frowning. "Or whether he was just trying to get a juicy story out. Something he could piggyback on with a more detailed interview from Julia and me."

"Hoping to blackmail his handlers into paying more to keep his mouth shut if things got too hot for them, would be my guess," Annabelle said. She poured herself a glass of iced tea.

"Too bad he's dead. We'll never know." As she accepted a glass of iced tea from Annabelle, Celine knew her words sounded callous. But Jonah had tried to kill her. It was hard to regret his untimely death. The only person she felt sorry for was his mother.

She made a mental note to have Charles Durand, her lawyer, look into taking over the nursing home payments. And maybe, Annabelle or Bryan could be persuaded to visit the lady when they were in town.

Was there a way to discover who the insider in the Gardner Museum had been—Hugh Norton or the General?

But as soon as it occurred to her, Celine shrugged the thought away. That was a question for Julia and Blake to explore. Not for a businesswoman who was a part-time psychic.

Turning to Bryan, she smiled. "Apology accepted." She stretched out her hand. "Friends?"

"Not friends." Bryan grasped her hand in both of his. "Family. Simon looked upon you as a daughter. That makes us family, Celine."

❧

The Gardner theft took place in March 1990. The thirteen works stolen are still lost. I hope this story provides closure—and the expectation that the Gardner's treasures will one day be recovered.

Celine's story will continue. Stay with her as she delves deeper into the heist. If you haven't read Visions of Murder, you'll want to get a hold of it.

The stunning prequel to the series traces Celine's journey from psychic artist to psychic sleuth and ends with her first brush with the shocking Gardner theft.

And if you enjoy exciting, well-plotted mysteries, give the Joseph Haydn Series a try. In Haydn's world, music is murderous, violinists treacherous, and operas deadly.

Visit ntustin.com/books for your next read!

Happy Reading,

Nupur